A DEADLY FORTUNE

STACIE MURPHY

PEGASUS CRIME
NEW YORK LONDON

A DEADLY FORTUNE

Pegasus Crime is an imprint of
Pegasus Books, Ltd.
148 W 37th Street, 13th Floor
New York, NY 10018

First Pegasus Books edition January 2021

Interior design by Maria Fernandez

Library of Congress Cataloging-in-Publication Data is available.

ISBN: 978-1-64313-630-1

10 9 8 7 6 5 4 3 2 1

Printed in the United States of America
Distributed by Simon & Schuster
www.pegasusbooks.com

For Audrey, who taught me about the passage of time,
and for Hillary, who persists.

Fate leads the willing; the unwilling it drags.

—Lucius Annaeus Seneca

1

Late February 1893

She had him. She was sure of it. Amelia studied the young man from beneath her eyelashes. He perched on the edge of his seat, hunched forward and eyeing the deck of cards as though it were a coiled serpent. She let the weight of the moment hang for another breath, then slid the stack across the table with an abrupt little movement. He flinched. The corner of her mouth twitched, but she smothered the smile before it could emerge.

"We might try again," Amelia said, her tone warm and encouraging. "Perhaps the second card will reveal what the first could not."

He swallowed hard and reached to cut the deck with a hand that did not quite tremble.

Amelia gave the cards a final shuffle. Their worn edges, full of tiny nicks and creases, were as readable as labels. With the barest glance, she chose the card she wanted. A practiced flick of her fingers floated it to the top.

She drew and turned: the Chariot, reversed. She sighed, a hint of regret in the sound.

His head jerked up. "What do you see?"

"I'm sorry." Her face was grave. "The answer is much the same. This is a card of uncertainty. Risk. It implies a journey." She hesitated. "It's also a water card, although—"

He leapt to his feet, knocking his chair to the floor. With a wild look around the room, he rushed for the door.

"Fate has a plan for us all," she called after him, half-standing. "All we can do is meet it with fortitude."

A muffled curse and a slammed door were the only response.

Amelia lifted her chin and allowed herself a satisfied grin. Served him right.

The sound of his exit had barely faded before the door began to open again. Amelia hurriedly resettled herself on the upholstered chair, spreading the skirt of her gown so the green silk puddled around her, shimmering in the gaslight.

She looked up, her face and posture inviting.

"What on earth did you do to that one?" Jonas said as he appeared in the doorway. "He lit out of here like the hounds were after him."

Amelia dropped her languid pose and straightened with a look of frank welcome. "I told him I saw him at sea during a storm."

"Was it real?"

"The sea voyage is real enough. I saw the top of a Cunard ticket sticking out of his waistcoat pocket when he sat down. As for the rest . . ." She shrugged. "Storms are common on the crossing. And he's nervous enough that if there's so much as a cloud in the sky he'll see Christ and his angels coming. He'll think I told him true either way."

"So nothing tonight."

"No, but the take has been good anyway."

"It's been a while since you had a real one."

"Not so long. There was the woman a few weeks ago," she reminded him, standing. "I told her that her husband was on his way home and she'd best move her new friend out of her bedroom. That one was real."

"I'd forgotten about her. It was a footman, wasn't it?"

"Yes." Amelia crossed to the window and pulled aside the heavy drapery. Her skirt rustled as she leaned forward to peer down at the street. The electric streetlights the city had begun installing were still confined to the main thoroughfares, leaving side streets like theirs bathed in the soft glow of gaslight, which danced over a row of hansom cabs in front of the building, horses dozing with their heads down, drivers clustered by the doorway.

"I've been busy so far tonight. How has it been on the floor?" She let the curtain fall and turned to Jonas. He stood before the mirror, brushing invisible flecks off the nap of his jacket.

"Busy there as well," he replied, without turning from his reflection. "I've been run half off my feet already. And Niehaus is here again. He's been pestering me all night—at my elbow every time I turn around."

"He's the one doing the statue of Moses?"

He nodded.

She snorted. "That's positively indecent—*you* as the model for anything biblical."

"I know. Isn't it delicious?" He looked at Amelia and grinned. "He's raised his sitting fee. I said I'd consider it."

Amelia knew she was pretty, if unremarkably so. Jonas, though. He had already been sculpted twice and painted more times than she could count. Tonight's midnight blue coat matched his eyes and emphasized the breadth of his shoulders. Coal-black hair curled over his collar. An adolescent break had left him with a slight crook to his nose. It made him snore terribly but saved his face from dull perfection.

He looked her over. "I was right about that color. It suits you. You should wear it more often. I came up to see if you want to watch Lina's last show. She's on in a few minutes, and you don't have anyone else waiting."

She stretched. "All right. I could use a break."

They crossed to the doorway and started down the corridor. The private gaming rooms were full, if the haze of cigar smoke and the waiters gliding in and out delivering drinks and small plates of delicacies were any indication. A lucrative night all around.

"Why didn't you tell that fellow he'd reach port safely?" Jonas asked. "Why did you let him leave so upset?"

Amelia grinned. "I heard him talking in the hallway before he came in. He made a rude joke about Tommy," she said, referring to the club's Black doorman. "I decided he deserved to sweat a little."

Jonas glanced down at her and grinned back, his left cheek dimpling.

They reached the balcony overlooking the main floor, and Amelia peered over the rail at the noisy throng. "Sabine's in her parlor?"

"Yes, and my sympathies to anyone who has to ask her for anything tonight," he answered. At her raised eyebrow, Jonas explained. "She tried one last time to convince Lina not to leave. It didn't go well."

It wouldn't have. The pretty young woman had announced she was leaving for San Francisco with one of her regulars, an older man who swore he would marry her—though Amelia had her doubts about that. Annoyed at the prospect of losing one of her most popular girls, and perhaps even genuinely concerned for Lina's welfare, Sabine had not taken the news well. The resulting shouting match had fairly scorched the walls, and Lina had required soothing to convince her to stay for a series of farewell engagements.

Now the girl received a raucous welcome as she took the stage for the last time, wearing a feathered satin dress that revealed a scandalous length of perfect leg. As Lina began a teasing dance to the accompaniment of the piano, Amelia surveyed the scene below and marveled—not for the first time—at how fortunate she and Jonas had been to find a place here.

Two years earlier, they'd been standing on a street corner, Amelia telling fortunes while Jonas watched over her and entertained passersby with quips and sleight of hand. Sabine had waited for a lull in business and approached Amelia with an offer.

"I own a club off Washington Square. You two should think about coming to work for me. I'm always looking for pretty girls. And pretty boys." She cast an appraising look at Jonas. "You could—"

"I'm not a whore," Amelia interrupted, accustomed to fending off such proposals. "I don't—"

"That's fine," Sabine said. "I have plenty of others who do. You put on a good show. If I get you cleaned up and properly dressed, you could do well." She nodded at Jonas, who, as usual, stood far enough back not to loom, but close enough to intervene if needed. "Your man there . . ."

"My brother," Amelia told her, more or less truthfully.

Sabine ran a skeptical eye over the large, black-haired man before turning back to Amelia's own petite blond form. "Well, whatever he is, he has a way about him. I can always use that. At any rate"—she raised her voice to address the pair of them—"I'm willing to try you out for a few months; then we'll see where we are."

Amelia and Jonas exchanged a look. They hadn't survived by ignoring good chances. And they had plenty of experience getting out of bad situations.

Sabine was as good as her word. After those first few months, they'd moved into a set of small rooms in the old carriage house behind the club. Jonas worked the floor, appearing whenever he was needed to charm new guests or eject those who became unruly. Amelia held séances and told fortunes. And if her unreliable gift rarely showed itself, she'd long ago learned to compensate.

She had her seer's crystal, useless lump of rock though it was. And she had the cards, with their intricate swirls of color and stylized pictures. They were ink on paper and nothing more, but they were pretty. The clients liked them. And when the clients were happy, the coins flowed like water.

The club was a world unto itself, where the strict social hierarchy that ruled outside the doors was temporarily suspended. No few of Mr. McAllister's Four Hundred were frequent guests of Sabine's. They mingled with artists and drank with actors and conducted liaisons that would have gotten them struck from invitation lists throughout the city were they to become publicly known. To that end, various city officials received envelopes fat with cash each month. In return, they happily turned a blind eye to the misdemeanors taking place beneath Sabine's roof.

The moral crusaders were another matter. Tommy managed them. He stood guard at the front door each night, as immovable as St. Peter. He turned away temperance advocates, anti-vice crusaders, and other assorted Comstockian zealots, as well as the rowdier university students and anyone else who looked likely to make too much trouble—although Sabine believed *a little* trouble kept the place lively.

Onstage, Lina finished her performance with a final flourish and blew a kiss to the cheering audience. The girl leaned down to accept an enormous bouquet of roses from a woman with a mannish haircut and a severely tailored suit. She whispered something in Lina's ear, and the girl laughed and shook her head.

Although the men and women who worked for Sabine weren't techni-cally whores, nearly all of them were willing to entertain offers. Lina, it appeared, had just declined a final overture from a former client.

"Sabine's right. She's making a mistake," Amelia said, as Lina's would-be suitor turned away with an air of resignation.

Jonas was scanning the crowd with an avidity Amelia recognized from recent experience. Looking for Sidney. Amelia suppressed a sigh. Jonas was selective, but he often took advantage of the offers that came his way. He'd left a trail of broken hearts and lightened wallets in his wake. He'd always been diligent about preventing attachments from forming—on his side, at least. But this most recent entanglement left Amelia on edge. She'd seen the young man once or twice from across the room and hadn't been impressed. But Jonas seemed to like him. They'd even met away from the club, although Jonas still thought she didn't know about that.

"Maybe," he said finally.

"Maybe?" Amelia turned toward him. "Lina's giving up her freedom, her ability to make her own money. And for what?"

"Maybe she loves him."

Amelia snorted. "More fool her, then." She pushed away from the railing. "Come on. We have to get back to work."

⁓

Hours later, after a particularly lengthy reading, Amelia stood with a groan as Jonas entered the room. She cast a baleful look at the sparkling chunk of quartz on the table. "Enough. I can't look at another card or stare at that blasted thing any longer."

He crossed the room and began to massage her temples as she leaned against his chest. Eventually she sighed and pulled away.

"Let's see if there's anything left in the kitchen and call it a night," Amelia said. "I want something for this headache, and I want my bed."

They made their way down the staircase and through the front room. The crowd had dwindled, although a few people still sat finishing their drinks and pulling out wallets and purses to pay what were certain to be, in some cases, truly enormous tabs. Tommy stood by the front door, ready to help inebriated guests into waiting cabs.

They passed the shining oak bar at the back of the room and nodded to one of the bartenders as he wiped glassware and whistled to himself.

"We had a good night," Amelia said. When Jonas didn't respond, she turned and found him scanning the thinning crowd once more. He stiffened when he saw her watching.

She couldn't stop herself. "Sidney wasn't here tonight?"

"No."

She couldn't think what to say, so settled for: "Are you sure it's—" in as neutral a tone as she could manage. It was not neutral enough.

"Don't. You've been clear about what you think. I don't need to hear it again."

Stung, Amelia let it drop as they entered the kitchen. The staff were cleaning with the manic energy of people who'd already worked all night and knew they needed one final push before they could leave. Jonas wove around busboys carrying dirty linens and stacks of clean plates, Amelia in his wake.

"Lina was here earlier," Jonas said, reaching a side table where a paper sack sat beside a roll of fabric. "She was giving away most of her things. Said she's getting a whole new wardrobe when they get to California. I snagged this for you." He shook out the cloth bundle to reveal a heavy velvet cloak. "It'll be long on you, and it's got her name stitched inside, but you can pick that out," he said. "It's quite a bit nicer than yours."

Amelia reached for it. "Thank you. Is there supper?"

He held up the sack.

They walked out the back door, crossed the courtyard, and climbed the stairs to their apartment in silence, the air between them still thick. Amelia hung her new cloak on the hook beside the door and smoothed the heavy fabric with the back of her hand. The paper sack held a pair of cold meat pies, the flaky crust only slightly toughened after sitting for several hours. After they ate, they took turns using the tiny washroom. Jonas disappeared into his room without saying good night.

Amelia undressed in her narrow room, pulling off her gown and sighing with relief as she released the hooks on her corset. She tossed both garments onto the spindly wooden chair in the corner, then reconsidered with another sigh and hung up the gown properly. She brushed her hair out of its chignon and wound the honey-colored strands into a loose braid. She climbed into bed in her shift, still troubled. She didn't like being crosswise with Jonas. They rarely apologized to each other, generally tending to let their disagreements slough away unremarked upon. As she considered getting up to make an exception, Jonas knocked on her door and stuck his head into the room, already in his nightshirt.

"Would you like to listen to me read for a while?" he asked, his tone casual.

A truce, then. Something in her chest relaxed. "What is it?" she asked warily. "One of your science magazines?"

"No, but I can get one of those, if you'd prefer. This," he replied with a grin, holding up a slim volume with a flourish, "is trash. A novel of mystery, seduction, and ruin. Orphans and waifs and men with bad intentions. Probably someone will die of a broken heart before it's over, and the wicked will get their comeuppance."

"No," she said through a huff of laughter. "I've had more than enough of those. This one is all yours. You can read me the next one."

"All right." He pulled the door closed as he left.

Smiling, Amelia doused the lamp beside her bed and put her head on her pillow. She was asleep in seconds.

∞

She woke before noon to a gray, lowered sky and a nagging unease in her belly. The apartment was quiet, the only sounds a pair of muffled voices from the yard.

Amelia rose and dressed in a plain gray muslin day dress, one designed to be worn with a comfortably loose corset. Jonas was already up and gone, judging from the disorder in the front room. The previous night's novel sat on the table, the cover speckled with crumbs. He'd probably finished it during breakfast and taken another with him when he left. Or maybe one of his indecipherable journals. Some of the club's regulars saved their periodicals for him, and he devoured them all—everything from old issues of *Penman's Gazette* to the *Journal of Metallurgy*. He'd been the only street tough she'd ever known who picked pockets looking for a library card.

Amelia brushed the crumbs off the cover of the book and picked it up. A piece of paper slipped out and fluttered to the floor. She retrieved it, intending to tuck it back into the book, then hesitated. She could not quite stop herself from looking at it.

The paper was of fine quality. The hand was unfamiliar and distinctly masculine.

I thought of you when I read this last night. I know you said you needed time, and I want you to take as long as you need to decide, but please do think about it. I'd love to show you Paris.
—Sidney

There was a scrap of poetry beneath the signature.

Alarm bloomed in her chest. This was more serious than she'd realized. It was baffling; Jonas was usually so practical in his affairs. Other lovers had made him promises, sent him gifts. He always showed them to her. They'd laughed together at the idea that anyone could be taken in so easily. But now this rich, idle charmer was offering to take Jonas to Europe. And he hadn't even told her.

Amelia shoved the paper back into the book, wishing she'd never seen it.

Was he really considering— No. Jonas would never be so foolish. But why hadn't he told her? She thrust away the worry aside as she tossed the book back onto the table. He knew better. Nothing would come of it.

But the hollow feeling in her stomach lingered.

∽

The club was packed again that night. Amelia took a break at midnight and was about to go to the kitchen for something to eat when Jonas walked in. "I'm starving, have you—" He got no further.

"Jonas!" There came a frantic shout from the hall, and a busboy appeared in the doorway, his skinny chest heaving.

"What is it?"

"Some a' them Eastmans has caught a couple fellas in the alley. They're near 'bout beatin' 'em to death. There ain't nobody out there," he said, panting. "You gotta come quick."

"Sporting with the fairies" was a popular entertainment for some of the lower-tier members of the local gangs. It rarely escalated beyond taunts and shoves; Sabine's security knew their business. But there was always a risk. Tonight's ruffians could have come looking for a fight, or they could have stumbled across this one on their way somewhere else. It didn't matter; once a fight like this started, it usually ended with bodies on the ground.

"Bastards," Jonas seethed. He lunged for the stairs. "Stay here!" he ordered Amelia over his shoulder.

As he dashed out of the room, the dull foreboding Amelia had felt all day flared to life. Her breath caught in her throat. She darted after him.

"Go find help!" she ordered the busboy, not staying to see if he obeyed.

Jonas took the stairs at a run and vaulted over the railing near the bottom. His hurtling bulk cleared a path through the throng, but it closed in again behind him. Amelia shoved her way through the crowd, all pretense of elegance forgotten. Panic drove her, as the certainty that something terrible was about to happen rang in her head like a gong.

She dashed out the front of the club and around the corner, taking in the scene in an instant.

A silver-haired man in evening wear lay curled on the ground, bloody and still, being kicked with obvious relish by a dirty-looking fellow in a stained shirt. Two men were holding his younger companion, twisting his arms behind his back while a third slapped and taunted him. The younger man's face was desperate as he struggled.

Four on two, she thought with disgust. *Cowards.*

Jonas seized the kicking man by the arm and spun him around, planting his fist in the assailant's gut. The man folded in half with a grunt. Jonas dropped him and turned on the others.

The one who'd been doing the taunting grinned, revealing a mouthful of unfortunate teeth.

"What's this? Another fairy wants to join the party?" he asked with a faux lisp.

With an inarticulate sound of rage, Jonas surged toward him.

The young man being held took advantage of the distraction, yanking free of his tormentors and seizing one of them around the waist, dragging him to the ground to grapple on the cobblestones. The other assailant hesitated, as if unsure which of his companions to help.

Jonas settled the matter by tackling the lisper and driving him backward into his friend. They both crashed against the wall of the alley and fought to remain upright, stumbling over each other and the pair of men struggling on the ground.

The man Jonas had punched had recovered enough to reach into his boot. As he straightened, Amelia caught the glint of metal in his hand.

"Jonas!" she shouted. "Knife!"

Jonas ducked at her warning. The knife sank in near the top of his shoulder and came out red. The man went in for another stab. Jonas grabbed his wrist, twisting his arm behind him and forcing the blade away.

Shouts and the sounds of running feet echoed across the mouth of the alley; help was coming. The two attackers still on their feet must have heard the reinforcements approaching and decided they'd had enough. They turned and sprinted for the street, Amelia in their path. The larger of the two flung her aside with a meaty arm. She flew backward into the alley wall. Her head hit the bricks with a crack. Pain exploded in her skull, and the world went black.

2

"There is nothing more I can do. She will either wake, or she will not." Jonas scowled at the doctor and considered punching him. The impulse must have shown on his face, because the man eyed him warily and moved away from Amelia's bedside.

In the front room of their apartment, the doctor continued. "Injuries of this kind are unpredictable. There is a great deal medical science still does not understand about the brain. The skull might have had a minor fracture, but if it did, it is healing. Her eyes react normally to the light, which indicates that her brain is intact. I don't know why she does not wake. All you can do is keep her comfortable and wait."

Jonas only half listened, having heard some version of the refrain near daily for the past three weeks. It had not grown more hopeful, or for that matter helpful, since the first time.

The doctor gestured to a chair. "Sit. I want to have a look at your shoulder."

Jonas scowled again but removed his shirt and did as he was instructed. The doctor lifted the bandage covering his half-healed wound and sniffed.

"There's no sign of infection. It's healing well, although you're fortunate not to have torn it open again, using it as you have." He glanced back toward the room where Amelia lay.

Jonas ignored the rebuke. He had been forced to accept the help of a nurse in the days immediately after their injuries, when his arm had been immobile and he'd needed laudanum to quell the pain, but he didn't like having a stranger around and sent her away as soon as he was able. He'd nursed Amelia by himself after that.

Well, almost by himself. Tommy's mother kept him fed, and she had insisted on coming over several times to sit with Amelia. Mrs. Franklin was a powerful force for such a frail old woman. She'd ordered him out of the apartment when she arrived, and he'd been intimidated into obeying. He returned to find the place scrubbed and shining and Amelia lying on clean sheets. She'd been far more help than the doctor, with his lectures on the mysteries of the human brain.

"Keep the wound clean, and it should heal without loss of function." The doctor reached for his hat. "You were lucky. Any lower and it would have hit something vital."

Jonas showed the man out with as much politeness as he could muster—it wasn't much, he knew—and returned to Amelia's bedside. *Lucky.* He didn't feel lucky.

Seeing her fall had been the worst moment of his life. Terror had swamped the pain in his shoulder. He'd wrenched the arm of the man he held until it popped and shoved him away, only dimly aware of the man's howls and Tommy's arrival. The man and his companions, who hadn't gotten far, had received a thorough lesson in the folly of attacking Sabine's guests. Jonas would have enjoyed helping impart that lesson, but he'd missed the rest of the action. With blood streaming from his shoulder, he had managed only to stagger over to where Amelia lay and reassure himself that she was breathing before he collapsed beside her.

He would be fine. But Amelia might not. Jonas looked at her in the weak afternoon light. She had grown alarmingly gaunt in the weeks since her injury. She swallowed when he trickled water into her mouth but had taken no other nourishment. Her cheekbones threw deep hollows in her face, and her breathing remained so shallow that more than once he'd held his hand beneath her nose to reassure himself that she still lived. If she didn't wake up . . . Or, he shuddered, if she did but wasn't *there* anymore.

They'd known a boy back at the Foundling, when they were children, who had fallen from a tree and dented his skull. He lived, but it was a shadow-life. Jonas knew Amelia would prefer a pillow pressed to her face to living like that.

But what if she stayed as she was now? How long could she live like this? How long could he afford to care for her? He wasn't working, and Sabine had already brought in another fortune-teller to use Amelia's room.

"I can't have it standing empty," she'd said when he complained.

He and Amelia had savings enough to keep paying their rent for a while longer, but the money would run out eventually. His jaw clenched. She had to wake. She had to recover. He'd promised to take care of her, and if he failed . . .

Jonas closed his eyes, pushing away the dread and forcing himself to take a deep breath. Releasing it with a sigh, he picked up the book he'd left at the foot of the bed. He found his place and continued to read:

> Dantès rose and looked forward, when he saw rise within a hundred yards of him the black and frowning rock on which stands the Château d'If. This gloomy fortress, which has for more than three hundred years furnished food for so many wild legends, seemed to Dantès like a scaffold to a malefactor.
>
> "The Château d'If?" cried he, "what are we going there for?" The gendarme smiled.
>
> "I am not going there to be imprisoned," said Dantès; "it is only—"

"Haven't we read this one before?" A weak voice from the bed shocked him to silence. He froze for a moment, then dropped the book and leaned forward. Amelia's eyes were shadowed but lucid.

"You're awake! And you're you. Thank Christ." His voice shook.

"Sister Martha would wash your mouth out for that. What happened?"

"What happened? You nearly got yourself killed, that's what happened. You've been lying there closer to dead than alive for weeks. How do you feel? The doctor just left." He leapt up. "I'll get him back."

"No, don't, there's no need," she said.

"How could you possibly know that?" he said with sudden irritation. "You weren't the one sitting here worrying you weren't ever going to wake up. Worrying that if you did you'd be feeble. I've been half out of my mind—"

"Could I have some water?"

"Oh. Oh, god. Yes, of course."

He dropped his pique and hurried off, returning with a cup. He helped her sit up to drink, holding it to her lips as she leaned forward.

"Little sips. That's right."

She finished it all and sat back. "Thank you."

Jonas looked at her in silence, then squeezed her hand. After a moment, he stood. "You should eat."

She nodded.

He came back a few minutes later carrying a steaming bowl of Mrs. Franklin's stewed chicken. Amelia was asleep again. This time, however, she was curled on her side and breathing with a deep and satisfying regularity. Jonas muttered a prayer of thanks to a god he was fairly certain didn't exist, then took his book and crept from the room.

∞

Amelia recovered. Each day she remained awake longer, spoke more. Jonas kept nursing her. By the next week, she was up and moving around.

Jonas spent part of a night away from the apartment and returned wearing a beautiful silk scarf, his initials monogrammed in one corner. Something tightened in Amelia's chest when she saw it. She looked away, her lips pressed into a thin line.

Late that afternoon, they were in the yard enjoying the last of the sunshine—Jonas sitting on the third step and Amelia in the chair he'd insisted on hauling outside for her—when Tommy and Mrs. Franklin appeared at the mouth of the alley. Jonas waved to them, and the pair turned, identical looks of pleased surprise spreading over their faces.

"Miz Amelia," Tommy called as they neared. "Good to see you out."

"It's good to be out." She smiled at them. "I'm glad to get a chance to thank you," she told Mrs. Franklin. "Jonas says you were a great help to him while I was ill."

The old woman waved off the thanks. "People got to help one another. And besides, you've been good to my boy—he told me you treat him right."

They chatted for a few minutes more before mother and son made their farewells. Mrs. Franklin patted Amelia on the arm with a gnarled hand, her thumb brushing against Amelia's wrist as she withdrew. Amelia's vision darkened at the touch, and half a dozen images roiled inside her head, layered one over another, all stinging and urgent. It was over in an instant, before Amelia could so much as gasp in surprise.

Mrs. Franklin had already turned away, but Tommy still faced her. Before he could take a step, Amelia's hand shot out as if of its own volition and clamped onto his wrist with a desperate, viselike grip.

Tommy looked at her. "Miz Amelia?"

"Don't leave her," she said, her voice hoarse and low.

Tommy glanced at Jonas, who had half-risen from his perch.

"Don't leave her," she repeated. "Not tonight. Something's wrong."

Something in Amelia's face must have convinced him. He shot a worried look at his mother, then nodded at Amelia and gently disengaged her hand from his arm. "I won't. I'll take her home right now, and I'll stay with her."

Jonas sat back down as they left. "What was that?"

Amelia frowned. "I don't know. I never felt anything like it before." The sun fell below the roofline and cast them into shadow. She shivered. "Let's go inside."

⁓

Tommy knocked at the door the next day, his eyes tired and his voice awed. "You saved her," he said, looking at Amelia. "We'd just got home and she'd gone to start dinner. I heard her fall. She was on the floor when I got to her, gaspin' and holdin' her chest. I ran for the doctor, and he said it was her heart. Gave her somethin'—put it under her tongue. It brought her around after a few minutes. Doc says she'd probably have died if I hadn't been there." He took Amelia's hand in a crushing grip. "She would have laid there on the floor alone. You saved her."

When he'd gone, Jonas looked at her, his expression odd. "She touched you yesterday, and you knew something was going to happen. What did you see?"

Amelia shook her head. "I didn't *see* anything, not exactly. I didn't know what was going to happen."

"But you knew something would," he said, thoughtful.

When she came to the table for dinner that night, her cards and crystal were sitting in its center.

"What are these doing here?" She looked at him.

"I thought you might like to practice. I've had them in the cabinet since you got hurt. Sabine has had someone working out of your room," he told her. "A sort of substitute."

"A substitute," she said in a flat tone. "I should have realized. Have I lost my place?"

"I don't think so. She's not a patch on you. But she brought her own props. Although she calls them 'gateways.' She claims different tools connect to different levels of the spirit realm," he said with disdain. "Makes these grand pronouncements in the most awful fake accent—"

As Jonas went on, describing the manifold deficiencies of her successor, Amelia brooded. Too many things were slipping from her grip. She needed to get back to work. That would start to set things right. She leaned forward across the table to touch the crystal with one finger, then pushed it away and slid the cards out of their wrapping. She held the deck and stroked her thumb over the slick back of the top card, only partly listening to Jonas.

"—the most obvious old fraud you could imagine," he continued with relish. "Terribly dramatic."

Amelia idly shuffled the deck and drew without looking. She glanced down: the Tower, signifying misery, adversity, calamity. Appropriate enough to their circumstances. Perhaps more to come if she couldn't get her place back. She shuffled and drew again: the Tower. With a prickle of unease, Amelia shuffled a third time, carefully averting her gaze from the telltale markings on the cards. When she drew, the Tower appeared once more. Her heartbeat was suddenly noticeable in her chest. Jonas had gone silent, looking down at the card in her hand. He knew their meanings as well as she did.

"That was . . . odd," he said finally, subdued.

Amelia avoided his eyes. She stood to stack the cards and put them away.

"Do it again."

"I don't—"

"Please," he said with uncommon gravity.

She met his eyes and sighed. "Fine." She shuffled slowly, the deck warm in her hands, and drew the card. The desolate gray crenellations of the Tower stared up at her, lightning kissing the spire at the top, desperate figures falling from its heights. Neither of them spoke.

After a frozen moment, she put the cards away. "I'm going to bed."

The first dream came hours later.

She stood on an open plain, the night pressing in on her with a palpable weight. The tower loomed before her, its top a roaring inferno. A man leapt from its heights, screaming. She turned away before he hit the ground. Behind her, it was midday. She watched as a woman followed a yellow cat into a field of riotously colored flowers and was swallowed up, vanishing as though she'd never been. Another woman rose up in her place, pale and armless, like an ancient statue. With a banshee shriek, she turned to Amelia, her eyes imploring, before drying up like a husk and crumbling to dust. A third stood behind her, this one weeping from eyes as black as night. Amelia leaned forward to brush away the tears, and the woman snapped out of existence with a hollow pop. Amelia looked down at her hands—her palms were streaked with blood. She gasped and scrubbed them against her dress, a rough gray thing with black smudges at the hem. The flowers faded, and a man dressed in the robes of a monk bloomed in their place. He stood mute and unhearing as yet another woman circled him, pleading. Amelia blinked, and they were gone. A scraping, scratching noise behind her, and she turned again. Her breath caught in her throat. An impression of limbs, withered and gnarled, sinews standing out against leathered hide. Fur and scales and long, matted hair trailed on the ground. A knob at one end for a head, and when it raised itself toward her, it had no face, only an open pit lined with glistening fangs. She whirled to run, fell, looked down her body.

The creature's hands were around her ankles. She howled, an animal sound, raw with terror. The hands moved up her body, gripped her shoulders. . . .

Amelia woke with a gasp. The sheets were twined around her legs, damp with sweat despite the cool night air. A dim outline leaned over her in the moonlight—Jonas, both hands pressing her shoulders into the mattress.

"You were screaming," Jonas told her, concern heavy in his voice. He released her and leaned back. "I had to shake you hard to wake you up."

"I've never had a dream that vivid." She took a deep breath and brushed sticky strands of hair off her face. Her hands were trembling.

"Do you want to talk it through? Do you think . . . was it—"

"No!" She shuddered and softened her tone. "No, I— It was just a nightmare. I'm fine. Go back to bed."

With a doubtful look, but without comment, he left.

In the light of the next day, it was possible to believe it had been only a dream. There'd been the excitement with Tommy's mother. And the strange coincidence with the Tower card the night before. She was worried about her job, about Jonas. It had influenced her, caused her mind to create that *thing*. Everyone had bad dreams sometimes. It meant nothing.

But it came again the next night. And the next. And each night thereafter.

The details changed. Once Jonas was the man falling, trailing fire as she screamed his name. Once the lurching monster had her own face, distorted but recognizable. Each time Jonas woke her. Each time she refused to talk about it.

For the first few days, they pretended nothing was happening. Every morning, Amelia sat and drank coffee as Jonas read the paper, relaying bits of news out loud and adding commentary to items he found interesting.

"There's a smallpox outbreak at the almshouse in Jersey City. 'Health authorities were thrown into a state of alarm'. . . . I should say so. . . . A former congressman is divorcing his wife and asking for $50,000 in damages from her lover—apparently she's been carrying on with a banker. . . . The *London Times* liked President Cleveland's inaugural address. . . . The Princess of Wales and her children had an audience with the Pope. . . . The body of a young doctor was found in the river. . . . Lily Post has taken over the role of Gianetta in *The Gondoliers*. I like her. We should try to see that."

This relentless pursuit of normalcy soothed them both, for a time.

But the nightmare was always waiting, as vivid and terrible each time as if it were new. As the days passed, the strain began to tell on both of them. Sleep became difficult, Amelia lying awake in her room and Jonas in his, both dreading what they knew would happen when she closed her eyes.

Jonas stopped chattering over the paper in the mornings, instead clenching its edges in whitened fists and casting furtive glances at Amelia over the top of the page when he thought she wasn't looking. There was something speculative in his gaze.

Three more times that week, he brought her the cards and nagged her into drawing. Each time the Tower fairly leapt from the deck.

They became snappish with each other. Amelia withdrew, ignoring all but direct inquiries and answering in monosyllables. Jonas stopped going out and began to find increasingly pallid excuses not to leave her alone. Their apartment took on the choking atmosphere of a city under siege.

She refused to draw a card the fourth time he offered them, waving them away with a scowl. He muttered something under his breath as he put them away. Their tempers frayed, each of them spent the rest of the day brooding, looking away whenever their eyes met.

On the ninth day, a package arrived for Jonas: two books, one a beautifully bound copy of *Leaves of Grass*. The other, Amelia saw before he hastily covered the front, was a popular traveler's guide to Paris. He read the note it contained, then shoved it in his pocket, glancing at Amelia as if to gauge whether she'd noticed. She made a point of averting her gaze, her jaw clenched against the words threatening to spill from her mouth. The air between them darkened.

That afternoon, Jonas offered her the cards once more.

"No," she snapped, knocking his hand away and spilling the deck to the floor. "I'm not drawing again. It means nothing! And you've got to stop this damned *hovering*. Everything is fine. Nothing has happened. Nothing is going to happen. I'm recovered. You should go and tell Sabine we're ready to come back to work."

"I will do no such thing. None of this is fine," Jonas spat, gesturing at the scattered cards. "This thing with the Tower, it's important. And you know it. That's why you won't talk about it—because it's scaring you. All of it—Mrs. Franklin, and the cards, and that god-damned nightmare." He nearly shouted the last. "And you are not recovered. You're thin as a rail and pale as milk, except for those black circles under your eyes. I doubt you could make it all the way out to the street without falling over, let alone work a full night. You're exhausted. You can't—"

"I can do whatever I damned well want," Amelia shot back. "I want to get back to work. I want things to get back to normal, and that isn't going to happen until—"

"It isn't going to happen at all," he cried. "Don't you see? Things are different now. *You* are different."

"Nothing is different. It's just a dream. It's just a stupid dream, and this," she said, plucking up the Tower card, where it had fallen face up at her feet, "is just paper." She ripped it in half and flung the pieces at him.

Jonas scoffed. "You know better than that." He shoved her seer's crystal across the table at her. "I'll bet if you tried, you'd see something in it now. But you won't, because you're terrified I'm right. Something's happened to you, Amelia. Lying to yourself about it won't help anything."

She batted the crystal back at him. "I'm not the one who's lying."

"What are you talking about?"

"You think I don't know? About the gifts, and the poetry, and Paris?" The last word was a sneer. "Are you a fool? You're his toy, and when he's tired of you, he'll drop you."

"You don't know what you're talking about. You've never even met him, for god's sake, you don't know—"

"I know enough. I know he wants you to leave with him. And you're thinking about it, aren't you?"

He hesitated for an instant, and the pause was answer enough. Rage swept over her.

"What's happened to you? I never thought you'd be content to be nothing but someone's whore!" She hurled the last word like a knife.

Jonas looked as stunned as if she'd slapped him. His face flushed red. Without a word, he turned, stalked out of the apartment, and slammed the door behind him. Amelia seized the crystal and heaved it after him. It shattered against the doorjamb. She kicked the table's leg, earning herself nothing but a bruised foot. "Damn it," she hissed, rubbing the injury.

She threw herself down into a chair, let out a shuddering breath, and buried her face in her hands. Her anger drained away, replaced by a searing mixture of guilt and shame. Her barbed words still echoed through the empty room, pricking her anew with each reverberation. She felt as if she might climb out of her own skin.

Enough. She had to get out of here. She stood, snatched up her new cloak—still hanging on the hook by the door since the night of the brawl—and tied it on as she made her way down the stairs.

Amelia was winded by the time she reached the bottom. She swore again with more force, irritated anew that Jonas had been right. She looked up at their door but couldn't bear the thought of sitting alone in the oppressive silence.

I'll go for a walk, she thought, squaring her shoulders. *It will be good for me. If I tire myself out, then maybe tonight I won't*— She cut herself off, her mind skittering away from the subject of her dream.

She crossed the yard and started down the alley. As she passed the spot where she'd been injured, regret for the things she'd said to Jonas stabbed through her. She'd gone too far. He worried about her. He didn't deserve the way she'd spoken. As she reached the street, she promised herself she would apologize as soon as he returned.

The resolution made, she set off feeling if not unburdened, then at least lighter. The season had begun to change while she'd been stuck inside, and the air held a faint hint of spring, though the breeze was still chilly enough to make her glad of the cloak. At her favorite café, she bought a sausage on a soft roll and a cup of cider. She sat at one of the outdoor tables facing the park, watching the passersby and enjoying the salty meat and the mild alcoholic bite of the cider. She finished her meal and turned her face up to the sun.

The green expanse of the park beckoned, and she stood, surprised and amused to find the drink had gone to her head. She crossed the street and wandered along a graveled path, crossing a wooden bridge over a rocky spot where a trickle of water flowed. The sounds of the city faded, replaced by birdsong.

Inattentive, she was only steps away when she saw it: people drifting off the path up ahead, flowing around a roundish, empty space like water around a rock in the middle of a river. Amelia stepped closer, the air pressing in on her, every sound magnified until there was nothing but a roar in her ears. She focused on the empty spot and froze.

The space wasn't empty at all. Something gray and translucent swirled in the air. It began to take shape even as Amelia blinked in disbelief. Within a moment, a young woman, no older than Amelia herself, stood in the spot. Her features were sharp, although she remained oddly faint and colorless. She wore a shapeless dress and a round cap in a style fifty years out of date and shabby even for a servant. Around her neck was a knotted rope, its ragged end trailing on the ground.

Amelia gasped. The woman's head turned with a jerk. Her eyes widened as they locked on to Amelia's. Startled recognition swept over her face, followed an instant later by an expression of eager anticipation. An itch began somewhere behind Amelia's breastbone, and the girl began to move toward her. Or rather, she must have moved, though it seemed more as if the space between them simply contracted.

The itch grew. Intensified. Within moments it felt hideously like something was boring through Amelia's chest, tugging at her sternum from behind. She knew, with an awful certainty, that something terrible would happen when the apparition touched her.

Amelia ordered herself to move, to turn and run, but her legs refused to obey. It was as if she were rooted to the spot. Amelia tried to ward the thing away, but her arms remained locked at her sides. The girl reached out a hand, and an alien, suffocating presence enveloped her. Something clenched around Amelia's neck, and her breathing became a desperate wheeze.

The world tilted. The cold ground pressed against her back. The shade drifted toward her, the gray hand still reaching. Amelia felt a frozen touch on her cheek, and then she was gone.

3

Amelia thrashed in the space between dream and waking, drowning in the void, unable to fight her way to the surface. Awareness faded and sharpened in ragged beats. Snatches of conversation stitched themselves together, the pattern incomprehensible.

—*found her in the park—*

—*drunk? Smells like she—*

—*fought like a wildcat. Screaming about how she never meant to burn them up—*

—*scratched the hell out of Hanlon when—*

—*Put her in a cell. Maybe someone—*

—*the hell is she still here?! We can't keep every stray—*

—*here today? Have him take a look. Maybe he can—*

—*raving when she came in. Still hasn't spoken any sense—*

A thumb lifting her eyelid.

—*Miss Casey, can you hear me? Carolina?—*

—*my count, gentlemen. One, two—*

A jolting motion, a sickening weightlessness, a swaying. She fell away again.

4

Amelia returned to herself a sense at a time.

First a woman's voice, brusque and echoing: "This way please, gentlemen. Set her down, thank you. We'll take her from here."

Throbbing pain filling her head to bursting. Mewling with it, clutching her temples with her hands. A foul taste in her mouth and a stench in her nostrils that she dimly recognized as coming from herself. Filth and bile and rust. Slow, shallow breaths. Slitted eyes opening against piercing light.

She blinked slowly, orienting herself. She was lying on the floor—on a stretcher—in a large, tiled washroom. And she was not alone. Three women wearing identical brown-striped dresses and stern expressions looked back at her. One opened the folder she held and looked down, making notes with a pencil. The scritching sound was as loud as a scream in the echoing room. The second held a cloth bundle and a limp canvas sack. The third stepped forward.

"Good. You're awake. Do you understand me?"

Amelia tried to speak but found her voice wouldn't obey. She managed a shadow of a nod.

"Do you know where you are?"

Shaking her head was beyond her capacity. She closed her eyes again. Frowned.

"This is the city lunatic asylum at Blackwell's Island."

Shock forced Amelia's eyes wide open. The light assaulted her, sent a bolt of pain through her head, forced a strangled groan from her throat. Her stomach heaved, but it was empty, and all she did was retch pitifully.

"None of that. We'll not be cleaning up after you."

One of the others spoke. "Let's get her seen to."

Hands pulled her upright, and the room whirled sickeningly. Amelia closed her eyes again.

One of the women probed at her head, yanked at her tender scalp. "What on earth have you done to your hair?"

Amelia reached up with a trembling hand. Felt coils of hair, stiff with filth.

"I'm not going to waste all day trying to get this mess cleaned and combed out. We're going to have to cut it off." The speaker nodded to the one with the folder. "Make a note: there was an infestation of lice."

Amelia ignored their chuckles as the woman reached into her pocket and produced a pair of scissors. Clumps of hair fell to the floor.

"There. Let's get her cleaned up." Two of them held her on her feet while the third stripped her, grumbling over the muck caked on her clothes. Naked, she was lifted into an enormous tub. The water was cold.

"In with you," one of them muttered, prodding her hard in the back.

Amelia's feet slipped out from under her, and the frigid water closed over her head. Her breath went out in a rush. She came up sputtering, the chill already seeping into her bones.

But it brought her further back to herself. She took more note of her surroundings as she was scrubbed with stinging soap and a coarse brush. Her hands and feet were blue with cold when the women finally lifted her out of the tub. She shuddered as they dried her with a length of rough toweling. They dressed her in a coarse linen shift and shapeless calico dress made for someone much taller. There was writing along the hem, illegible from her vantage point. A white cap and a pair of thin slippers completed her new wardrobe. Amelia's own clothes disappeared into the sack, probably fit only to be burned.

"Now then," the one with the folder said. "Carolina Casey, found in fits in a public park, possibly drunk, uncommunicative." She tutted. "No known family or friends, adjudged destitute, committed by judicial order until such time as the asylum superintendent finds her fit to be released."

Carolina. Who was . . . ?

"Lina," she muttered. The cloak Jonas had saved for her. It had Lina's name in it.

"Lina," one of the nurses repeated, scratching something in the file.

Amelia opened her mouth to protest, to tell them her real name, to insist they let her go. Then some practical part of her mind, awake now for the first time since the park, realized how it would sound—half the women here must insist all those things with their every breath. No one would believe her; anything she said would be only further evidence of her madness. And Lina had no further need of her cloak or her name. She was gone to California. Amelia stilled, keeping an iron grip on the terror beating its wings against her chest. Her name didn't matter. She could be Lina for now.

She was compliant as they led her from the washroom, feigning continued confusion. But though she kept her head lowered and her steps tentative, she darted glances in every direction, taking in as much as she could. One nurse led the way while the other two supported her as she stumbled down the long stone hallway. Amelia squinted against the noonday light coming in through the high, narrow windows lining one side. It penetrated only weakly into the barred cells along the opposite wall, painting the occupants in graded shadows. Some were nothing more than dark forms huddled away from the doors, despair wafting through the bars. Others pressed themselves forward, hands outthrust and imploring.

One woman flung herself at the door as they passed, hands clawed and digging bloody furrows down her own arms. "A knife. Please, a knife. They're under my skin. You have to help me," she begged.

The nurse in the lead chided her. "You'll have to go back into the jacket if you don't stop that." They walked on.

"My baby, my beautiful boy. I want my baby."

There were repeated thuds as one woman rocked on the floor, her hands over her face, her body thumping hard against the wall of the cell. "*Hilf mir. Hilf mir. Bitte!*"

Another shouted. "Water! Water, for the love of God, I'll burn up!"
The nurses ignored her.

"I want to go home. Please let me go home."

Women shrieked. They moaned. They sobbed and swore and gibbered. They sat in frozen silence and glared with murderous intent.

One caught Amelia's look as she passed. With a growl, the woman flung herself at the door. "You *cunt*. You dare to look at me? I'll rip your eyes from your face. I'll open your chest and tear out your heart." Her threats followed them as she faded from view.

A few more steps and there came a low, pleading voice.

"I have to get home to my cat. She'll wonder where I've gone, my sweet little kitty. She needs me."

The next cell stood open. Waiting. Wild laughter echoed from farther down the narrow hallway. The nurses guided Amelia into the empty cell, then turned away without a word.

The hinges screamed, and the door swung closed with a crash. It was the most final-sounding thing Amelia had ever heard.

5

Andrew Cavanaugh stood at the ferry's bow as it drew toward the island's northern dock. He'd been asked to arrive by eleven o'clock and assured someone would meet him, but the area around the weathered wooden structure was empty. It looked as though he would have to find his own way to the asylum.

The boat bumped to a stop against the pylons, and the ferryman appeared beside him and tossed a loop of rope over the one nearest the boat.

"This'll be your stop." He gestured to Andrew's medical bag and the large carton of books beside it. "I'm sorry I can't help with those," he said, not sounding sorry at all. "But I've a schedule to keep."

Andrew cast one last discouraged look past the dock, then bent to lift his things over the side. "I'm not sure where to go."

"The Octagon. Straight up the path there and to the left." The man pointed. "If you hit the lighthouse, you've gone too far."

Minutes later, Andrew was alone on the dock, the chuff of the ferry fading as it steamed back across the river. He sighed, then hoisted the box onto one shoulder and, taking his medical bag in his free hand, stepped onto the island.

The walk was not a long one, but the wind off the river was freezing. Andrew's ears and fingers were stinging with cold by the time he spotted his destination ahead. The building was rough-quarried gray stone, darkened by the rainy weather. Two straight wings spread out at right angles from the central building the ferryman had called the Octagon. It was indeed angled, with a high-domed roof. A wide paved walk and double staircase led to the entrance. Tall windows arranged on top of one another gave the appearance of glass columns. As he reached the doors, they swung open to reveal a stern-faced, balding man with a pair of spectacles perched atop a hawklike nose.

"You must be Dr. Cavanaugh."

"Yes." Clumsy with the cold, Andrew attempted to maneuver the box so he might offer his hand.

"I'm Simon Harcourt, asylum superintendent and head physician. Welcome." Harcourt motioned to a passing orderly with an acne-scarred face. "Russo, take Dr. Cavanaugh's things up to Dr. Blounton's—" He cut himself off. "To the small office on the third floor," he finished. Harcourt turned back to Andrew. "I'm sorry there was no one there to meet you with the wagon. We're dreadfully shorthanded."

Andrew's first sight of the inside of the Octagon brought him to a standstill, his mouth dropping open with surprise. Harcourt paused, apparently accustomed to the reaction.

"Unexpected, isn't it?"

"Very," Andrew replied. *Unexpected* was hardly the word. It felt inappropriate to call such a place *exquisite*, but it was the only word that came to mind. The ceiling rose above him all the way to the top of the dome. Wide, gleaming staircases spiraled through the rotunda to open balconies on each floor. Ferns stood on small tables against the walls, and a burnished wood door along the wall to his right stood open to reveal a comfortably appointed parlor. Other doors, most of them closed, lined the gently curved walls. After a moment, Andrew collected himself and turned back to his host.

"My apologies."

"It's a common enough reaction." A smile softened Harcourt's harsh features. "Come, I'll point out the essentials on the way to your office.

It's a bit small, I'm afraid. Once you've settled in, we can have a more detailed tour. I've also arranged a luncheon, where you can meet the other doctors. They're the ones you'll be working with the most. I see some patients, but I am much preoccupied with administration. Come."

Harcourt narrated as they walked. "Here on the first floor, there are parlors and receiving rooms for visitors and official guests, as well as the staff dining rooms. There are entrances to the patient wings on each floor."

He opened a polished wood door to reveal a short vestibule with another door at the other end. In contrast, that one was heavy steel, with a barred, square viewing port and a formidable-looking lock.

"We have over twelve hundred patients, all women, of course," Harcourt went on. "The men were moved to a facility on Wards Island several years ago. We have a staff of sixty-five—mostly orderlies and nurses. There are three resident doctors, in addition to myself."

"So few? That seems inadequate for the need."

"Oh, it is," Harcourt replied. "It's far too great a load for the staff we have. We leave most of the routine care to the nurses, and even they're stretched thin. The asylum was never intended for so many patients. There are only four physicians' apartments—hence my inability to offer you living quarters along with the job." They started up the stairs.

"Technically, we're not even budgeted for a fifth physician. I've scraped together the salary out of discretionary funds. You're fortunate to have some independent means." He glanced at the fine wool of Andrew's suit.

"Yes," Andrew said, uncomfortably reminded of the falsehood he'd told during his interview. In fact, thanks to his recent estrangement from his family, he had nothing but his own savings to supplement the admittedly tiny salary. But Harcourt had seemed somewhat suspicious of his willingness to accept such a paltry figure, and Andrew had been desperate to get the job, so he'd tossed off a line about income from a family trust.

Andrew changed the subject. "What about my predecessor? Where did he go after his time here?"

Harcourt blanched. "Unfortunately, the position became vacant due to the death of the previous occupant."

"Oh dear. I'm sorry to hear that."

"Thank you—it was a shock and terribly sad."

Harcourt continued as they passed the second floor. "We have a central administrative office here. There is also a small medical library and private doctors' parlor, both of which you are, obviously, welcome to use. Resident physicians' apartments are here on the third level—as is the office we have set aside for you. I hope it will be adequate."

As he finished, Harcourt opened a door down the hall from the stairs and stepped inside. Andrew followed. His bag and carton of books sat on a battered desk beside the narrow window.

"I had it cleared out for you," Harcourt said, tugging at one of the drawers. It opened halfway, then stuck. He shoved it closed with a screech. Both men winced at the sound.

"I can see about finding you a different desk, if you like."

"I'm sure this one will be fine," Andrew assured him. Behind it sat a wheeled wooden office chair. A second chair and a long table were the only other furnishings.

There was another door opposite the desk. It led to a narrow room with shelves and wooden cabinets lining the wall. Stacks of files covered every surface, and a folding cot sat in the corner. Andrew looked back at Harcourt, a question on his face.

"Records storage," Harcourt explained. "The patient wings are so crowded we've had to find space wherever we can. Current patients' files are in the treatment wings, but the older records are more scattered."

"And that?" Andrew gestured to the far end of the room, where a metal ladder, bolted to the wall, terminated beneath a hatch in the ceiling.

Harcourt leaned around him. "Ah, yes. An access hatch for the roof. There are several on this floor. The dome is impressive, but it requires an impractical level of maintenance." He checked his watch. "I believe lunch will be waiting, if you are ready?"

The meal was served in a pleasant dining room on the first floor. Two other men were already seated at the long table when Andrew and Harcourt arrived. The elder of the two, a wizened man with ink-stained cuffs, paid them no mind, his attention fixed on the notebook before him as he scratched away with a pen. The other, perhaps in his forties, with a stocky build and gingery side whiskers, stood as they entered.

"Dr. Tyree," Harcourt said. "Please, sit. This is Dr. Andrew Cavanaugh."
Andrew leaned across the table to shake the man's hand.

"Welcome," Tyree said as he retook his seat. "William Tyree." He
indicated the man seated to his left. "This is Dr. Donald Lawrence."
Tyree tapped him on the shoulder. "Lawrence, would you join us for a
moment, please? The new doctor is here."

Lawrence looked up with an absent expression, his fine white hair
floating around his head like dandelion fluff. "Hmm?" He focused on
Andrew, then started. "Oh, yes, pardon me. Welcome. Dr. Donald Lawrence." He shook Andrew's hand, then seemed to forget him, turning
back to his notes.

"You'll have to pardon Lawrence," Tyree said with a sigh. "He lives
on a different plane than we mortals. You watch, if we don't stay after
him, he'll forget to eat. Myself, though, I'm hungry. Where's Klafft?"

"Right here," said a new voice. A spare, nattily dressed man with
smooth silver hair stood in the doorway, an edge of irritation in his patri-
cian features. He entered and took the seat to Andrew's left. "Dr. Roger
Klafft." He shook Andrew's hand with starchy formality.

A silent young man in a threadbare suit had entered behind him.
He took up a position against the wall behind Klafft's chair. No one
introduced him.

"Well," Harcourt said. "Now that we're all here, let's eat."

The food was plain but good—roasted chicken, potatoes, peas. There
were fresh rolls and butter on the table, along with a wedge of cheese
and a dish of preserves.

Harcourt spoke as they began to fill their plates. "I thought this would
be an excellent opportunity for all of you to meet Dr. Cavanaugh and
help him prepare for his work."

Klafft lowered his fork. "What work is that, precisely, if I may ask?
You were an internist in Philadelphia, were you not?"

"Yes." Andrew paused to pass a platter to Tyree, who nodded his thanks.
"I grew up there. After college in Boston, I returned home for medical
school. Once I finished, I was invited to join an established practice."

"Why did you leave? I would have thought that a fine prospect for a
young physician."

"It was. But after my . . ." Andrew stumbled, then cleared his throat. "Due to some personal circumstances, I became interested in diseases of the mind, specifically as they manifest in women."

Personal circumstances. What a pallid way of describing the abrupt upending of his entire life. His father had been furious when Andrew announced he was leaving. His mother had sobbed and begged him not to go. Ending his engagement had been far less difficult than it should have been, if he were honest with himself. Cecilia had been angry but far from heartbroken. She'd been more concerned with the embarrassment than with the loss of the relationship itself. *Everything is arranged! Have you even stopped to consider how humiliating this will be for me?*

She'd rebounded quickly. It hadn't taken long before all of Philadelphia society knew *she'd* thrown *him* over for unspecified but clearly just reasons. Between that and his obvious schism with his family, by the time he left, most of his acquaintance had started pretending not to see him in public.

He didn't care. He'd wanted out. Out of the engagement, out of the city, out of the constricted little life he'd been so busily building for himself. He'd begun making plans to leave even before the funeral—had been willing to go anywhere to get away. He'd even considered going abroad.

"I saw the advertisement for the position here," Andrew explained. "It seemed the perfect way to gain experience with the kinds of cases I wished to study."

"And what are those, precisely?" Klafft asked.

"All mental disorders are fascinating, but my particular focus is the phenomenon of dementia praecox. I hope to produce the first American monograph on the topic. There are some recent clinical reports out of Prague, but—"

"Oh!" Lawrence looked up from his writing. "Have you read Pick's work? I've been quite interested, but my German is dreadful. I was unable to get the details of the cases he reported. You must tell me all about them." He turned to a new page in his notebook, pen poised, and looked up at Andrew, intent. "I understand he views it as a form of hebephrenia. How does his classification differ—"

"Please, Lawrence, not now," Tyree interjected. He reached for another roll and looked at Andrew. "He'll have you reciting the entire contents of those reports if you let him. He'll fill a notebook, the rest of us won't get another word in, and you'll not get another bite of your lunch."

"But his theories are fascinating," the older man protested. "Why, an identification and classification of various forms of dementia praecox would revolutionize our understanding—"

"What rubbish," Klafft snorted and set down his fork.

Andrew looked at him, surprised. "How so? I found the concept quite logical. Categorizing symptoms may help us understand the causes of various forms of insanity and might even help us learn how to treat them more effectively."

Klafft made a derisive noise. "Far better to classify them by the source of their problems."

"What do you mean?"

"Inebriates, hysterics, syphilitics, and malingerers," Klafft replied, counting them off on his fingers. "Nearly every patient here is one of those. Oh, there are some cases of congenital insanity, I'll grant you, but most of the insane are victims of nothing but their own bad choices and innate low instincts. As for treatment—"

"Roger has a somewhat more, let us say, *old-fashioned* approach to psychiatry, as you may perceive," Tyree interjected.

"Must I remind you, yet again—"

Tyree sighed. "Yes, I know. I do beg your pardon, Dr. Klafft."

Andrew looked between them.

"I prefer a certain degree of formality," Klafft explained stiffly. "I do not think it appropriate to be overly familiar with one's colleagues."

There was a moment of silence after this pronouncement. Harcourt cleared his throat. "Dr. Tyree, I wonder if you might be willing to let Dr. Cavanaugh accompany you this afternoon? I have a mountain of paperwork waiting, and there's still so much of the facility he hasn't seen. I'd rather not leave him to wander without a guide on his first day."

"Of course. I'd be delighted."

After a dessert of apple tart with cream, Andrew followed Tyree up to the second floor. A gangly young man in his twenties sat behind a desk inside the doorway. He brightened as he saw them and stood, nodding to Tyree, then turned to Andrew.

"You must be Dr. Cavanaugh. Herbert Winslow," he said, extending his hand.

"Winslow is our head clerk," Tyree said. "He's really the one who keeps the place running. You should have seen what a shambles it was before he got here. You'll probably find him a great help to your research—he's a genius at tracking down misplaced paperwork and such."

The young man waved away the praise as he settled back into his chair. "It only seems that way because you always misplace your paperwork in the same places, and I just happen to know where they are." He turned to Andrew. "I am, however, at your service, should you need anything."

"Dr. Cavanaugh will be joining me on afternoon rounds," Tyree said. "Where are we headed?"

"Wards one and three." Winslow handed him a sheet of paper. "And the reconciliation was yesterday, so this should be accurate."

Before Tyree could respond, a metallic clamor split the air. Andrew started at the sound, and Winslow leapt to his feet with an apologetic grimace. "The telephone," he explained, hurrying toward an alcove on the wall.

Tyree looked at Andrew with a sympathetic grin. "Awful racket, isn't it? We've had the thing for over a year, and I'm still not used to that noise. No denying it's useful—when it's working properly," he added, as Winslow's raised voice carried across the room. "There are days when the connection is dreadful." Tyree turned his back on the young man's technological struggles.

"What is the reconciliation?"

"Winslow's Sisyphean attempt to impose order on chaos." Tyree rummaged in a drawer and came up with a battered clipboard. He attached the page Winslow had given him. "Patients get moved from ward to ward, but the transfers aren't always reflected on the ward lists. Each patient has a file as well, which is meant to be kept in the ward with her, but you can imagine how frequently those go astray. So once a week, there's an audit of sorts. A head count and roll call in each ward. Then the lists get updated and the files moved. Winslow instituted it not long after he arrived. It's made a world of difference." He tucked the clipboard beneath his arm.

"Now, if you're ready, we can get started. We have wards one and three. The malingerers and the hysterics, as Klafft would have it," he said, with a sardonic glance at Andrew, who smiled.

"So the patients *are* separated by diagnosis?"

"Oh, nothing so formal. We do our best to keep the violent away from potential victims. We try to identify the patients who can safely be released." He sighed. "And Klafft is correct that a great many of the residents here are inebriates of one kind or another. Or, yes, former prostitutes. It's not at all uncommon for women to split their time between the city streets and the asylum. Many of them have nowhere else to go."

Andrew followed Tyree out of the office and back toward the staircase.

"The asylum opened in 1839. It was the first city asylum in the country. Before that, there had been only state and private institutions." He gestured to Andrew to take the stairs down ahead of him.

"The ferryman mentioned a lighthouse. Where is that?" Andrew asked.

"On the northernmost point of the island. Supposedly built by an asylum inmate, although that was before my time. Before any of us, actually, even Lawrence, and god knows he's been here an age. Twenty years or more, at least. He likely couldn't tell you exactly himself. Brilliant mind, in his day, but I'm afraid he's grown increasingly, ah, *abstracted*, I suppose, is the proper word for it."

"And yet he's still caring for patients?" Andrew asked.

Tyree caught his meaning. "Yes. He's not incompetent, merely eccentric. *More* eccentric," he corrected himself. "I'd guess he was always a bit of an odd duck. Although, really, we all are, to some extent. One has to be, to work here for very long."

"I suppose it can be a difficult environment."

"Indeed. And working here also means living here, present company excepted. Makes it difficult to have a normal life. One couldn't very well have a wife and children living here, for example."

"How long have the others been here?"

"Well, I'm coming up on seven years. Klafft . . . let me think. Twelve, perhaps? I'm not certain. Harcourt arrived only about three years ago."

They reached the ground floor, and Tyree directed him toward one of the doors to the wards Harcourt had shown Andrew earlier. "A bit of a surprise that he applied for the position, actually. He'd been on the verge of retiring, or so I heard. Klafft was furious when the board of governors chose Harcourt over him." Tyree opened the ward's first door, stepped inside the vestibule, and rapped on the metal door.

"Lawrence kept misplacing his keys," he explained. "So now none of us carry them."

Andrew nodded and returned to the earlier topic. "Dr. Klafft had applied as well, then?"

"In a manner of speaking. He presumed he would get the job."

"Why didn't he?" Andrew asked.

Tyree glanced around, then lowered his voice. "I heard his interview with the board went terribly. His belief in his own superiority was on full display. You can imagine how they responded. He makes no secret of the fact that he regards their decision as a mistake."

"That must make things awkward for Dr. Harcourt."

"Indeed it does. But it was for the best. Roger is a terrible doctor," he said. "Not bad enough to warrant dismissal, especially since it's damned difficult to find people willing to work here at all. You know, when the asylum first opened, they used convicts to care for the patients. I've often thought Roger wouldn't blink at reinstating the practice."

"His view of the patients did seem rather harsh."

Tyree muffled a chuckle as he knocked on the door again. "That was diplomatic of you. He's more like a character from a Dickens story than a modern practitioner. Honestly, I don't think he ever actually wanted to be a doctor, and certainly not an asylum physician. But can you imagine him in a private practice?" Tyree shook his head. "He'd be a disaster. Here, he's an authority. And his patients are in no position to complain about his manner toward them."

Tyree quieted at the sound of the lock turning. "Malingerers first," he said, with a wry glance at Andrew as the heavy door swung open. "We'd best ease you into it."

6

The first night of her captivity passed more easily than Amelia expected. She woke to a noise at the cell door. A young man stood there, fumbling with a ring of keys and holding a tray. She sat up carefully, relieved to find her headache gone. She stretched and swung her feet to the floor. As the man entered, Amelia tried to speak but produced only a rusty whisper.

"Good morning."

He looked up. "Good morning, miss. I have your breakfast." He stepped forward, set the tray at the foot of her bed, and turned to leave.

"Could you tell me what's going to happen?" He looked at her, uncertain. "I mean," Amelia continued, "can you tell me the normal order of things here? I'd like to know what to expect."

"I'm not supposed to talk much to the inmat—the patients. The nurse will be along in a minute," he said in a low voice. "She won't like it."

"Please," Amelia said. "It's very frightening not to know what's happening."

With another quick look out the door, he relented. "Well, you're new, so you're in the isolation cells. You'll be here for a bit while the doctors watch to see if you're dangerous. Them that are—the ones who hurt themselves or attack the other patients—they stay here. If you aren't, and if you don't give nobody no trouble, they'll move you to one of the open wards. Some of them ain't so bad. The women there sew, and sometimes they go outside to walk or work in the gardens."

Amelia was a great deal more concerned about the wards where they *didn't* sew or go for walks, but she knew she'd gotten as much as she could from the man.

"Thank you." She gave him a faint smile as he left.

Her stomach growled as she examined the tray. It held a bowl of mashed oats, a hunk of dry brown bread, and a tin mug of what looked like either tea or weak coffee. Unappetizing under most circumstances, but it was anyone's guess how long it had been since she had eaten. She apparently wasn't permitted cutlery, so she used the crust of the bread to scoop the cold oats into her mouth.

When they'd left her the day before, she'd been unable to do anything but lean against the wall, trying to master her panic. Amelia had nearly added her own voice to the chorus of wails and shouts coming from the hallway. Finally, she'd stumbled to the narrow bed and lay down, her knees pulled to her chest. She stayed there, as still as a hare in the shadow of a hawk. Eventually she must have fallen asleep, although she had been in such a state she was frankly surprised. But the long, dreamless—

She went still. Dreamless. The god-awful nightmare of the Tower hadn't come last night. Had it been a premonition? She tore off a chunk of bread with her teeth. If so, it hadn't proven at all useful. Flowers and armless women and that slithering creature.

And then the apparition in the park. She shuddered, recalling the feeling of invasion, the wrongness of that thing pushing into her head. She'd had unnerving experiences before—no few of them in the past several weeks. But nothing had ever come close to that. Jonas had been right, as usual. Her gift had changed. And this was where it had led her.

She sipped at the mug—tea, weak and unsweetened—as she studied the cell. The walls and floor were rough gray stone, and the low ceiling appeared to be wooden beams mostly buried in thick plaster. The only light spilled in through the barred door from the window across the hall. The mattress beneath her was stained and the blanket was thin and rough, but both smelled of lye soap. They must be careful of lice and other vermin in a place like this. That was something to be thankful for, at least. She leaned forward to peer beneath the cot. A metal chamber pot sat under its foot. She shifted in sudden discomfort, hoping someone would take her to the washroom before she had to make use of it.

I've gotten soft, she thought in chagrin. Not so long before, chamber pots had been a fact of life.

Amelia pulled her attention back to the matter at hand. No one knew where she was. Jonas would be frantic. He would search for her, but with no way of knowing where she'd gone or what had happened to her, finding her would be difficult. She sighed, regretting anew her cruel parting words. If she couldn't get out of here. . . . No. She would get out. She would convince whoever was in charge she was perfectly sane, and they would let her go.

Amelia practiced her plea as though it were a catechism. Writing and rewriting her lines in her head, adjusting her tone and delivery until it was note-perfect. When the doctor came, she would explain. She'd been ill. She had believed herself recovered and had gone for a walk in the park, where she'd fainted. She had friends. She was no vagrant, no inebriate. She did not belong in an asylum. There had been a terrible misunderstanding. She would send word, and Jonas would come for her.

She sat and watched the pale light move across the floor. The din from the other women rolled through the ward like waves on the ocean, never ceasing, retreating for only moments at a time before swelling again. A pair of nurses came to take her to the washroom. A second meal appeared, no more appetizing than the first. People passed in the hallway, but none of them looked at her.

Amelia was careful to maintain a genial expression and correct posture, ready for the doctor whenever he should come. By the time a third meal arrived, she realized none would. She slumped on her cot and reached for the tray. She ate the bland food without interest, but the first swallow from the tin mug brought her upright again with a cough. Water, with a bitter, medicinal aftertaste. Laudanum, and a hefty dose of it. She set down the mug. She had no interest in another episode of insensibility if she could avoid it.

As night fell, the ward quieted. Clearly, she had not been singled out to receive the drug. She wondered at the other patients. The taste had been obvious. Those who drank it must have been too deranged to care. Or perhaps, she considered with a chill, sane enough to embrace any means of escape, however temporary.

∞

Days passed, leaden and sluggish. The drug-laced water appeared twice more, following no appreciable pattern. Fearful someone would notice her refusals, whenever Amelia detected the telltale bitterness, she poured the tainted water into the chamber pot. The ward was as silent as a tomb those nights.

There were no additional manifestations of her altered gift, and Amelia developed a faint hope it had left her. She tensed and readied herself each time footsteps sounded in the hall, but the only ones that stopped at her door were those of a rotating cast of orderlies and nurses.

That morning's nurse was one of the talkative ones, keeping up a steady stream of commentary as she went about her work. Amelia watched between the bars as she returned her neighbor to her cell. The woman's face was slack and haggard, with limp hanks of graying hair hanging around it.

"Your damned cat is right here." The nurse scooped something from the floor and pressed it into the woman's hands. The patient gave a low cry, and the nurse swung the door closed with a shake of her head. "She asks for her cat, we give it to her, and what does she do but fling it on the floor."

She unlocked Amelia's cell as she spoke, and Amelia shifted in anticipation. Meals arrived at more or less the same times each day, but visits to the washroom were sporadic. She had several times been forced to resort to the chamber pot, much to her own disgust.

Amelia stepped meekly out of the cell and started down the hallway. She glanced into her neighbor's cell as they passed. The woman was curled on her bunk, keening. The stuffed cat, a pitiful, grayish lump, lay abandoned. They walked on.

"And you," the nurse said to the next cell's occupant. "Told you you'd be back in the jacket, didn't I? Gave you proper warning, but here you are anyway, and with none but yourself to blame."

That woman, shrouded like a corpse in white canvas and leather straps, was oblivious to the reproach.

The nurse quieted as they passed the next cell, and both she and Amelia quickened their steps. The woman who'd threatened Amelia the first day was young, not much older than Amelia herself, from the looks of it. She might have been attractive, were it not for the unfocused fury twisting her features. She had an impressive store of profanity, and she was generous with it, hurling obscenities at anyone unwise enough to look in her direction. And words weren't the only thing she hurled—she plainly did not have reservations when it came to the use of the chamber pot.

In the washroom, Amelia found herself standing at the sinks next to the young woman who always cried for her baby, brought there with her own pitiless escort. As the two nurses gossiped by the door, Amelia washed her face and tried her best to ignore the girl, who stood mute as tears made shining tracks down her cheeks. Despite her resolve, she could not help herself in the face of such misery.

Amelia reached out and squeezed the girl's hand. Time halted at the touch.

Though neither of them had ever learned to swim, she and Jonas had once taken a day-trip to Brighton Beach. With a packed lunch and a pair of borrowed bathing costumes, they'd boarded a train in the dark of the early morning. They dozed in a cramped compartment and arrived just after the sun came up.

Enthralled by the view of the horizon, Amelia ignored the bathing boxes and walked out into the surf, enjoying the gentle tug of the waves and the sliding sand beneath her feet. Unwary, she went out too far. A rogue swell knocked her off her feet, and in an instant everything went mad. She clawed at nothing as she spun in the foamy water, buffeted against the ocean floor and terrified of being dragged out into the deep. There was nothing but rough sand and frothing water and naked desperation.

Taking the girl's hand felt like being swallowed by that wave. A torrent of images, vivid and wrenching, poured through Amelia's mind and became as real to her as her own thoughts. She knew why the girl—Mara was her name—wept, what she'd lost. She felt what Mara did, the boundless sorrow, the scouring shame, and the utter certainty that all the world in every direction held only more of the same. Panic gripped her for a moment as she was nearly swept away. But like the wave that day at Brighton, almost before it had begun, it ended, and she found her feet again.

Amelia blinked. No more than a second had passed. The nurses had not paused in their conversation. She let out a shuddering breath. So much for hoping her new abilities had gone. She looked at Mara, and the pain in the girl's eyes made Amelia's heart lurch.

She gave the hand she still held another gentle squeeze and let go. "It wasn't your fault."

The nurses looked over at the words. One of them snorted in contempt. "Says the likes of you." She turned on the young woman. "And you. Always wanting us to bring you your baby. Can't, can we? And well enough you know it, since you were the one what killed it. Oh, you fooled the judge, but you'll not fool me."

Scowling, the nurse jerked Amelia away and hauled her back to her cell.

That afternoon, Amelia lay on her cot, trying to make sense of it all. Before her injury, the most dramatic display of her ability had been the time she told Jonas to bet on Henny Pritchard's little brindle bitch to win in the ring. He'd looked at her doubtfully but done it. The skinny dog had taken down an ugly, snarling cur twice her size, and they'd won what was, for them, a tidy sum—they'd slept indoors, with full bellies, for most of a month off the winnings.

That had only happened the once, despite their many attempts to recreate the feat. Her whole life, Amelia had sometimes known things she shouldn't have. But as often as not they were silly, useless things. Oh, she and Jonas used her flashes whenever they could, but it was never very often. Her ability simply wasn't reliable. And it had certainly never shown her anything like the things she'd been seeing since her accident.

The cards and the dream seemed to speak for themselves. They'd been a warning of her coming incarceration, for all the good it had done. Touching Mrs. Franklin and Mara had triggered something, but there was more to it than that. She tried to count all the people who'd touched her since she woke. Jonas, obviously. The doctor. Tommy. The nurses who'd stripped and bathed her when she'd arrived and a few of those who'd escorted her through the halls. She'd seen nothing with any of them. So it wasn't as though every touch brought it on, and thank god for that, or she'd go mad in truth before long. The spirit in the park had affected her even before it touched her, but she hadn't seen anything like it since—and fervently hoped she never would again.

Amelia brooded for a while, then set it aside with a sigh. It wasn't as though there was anything she could do about any of it at the moment. She and Jonas could talk it through once she was free. He would come for her. She knew, knew to her bones, he would never abandon her.

With every day, however, her certainty grew the slightest bit fainter. At night, when the ward was ghostly silent and the shadows invited doubt, she could not master her traitorous mind. Jonas was coming, she reminded herself in the daylight. But at night she lay in her cell, remembering her goading words, imagining him boarding a ship for Europe, walking the streets of a foreign city. Each morning she shamed herself for harboring such thoughts. Then night fell again, and they wormed their way back into her mind, the images crisp and haunting.

She edged ever closer to despair.

By Amelia's admittedly imprecise reckoning, it was the fourteenth day of her captivity before she finally caught sight of a doctor. He stopped outside her door, a nurse by his side. She straightened and readied herself to speak, her heart pounding. The doctor wore finely tailored wool, and his silver hair was smoothed back with pomade. She fought down a feeling of instant dislike.

"Carolina Casey," the nurse read off a clipboard. "Vagrant, possible dipsomaniac."

The doctor made a noise. "Any incidents since her arrival?"

"Nothing of note."

"Move her to the wards, then. Number three. See how she does there." He began to move away without ever having looked at her.

His dismissal was like a slap, and Amelia leapt to her feet. "Doctor! Please, I need to speak with you."

He stopped, turned. His gaze flickered over her, settling on a point somewhere behind her head. "Yes?"

Her carefully prepared speech fled in the face of his disinterest. She groped for a moment before picking up the thread. "I . . . I shouldn't be here. I'm quite well. I was ill, you see, but—"

He cut her off. "Yes, yes, of course. You aren't ill any longer, you have friends who would care for you, you certainly aren't insane, you are here through mere happenstance, no fault of your own, and I should release you immediately. Is that what you were going to say?"

Startled, she blinked at him. "Yes, I—"

He interrupted again. "Miss . . ." He looked at the nurse.

"Casey," she supplied, after a swift glance at the paper.

"Miss Casey, you cannot expect to be the judge of your own condition. And I assure you, if those things were true, you would not have been brought here in the first place. You should be grateful those who know better are able to look after you."

He turned on his heel and walked away, the nurse hurrying after him.

7

The suggestion was so lewdly graphic that Andrew felt his eyebrows climb toward his hairline. He regained control of his expression, if only just, but couldn't stop a flush from spilling across his cheeks and down the back of his neck. The patient cackled at his discomfiture before settling back onto her cot with a satisfied grunt.

He gave her a quelling look and finished his review of her file without further interruption: a long history of arrests for prostitution and drunkenness; no known family; committed to the city lunatic asylum after repeated public indecencies.

He sighed and closed the folder before handing it back to the waiting nurse.

He'd already seen more than a dozen cases of advanced neurosyphilis in his first two weeks of work. This one offered nothing new. Medically, nothing could be done for her. The asylum was as good a place as any to keep her fed and housed until the end, which—judging from the yellow tint to her skin—was not long in coming.

Andrew started for the door at the other end of ward five, known unofficially as the incurables wing. It was a depressingly apt designation. His eyes roved over dozens of other patients as he went. Some were quite clearly ill, raving and weeping; a few were even wearing restraints. Others merely sat, mute and unseeing. He fought the urge to stop, to try to speak to them. To offer some measure of comfort. It would do no good.

Tyree had told him the truth that first day—the "malingerers" had been a gentle introduction to the asylum. In the two weeks since, he'd seen more depravity and more anguish than in the whole of his life up until then. There were so *many* patients, with more coming in each week, and so few effective means of helping the sickest of them. He reached into his coat pocket and rolled the hard rubber cylinder he found there between his fingers. It contained a syringe loaded with chloral hydrate, which he'd begun carrying on Tyree's recommendation. "There will be times when you'll want it quickly," the other physician advised him. "Best to have it ready." So far, Andrew had not been forced to use it, but there had been several times he'd come close.

One of the nurses swung open the outer door as he approached. He nodded his thanks to her and stepped out into the main hallway. He sighed as the door closed behind him and raised a hand to rub at the back of his neck.

"You look as though you could use a drink."

Andrew turned. Tyree walked toward him, a knowing expression on his face.

"It shows, does it?"

"One comes to know the signs. Are you finished for the day?"

Andrew nodded. "I was about to get my things and head to the ferry."

Tyree pulled a watch from his pocket and clicked open the cover. "Well, you'll have missed the six o'clock. May as well come up and have a drink while you wait for the next one. You can tell me about it." He gestured toward the ward door.

Andrew's face heated again as he thought of the woman's proposition.

Tyree grinned. "Must have been a good one."

Andrew relayed the story as they walked, and by the time they reached the stairs, the other man shook with barely suppressed laughter, his face nearly as red as his hair. Andrew felt a smile pulling at the corners of his own mouth.

They passed Dr. Klafft on the way up, trailed by Connolly, the young man who'd stood behind him at lunch the first day. He was, Andrew had since learned, employed by Klafft. "Paid from my personal funds," Klafft informed him upon discovering Connolly completing some trivial task Andrew had unwittingly assigned him. He seemed to be a sort of secretary-cum-valet. "A dogsbody," according to Tyree. He assisted Klafft in the wards, but he also saw to the doctor's wardrobe, kept his social calendar, and—if Tyree's somewhat acerbic commentary was to be credited—even shaved him in the mornings. He allegedly lived off-island, although Andrew found it difficult to believe, ever-present as he was.

The older man gave the pair of them a disapproving look before continuing on his way, his silent, harried shadow scurrying in his wake.

"Here we are," Tyree said moments later. He unlocked the door and gestured for Andrew to enter ahead of him.

They stepped into a comfortable-looking parlor, with plush furniture and decent rugs on the floor.

"Help yourself to whatever you like." Tyree pointed to a shelf containing several bottles. "Pour two. I'm going to wash up before I join you." He disappeared through another door at the back of the room.

Andrew examined the selection and poured two glasses of what turned out to be entirely undistinguished whiskey. Leaving one on the table, he took the other with him as he made an aimless circuit of the room. There were several prints on the walls, but no photographs. The only sign of disorder was a pair of boxes on the floor in front of a deep shelf of books and curios. Andrew examined the volumes on the bottom shelf: several popular novels, some poetry. Propping them up at one end was a glass-topped wooden case with a tarnished brass latch. Inside, resting in velvet-lined cradles, sat several pistols, some obviously quite old.

"Inherited from my father," Tyree said from behind him. Andrew turned back to the other man, who took a drink and sighed with evident pleasure. "Never saw the appeal myself, but after he died it seemed wrong to sell them. Are firearms an interest of yours?" He gestured to the case with his glass.

"Not particularly," Andrew replied. "An uncle taught me to shoot when I was a boy, but I never showed any aptitude for it."

"You're still ahead of me, then. I've never taken them out of the case." Tyree seated himself in a worn leather chair. "So, apart from obscene suggestions, how are you finding your time here?"

Andrew cast around for the right word as he sat. "Enlightening."

"Not what you expected?"

"I'm not sure what I expected. I suppose I was not prepared to see so much intractable illness. So many of the patients seem so far removed from reality," he said. "I don't know that anyone can help them. It's disturbing."

"Do you regret taking the job?"

"No," Andrew said after a moment. "There are patients here who can be helped. It is a fine thing, for the city to have a facility such as this to care for the poor. And from the perspective of my research, it's ideal. The wealthy have many of the same problems, but they're far better at keeping them secret. It isn't—"

Andrew cut himself off and glanced at Tyree, hoping the bitterness creeping into his tone hadn't caught the other man's attention. But no, Tyree didn't appear to have noticed anything unusual. Relieved, he went on. "At any rate, I feel quite fortunate my situation has worked out as it has."

"Even if you do have to spend some of your time in ward five?"

"Even in ward five there may be those who could be treated, if only there were resources enough."

"You sound like Blounton." Tyree shook his head, a flicker of emotion passing over his features.

"I presume he is the doctor who passed away?" Andrew asked after a moment's hesitation.

Tyree nodded. "Dr. John Blounton. A fine physician. Quite dedicated to the patients. He could have had a bright future somewhere, but he wanted to be here."

"He was young, then?"

"Indeed. Just two or three years out of medical school. He was only here for a few months, but I liked him quite a lot." Tyree stared into his glass. He hesitated, then seemed to decide something. "Officially, his death was an accident."

"Officially?"

Tyree sighed. "I don' like to tell tales, but . . ." He took a swallow of whiskey, then continued. "I believe I would be remiss not to offer my advice." He looked at Andrew, his gaze direct. "Working in a place like this, one needs to be able to keep a certain professional distance. I don't mean like Klafft, insisting on being addressed as 'Doctor' even at lunch with his colleagues. Ridiculous man." He snorted. "No, I mean from the patients, from their histories, from the weight of the place itself. There are a great many sad stories here. If you let them affect you too much . . . Well, Blounton was young and idealistic. He didn't understand that however much he wanted to help the patients here, it wasn't always possible to do so. I saw it happen. He hadn't been here long before the place began to drag at him. He grew quieter. And then . . ."

"Do you mean to imply—" Andrew floundered, unsure how to continue. "Forgive me for asking so bluntly, but how did he die?"

Tyree grimaced. "It was ruled an accident, as I said. He was known to be in the habit of taking walks along the island's seawall, and the verdict at the inquest was that he must have slipped and fallen in somewhere. Hit his head on something and drowned. But I've wondered ever since if that's the truth of it. He had changed so much. And I feel a certain degree of guilt about it, as well."

He stood and crossed to the decanter, where he poured himself another drink, raising an eyebrow and pointing to Andrew's glass as he did so. Andrew declined with a small shake of his head.

Tyree sat back down. "I should have pursued the matter when he began to pull away from our friendship. But I'm afraid I was rather hurt by it. I didn't see it for what it was. If I had said something to him, or if I had been here when it happened . . ." He shook his head with regret.

"You were away?"

"Yes. I was attending a conference that week. In Philadelphia, as a matter of fact. It was such terrible news to come home to." He sighed. "Ultimately, there's no way of knowing exactly what happened."

He indicated the boxes by the shelf. "I packed up his things afterward. I found nothing to indicate he'd planned to harm himself. But one doesn't always."

"No," Andrew said quietly, "one doesn't." He took another swallow of his drink, trying to dissolve the knot that had suddenly appeared in his throat.

There was a long moment before Tyree spoke again. "I haven't shared my suspicion with anyone else. I would hate to cause further grief to his family. I hope you will honor that desire."

"Certainly."

"I wouldn't have even brought it up, but as I said, you remind me of him. I know you have little experience with such things, and I know how important it is for you to guard yourself from too much sentiment. We have all had to learn. Klafft manages by virtue of his own unpleasantness—he blames the patients for their condition, so they aren't worthy of sympathy. Lawrence records minutiae and natters on about nothing and floats above it all. Harcourt avoids the wards by burying himself in administrative work."

"And yourself?" Andrew asked. "How do you manage?"

Tyree considered his now-empty glass. "I strive always to remember why I am here. I keep my distance. I do my job, and I walk away."

They finished their drinks in silence, and Andrew thanked Tyree for his hospitality and bade him farewell. As the sun fell toward the horizon, Andrew made his way back across the river and to his rented rooms, his heart heavy. When he arrived, he took off his coat and lowered himself into a ratty armchair, lost in thought.

He found himself staring at one of the cartons he'd never gotten around to unpacking after his hurried flight from Philadelphia, then reached out and hauled it nearer. He tore open the flaps and rummaged, sitting up a moment later with a small wooden box in his hand.

He opened the lid and read the brief note first, although he'd long since memorized every word.

My dearest Jamie—
 I'm so sorry. This isn't your fault.
 Please forgive me.
 I love you always.
 Susannah

Beneath the note was a silver oval—a locket on a chain. The metal was smooth and cold beneath his fingers. Finally, the photograph. By then it was as familiar to him as his own face in the mirror: a little boy, wrestled into his best suit of clothes and standing, stiff with resentment, next to a smiling older girl in a ruffled dress. The locket was visible, hanging around her neck. Andrew traced her face with a finger before he flipped the photograph over and ran his thumb across the faded words their mother had inked there years before.

Susannah Grace Cavanaugh, age 12
Andrew James Cavanaugh, age 8

Tyree had warned him to avoid involvement. There was wisdom in the advice, but Andrew knew he would never be able to embrace it. He'd kept his distance once before, and the price had been far too high.

8

W ard two was one large room, broken in half by a low wall. Behind it, iron cots crowded against one another, so close each woman felt the breath of her neighbor on her face as she slept. In the front were rows of hard wooden benches, backless and rough, where the patients—some two hundred of them, by Amelia's rough count—spent the bulk of their waking hours pressed shoulder to shoulder.

It took Amelia less than a day to decide she vastly preferred her cell.

The crowding would have been unpleasant under any circumstance, but it proved an especial torment to Amelia. It was impossible to avoid touching the other women: a brushed hand as they reached for a bowl or steadied themselves on the benches, an outflung arm in the night. Twice that first day in the new ward, the unexpected contact sent a jolt of insight through her, as it had with Mara. The first time, Amelia relived a woman's memory of being held facedown in a washtub, a man's large hand on the back of her head as she struggled. It ended as she breathed in, and Amelia came back to herself with a choked gasp, her heart hammering against her ribs.

The second time was worse.

Desperate to keep it from happening again, Amelia held herself rigid on her bench the rest of the day. That night she lay vigilant on her narrow cot, starting at every movement. By morning she was skittish and haggard.

Shortly after breakfast, Amelia was sitting beside the wall, grimly determined to touch no one, no matter what the cost, when the ward door swung open to admit a quartet of nurses. All had at least half a dozen wide leather belts looped over each arm, which they began to lay out two by two on the floor.

"What's happening?" Amelia asked the woman nearest her.

"It's the Promenade. Haven't you been before?"

Amelia shook her head, frowning as two of the nurses began threading a heavy rope through the canvas loops attached to each of the belts. The other two began herding patients toward the front of the room.

"I was in isolation until yesterday." Amelia went silent in appalled astonishment as the nurses began to harness—there was no other word for it—patients into the contraption.

The other woman apparently noted Amelia's horror. "It's not so bad as it looks. It's outside air, a chance to move around without bumping into anyone or having their elbows in your ribs."

Amelia considered her words as the first group departed, hitched two abreast like horses to a plow and driven out of the hall. When they returned, she hesitated, then set her teeth and stood. She followed the woman who had reassured her and joined the queue for the second group.

"I'm Elizabeth," the woman said as they stood waiting to be fitted with their belts.

"Amelia," she replied after an odd, strangled pause, suddenly tired of the pointless "Lina" charade.

Before Elizabeth could reply, the ward door swung open and a large woman stepped inside. Dressed in a more formal version of a nurse's uniform, her doughy face was broad and empty of expression. Her steel gray hair was scraped into a tight knot. A frisson of something ugly rippled through the room at her appearance, raising gooseflesh on Amelia's arms. She went still, transfixed by the air of absolute menace emanating from the woman, palpable even at a distance. Even the nurses seemed to shrink before her.

"What's the delay here?" the woman asked.

"No delay, Mrs. Brennan," one of the nurses said as she fumbled with the belt on the woman in front of Amelia. She yanked it tight, and the patient let out a grunt at the abrupt pressure around her middle. "Just these last two." She gestured to Elizabeth and Amelia. "And then we'll be ready."

Mrs. Brennan watched silently as the two women were buckled into their belts, then left the ward.

There was an audible sigh of relief in the wake of her departure.

"Who was that?" Amelia asked, after the nurse moved away.

"Mrs. Brennan, the nursing matron," Elizabeth replied. She paused. "It's best to stay out of her way, if you can."

In their traces, the women were led out of the building and on a circuit of the grounds. The morning's fog hadn't fully burned away. Near the kitchen gardens, they passed a group of more privileged patients working under a nurse's supervision, clearing away the winter's debris and turning the soil in preparation for planting. These women shied away from the group as though they carried lepers' bells. Amelia's cheeks burned. As if the same couldn't happen to them.

A group of orderlies clustered under a tree, smoking and trying to flirt with the younger nurses. One was taller than the others, with a shock of black hair. Hope surged in Amelia's breast, and she twisted in her belt. *Jonas.* But the man turned his face away as they passed and blew out a stream of smoke. Her heart plummeted. Jonas hated smoking. The nurse at her side wrenched her back into place with a pinch and a muttered threat, and Amelia walked onward in bitter disappointment.

It was quite possibly the most humiliating experience of her life. And she knew when she next got the chance, she would line up for it all over again. For the promise of clean, cold air and an hour's freedom from the risk of seeing another woman's ugliest memory, she would willingly surrender every shred of dignity.

She might have tried to convince herself it was because the outings would help her escape. But the excuse rang hollow. She'd already seen enough to judge it impossible. Even if she could free herself from the restraints, if she could walk away from the group unseen, where would she go?

Amelia imagined attempting to board the ferry wearing her trailing sack of a dress—with CITY ASYLUM, BLACKWELL'S ISLD stenciled across the bottom in thick black letters, no less. And unless she could steal and somehow learn to pilot a boat, the ferry was the only option, with swimming out of the question. It was excruciating; the city skyline was visible across the water but as far away as the moon.

The group was near the northernmost end of their route when Amelia felt it: the same strange itch she'd felt in the park before she encountered the girl's spirit. She stumbled and avoided going to her knees thanks only to Elizabeth, who darted out a hand and caught her by the elbow.

"Amelia?"

Amelia ignored her, trying to find the source of the sensation. They were at the bottom of a gentle slope; whatever was on the other side was invisible from their vantage point. A small copse of trees grew a stone's throw from where they stood.

The spirit in the park had looked like fog before the girl's shape formed and began to advance. But here, there was nothing. The lead nurse called for them to turn, and as they did, the feeling in Amelia's breast faded. She breathed a perverse sigh of relief when they reached the asylum, and the gray stone walls lay between her and whatever it was that had nearly found her.

9

His head half buried beneath his pillow, Andrew squinted at the window. Well before noon, based on the angle of the light.

The knock came again, followed by his landlady's muffled voice. "Dr. Cavanaugh, are you in?"

"Just a moment." He threw back the covers and hauled himself upright. He padded to the door, tying on his dressing gown.

Mrs. Danbury looked taken aback as Andrew peered at her through a crack in the door.

"Oh dear. I didn't mean to wake you. I've just come back from church, you see, and I wasn't certain you were here."

"It's quite all right." He heard his tone and made an effort to soften it as he continued. "Was there something you needed?"

"There's someone—a gentleman—in the parlor. He says he's a friend of yours. A Mr. Edward Glenn?"

Andrew frowned. "I don't think I— Wait." His half-wakened brain snagged on a thought. Ned Glenn had been a friend in college, but he still lived in Boston, the last Andrew had heard. What was he doing in New York? And how did he know Andrew was here? "Please tell him I'll be down directly."

He shaved and dressed quickly, gooseflesh stippling his arms. Mrs. Danbury was a widow who claimed she took in boarders only because she felt safer with men in the house. Her parsimoniousness with things like heat suggested other motives.

Minutes later, Andrew made his way down the stairs as Mrs. Danbury emerged from the kitchen holding a tray with a coffeepot and a pair of cups.

Andrew reached for it. "Allow me."

She relinquished her burden with a grateful smile and disappeared back into the kitchen. Andrew shouldered open the parlor door and stepped inside. Like its mistress, the room showed evidence of having once been grander than it now was. A pair of tufted sofas, their velvet upholstery worn smooth in spots, faced each other across a low table flanked by chairs with needlepoint covers and arms of dark, shining wood.

A man's coat and hat lay across the back of one of the sofas, and the man who'd shed them stood looking out the window. He turned as Andrew set the tray on the table. His face was thinner than Andrew remembered, and there was an unfamiliar degree of strain in his expression, but it was unmistakably his old friend.

Andrew smiled and shook the hand Ned offered, then gestured for him to sit. "This is quite the surprise. I thought you were still in Boston."

"I am," Ned said, settling uneasily on the edge of a chair. He nodded his thanks as he accepted the coffee cup Andrew offered. "My wife—I don't suppose you knew I'd gotten married?"

"I didn't," Andrew said. "Congratulations."

"Thank you. And to you as well," Ned added, his face brightening in sudden recollection. "I believe I heard you were engaged?"

Andrew tried to suppress a grimace. Cecilia's family had announced their engagement in several cities' newspapers. Word of its end hadn't spread quite as far, it seemed. He busied himself adding sugar to his own cup. "I was, briefly. But not any longer."

There was an awkward beat before Ned cleared his throat and went on. "Well, at any rate, my wife's family is in Boston, and she didn't want to leave. But I was born here, though there's no reason you would have remembered that."

Andrew hadn't, in fact. "So you're visiting?"

Ned's posture stiffened, and he toyed with his cup. "Not exactly," he said, setting the cup on the tray with precise movements. "It's rather sensitive. I must ask for your discretion."

Andrew straightened, realizing why Ned must have come. It was a hazard of his profession, being approached for help with embarrassing medical problems. Ned was recently married. Perhaps he and his wife were having conjugal difficulties. Or it could be something worse. Andrew had been approached several times by men suffering ill effects from extramarital dalliances. "If you're experiencing a medical issue, surely the place to start would be with your own physician. I'm hesitant to—"

"It's nothing like that," Ned interrupted. "It's not about me." He took a breath. "It's my sister, Julia. She's missing. I think . . . we have reason to believe she may be in the city asylum."

Whatever he had been expecting, it was not this. Andrew groped for an appropriate response. "I don't see how that could be," he said finally.

"I know it sounds mad." Ned shot him a tight smile. "Just hear me out."

Andrew sat back. "Very well."

Some of the tension went out of Ned's shoulders. "Thank you." He took a breath, then stopped, seeming uncertain how to begin.

"Why don't you tell me a bit about her?" Andrew suggested.

"Oh. Well. Julia is my elder by nearly ten years." Ned smiled slightly. "Growing up, it was almost as though I had two mothers. We've always been close. Six years ago, she married a man called Bryce Weaver."

There was something sour in his tone when he said the man's name.

"You don't like him?" Andrew asked.

"No," Ned said frankly. "I never have. I met him for the first time shortly before the wedding, and the whole business struck me as odd. He's several years younger than Julia, for one thing. And much as I love her, the fact is that Julia was always plain. Quiet. Something of a wallflower. She'd never had a suitor before, and suddenly here was this charming, good-looking fellow wanting to marry her.

"I didn't trust it. But Julia was smitten with him—anyone could see it. And, really," Ned added, "how do you tell your sister you think she's not pretty enough for the man who says he wants her?" He shook his head. "I kept my worries to myself. They married, and my parents gave them some money to help them get started. Bryce has done well for himself—I understand that he's become quite wealthy in the last few years."

"And your sister?" Andrew asked. "Was she happy?"

"She seemed to be." Ned looked down at his hands. "I didn't see her more than two or three times a year, but we wrote often. There was nothing amiss in her letters. She has a little girl—my niece, Catherine. We call her Kitty. She's almost five now."

He hauled in a deep breath and ran a hand through his hair as he went on. "Four months ago, Bryce came to my parents. He told them Julia had been unwell for some time, and he'd waited as long as he could, but he'd finally made the decision to send her to a place upstate for treatment—for a 'rest cure,' he called it. They said Bryce wouldn't tell them much, but that he hinted Julia had been . . . inappropriate with men." Ned flushed and glanced at Andrew, who nodded for him to continue. "And he said she had terrible moods, laughing one minute and crying the next. He claimed she had horrible bouts of anger, screaming and breaking things. That sometimes when she spoke, she made no sense. But my mother had spent the afternoon with her only a few days before and says she was fine."

"There are illnesses that can come on suddenly," Andrew interjected in a cautious tone. "And it's certainly possible for a sufferer to appear well between bouts of madness."

"So I'm told," Ned replied. "And we might have had to accept it, but for everything that's happened since."

"What do you mean?"

"When my parents asked where Julia was, Bryce wouldn't say. He said the doctors believed she needed a period of solitude and quiet. My parents were obviously terribly worried, but they agreed. They didn't even tell me what was happening until weeks later. I think they were trying to save Julia the embarrassment. But if I'd known earlier, I might have been able to do something." He rubbed at his eyes and went on. "My parents kept asking, and Bryce kept putting them off. And then, a few weeks after he sent Julia away my mother went to the house to visit Kitty, and the servants wouldn't let her in. Bryce has completely cut off contact with them. It's half killed my parents," he added. "They look like they've aged twenty years since then. Most of the life has gone out of them."

As though he could no longer bear to sit still, Ned sprang from the chair and began to pace around the parlor. "Once my parents told me what had happened, I started looking for Julia on my own," he continued. "Bryce said 'upstate,' but I sent letters and telegrams to every place I could find in half a dozen states. She's not in any of them. I was considering hiring a private detective to search for her.

"But then," he said, "last month, my mother got a letter from Julia's lady's maid, Ellen. Her mother had been ailing, and so right after Julia was sent away, Ellen went home to Albany to take care of her. Three weeks later, Bryce fired her, even though he'd given her leave to go. So she stayed in Albany and had no idea about everything that happened after—with Bryce not telling us where Julia was and so on. Ellen said she'd finally heard about it from one of the other servants and was horrified. So she wrote to tell us."

"Tell you what?"

Ned stopped his pacing and dropped onto the couch opposite Andrew. His voice went flat and precise. "Ellen was there when Julia was taken away," he said. "She said two men half carried my sister out of the house; limp, and wearing a ragged dress Ellen had never seen before. No luggage. One of the men said something about meeting the ferry, and the other said the wagon would be waiting when they got to the island. They had to be talking about the city asylum. My parents telegraphed me as soon as they got the letter, and I got on a train."

"And you've been here since?"

Ned nodded. "Trying to find any information I could. I telephoned the asylum. The man I spoke to said Julia wasn't there. I didn't believe him, so I took the ferry to the island. I meant to look in the face of every woman in that building if I had to." His voice was ragged.

"And?" Andrew said.

Ned made a sound that was half disgust, half embarrassment. "I'm afraid I made a bit of a scene. A pair of large orderlies escorted me back to the ferry and made it plain I wasn't to return. I've been trying to think of another way ever since." He sat forward. "But then I heard you'd started working there."

His tone made Andrew's throat tighten. It was that of a drowning man who'd spotted a ship in the distance. A faint hope, but one too precious, too providential, to relinquish.

And yet it was almost certainly false. The city asylum was for the indigent. A wealthy man like Bryce Weaver wouldn't be allowed to place his wife there. Most probably, the maid was mistaken in what she'd overheard. Julia Weaver was likely ensconced in some private facility, tucked away in the countryside.

As if he sensed Andrew's doubt, Ned leaned forward to look him in the eye. "You have to help me. I can't give up. She's my sister."

Andrew's resistance cracked in the face of Ned's plea. It cost him nothing to look. And if, as Andrew suspected, Julia Weaver were not on the island, Ned would at least know for certain.

"Very well. I'll look."

Ned slumped with relief, then reached for his coat and dug a hand into the pocket. He extracted a large envelope.

"Here," he said, handing it to Andrew. "This is the last letter I received from Julia. You'll see there's no hint of anything wrong with her. I've also included Ellen's letter to my mother and a pair of photographs of Julia. Keep them as long as you need. Use them to find her. Please."

10

Amelia went on Promenade three times more over the following week. Each time, the faint presence near the north end of the island tugged at her, though it never revealed itself. Possibly the group simply never went near enough for it to do so. For that small blessing, Amelia was profoundly grateful.

Life in the ward remained a constant trial. The nurses came and went, each enforcing her own particular set of rules. Sometimes movement and quiet conversation were allowed. Sometimes stillness and silence were required. Minor infractions might be ignored, or they might invite violent rebuke. Slaps and pinches were common. Restraints and doses of chloral hydrate served for those patients who required further correction. Mrs. Brennan especially was quick with the needle. Patients unwise or unlucky enough to cross her often spent the remainder of the day drooling on their cots. Several had been dragged from the ward, one by her hair. None of them returned. Amelia did her best to be invisible whenever the matron appeared.

Ward two was intended for those whose madness was of a manageable kind. Patients who shouted at invisible antagonists or flew into fits of rage didn't stay; instead, they were quickly removed to other quarters. Those who suffered subtler afflictions, only appreciable under closer observation, might last longer. A great many, as far as Amelia could tell, were not mad at all—they were simply too old, or too feeble, or too damaged by poverty or drink to survive anywhere else.

There were a few who seemed entirely out of place. One girl, Janey, could not have been more than sixteen, though her mind was more like a child of three. Many of the ward's residents doted on her, seeing in the girl, perhaps, their own lost children.

It was Elizabeth who remained the greatest puzzle. She and Amelia were friendly, after a fashion, sitting together in the ward and arranging to be paired on their outings. The other woman carried herself with quiet dignity. Her speech marked her as educated. Her tone, when she spoke to the nurses, was polite without being deferential. Amelia might have asked how she had come to be here. But there was an unvoiced taboo among the patients against speaking of their lives outside the asylum, and Amelia was loath to explain her own presence, wanting neither to lie nor to be judged insane for telling the truth.

Amelia was chatting with Elizabeth on a Friday afternoon as the other woman brushed and braided young Janey's hair. The girl sat with her back to them, playing with a bit of string and humming under her breath. All three looked up as a pair of nurses entered. One carried a clipboard.

"Attention!" she shouted. "The ward is to receive a visit today from a group of Christian ladies. If I call your name, you are to come forward so they may speak with you. The rest of you will sit quietly on your cots while they are here." The glare she gave them conveyed the guarantee of consequences for disobedience.

Elizabeth sighed and patted the girl on the shoulder. "Janey, be a dear and stay right here. I'll come to you directly. If you're good, I'll bring you a sweet."

Janey smiled at the promise and went back to playing with her string.

Elizabeth stood, pulling Amelia with her.

"What's happening?" Amelia asked.

"Charity." Elizabeth's expression was resigned. "The Women's Christian Benevolent Association sends visitors every other month or so. They bring pamphlets and sugar buns and lecture us about the evils of drink and loose ways. I'm not certain what good they think they're doing," she added. "We're all safe from fornication and demon rum in here, and half the women can't read anyway. But they mean well, I suppose, and the buns are welcome." She glanced at Janey with a fond smile.

The nurse began calling names. Patients stepped forward—all of them women capable of coherent conversation and not prone to outbursts.

"Casey, Carolina!"

There was a second's pause before Amelia remembered this was supposed to be her. She moved across the room with a grimace. Elizabeth would certainly ask.

A second later, however, Amelia had questions of her own as the nurse called, "Fox, Anne!" and Elizabeth started toward her.

"Carolina?" Elizabeth asked under her breath.

"Anne?" Amelia countered.

The ward door opened before Elizabeth could reply. Mrs. Brennan strode in, leading a cluster of elegantly dressed women. The selected patients straightened and went quiet.

The visitors spread out from the doorway, their bright, velvet-trimmed gowns and feathered hats shocking against the gray of the ward. They looked like a flock of exotic birds fluttering among the chickens in a tenement yard. They tittered and cooed like birds, too, as they exclaimed over the patients. Amelia tried to maintain a pleasant expression in the face of their condescension.

One of the women—younger, pink-cheeked, and earnest—turned toward Amelia and Elizabeth. She flipped the cloth off the top of the basket on her arm, and a waft of yeasty, sugar-scented air puffed out. Amelia's mouth watered. The woman thrust a hand into the hamper and emerged not with the promised sugar bun but with a folded booklet. An improving tract, from the looks of it, doubtless full of essays on the virtues of temperance and chastity. Perhaps a few paragraphs on the importance of feminine modesty.

The woman offered it to Amelia, who clenched her teeth into a hard little smile and accepted with as much grace as she could muster. She could hardly do anything else, not with Mrs. Brennan watching. The woman pressed a second tract on Elizabeth before reaching into the basket again and offering them each a pastry. Elizabeth accepted with a murmured thanks. Amelia reached for hers, and her fingers brushed against the young woman's.

Smoke. Choking, billowing clouds of it abruptly enveloped them, blanking out the room and everyone in it. It stung Amelia's throat, burned her eyes. She gasped, then doubled over, coughing, as the soot and fumes poured into her lungs.

A sheet of flame danced across her vision. For an instant she could feel it licking her skin, and she lurched back with a wheezing shudder, turning her face away and closing her eyes against the searing heat. She heard the windows shattering, one by one. They would die, all of them. They had to get out.

Someone was pulling her away. "Amelia?"

Elizabeth. Elizabeth had her. Good.

"The fire," Amelia said, her voice rough and low. "We'll burn. We have to get out—"

Another step back and the heat and smoke were gone. Amelia shivered in the sudden chill and dragged in a lungful of blessedly clear air. She blinked, her eyes still tearing. Her throat felt scratched and raw as her eyes darted around the ward, seeking the blaze that had been there only an instant before. There was nothing.

Elizabeth was still holding her by the arm, leading her back to the cots, her face worried. The woman who'd given her the bun—now crushed into a doughy mass in her hand—appeared momentarily alarmed before seemingly deciding such behavior was to be overlooked in a madhouse. She turned to another patient and dipped her hand back into the basket. Mrs. Brennan's eyes followed Amelia and Elizabeth as they retreated, but when they made no further disturbance, she seemed to dismiss them.

Elizabeth led her to the cot beside Janey. "Here." Elizabeth handed the girl the bun before turning to Amelia. "Lie down for a moment."

"I'm fine," Amelia said, shaking and embarrassed. She tried to pull away, but Elizabeth held firm.

"You're not fine. You've gone white. Lie down. What was that about a fire?"

Weak at the knees and abruptly exhausted, Amelia submitted. "It's nothing," she lied as tears slipped from her eyes. She brushed them away with the back of the hand holding her own mangled bun. "I don't know what happened. I . . ." She forced herself to stop talking before she said more. Before she blurted out what she'd seen and what she feared it might mean. Perhaps she should speak. Probably she should. But the warning of a madwoman would mean nothing. Mrs. Brennan would punish her for it. Elizabeth would believe her no better than any of the others who raved and shouted. They all would. And perhaps she was wrong. She had to be wrong.

She lay on the cot until the visitors left, unable to look at them again. Elizabeth sat with her. Amelia fell asleep with the destroyed bun in one hand and Elizabeth's hand in the other.

∾

Two days later, Amelia and Elizabeth reentered the ward after Promenade to find a pair of nurses poring over a newspaper.

"It was the whole family?" one asked as they neared.

"Yes. I can hardly believe it," the other replied. "That pretty young girl, here just two days ago, then gone like that."

"How did it start?"

"The furnace, they think. It was in the basement. Whole house went up in the middle of the night."

Amelia stopped in her tracks, her blood gone cold.

An angry shriek at the other end of the ward attracted the nurses' attention, and they left their paper on the desk. Almost against her will, Amelia picked it up, the blaring headline leaping out at her: OVERNIGHT BLAZE KILLS FAMILY OF SIX.

Amelia tore her eyes away from the words, sickened. She had known. Not exactly what was going to happen, but enough. She should have said something. Tears pricked at her eyelids.

She lifted her gaze to find Elizabeth frowning at the newspaper. After a moment, she looked at Amelia, her expression thoughtful.

"You saw it," Elizabeth said. "You knew."

Amelia hesitated. "Some of it."

"Is that why you're here?"

Amelia nodded. Elizabeth said nothing, plainly waiting for more. Amelia swallowed. Here was what she'd been trying to avoid. She put down the paper and made her way to a relatively quiet spot along the wall. Elizabeth followed. When they'd seated themselves on the bench, Amelia related her story. How she and Jonas had always used her modest abilities, how things changed after her injury, and how she'd come to be in the asylum. It was a relief to finally tell someone.

Elizabeth was silent as she finished.

"I'm not mad," Amelia insisted after a moment. "You have to believe me."

"I do," Elizabeth said finally. "I wouldn't if I hadn't seen it with my own eyes. But I did see it. So no, I don't believe you're mad."

Amelia sagged in relief.

"Why do they call you Carolina?"

Amelia explained about the cloak. "I tried to tell the nurses that first day, but my head ached so, and I decided it didn't matter. So I stopped trying."

Elizabeth laughed, and the sound was bitter. "It wouldn't have mattered even if you'd kept on."

"Anne Fox?"

Elizabeth nodded. "My name is Elizabeth Miner, but I gave up arguing about it months ago."

"How long have you been here?"

"More than a year."

"A year," Amelia repeated, dizzy with horror at the idea. "Why? How did it happen?"

"It happened because I am a very great fool." Elizabeth looked away for a moment before she continued. "A bit over two years ago, I met Daniel Miner at a dinner party. He was very charming. Very polished. He began courting me. Around that same time, my father became ill. My mother died when I was a child, so it was just the pair of us. I used to go to his law office to help him. He called me his best assistant." A smile flickered across her face at the memory before her expression sobered.

Janey wandered over and sat on the floor, leaning against Elizabeth's legs. Elizabeth stroked the girl's hair.

"Looking back, I think he'd been ill for some time and had been hiding it," she continued. "He'd seemed tired for several months, but he brushed it off whenever I mentioned it. He never wanted me to worry. But whatever the truth of it, the doctors said there was nothing to be done. Father had a few months at most."

"I'm sorry," Amelia said.

Elizabeth gave her a small smile. "Thank you. It was a horrible time." She shook her head. "I could blame the circumstances for what happened next, but it's my own fault. I confided in Daniel, and he shocked me by proposing marriage. He said he knew it was sudden, but he'd already made up his mind and had only been waiting to speak for propriety's sake. He suggested we marry as soon as possible—it would give my father comfort to know I was taken care of, and if we waited, it would be a year or more before we could marry, since I would be in mourning.

"And, Daniel pointed out, once my father was gone, I wouldn't be able to live in the house without a chaperone. I'd have to find an older woman to come stay with me. I couldn't bear the thought of having some stranger in my home. It hadn't occurred to me yet," she added in a sardonic tone, "that Daniel was still essentially a stranger.

"I should have seen what he was," Elizabeth said, "but I was grieving, and lonely, and so tired with caring for Father. Father gave his permission, and we married at once." She paused and looked away for a moment before continuing. "Father died only a few weeks later. He'd left everything to me. Not a fortune, but a comfortable estate, and all in my name. I let Daniel manage things. I'd been accustomed to Father looking after the money for me, so it felt natural for Daniel to do it. But only a few months in, Daniel suggested we sell the house. I refused. I'd lived there my whole life. He argued. It worried me, his insistence. It woke me up. I looked at our accounts."

Amelia grimaced, already knowing what was coming.

Elizabeth caught the look. "Yes. He'd gone through the money like water. He'd presented himself as well-off, but he brought in almost nothing. Everything was purchased on credit. There were bills from the tailor, the wine merchant. We didn't even own my wedding ring outright. The house was the only thing left. I confronted him, and we quarreled.

"He insisted we sell the house. I told him he could insist all he liked, but it was in my name, and I would never consent to selling my home to dig him out of a mess of his own making. He alternated between railing at me and sulking for weeks, but I didn't budge."

"Good for you," Amelia said.

"Perhaps not, given what happened next. Daniel came home one evening acting as if nothing had ever happened. Kissed me on the cheek and said not to worry, he'd handled everything. The next week was the nicest since we were first married. He was so thoughtful. He brought me tea in bed every morning." The next words were precise, almost bitten off. "The last morning, it was quite bitter. He apologized for making it so strong and brought more sugar. I drank it. I fell asleep. And I woke up here, with everyone calling me Anne. I didn't have any idea what had happened. I thought at first there had been some terrible mistake. I hadn't realized what Daniel had done."

"The tea?"

Elizabeth nodded. "He'd laced it with laudanum. I realized it the first time they dosed me here. We'd never kept it at home—my father didn't like it—so I didn't recognize the taste. I was here for a week before I saw a doctor. I thought when I explained—"

"That they'd let you go home."

Elizabeth nodded. "But Dr. Klafft—he was the doctor I saw—said my file stated I was unmarried. He said my insistence that it was wrong was a sign of my illness. He said I was suffering from the Old Maid's Disease. That I wanted to be married so much I imagined I was. It had disordered my mind."

"Of course," Amelia said with a disgusted roll of her eyes. "And so you stopped trying?"

"Not completely. There was another doctor—Dr. Blounton—who I think might have tried to help me. But he died only a short time after we'd begun speaking. None of the others seemed likely to listen. For a time, I hoped Daniel meant to teach me a lesson, that he'd come for me after a few weeks. I'd have agreed to sell the house by then. I would have agreed to anything he wanted. But he never came."

Amelia opened her mouth to say something comforting, though she had no idea what.

Before she could speak, a nurse entered, holding a list and pushing a cart full of files. Mrs. Brennan followed, a scowl already creasing her wide face.

"Patients will move to the left side of the room!" the nurse shouted. "When your name has been called, you will sit and wait until the head count is finished."

The weekly head count was a tedious exercise at the best of times, and Mrs. Brennan's malevolent presence would hardly improve it. Amelia stood. Elizabeth tried, but Janey, still on the floor beside her, flung her arms around Elizabeth's legs.

"Janey dear, it's time to get up." Elizabeth untangled the girl's arms with some effort.

Janey resisted, a mulish expression on her face.

"Please? For me?" Elizabeth tried again.

Amelia cast a quick glance at Mrs. Brennan and found the woman looking at them through narrowed eyes. Her mood seemed even more sour than usual. Amelia tried to help Elizabeth pull Janey to her feet, but the girl remained obstinate.

Mrs. Brennan strode toward them. Janey went still, her face blank and her mouth dropping open in a wide *O* of fear. Mrs. Brennan took the girl by the arm and yanked her to her feet.

Janey went wild, struggling to pull away and making fearful, wordless noises. One of her flailing hands caught Mrs. Brennan with a glancing blow on the cheek.

The matron's reaction was immediate. She fisted one hand in Janey's hair and swung her around, clouting her about the face and shoulders with the other. The girl cowered and tried to cover her head with her hands. A wet patch spread on the front of her dress, and the sharp smell of urine wafted through the air. With a noise of disgust, Mrs. Brennan threw her to the floor. Janey landed at Elizabeth's and Amelia's feet.

Elizabeth bent to help her as Mrs. Brennan aimed a sharp kick at the girl. Her foot connected with Elizabeth's ribs instead, and Elizabeth let out a surprised *oof* of pain.

Amelia helped her friend to her feet, then looked at Mrs. Brennan. Something of her feelings must have shown on her face. Mrs. Brennan casually raised her arm and dealt Amelia a backhanded slap.

She spun and fell, and the side of her face struck the edge of the wooden bench where they'd been sitting. Agony flared white-hot across her cheek. She thought she cried out, but perhaps it was only in her mind. She heard the nurse's voice from somewhere far away, garbled words Amelia heard only as an echo, understood only after they ended.

"I've no time for any more nonsense. Get them out of here and get on with it."

11

Some unmeasurable time later, Amelia opened her eyes to find she was back in her cell on the third floor. She had an instant to wonder where Elizabeth and Janey were before the pain roared to life and drove every other thought from her mind. Her face throbbed in time with her heartbeat, and she reached up with careful, shaking fingers to touch it. Her cheek was puffy, and the eye above it was nearly swollen shut. Hurt like quicksilver ran in channels down into her jaw and up around her eye.

Her stomach roiled, and she fought not to be sick, afraid even to imagine what it would feel like in her current state. Finally, the nausea receded. With exquisite care, Amelia eased herself over, laying the uninjured side of her face on the mattress. Mara's familiar sobbing echoed through the hall. In the cell beside Amelia's, the haggard woman called for her cat. Amelia stared at the wall, counting her breaths and watching the light fade.

When the evening meal arrived, she slid the tray toward herself with desperate hope. She dipped her little finger in the mug of water and watched a droplet dance on the tip before she touched it to her tongue. Bitter. She nearly wept with relief. She tipped the vessel to her mouth and drank, one tiny sip at a time. She consumed most of the cup and lay back, closing her eyes and waiting for the angry little darts to stop shooting through her head.

As night came on, Amelia fell into a stuttering sleep, skipping in and out of consciousness like a stone across a pond, bodiless and floating between jolts of hurt.

Trapped somewhere in the space between dream and waking, she ran across a foggy plain, her chest heaving, pursued by apparitions she knew were there but could not see. She was safe in her cell, but something caught her and dug its claws into her face. She fought a damp, clinging creature shaped like the blanket covering her. She thrust it away and shivered in her victory. Footsteps echoed in the hallway outside the cell, and Amelia let out a soundless scream of terror. She fled as their echoes died behind her.

She blinked. A towering being cloaked in mist stood at her door. It floated, then melted away with a metallic shriek. Clouds passed over the moon. A shadow thinned and lengthened across the floor. A threat swelled in the air, and Amelia tried to call out a warning, but the drug stole her voice. The words died in her throat. Something rustled. There was a flutter in the air like a halting exhalation. It brushed past her face with a whisper.

A distant, lucid sliver of her mind chattered, trying to be heard. There was something here to be marked, it said. Something significant. Amelia sought to follow the thread, to track the feathered thing through the air, but it turned to smoke, dwindled, and vanished. She let go of the thought with regret as she floated away again.

In the morning, cries of alarm from the hallway roused Amelia from a fitful doze. She wrapped herself in the blanket and wobbled to the door, her head pounding, the deep ache in her cheek already promising another day's misery. Dull and listless, Amelia leaned her forehead against the cold bars. She watched as a stretcher was carried from the cell beside hers, bearing a still form wrapped in a gray blanket, the ragged stuffed cat perched on top. As it was borne away, something tickled at the back of her mind—the nagging unease of something important, forgotten.

12

Jonas pushed away from the tree he'd been leaning against and took a final pull from his cigarette, the burning end bright in the predawn darkness. He tossed the last inch to the ground and gave it an emphatic grind with his heel. The things tasted like death, and he was heartily sick of pretending to smoke them. But most of the other orderlies smoked, and along with a brief break for lunch, these twice-a-shift gatherings were the only time they clustered away from the eyes of their supervisors.

It was worth it. He'd found her.

Jonas had stayed clear of his and Amelia's apartment for the better part of two days after stalking away in the wake of their argument. When he came back, something crunched beneath his feet as he walked through the door—shattered bits of crystal, some ground to powder under his shoes. He frowned, recalling the crash he heard as he left. It wasn't like Amelia to leave a mess sitting for so long.

It was the work of a moment to determine she was not in the apartment. Alarmed, he crossed the yard to the club to ask if anyone had seen her. No one had. He went back to the apartment and sat fidgeting, hoping she would return. By nightfall he was certain: something had happened. He considered the possibilities. All were terrifying.

Jonas spent a long and sleepless night making a list of places Amelia might plausibly have gone; every shop she liked, every café. There weren't many, and the next morning he set out to check them. He found where she'd eaten the day they fought, but no one had noticed where she'd gone afterward.

The following morning, he placed an advertisement in the newspaper with her description and the offer of a reward. He was struck, when he went to the newspaper office, by how routine his request seemed. The clerk barely looked up from his form as he wrote the instruction. How many people disappeared in this city without ever being found? He suspected the number would appall him and promised himself that, whatever it took, Amelia would not be added to the tally. He *would* bring her home. The vow sounded pretty in his head, but it didn't help with the strangled panic thrashing in his chest.

He inquired at every police station and hospital in Manhattan. When he found nothing, he steeled himself and checked the morgues. *God save me from ever having to do such a thing again*, he thought as he trudged home afterward. The things he'd seen would stay with him forever. He bathed twice afterward, but the smell, or the memory of it, clung to him like a fog.

It was all the more difficult because he was facing it alone. Sidney delayed his trip—twice—hoping Jonas would be able to go with him, but he couldn't delay it a third time without a good reason. Sidney's male lover's psychic sort-of sister being missing didn't precisely qualify. He offered to find some excuse, some reason to stay, but there hadn't been anything Sidney could do. Jonas finally told him to go, unable to avoid a pang of regret and feeling immediately guilty for it. He thought he would be too busy to miss Sidney once he left, and for the most part he was, though in Jonas's rare quiet moments—the in-between moments—he was aware of a particular strain of loneliness he'd never known before. Sidney cabled once a week, asking for updates. For far too long, Jonas had nothing to tell him.

On his second visit to one of the police stations, Jonas found the only real clue. A plump Irish sergeant, one who'd not been there on the day of his first visit, stopped him as he left. He'd heard something about a girl fitting Amelia's description, and he was willing to talk, for a price.

After a brief negotiation, they'd settled on an amount that was probably at least a week of the man's pay. But if he had information, it was worth the cost. Jonas set his teeth and motioned for the man to get on with it.

The sergeant told the story with relish. "Fought like the very devil, she did. Raved and choked and left bloody scratches on the first poor lad who tried to take her in." He shook his head. "And her language. She sure didn't seem like no lady, you'll pardon me for saying so."

He gave Jonas a sly look and a nudge with his elbow. "But then, that'd be your business, whatever she is. I'm sure you've a good reason for looking for her, a wildcat like that."

Jonas ignored the innuendo. "You saw her when she was brought in? What did she look like?"

"I couldn't say, filthy as she was. But she was strong for such a tiny thing. But then, they say the mad have a wild sort o' strength, don't they? I remember one time, my first year with the force, when—"

"Where is she now?" Jonas asked through clenched teeth.

The man shrugged. "When they couldn't get her to make any sense, they sent her over the river—out to the madhouse. I'd guess she's still there. Sure didn't look like she was fit to be out in the world. What they ought to do is—"

Jonas did not stay to hear the end of the thought. He tossed the man his money and headed for the docks.

According to the sergeant, Amelia had been out of her head when she was taken away, unable to communicate. It had been weeks since she'd disappeared. Surely she'd have come to herself by now? If she was still unwell . . . He grimaced. It would account for why no one had sent for him. But in that case, would they let him show up and take her away? What if she didn't recognize him?

He stopped on the sidewalk, ignoring a muttered oath as someone behind him was forced to check his steps. He needed more information. There was a sign ahead for a doctor's office. Perhaps they would have a telephone he could use.

They did, along with a directory and a pretty young nurse who was no match for the full force of his smile. Jonas paged through the directory and lifted the receiver.

"How may I direct your call?" the operator asked.

"City 1028-18, please." He gave the nurse another quick glance. She blushed and busied herself with a stack of files.

There was a click as the call connected, then a half dozen shrill rings before someone answered.

"City Asylum, how may I assist you?" The voice was that of a young man, polite but distracted.

"I'm looking for someone. I believe she may have been brought to you several weeks ago."

"Name and date of admission?"

"Amelia Matthew," he said, "and it would have been on or shortly after March twenty-first. She may also have been unidentified when she was brought in."

"One moment, please. I'll check the ledger."

Jonas reminded himself to breathe.

"I'm sorry, there's no one here by that name. And there were no unidentified patients admitted that month."

"I was told she was brought to you," Jonas said quickly, sensing the man wanted to end the call. "She must be there. Could I come to the island to look for her?"

"Are you her husband or father? Because," he continued before Jonas could answer, "if the doctors have not cleared her for release, then only her father or husband can take custody of her without an order from the court. If she were here, which she is not."

Jonas considered. He was too young to be Amelia's father. "I'm her husband," he said. From the corner of his eye, he saw the nurse stiffen from across the room.

"Then, theoretically, if she were here, yes. You would bring your marriage certificate—"

"My marriage certificate?"

"Yes, or some other proof of the relationship. We can't release a vulnerable patient without it. But really," he said, a hint of compassion coloring his tone, "it's a moot point. Your wife is not here. I wish you the best of luck in finding her."

He hung up.

Jonas replaced the receiver and turned, not surprised to find the nurse now glaring at him. He fished some coins from his pocket and laid them on the desk as he left.

Back on the street, he started toward the dock again, mostly because he didn't have any better idea. He developed a vague notion of going to the island and trying to bluff his way through the lack of a marriage license. But he couldn't be certain Amelia was even there.

Thirty minutes' walk brought him to the dock, where he was surprised to find he wasn't alone. A number of other men, and a few women, waited with him. The men smoked and watched the women—obviously nurses, with their tidy uniforms and practical shoes. They stood apart and chattered in small groups, the younger, prettier ones making a show of ignoring the looks directed their way.

The men were dressed less formally, in nondescript brown tunics and heavy trousers. They varied in age and build, some hulking, others small and whipcord thin, but with obvious sinewy strength in their arms. Jonas flexed his own biceps under his coat as he worked out the best approach. By the time the ferry arrived and a similar group disembarked, he'd decided. When those on shore boarded, he followed.

Getting hired at the asylum was the easiest con he'd ever pulled. Apparently the turnover was appalling, because no one cared about his lack of qualifications. He'd been prepared to spin some sort of story, but the man who hired him merely looked him over, assessing the breadth of his shoulders and the muscles in his arms. He muttered something about faces that were too pretty before nodding.

"You can start tomorrow. Three dollars a week, and you bring your own lunch. You'll work some nights to start."

Jonas suppressed a grimace. Sabine wouldn't like that. He nodded, and the man went on.

"The job's simple enough." He looked Jonas in the eyes. "You do as you're told, and mark me: no bothering the nurses."

Jonas promised not to seduce any nurses, and that was that.

During the first week of work, he moved about as much of the facility as he could, trading shifts so he could work different wards and observe each of the doctors. Tyree was his favorite. He was the friendliest of the bunch, and he wasn't averse to answering questions about the work. He'd even allowed Jonas to borrow books from the asylum library. They made for interesting reading, even if they didn't help with his current quest. Harcourt was brusque and busy, almost never in the wards. Klafft was contemptuous and dismissive—and that bootlick of a secretary of his was no better. Most of the orderlies preferred working with Dr. Lawrence, who forgot they were there and, as a result, never required anything of them. Cavanaugh seemed decent enough, though Jonas hadn't spent much time around him.

Blending in with the orderlies was easy. He sat three times a day, cigarette in hand, taking an occasional pull to keep the tip burning and tapping ash onto the packed ground. He watched. He listened. And earlier in the week, his desperation and persistence had paid off: He'd spotted her. Amelia was there.

He descended from the little rise where the tree stood and broke into a jog to catch up with the group. Out of habit, he kept one ear on their idle talk. Every now and then he picked up a useful tidbit. Most of his mind, however, focused on the thing that occupied him day and night: how to get Amelia away from this place.

All legitimate channels were blocked. Jonas wasn't her husband or father. He wasn't technically a relative at all, come to that. And now that he was known by the staff, he couldn't attempt the bluff. He grimaced. He might have been too clever by half there, but he'd been desperate.

A bribe, perhaps. But he hadn't yet identified a potential target, and, more to the point, he wasn't sure they had enough money left. He hadn't worked steadily since before Amelia's injury, and two weeks of an orderly's pay wasn't going to tempt anyone.

He looked up in time to avoid bumping into the man ahead of him. The clump had drifted to a stop as they turned the corner to the staff entrance. Outside the wide doors, a horse and wagon stood, the pale wood of one of the asylum's cheap pine coffins just showing above the wagon's sides. As they watched, the driver hauled himself into the seat, took up the reins, and clucked the old horse into motion.

Deaths weren't exactly common on the island, but neither were they rare enough to be surprising. Last night's was the first since he'd arrived.

Some sort of heart ailment, he'd heard. A good number of the patients were elderly, or sickly, or simply worn down by the harsh lives they'd lived. And there were always some few who were suicidal. Jonas sketched a reflexive sign of the cross as the coffin passed, then caught himself with a wry chuckle. Perils of a Catholic upbringing.

He followed the group inside, glancing back one last time at the wagon carrying one of the only women he'd seen leaving the asylum since he arrived. As it disappeared over a rise, a little seed tumbled through his mind and took root.

13

The river was hammered bronze beneath the dawning sun. Andrew resisted the urge to check his watch yet again, knowing it wouldn't get him onto the ferry any faster. There had been a death on the island overnight, it seemed, and the dockworkers refused to unload the coffin until the city wagon arrived to carry it away. Fair enough. In their place, he wouldn't want to be left with a corpse and nothing but a promise that someone would come and take it away. But the delay—and its cause—only further increased his unease.

He'd woken shortly after midnight from ragged, ponderous dreams and tossed for several hours before resigning himself to wakefulness. He lit the lamp and sat at the desk to reread the letters Ned had given him, already knowing he wouldn't find anything new. The maid's—Ellen's—letter recounted precisely the story Ned had told him the day before, though he'd thought of several additional questions for her. He would ask Ned for the address, or perhaps have him write to her. Julia's letter was unremarkable. There was no hint of any mental distress or disordered thought. The letter was warm, full of news of her daughter and the little doings of her household. The kind any fond sister might write to a sibling.

The kind Susannah might have written to him someday, had things been different.

Andrew folded the letters back into their envelope without looking at the photographs. He remembered well enough what they showed. The first, a simple portrait, revealed Julia Weaver to be a plain-faced, solemn woman—though there was kindness in her eyes. The other was a wider shot of Julia seated, her arm around the shoulders of the little girl standing beside her—Catherine, presumably. Julia was turned toward the child, and the angle of her hat meant only part of her face was visible. It would be next to no use in identifying her. It could have been anyone.

The photos had lingered in his mind. In the most unsettling of the night's dreams—the one that drove him from sleep and spurred his eventual rising—Andrew opened a door and came upon the precise tableau in the second photograph. For a moment, his dream self was delighted—Ned had asked him to find Julia, and there she was. Then the woman turned her head toward him. The face beneath the hat's brim was Susannah's.

A little shudder ran through Andrew. He put his hand in his pocket and traced the outline of Susannah's locket with his thumb. He'd plucked it from his desk that morning along with Julia's photographs, which now resided in the pocket of his waistcoat. He had no idea why he'd brought both photographs, except that Ned had presented them as a pair, and so, to Andrew's hazy, overstimulated brain, a pair they must remain. He shook himself alert as the wagon arrived. Still holding the locket, he waited as the coffin was carried away, then boarded the boat.

Once on the island, Andrew fetched himself a cup of the asylum's burned, tarry coffee, dumped in enough sugar to kill the taste, and got to work.

By the time the head clerk, Winslow, arrived, Andrew had done a thorough review of the admissions register. There was no Julia Weaver or Julia Glenn anywhere in its pages.

He questioned the young man, just to be certain. What, precisely, were the admissions procedures? Did patients ever arrive without paperwork? What happened when a patient's name was unknown? Was Winslow absolutely certain that every patient in the asylum was in the register?

Winslow answered his inquiries, at first easily and then with a growing thread of carefully suppressed irritation in his voice. Andrew finally realized he was verging on insult and forced himself to break off the interrogation.

"Thank you," he told the young man, who nodded stiffly and handed him his ward assignment before turning toward the pile of paperwork on his desk.

Andrew left the main office strangely deflated. It seemed his initial instinct had been right. Ned's sister wasn't here. He would have to give his friend the news that evening. But perhaps he could still help. Andrew had contacts at other asylums, knew many of the small, private facilities that didn't advertise. Julia could well be in one of those. He could at least give Ned a list of other places to look.

That decided, Andrew glanced at the paper in his hand and couldn't suppress a sigh. Ward five again. His mood darkened further when he arrived to find Klafft already there, preparing to begin "cold treatment" of a catatonic patient. The older doctor's preferred methods were, according to everything Andrew had read, at least a quarter century out of date. But the man persisted in using them, and as Andrew had discovered, he was deeply resistant to newer theories.

The woman in question lay on the cot, her eyes vacant and staring. She appeared entirely indifferent to the fact that she was about to be repeatedly dunked in icy water, wrapped in a wet sheet, and left to lie in a frigid room for several hours.

But the plan struck Andrew as not only useless but actively cruel, so he ignored Klafft's warning scowl and attempted to intervene.

"I must question the utility of such a treatment," Andrew said carefully.

From the corner of his eye, he saw a pair of nurses exchange a knowing look. The two doctors' tendency to clash had been noted by the staff, and Andrew suspected many of them found it entertaining. He reminded himself to remain calm.

"Nonsense," Klafft snapped. "It's well-documented that cold baths are effective in treating the physical roots of hysteria and other feminine neuroses."

"But given Donkin's theory that such neuroses are often the result of intellectual repression—"

Klafft's face tightened. "Intellectual repression! What rubbish. The average female brain weighs five ounces less than that of the average man's. That alone must prepare us to expect a marked inferiority of intellectual ability—"

"But if—" Andrew began.

"—as well as greater risks from prolonged mental exertion," Klafft continued. "It therefore follows that such exertion would lead to poor outcomes. Women's minds and bodies are not equal to those of men. When they step outside their appropriate sphere—whether mentally or physically—they risk becoming unbalanced. Hysteria and other forms of instability"—Klafft indicated the patient without looking at her—"are the result. Physical treatments are a logical response."

Andrew's resolve failed him. "That is an utterly antiquated notion," he snapped. "Next you'll be prescribing cures for a wandering womb. Any modern practitioner should know better than—"

Klafft put up a hand, his face stony. "Enough. Dr. Cavanaugh, I have been treating mental disease for thirty years, and I will not be lectured to like a rank novice. Six months' reading and an overenthusiastic self-regard do not entitle you to question my judgment.

"You claim," he continued, "to have come here to learn, and to do a particular kind of research. But I cannot say I've seen you doing either. Instead, you persist in inserting yourself into cases I and the other doctors already have well in hand, and which clearly do not fit your so-called research criteria, all the while putting no apparent effort into finding those that do.

"You want to treat patients?" Klafft made a sweeping gesture with one hand. "There are more than enough of them here. Go find your own and leave off interfering with mine."

He turned his back in unmistakable dismissal.

Andrew swallowed a retort as the nurses whispered to each other and glanced in his direction. His face flaming, he left the ward with as much of his dignity as he could scrape together. Damn the man for a quack. Leeching that poor woman would do as much good as half freezing her.

He stalked through the main hall, brooding, though a touch of chagrin crept in as he neared the main office. Klafft might be a jackass and a poor excuse for a physician, but Andrew had to admit he was not entirely wrong in his observation about Andrew's work. It was true he spent much less of his time than he'd intended seeking subjects for his research. Partly, this was because all the cases were interesting in their own way. And with such overcrowding and poverty, his skills as a general practitioner were much in demand.

But it was also because he was a coward.

He'd meant to start at once. He wanted to understand, needed to. He owed it to Susannah to—

Andrew stopped in the hallway, his eyes stinging. He closed them and swallowed hard, then turned back toward the main office, determined to salvage something from this wreck of a morning.

Winslow was still there. He looked up as Andrew entered, and his face tightened, as if he expected Andrew to resume questioning him.

"Dr. Cavanaugh. Can I help you with something else?"

"Yes, actually," Andrew said, in as friendly a tone as he could manage. "I would like to examine some of the patients who have shown a particular set of symptoms. I need some help identifying them."

"What symptoms?"

"Abrupt shifts in mood or behavior. Sudden, deep melancholia. Auditory or visual hallucinations. Bouts of aggression without any apparent trigger. These would have begun to appear in adolescence or young adulthood, at the latest."

Winslow frowned. "There are a great many patients with at least some of those symptoms. It might be difficult to put together a list. But . . ." He walked to one of the desks and opened a folder. "I believe I heard something recently. I try to keep track when patients are moved between wards. I don't always hear about why—ha! Here it is!" He pointed to an entry, his pride in his accurate record-keeping melting away his earlier stiffness. "There was an incident in one of the wards a few days ago. Three patients moved into isolation. Two of them are younger. Perhaps while I'm looking for others, you might want to examine them?"

Andrew hesitated for only an instant. "Yes. I'll do that. Thank you."

Five minutes later, Andrew was following Mrs. Brennan, the stout, dull-featured nursing matron, down the noisy hallway of the isolation wing, trying to calm his racing heart. This was why he'd come here.

Mrs. Brennan came to a stop so suddenly he almost trod on her heels. She glared at him, and he stepped back, straightening his sleeves and trying to look nonchalant. He peered past her into the cell.

The patient lay on her cot, asleep, it seemed. But when the matron's heavy keys clanged against the lock, she did not start as if awakened, only rose smoothly to her feet and stood, waiting.

"Good afternoon, Miss Casey, is it?"

"Yes."

Andrew stepped into the cell and got his first look at her.

She was tiny. He was not particularly tall, and yet he doubted she would reach much past his shoulder. Young, obviously—she couldn't have been more than twenty. Painfully thin. Her hair was cropped and ragged beneath her cap. Bruises, purple and swollen, stretched from the side of her pointed chin up over her cheekbone, framing an eye swollen nearly shut. The other regarded him warily.

Without turning around, he asked, "Why isn't she in the infirmary, with an injury like that?"

Mrs. Brennan stepped into the cell, and the patient, who had been studying him as he studied her, snapped her attention to the woman behind him, naked hostility overtaking her face.

"She's a troublemaker," the matron said in a flat tone. "Best to keep her away from the others."

Andrew frowned. "That will be all. You may step outside."

Mrs. Brennan shot a poisonous glance at the girl but did as Andrew instructed, taking up a place outside the door.

The girl relaxed a fraction and shifted her eyes back to him. "I am Dr. Cavanaugh," he said gently. "With your permission, I'd like to examine you."

She opened her mouth as if to speak, but in the same breath her gaze moved away from him again and froze. Her eyes widened as they focused on something behind him. He glanced over his shoulder, ready to reprimand Mrs. Brennan for returning. She hadn't moved.

"I'm interested in cases such as yours," he continued in the same tone.

Her eyes flicked back at him for an instant before returning to the spot behind him. He almost spun to look again but controlled the instinct.

"I'm not sick," she said with a bitter laugh, her eyes still not meeting his, "and I very much doubt you've ever seen a case such as mine."

"I'd like to start by taking your pulse." Even from where he stood, he could see it beating a rapid tempo at her throat.

She paused. "Very well."

Her gaze never moved from the spot behind him as he stepped forward and took her wrist.

She gasped as he touched her, and her eyes rolled white. He only just managed to catch her before she crumpled to the floor. Before he could lower her to the cot, even before Mrs. Brennan, watching like a waiting vulture, had taken a step from her place by the door, she recovered. Her face and body were relaxed, nothing like the watchful, tentative demeanor of a moment before.

She focused on him. And smiled. Recognition—and profound relief—flared in her eyes as her hands clutched at his shoulders.

"Jamie!" she breathed. "Thank heaven you're here. You have no idea how awful it's been."

Andrew's own breath all but froze in his lungs at the sound of her voice. The timbre, the pitch. If he'd closed his eyes, he would have thought Susannah stood in the cell with him.

His head throbbed as blood rushed to his face. His heartbeat pounded in his ears. His vision grayed.

He nearly dropped her as she went on, taking no notice of his shock.

"You have to tell Mother and Father not to make me go back. Make them understand. They'll listen to you." Her tone was low, confidential, and heartrendingly familiar. "I'm so glad you're here. You can tell them. You will, won't you? I can't bear the idea of it. That place." She shuddered. "There's no need for it. I'm perfectly well now, you know, and if they let me stay, I'm sure I won't . . ."

She trailed off as she seemed to catch sight of the cell, to all appearances for the first time. Her jaw dropped, and she looked up at him in horror. She thrust him away and stumbled backward. He took a half step toward her. She shrank into herself, her hands coming up to ward him off. That, too, was so familiar his chest clenched. She looked around in wild, panting terror, betrayal etched on her features.

"What . . . How . . . How did I . . ." She choked on a sob. "This isn't . . ." She stopped. Her eyes narrowed as they swung back around to focus on him, flashing with sudden fury. "You did this. I don't know how you did this, but you did. You tricked me," she said, rage and accusation in her tone, outrage in every line of her face. "Somehow you brought me here, and now— Oh, what did you do? You drugged me, didn't you? It had to be you. No one else could have. Jamie, I trusted you. I *trusted* you! But you're working with *them*."

She sprang at him with a low growl, her hands clawed, fury radiating from her. Too stunned to react, Andrew barely felt it as her fingernails raked the side of his face.

He stumbled back and got his hands up only as she drew back for another assault. She flung herself at him again, and he caught her, pulling her body into his chest and wrapping his arms around her own, pinning them to her sides. She thrashed and kicked, cursed him with every breath.

"Use the chloral!" Mrs. Brennan shouted from the doorway. "I'll call for the restraints." She disappeared down the hall as the girl slammed her head into his chest.

Andrew sucked in a wheezing breath. Desperately, instinctively, without thinking, knowing he had to quiet her, he lowered his mouth to her ear and spoke. "Susannah. Susannah, please. You must listen to me."

Shocked into immobility by the words he'd spoken, he went as still as she did, his mind scoured of rational thought. The sound of their breathing, ragged and discordant, filled his ears. Her heartbeat against his chest was as rapid as a bird's. They remained frozen there for a long moment, until she made a little noise, almost a sob.

The sound nearly drove Andrew to his knees, but it woke him from his stupor. He tried to swallow past a knot in his throat as something hot and terrible bloomed inside his rib cage. The backs of his eyes stung. His head buzzed. He licked his dry lips and set her carefully on her feet. He stepped back, raising his shaking hands more in denial than in defense against another attack.

She turned to face him again, and her eyes were terrified, full of questions. Lost.

"Jamie?" A tiny voice. She looked around again, down at her hands, slow horror spreading over her face. "These aren't mine." Her eyes welled with tears. "She's here. And I'm not. I'm not here." A low moan started in her throat. Built. Erupted from her mouth in a howl of despair.

Unable to stop himself, he stepped toward her again and took her in his arms, rocking her against his chest as she cried. Tears leaked from his own eyes as he struggled to breathe through a fog of disbelief. Of guilt. After a moment she quieted, then reached up with one trembling hand and brushed the hair away from his forehead. The gesture was so tender, so familiar, his heart broke inside his chest, and he had to will himself to breathe.

As she moved, the scent of the asylum's harsh soap wafted from her skin and pinned him to the moment. Andrew clung to it like a man anchoring himself against a gale. She stepped back, pulling out of his embrace, and, numb, he forced himself to let her go.

"It was the voices," she said in that same small voice, sorrow and regret in every feature. "They were so loud. I had to make them stop. But now I'm not here, and I can't stay. I'm so sorry. I'm not . . . I can't . . ." She clutched her head, groaning. The muscles of her face twitched, and her hands dropped to her sides. Then her eyes went white again, and this time Andrew did not manage to catch her. She landed on the floor in a heap.

14

Andrew all but ran from the cell. He kept his head down, a handkerchief pressed to his bleeding cheek. He was aware of nothing but the roaring in his ears and a desperate need to flee. The nurse at the end of the hall saw his face as he approached and leapt to open the steel door for him.

He spilled out into the Octagon with a spasm of vertigo, a fissure opening between the Andrew who stood in that too-lovely space and the one still back in that cell. He swerved into a nearby washroom and vomited into the basin. His hands shook as he rinsed his mouth and dampened the handkerchief to dab at his cheek.

Andrew straightened, and as he looked at his own colorless face in the mirror, an overwhelming urge to leave swept over him. He could go out the doors and straight to the dock. Back to the city. Perhaps even back to Philadelphia. He could apologize to his family, rejoin his practice. Pretend this whole chapter of his life never happened, pretend he'd never seen . . .

The hairs on the back of his neck were standing at attention. His scalp prickled, and the sheen of sweat coating him went sticky and cold. He shuddered and stepped away from the sink on trembling legs. He strode back to his office, closed the door, and sat down in his creaking chair. He held utterly still, listening to his own hammering heart as it thundered in his ears. This couldn't be real. Perhaps he'd never woken from last night's dream after all, and this whole day had been nothing but a construct of his sleeping brain. He looked at his hands, resting on top of his desk. His movements deliberate, he used his right hand to give the flesh on the back of his left hand a vicious pinch.

Andrew grimaced and sat back in his chair, shaking away the pain. No good. He was awake. He had to get ahold of himself. He wished he were one of those men who kept a bottle in a desk drawer. A stiffening shot of something would be welcome. Perhaps Tyree would—but no. He couldn't explain this to anyone, didn't even want to attempt it. At any rate, his legs felt so weak he doubted he could stand back up.

Andrew reached into his pocket for Susannah's necklace and placed it on the desk. He stared at it until his eyes swam out of focus. He tipped his head down and closed his eyes, began to count his breaths. He recited every chemical formula he could remember. He listed all the bones in the human skeleton, all the elements of the periodic table. Gradually, he calmed.

With a final breath, he opened his eyes. "All right, then. Let's think about this," Andrew told the empty air. There were those who believed in ghosts and mediums—even some so-called men of science. But he had never been one of them. Such things were not real.

Susannah was dead. Whatever it was he'd just seen in that cell, it wasn't his sister. It couldn't have been. Therefore, this was some sort of hoax. A cruel prank perpetrated by someone who knew of his recent loss. Someone had told her what to say.

But he could not quite believe it. The chain of events that had led him there, to that cell, to that woman, at that time, had been so implausible. He could count on one hand the number of people who knew the full story of Susannah's death. And none of them would have told it, not for anything. The more he considered it, the more certain he became that no one could have orchestrated that encounter. Someone might have told the woman what to say, but how could she have known how to pitch her voice to sound like Susannah's? How to hold her body? And Susannah was the only one who'd ever called him Jamie.

The thought started his heart racing again before he squelched the feeling. He was a scientist. There was a rational explanation. He just had to find it.

Andrew wandered through the rest of the day in a fog. When he left the island that evening, he went directly to the nearest telegraph office, where—for an exorbitant fee—he made a long-distance telephone call.

"Philadelphia, please." He gave the clerk the number. It was late, but he suspected Dr. Lindman would still be in his office.

He was.

"Andrew, my boy," he said, his Dutch accent pronounced. "How is life among the madwomen? Are you ready to come back home yet?"

"I understood you'd already taken on another physician." The shadow of a smile crossed his face at the fondness in the man's tone.

"I have." The gruff voice softened. "I understood your desire to leave. Entirely natural that you would need some time. But if you're ready to come back . . ." The old man cleared his throat. "Well, you will always be welcome."

Andrew swallowed past the lump in his own throat and took a breath. "I must ask you something. And please forgive the implication. Did you speak to anyone here about the . . . the details of my situation?"

"Certainly not," Lindman replied, a hint of reproof in his voice. "You told me in confidence. I would never betray such a trust."

"You're certain?"

"I've said nothing of it, to anyone. I would not speak of such a personal thing, even if asked. And no one has. Your Dr. Harcourt called to confirm my letter of reference. He wanted to know my opinion of your medical skills, and if I believed you to be of generally sound character." Lindman chuckled. "Although I got the impression he would have welcomed you even if I had said you were a drunkard and degenerate." He sobered. "Now, what's all this about?"

Andrew hesitated. "I've begun to wonder if perhaps the story did not follow me here."

The response was immediate. "I don't see how it could have. Whatever your feelings toward your parents right now, your father did a very thorough job of suppressing the details. I've heard no talk at all of it here, beyond sympathetic murmurs. I can't imagine anyone in New York could know." Lindman's tone turned paternal. "Now, I must ask, have you spoken to them? Your parents?"

"No," Andrew said shortly, "and I would appreciate it if you did not mention my call."

"If it is what you want, my boy, I'll not say anything. But I wish you would reconsider—"

Andrew interrupted before he could be reminded of his filial obligations. "Dr. Lindman, I must go." He hesitated. "Thank you. It was good to speak to you."

The older man sighed as he ended the call, and Andrew felt a flash of regret for the life he'd given up. But it hadn't been a choice. That life ended with one early-morning knock at his bedroom door.

He shook off the memory and handed over a palmful of coins to the hovering clerk. Andrew walked out of the telegraph office into a thick, misting rain and headed toward his rooms in brooding silence. Dr. Lindman's denial rang true. And his parents, who'd gone to extraordinary lengths to suppress the story, would have died rather than see it spread about.

But an asylum patient channeling Susannah's spirit was impossible.

Therefore, it was a trick, and someone was responsible.

Each time he came to that conclusion, the treacherous voice in his mind whispered to him again, and he saw the recognition flaring in the girl's eyes, and he wondered, and cursed himself for a fool.

The rain grew worse as he walked. The streets emptied. He could have flagged a cab, but the weather and the solitude suited his mood. Sherlock Holmes said that when one had eliminated the impossible, one must accept the improbable. But what to do when there seemed to be only impossibilities? Two unfathomable options bounced like rubber balls inside his skull.

Andrew looked up to find himself outside the saloon a block from his lodging house. Warm light and merry babble spilled into the street as he stood there being pelted by cold water. With a muttered oath, he pushed open the doors and went in.

15

Amelia lay on her cot with her eyes closed, as uncomfortable as she'd ever been in her life. Her arms, pinioned by the heavy canvas sleeves of the straitjacket, had long since gone numb. The ache in her shoulders, however, went bone-deep. The straps squeezed her torso, pulled far too tight and fastened by heavy metal buckles at the middle of her back. The injection they'd given her before they put the straitjacket on her, much as she hated them for it, was the only reason she'd slept at all. Even now, it clung to her mind like mist, blurring the edges of her thoughts and lending an otherworldly air to everything around her.

One thought was clear: it had happened again. Not quite as it had in the park, but near enough. She remembered the doctor—Cavanaugh, she thought she'd heard—coming into the cell. She remembered Mrs. Brennan leaving. And then as he spoke to her, the silvery mist had gathered behind him and taken shape. He touched her, and it surged over her.

And the next thing she knew, she was lying on her cot and the cell was full of people. Cavanaugh was still there, pale and shaken and holding a blood-spotted handkerchief against his cheek. Mrs. Brennan was behind him, and two orderlies were in the doorway, one holding a syringe and the other a bundle of white canvas, straps trailing down.

"What happened?" she rasped.

Cavanaugh only looked at her with wide, stunned eyes.

"You had another of your fits," Mrs. Brennan said, with a smug glance at the doctor's back. "You see?" she told him. "She's dangerous. You'll want to tend to your face. Leave us to see to her." Mrs. Brennan jerked her head toward the orderlies, who started forward. Amelia shrank back against the thin mattress.

"No," Cavanaugh barked, waving them away. "No," he said again in a more measured tone. "She's done no real harm, and none at all intentionally. You're to leave her be."

He gave the cell a wild glance and backed toward the door. He turned, pushed past the others, and strode out.

Mrs. Brennan scowled after him, then turned back to Amelia. A moment later, the sound of the heavy ward door closing echoed down the hall.

The matron motioned to the orderlies. "Get on with it."

They looked at her in confusion. "But the doctor said—" one of them began.

She rounded on him with a ferocious glare. "The doctor"—the word was a hiss—"isn't here. I am, and I'm telling you to get her jabbed and wrapped, or you'll be off the island and out of a job by dinner."

Amelia had tried to fight, but her head throbbed with every movement. The two of them would have been more than a match for her in any case. One held her as the other stuck the needle into her arm. By the time they stepped back, her head was foggy and her vision was blurring. From far away she heard one of the orderlies ask if the restraints were necessary.

"She don't look to be in any shape to cause trouble," he said.

Mrs. Brennan let loose with a stream of invective. Both men flinched and moved to obey. Unable to hold them open any longer, Amelia let her eyes droop closed, thinking vaguely that at least now her face didn't hurt. The last thing she felt before she lost consciousness was the orderlies threading her limp arms into the stiff white canvas.

Now her stomach roiled and her head throbbed. The endless noise of the ward seemed to have magnified and somehow concentrated into a solid mass that pressed against the insides of her ears. How much of this new sensitivity was an effect of the injection, and how much was a result of yesterday's encounter? The scrape of a key in a lock sliced into the thought and sent a bolt stabbing through her head. She groaned, pressing her forehead against the thin mattress.

Amelia steeled herself and opened her eyes. One of the younger nurses stood in the doorway of her cell. Cavanaugh stood behind her.

He was through the door before it had opened much more than a crack, resolve on his face. Another step, and his eyes widened. Without taking them off her, he spoke to the nurse in a voice like the crack of a whip.

"I specifically said she was not to be restrained. Who ordered this?"

"I don't know, Doctor, I only came onto the ward this morning."

He pressed his lips together. "Leave us."

As the nurse scurried out of the cell, Cavanaugh stepped forward. "Are you able to sit?" His voice was tight.

She didn't reply, too busy scanning the space behind him. There was nothing. She relaxed the tiniest fraction and finally focused on him. His eyes were shadowed, his face drawn and pale. She wormed and twisted until she was sitting upright on the cot. He watched and made no effort to help her.

The movement sent darts of pain through Amelia's head. She did her best to ignore it and turned halfway so he could reach the buckles at her back. There was a momentary hesitation—he didn't want to touch her, she realized. She looked back over her shoulder at him as he finally leaned in, his jaw hard.

He'd nicked himself shaving and missed a thin strip of beard over the pulse in his neck. He wore far too much cologne, no doubt in an attempt to mask the odor of stale whiskey seeping from his pores. It seemed she wasn't the only one suffering from a heavy head this morning.

She might have enjoyed his discomfort if her own had not been growing with every minute. She tasted the sticky floral scent on the back of her tongue. Her stomach lurched. She swallowed hard and turned her head away as he worked.

After another moment, the buckles loosened, and he moved back, taking his eye-watering cloud with him. Amelia took a relieved breath and wriggled out of the restraints. She flexed her shoulders with a sigh—then grimaced as the blood rushed back into her arms. She must have made a sound, since Cavanaugh leaned forward. The slick of artificial scent engulfed her, and suddenly it was all too much. Her stomach failed her, and she bent forward, retching, producing only a thin stream of acid and bile.

Once she regained control of herself, Amelia wiped her mouth on a corner of the straitjacket and shoved the thing away. She leaned against the rough stone wall, the thin, sweat-dampened fabric of her dress offering no protection from its chill. She shivered.

"What do you want?" she asked, not really caring.

He hesitated, his expression caught somewhere between concern and resolve.

"I want to know who told you what to do," he said finally. "Yesterday, you—I don't know how you—those things you said . . ." His voice trailed away, but his eyes never moved from her face.

"What did I say?"

His expression darkened. "Do not play games with me."

"Games." Amelia tried to imagine what he would say, how he would react, if she told him the truth. She knew, of course; he would think she was mad. Elizabeth had seen and believed. But this man, this doctor, flush with learning and superiority, would not. Amelia laughed, and it was a bitter, humorless sound. "I'm not playing games, Doctor. I don't know what I said."

He began to pace the length of the cell. "Did someone promise you something? Threaten you? I can help you, but only if you tell me the truth."

The taut strands of Amelia's patience frayed. "No one told me anything." Her tone was sharp around the edges. "I told you, I don't know what I said. Whatever happened yesterday, whatever—or whomever—you saw, whatever she said—"

He froze in his tracks and whirled to face her. "She." He pounced on the word. "You claim not to know what you said, but you know the words were a woman's?"

He thought he'd caught her. He would never listen to her denials now. All the weeks of careful, calculated behavior. All the endurance and the restraint. All of it had bought her nothing. Tears of anger and frustration pricked at her eyelids. Amelia blinked them away in sudden conviction.

If he wanted the truth, she would give it to him, and damn the consequences. She squared her shoulders and looked up at him.

"She stood behind you yesterday." Her voice was clipped. "A young woman. Pretty. I don't know who she is—or was, since I suspect she's dead."

He flinched, and his face went white.

Amelia went on with a rush of savage joy. "I see you recognize the description. I do not know what I said. She was the one who spoke."

Only years at the cards could have taught her to decipher the stream of expressions pouring across his face. Shock and sorrow. Guilt. And a flash of something soft. Hope? It touched his face and flitted away, fast as a hummingbird. Anger rushed in behind it.

He stepped toward her, flushed and shaking.

"You are lying," he said in a low, passionate tone. "You are lying, and someone has put you up to it. I want to know who, and I want to know why. You will tell me." His face was tight with anger, but there was a desperate edge to his voice.

A wave of fury rolled over Amelia and swept away her aching head and raw stomach. She leapt to her feet. All the fear and hopelessness of the past weeks, all the humiliations, the cruelties, the loneliness, and the desperation—they gathered inside her chest and swelled like water against a dam. And then they burst free.

She heard herself shouting as if from a great distance. About the infernal arrogance of men who demanded truth, then refused to hear it. About doctors who decided the course of women's lives without looking at them. About nurses who took pleasure in cruelty. About stolen names. About Promenades and chamber pots. About straitjackets and icy baths and drugged water. About purgatory and hell and hard benches and stone walls and the stupidity of men who made such places and demanded women thank them for it.

A tiny, horrified corner of her mind begged her to stop. With every word, every accusation, she confirmed her own madness and destroyed any chance she might have had of getting him to believe her. But he would never believe her, another, colder voice reminded her. She'd told him the truth, and he'd called her a liar. It drove her on. Amelia poured her rage at his feet like burning pitch.

He drew back from her, shocked. Her anger began to wear itself down, until finally the remnants drained away, and she slumped, breathless and exhausted. She felt a twinge of regret and crushed it with a ruthless fist. It didn't matter; he would never have listened. Never would have believed her. Never could have. She had lost nothing.

The rest of the ward had gone silent during her outburst. Now, in the hush that followed its conclusion, renewed sobs, wracking and piteous, began to filter through the hallway. Mara, continuing her ceaseless mourning.

"You'd do better to let the dead go," Amelia said, and jerked her chin toward the girl's cell. "She can't, and look what it's done to her. And if you actually want to help someone," she added, and noted his tiny flinch, "you should start with her. If all you can do is call me a liar, then you can get out and leave me be."

She turned her back to him. Moments later, the cell door crashed closed, and his footsteps echoed as he retreated down the hall.

16

Two days later, Amelia looked up from her breakfast as the sound of a masculine voice filtered down the hallway. The words themselves were lost in the general din of the ward, but the pauses indicated a conversation, and the tone was unmistakable. It was instructional, pleasant enough without any degree of deference. A doctor, for certain. The orderlies, when they spoke, murmured. Short. Obedient. Amelia held still, listening, but the voice grew no louder. Whoever he was, he'd stopped before reaching her cell.

After driving Cavanaugh away, Amelia had thrown herself back onto her cot and stewed until a nurse finally came to take her to the washroom. On the way, she peered into every cell they passed and confirmed that both Janey and Elizabeth were in the isolation ward as well. Amelia spent the rest of the morning trying to think of a way to communicate with Elizabeth, but her still-pounding head and sour stomach eventually forced her to set the problem aside.

Now, as she scraped up the last dregs of sticky porridge with her bread and popped it into her mouth, a momentary lull brought her a snippet of the conversation taking place down the hall.

"—quite certain. I will take full responsibility."

Amelia straightened. It was Cavanaugh.

She stood and crossed to the door. She wavered between stubborn defiance and self-reproach every time she thought of their last encounter. She had no interest in repeating it. Why was he in the ward?

Amelia tilted her head to peer through the bars. Cavanaugh stood down the hall. A nurse stepped in front of him to open a cell, and Cavanaugh disappeared inside. Perhaps five minutes passed before he reappeared, shepherding the cell's occupant before him.

Mara.

Amelia pressed closer. What was he doing? Mara hunched in on herself and shied away from his touch, blinking in the relatively brighter light of the hallway. He guided her down the corridor as if she were made of glass, and Amelia watched until the pair disappeared from view. A minute later, the ward door crashed closed. Amelia paced her cell until they returned, some two hours later. Cavanaugh led Mara back into her cell, conferred with the nurse, then left the ward again, alone.

He never looked in Amelia's direction.

He returned again the next day. And the next. And each day after that.

He spoke with other patients on the ward. He frequently drew something from a pocket and offered it between the bars of the cells. A few women—the ones prone to violence or threats—Cavanaugh spoke to from the hallway, quiet words Amelia could never make out. Most, like Mara, he removed from their cells for an hour or two at a time. Sometimes he carried a cloak over one arm, and the women returned pink-cheeked and smelling of the outdoors. Janey went more than once and always came back smiling. There was no pattern to the visits, save that he never skipped them for more than a day.

He made no attempt to interact with Amelia.

She wondered at his silence. Once or twice there was a tiny hitch in his stride as he passed her door, as if he might turn toward her, but he never did.

Mrs. Brennan happened to be in the ward when he returned with Mara one afternoon. She reached for the girl, who flinched away. With a scowl, Mrs. Brennan took a rough hold of her arm and gave her a shove in the direction of her cell. Cavanaugh spoke.

"I'll see her settled. You may wait for me over there." His voice held that note of command again, and on this occasion, Amelia found she did not object to it.

When he finished with Mara, he strode directly to Mrs. Brennan, standing halfway between Mara's and Amelia's doors and wearing an expression as sour as curdled milk.

"I do not wish to see you handle a patient so harshly again," he said in a firm voice, "especially one who is in need of neither restraint nor correction."

He looked past the matron, and his eyes caught Amelia's. Her chest tightened, and something flickered on Cavanaugh's face for a moment before he looked away.

Mrs. Brennan followed his gaze, her frown deepening. Despite an overwhelming urge to shrink back, Amelia stood her ground.

"Additionally," Cavanaugh went on, "I'm aware that you've disobeyed my explicit orders at least once. I don't wish to find that it's happened again." The warning was clear in his tone. He waited until the matron looked at him. "Is that understood?"

Amelia winced. Someone would pay for that, and there was every chance it would be Amelia herself.

The older woman's face flushed an unpleasant shade of red. Her jaw clenched, but she muttered something that must have been agreement before striding away.

Cavanaugh watched her retreating back for a moment. Amelia found herself hoping he would look at her again, but he only turned, nodded once to Mara, and left.

That evening, Amelia lay on her cot as the ward sang its chorus. Mumbles and shouts echoed. A burst of laughter pierced the air and trailed away. Threats and curses threaded through the hall. But something was missing. It came to her as she drifted into sleep. Mara's crying. The anguished sobs that had been such a constant part of the ward's discordant harmony.

They'd stopped.

17

Andrew started at the knock on his office door. "Come in," he called. An orderly entered with a stack of mail, handing it over with a nod. Andrew thanked the man and glanced at the clock as he left.

He'd done it again.

He turned his attention back to the stack of files on his desk. All of them needed updating before he left for the night. The one on top was Mrs. Dennis, who insisted the archangel Michael whispered messages from the dead into her left ear.

Messages from the dead. It seemed he couldn't get away from them.

Mrs. Dennis was quite insane, of course. Andrew very much doubted the archangel Michael instructed her to burn down her neighbor's chicken coop in broad daylight, or to threaten a pair of police officers with a knife when they responded to the neighbor's complaint. But the notion of the dead speaking through the living had proved impossible to dismiss since his initial encounter with Miss Casey. Their second meeting only made things worse. Her tirade had been shocking. It should have been enough to convince him of her madness. But it was her earlier words that shook him. Not only had she refused to admit the lie, she'd taken it further, describing . . . well, describing Susannah.

Andrew had fled from the ward and spent a pair of restless nights struggling to come to some sort of resolution. What he believed to be possible and what he knew he'd seen fought in his mind like a pair of dogs with their teeth locked on each other's throats.

He rose on the third morning, his mind exhausted by the struggle and something else she'd said ringing in his head.

If he wanted to help someone.

He did. And this fruitless obsession with an impossibility accomplished nothing. He would let it go and focus on what he'd come to the asylum to do. And, Andrew thought with a flash of something like defiance, he would start with the very woman Miss Casey had pointed out.

Mara Roark's case—along with some dozen others he adopted as his own—quickly consumed him. The interviews took time and attention, and there was all the reading and research necessary to teach himself about their conditions. He was making good progress with some of them. It was rewarding, and the work left him with no time to worry over the paradox of Miss Casey and her impossible claims.

Except, much as he told himself so, he knew the last bit for a lie.

This wasn't the first time he'd looked up to find he'd wasted an hour imagining what he would say to Susannah if he had the chance. If it were truly possible to speak with the dead.

He gave an irritated sigh and turned to the stack of mail: a circular for a medical supply company, the newest volume of the *American Journal of Psychology*, and a thin letter with a Philadelphia postmark.

Andrew glanced at the return address, then ripped open the envelope with suddenly shaking fingers. The letter within was brief:

Dear Dr. Cavanaugh—

I received your letter of April 19 with great pleasure. You have been much missed since your departure, and we are all pleased to hear you have found satisfaction in your new home.

I will admit your request came as a surprise. There are already so many in our own city who have suffered, and who have need of our care, it has never been our habit to accept the *sort of transfer you propose. But your account of these poor women's misfortunes touched the hearts of many here, and we resolved as a community to pray for guidance in the matter.*

We believe we have received such direction. Pending agreement of the relevant authorities, we will accept both Mrs. Roark and Miss Mayfield into our community.

Please forward details of any necessary arrangements soonest, and we will make ready to receive them.

I remain,

Yours,

Mother Mary Benedicta

Sisters of St. Joseph, Philadelphia

Andrew smiled as he reached the end of the letter. St. Joseph's was situated on a beautiful piece of ground in the eastern part of the city, leafy and quiet. They had a well-run school and convalescent home with a fine track record. It was exactly the right sort of place for Jane Mayfield. And Mara Roark could have a real chance at making a new beginning there.

"Still here, I see."

Andrew turned. Harcourt stood in the doorway behind him. He started to rise, but the older man waved him back down.

"No, no, don't get up. May I?" Harcourt gestured to the straight-backed chair beside the desk.

"Of course." Andrew swept an untidy tower of books off the seat and resettled it on the floor by the desk. The pile teetered until he reached out to steady it with a foot. This accomplished, he turned his attention back to his visitor, who had seated himself and was now gazing around the office with a thoughtful expression.

"You seem to have relocated quite a bit of the asylum's library."

Andrew looked around the cramped space. Stacks of books sat on every surface. Half a dozen lay open on his desk, and around the room were at least thirty more—closed, but bristling with slips of paper marking passages he meant to read again.

"I suppose I have gotten a bit carried away," he admitted with some chagrin. "I keep coming across things I need to research further. When

I do, I find there's yet more to study. And all of it fascinating. But if I've inconvenienced the other doctors, I'll—"

"No, no, the books are no issue. I'm glad you're finding them useful." Harcourt paused, then took a breath and continued. "There is a somewhat delicate matter I must address with you."

Andrew straightened at the other man's tone.

"I have received several complaints."

Andrew blinked, taken aback. "Complaints? About me?"

"Yes. It seems some of the staff feel you are overcritical of their work. And I understand you have expressed rather vehement disagreement with some of our methods of patient care."

Andrew nodded slowly, thinking of Klafft and his barbaric prescriptions. "I have doubts about the efficacy of some of the treatments I've seen being used. Many of them seem unlikely to be helpful. Some seem as though they could only make things worse."

"You believe you have the expertise necessary to make such judgments?"

"I do not believe it is a matter of expertise—more of common sense. I do not see how repeated ice baths, for example, could possibly cure a case of melancholy."

"But perhaps this is precisely because you lack the necessary expertise," Harcourt suggested. He forestalled Andrew's reply with a raised hand. "Your enthusiasm and your concern for the patients do you credit. But you are new to this work, and I must insist you do your best to be mindful of that fact when dealing with the senior staff. I cannot have you countermanding their orders or contradicting them in front of the patients."

"I don't believe I have done any such thing," Andrew said, startled. "I may have allowed my frustration with Dr. Klafft's treatments to show on occasion, but—"

"I am not speaking only of Dr. Klafft," Harcourt interrupted, "although his many years of experience should certainly entitle him to some deference from you. No, I am referring to your behavior toward Mrs. Brennan."

"Mrs. Brennan?"

"I'm told you berated her before several members of the nursing staff."

Andrew chose his words carefully. "I would not say I berated her. But I have been disturbed by her manner toward some of the patients.

In my view, she is overly harsh. And I know of at least one instance of her placing a patient in restraints, despite my having deemed them unnecessary."

"Perhaps they later became necessary," Harcourt said, a trifle impatiently. "You must have seen by now how quickly a patient's behavior can change. At any rate, if she judged it necessary, I see no reason to doubt her conclusion. And as to her manner, I will grant it is not warm. But she is not here to mother the patients. She is here to oversee the nursing staff, and it is a difficult enough job without having her authority undermined in front of them. I take it you understand my meaning?"

Andrew nodded once. "I do."

"Excellent." Harcourt stood, and the corner of his coat caught the letter on Andrew's desk and swept it to the floor, along with another sheet of paper—the list of asylums Andrew had made for Ned. Both landed faceup.

"What are these?" Harcourt asked as he retrieved them.

"The letter is from a Church-run refuge in Philadelphia," Andrew said. "They take in widows and orphans, along with others in need. I was one of the physicians they sometimes called in to see to their charges, and I grew to know many of the staff. It's an excellent establishment. I wrote to see if they might be willing to take two of our patients. The answer only arrived today."

Something in Harcourt's face tightened, and he looked back down at the page. "This is extraordinary," he said a moment later, looking up.

Andrew's smile faltered at the other doctor's expression. He was incensed, his eyes burning behind his spectacles.

"I see," the superintendent began, in a voice so cold it crackled, "that complaints about your arrogance and presumption were not unfounded. The situation is, in fact, more egregious than I had understood. What on earth would give you reason to believe you have the authority to remove patients from this facility? And this," he went on, holding up the list. "Part of a wider plan? Have you determined which patients will go to these facilities as well? Merely waiting for their answers?"

"No, no, nothing like that," Andrew said. He meant to sound definite. Instead, to his horror, he sounded defensive—a man denying plain evidence of his own guilt. "That list is part of a personal project—nothing to do with patients here." He tried to explain, but in his haste the story emerged garbled and preposterous.

Harcourt looked disbelieving and, if possible, even more furious.

Andrew pivoted to the letter. "At any rate, I assure you, I had no intention of attempting to transfer anyone without your consent. I would never have done so. I was merely looking into alternative situations. I don't believe the asylum is the proper place for them. The details of their cases suggest—"

"I do not care." Harcourt stepped toward him. "It is not your decision to make. You may be a doctor out there," he said, waving vaguely in the direction of the city, "but when it comes to this sort of work, you are very nearly a trainee. You presume too much. You have neither the experience nor the authority to make major decisions about patient care. You have stepped far beyond the bounds of your appropriate role, and it will not be tolerated."

A lead weight dropped from the sky and landed in Andrew's gut. Harcourt was going to fire him. He'd have to leave the island. He'd never know what happened to his patients. He'd never know if he could have helped them. He'd never have the chance to speak to Miss Casey again, to find out for certain if that had been Susannah speaking through her.

The last thought nearly brought him to his knees.

"Please." The word was a desperate whisper, forced out before Harcourt could go on. "Give me another chance," Andrew said. "I understand that I've made mistakes. But I've also been of use here—I know I have. Please, let me stay. I'll accept whatever conditions you set. I just—" He broke off as Harcourt held up a hand.

"I will accept part of the blame," Harcourt said, his tone somewhat calmer. "I failed to set clear boundaries for your work when you arrived. Let me do so now. You may continue to examine patients and note your observations. You may treat minor physical ailments. You may assist the other doctors in their evaluation and treatment. If you have ideas, you may suggest them. But going forward, you will initiate no treatments without the supervision of another doctor. You are not to countermand or interfere in any way with orders given by senior staff. And under no circumstances are you empowered to remove or make plans for removal of any patient from this facility. Is that understood?"

"Yes. Yes, I understand." Andrew tried not to sag with relief.

Harcourt regarded him for a moment. "Mark me. This is your second chance. There won't be a third." He turned and strode from the room without waiting for a response.

∽

Hours later, Andrew sank into what had become his customary chair as Tyree poured their drinks. They'd finished his original supply of whiskey some weeks before, and Andrew had replaced it with a new—much better—bottle. Tyree accepted the gift with the unalloyed pleasure of a man who has not recognized an implied criticism.

"I hear you got a thorough dressing down today." Tyree handed him the glass.

Andrew took a grateful drink and tipped his head back against the pliant leather. "I suppose the whole asylum knows about it?"

Tyree took his seat. "I should say so."

Andrew closed his eyes. "Wonderful."

Gossip on the island was like smoke in a closed room—with nowhere to go, it recirculated endlessly. He opened his eyes and looked at Tyree, who seemed unconcerned.

"Don't worry. It will be forgotten. Something else will happen in a day or two."

"Like what?"

"I don't know." Tyree shrugged. "Most of the younger nurses are stalking that new orderly. Perhaps one of them will catch him. That might be enough."

"I don't understand why Harcourt reacted as he did," Andrew said.

"That's easy enough to explain." Tyree sighed. "Do you remember my telling you Klafft originally wanted the superintendent job?"

"Yes."

"He's never really come to terms with it. Watch him around Harcourt. Klafft needles him, questions his decisions—including the decision to hire you, I might add. Does everything he can to undercut his authority. It's subtle, but it's always there. And it's not just pettiness. He's looking for anything he could use to damage Harcourt with the asylum's board of governors. If it appears he's lost control of the staff, that might do it."

"So what I did—" Andrew began.

"Felt to Harcourt like an attack on two fronts," Tyree finished. "A second doctor gone rogue, and giving Klafft more ammunition to boot."

Andrew sighed. "I did exactly the wrong thing."

"Yes," Tyree agreed. "What possessed you to do it at all?"

"Are you familiar with the patients in question?"

Tyree shook his head.

"Jane Mayfield is feeble-minded, not insane. There's no good reason to keep her here, but she can't take care of herself. Her file says she has a brother somewhere, but there's no record of him visiting."

"And the other?"

"Mara Roark." Andrew swallowed the remainder of his drink and told Tyree the story he'd pieced together from the testimony of a half dozen neighbors and Mara's own tearful recounting. She'd been an only child. She married, and her father got her new husband a job at the factory where he worked. Soon enough, there was a baby on the way. About two months before the birth, an accident at the factory. Father and husband, both lost. The baby came early, sickly and puling, and his mother couldn't stop crying.

Mara's own mother did what she could, but only six weeks later, she was gone as well, the grief and strain too much for her. Mara had worn her best dress—the one she'd worn for her wedding—to all three funerals, because there was no money for black. She went back to the apartment. The rent was due, and she didn't have it. Probably it would be the work-house for her, or the streets. She'd opened the gas jets and climbed into bed with her baby. Neighbors smelled it and knocked down her door in time to revive Mara, but the baby was already gone.

Tyree was shaking his head as Andrew finished. "Puerperal melancholy, obviously. A classic presentation, complicated by the other losses in such close proximity."

Andrew nodded. "That was my diagnosis. She'd likely have recovered in time—the literature suggests most women do." He sat forward and went on in an earnest tone. "As it was, she was quite overwhelmed. Clearly not entirely responsible for her actions. It's obvious she is still feeling enormous grief and guilt, but she isn't insane. St. Joseph's is the ideal place for her. But by going about it the way I did, I've ruined any chance of getting Harcourt to agree." He bounced a fist off the padded arm of the chair.

Tyree considered. "Perhaps not. I'll evaluate both of them myself and talk to Harcourt. Going ahead with the transfer might be his best move. It could be made to look like his own idea. If it's stopped, it will be obvious it wasn't. Everyone knows the asylum is overcrowded. If another facility is willing to take charge of these women and is qualified to do so, why shouldn't he let them go?"

Andrew closed his eyes and breathed a sigh of relief. When he opened them, he found Tyree studying him.

"You seem quite invested in these cases," the older doctor said. "And they aren't the only ones to attract your interest, apparently."

His voice was mild, but Andrew shifted under the other man's gaze. "I'm working with quite a few patients."

Tyree nodded. "And often in your office, rather than in their cells or the examination rooms. I believe you've even taken some on walks about the grounds?"

"The ones who are stable enough, yes. The wards are noisy and uncomfortable. My office is less intimidating than the examination rooms. And yes, sometimes I take them outside. What of it?" Andrew tried not to bristle.

The other man made a calming gesture. "I'm not implying anything improper, but it does suggest a certain disregard for procedure. I also hear you've been sleeping in your office."

It was true. Andrew had stayed late enough to miss the last ferry more than a handful of times and had been forced to drag the rusty old cot out of the storage closet. He'd also taken to keeping a fresh set of clothes in one of the drawers.

"The work is absorbing." Andrew shrugged.

"Tell me: When was the last time you attended any sort of social engagement?"

"I beg your pardon?"

"The theater? Dinner with friends, perhaps? *Have* you made any friends in the city since you've been here?"

Andrew studied the bottom of his glass.

"As far as I can tell," Tyree said, "you spend nearly every waking moment—and no small number of the sleeping ones—here on the island. You're in the wards before breakfast; you're at your desk late at night. It's not good for you."

Andrew looked up, stung. "You live here."

Tyree sighed. "Yes, and see what it's gotten me. A pair of rooms and every third weekend at liberty. It's a living. I've made my peace with it. But you"—he sat forward and pinned Andrew with a look—"are far too young to do so. You mentioned that personal circumstances led you to move to New York."

Andrew's heart lurched at the abrupt change of subject. He'd never spoken of Susannah to any of his colleagues. Did Tyree know? Was he the source of Miss Casey's uncanny knowledge? The palms of his hands tingled.

"A broken engagement, I believe?"

Andrew blinked. Twin pangs of relief and disappointment hollowed his chest. "My engagement," he repeated.

"I don't mean to pry, but if you're throwing yourself into your work as a remedy for a broken heart—"

Andrew barked a surprised laugh. "I'm not pining for a lost love, I assure you. I was the one who ended it. She was . . . well, it became clear we were ill-suited to each other."

Tyree nodded. "Then I applaud your prudence. There is nothing more dangerous to one's happiness than choosing the wrong marriage partner." A shadow passed over Tyree's face, and he sat back. "But my ultimate point remains. You cannot allow your work here to consume you."

Andrew nodded, though he knew the admonishment had come too late.

After a few minutes more, he wished his friend good evening and went back to his own office. He surveyed the stack of unfinished paperwork and decided to leave it for the following day. A tin of hard candies sat on the desktop, nearly empty. They made a wonderful lure for reluctant patients.

And sticky-fingered orderlies. The last tin had disappeared overnight when he left it on the desk. Andrew tugged on the desk's right-hand drawer, intending to leave the tin inside. It opened a few inches and then stuck fast. He jiggled it, unable to either open it farther or close it fully.

Irritated, he braced one hand against the edge of the desk and gave the handle a hard yank. The drawer came loose with a shriek of protest, slid entirely out of the desk, and tumbled to the floor with a loud bang.

A scrap of paper fluttered free, crumpled and battered and obviously torn from a larger sheet. Andrew reached for it, then froze as his eyes fastened on the words it held.

Julia Weaver—$250. The number terminated in a ragged edge. It was obvious there had once been more text below, but only the tops of the letters remained. His mouth gone dry, Andrew sank to his knees and listened to the blood pounding in his ears as the implications became clear.

He'd been wrong. Ned's sister was in the asylum after all.

And someone here knew it.

18

Amelia woke in the dark to a hand clamped over her nose and mouth. Thrashing in terror, she clawed at the wrist until a familiar voice hissed, "Ow! Stop that!"

She stilled.

"Do you know who I am?"

She nodded, her heart still racing. As soon as his hand withdrew, she sat up and flung her arms around him. "Jonas!"

She felt him sag.

"Thank god." He returned the hug for a long moment before drawing back. "I'm sorry for scaring you. But I didn't know what kind of state you were in. I couldn't risk you screaming if you didn't recognize me."

"I can't believe you're here. How did—" Amelia stopped as her eyes adjusted to the dim light. She reached out and fingered the rough fabric of his orderly's jacket.

"So it *was* you I saw that day when—" She flushed as she recalled exactly where she'd been when she'd seen him.

"Yes." There was anger in his voice. "I was going to try to catch your eye, but at the last minute I realized I didn't know how you would react."

"I can't believe you're here," she said again.

He squeezed her arm. "I'm sorry it took me so long. You were hard to track, and even once I knew you were here, I couldn't get to you right away. But then tonight—"

"Was a laudanum night," she finished.

His tone was disgusted. "For three of the wards on this side of the building. No one's walking them. The nurses are drinking sherry in one of the parlors, and the orderlies are gambling in the staff room. They'll eventually notice I'm gone, but we've got some time. This place." He shook his head. "How in god's name did you wind up in here?"

Amelia huffed out a bitter little laugh. "I went for a walk." She told him what she remembered about the figure in the park and the other incidents since she'd been in the asylum. "You were right," she admitted. "My gift has changed. It's different now."

Jonas whistled between his teeth when she told him about the vision she'd had of the fire and her subsequent discovery of the girl's death.

"I don't know how I would have stood it if Elizabeth hadn't been there."

"It wasn't your fault." He covered her hand with his. "You couldn't have done anything."

"Maybe not, but I should have tried."

"Let it go. It's done, and you can't change it. I need you focused. We've got to figure out how to get you out of here. A husband or another relative might be able to claim you, if you had one. I might have been able to mock up some kind of paperwork they'd accept, given some time, but—"

"But you can't play the part, since you're known here now." Amelia shrugged. "So we need someone else."

Jonas nodded, and she grimaced, thinking of their limited—and disreputable—circle of acquaintance. Except for Tommy, who obviously couldn't do it, there wasn't a one of them she'd trust to handle something like this.

Hating the notion, but having no better idea, she took a breath. "I don't suppose Sidney would—"

Jonas interrupted. "He's in Europe. He left a week or so after you disappeared."

Amelia gaped at him. Sidney had waited until she'd disappeared, and then up and left Jonas worried and alone? Outrage stabbed through her. She'd known he was no good, had wished to be rid of him. But like this? How dare he? Damn the man.

Jonas went on. "I have a couple of ideas, but I can't see how to make any of them work just yet. If we had someone here we could trust, then maybe."

Cavanaugh's face flashed through Amelia's mind. She dismissed the thought with a shake of her head. "I think it's just us."

Jonas's voice was determined. "Doesn't matter. We've always managed before. We can do it again. Don't worry. I'll come up with something."

Amelia stood and followed him to the door, the blanket wrapped around her. A pungent odor hung in the air, out of place among the mingled scents of lye and old soup and half-rinsed chamber pots.

She finally placed it. "That's how you got into the cell without waking me." She swung the door a few silent inches. "You oiled the hinges."

Jonas patted one of his pockets. "I palmed a syringe a while back. I filled it that night, and I've been carrying it ever since."

Amelia smiled. The expression felt foreign after so long. "And the lock? Did you palm a key as well?"

"Please," he said in mock offense. "If I couldn't pick a lock like this, I ought to be ashamed of myself. I'm surprised you haven't done it."

She indicated her raggedly cropped hair with a wry gesture. "A shortage of hairpins. And besides," she went on, as the humor leaked away, "without somewhere to go, there was no point."

They both went silent. A moment later, Jonas drew her into a crushing hug. "I was so worried," he said into the top of her head. "I thought . . ."

Amelia clung to him, blinking back tears.

With a final squeeze he let go and turned to leave.

"Jonas?" Her voice quavered.

He turned back.

"I have to—" She stopped, then continued in a rush. "I'm so sorry for what I said. That day. All of it. I never meant to—"

He raised a hand. "I know. I forgive you. I'll come back as soon as I can. Don't worry. I'm here."

He squeezed her shoulder once, then left as he'd entered, closing the door and relocking it behind him. He padded back down the hallway and melted into the shadows.

Amelia crept back to her cot. She closed her eyes and lay buoyant in the dark, tears of joy and relief sliding from beneath her lids and trailing unchecked down the sides of her face.

19

Six days later, Amelia found herself once again standing beside Mara in the washroom. The girl's nocturnal silence had continued, but this was the first time Amelia had seen her up close in weeks. Mara's face was still lined with grief, but the dense aura of misery that had once enveloped her seemed, if not gone, then at least lighter.

Cavanaugh was responsible. His visits to the ward had continued without interruption after his confrontation with Mrs. Brennan. After his single lapse that day, the doctor returned to his habit of never looking in Amelia's direction. It bothered her now in a way it hadn't before.

Both women's eyes swung toward the washroom door as it opened. A nurse entered, carrying something under one arm.

"Here." She shoved the bundle at Mara, who dropped it with a muffled thump.

"What—" Mara began.

"Dress yourself, and be quick about it. You." She turned to Amelia. "Help her. They're waiting."

Amelia bent to retrieve the fallen items: a dress of dark, plain wool and a linen shift, along with a pair of sturdy black shoes.

Mara removed her asylum shift with shaking fingers and drew the new garments on. They were ill-fitting but clean, and the girl plucked the fabric between her fingers as if she didn't quite believe it was real. Her blue eyes were wide with uncertainty.

The waiting nurse took her by the elbow and hustled her out of the washroom. Amelia hesitated, torn between curiosity and caution. Wherever they were taking the girl, it was nothing to do with her. And yet . . .

She turned and hurried after them.

The ward door was open. Cavanaugh stood just outside with a nurse, both of them wearing coats and hats. To Amelia's surprise, Janey stood between them, similarly attired and directing a worshipful gaze in Cavanaugh's direction. Mara and her escort approached, and he held out another coat and said something Amelia could not hear. At a nudge from the nurse, Mara turned and allowed him to help her don it, her face stunned and white. At his gesture, the waiting nurses stepped forward and began to guide the young women away.

Amelia rushed toward them. "Where are you taking them?"

Cavanaugh turned, and his eyes widened when he saw her. The nurse who'd brought Mara from the washroom hissed and grabbed Amelia's arm. Amelia struggled against her.

"Where are you taking them?" she asked again.

Cavanaugh motioned for the nurse to release Amelia. "Go ahead and take the ladies down, please. I'll be just a moment." He turned back to Amelia. "They're being transferred elsewhere."

Closer to him than she'd been in weeks, Amelia was startled to see how tired he looked. There were dark smudges beneath his eyes and lines of strain on his face she would swear had not been there before, even on the day he'd reeked of alcohol. What had taxed him so since that day?

He raised an eyebrow, and she realized she'd been staring. She dropped her gaze, self-conscious. "Is it better than here?"

With a glance at the ward nurse, who was approaching from her station beside the wall, he lowered his voice to reply, "Yes."

Amelia let out a breath she hadn't known she was holding. "Good." She hesitated. "Mara's better than she was. You've helped her. It seems I misjudged you somewhat."

"Somewhat?"

"Do you still believe me to be lying?"

He flushed, and the careful mask of his expression slipped. "I don't know." His voice was so low it was barely audible. He wouldn't look at her.

A spark bloomed in her chest. Amelia's throat went dry, and her voice, when it emerged, was hoarse and tentative. "Would you like to speak again?"

For a moment Cavanaugh looked hunted. Or perhaps *haunted* was the more appropriate word. Then his jaw tightened, and he nodded once. "I'm overseeing the transfer today. I'll be back tomorrow."

"Tomorrow, then."

20

Andrew struggled not to fidget as Miss Casey seated herself on the chair beside his desk. He'd risen that morning with a belly full of snakes, half-sure he was being played for a fool and yet entirely willing to take the risk. He'd gotten off the ferry and gone directly to the isolation ward with no idea how to approach the conversation he was about to have. Since his discovery the week before, he'd barely slept. Now buzzing anxiety had pushed aside the dull fatigue.

He followed Miss Casey's gaze as she examined every corner of the room, from the stack of files on the table to the tray of heavy cream stationery with its silver pen holder and inkwell. The set was a gift from Susannah on his college graduation. Each of the pieces bore his initials, formed into an ornate, curling monogram. "Suitable for an educated gentleman," she'd teased.

The letters blurred. He swallowed and turned to find Miss Casey studying him no less intently than she had the room.

He forced himself to sit, feeling, as he did, the outline of the tin of sweets in his pocket. He extracted them.

"So that's what you use to bait the ones who won't talk to you," Miss Casey said.

He offered her the tin without speaking, and she took her time selecting a yellow candy before popping it into her mouth and closing her eyes in evident pleasure.

The silence stretched between them.

Her voice broke it. "Ask me what you really want to know."

"Is she here?" The words were out before Andrew could stop them. They hung in the air, absurd. Urgent.

"No," she said softly, never taking her eyes from his. "There's nothing here now."

"But before. In your cell. There was?" It was only half a question.

Her lips tightened, and her chin dipped a fraction. "Yes."

"How?"

"I don't know. I don't have any control over it. It was only the second time I ever saw such a thing."

"The second? When was the first?"

"Just before I was brought here."

"Tell me."

"I've always had a degree of ability," she began. "The second sight, clairvoyance, whatever you want to call it. For most of my life it was so slight it barely mattered. But about two months ago, something happened."

She went on, Andrew studying her expressions and the tone of her voice. A job as a medium in a tony Greenwich club, the injury, a long convalescence, and the discovery of her heightened abilities. She paused now and again, searching for the right word, the right way to explain something she readily conceded was inexplicable.

A solitary walk in a city park. She stumbled a bit, trying to describe the phantom she claimed to have seen. Her voice trembled slightly as she spoke of it, and the pulse at her neck beat faster. Her hands, folded in her lap, tightened until the knuckles went white.

She spoke of waking in the asylum, of her fear and confusion, of her vain attempt to convince one of the doctors—Klafft, from her description—of her sanity. She described what had happened when she'd touched Mara's hand, recounted for him what she'd seen while she was in the ward. And she told him, again, what had formed behind him when he came into her cell the first time.

"Then you touched my hand, and you know the rest."

Andrew struggled to breathe. Her words seemed to have filled the room to bursting, swelling in their freedom and crowding against him on every side.

It was madness, this story she told.

And he believed her.

It was clear there were things she was leaving out, places where she'd hesitated in the telling, gliding over details so smoothly he'd never have noticed, had he not been so utterly focused. He marked them. None of it mattered.

The rational part of Andrew's brain railed against it. He was a dupe, a fool. But on some elemental level, he knew she was telling the truth.

He tried to hide it from her, standing as she finished and turning his face away, fussing with his jacket. But his trembling hands betrayed him.

"You believe me." Her voice shook, but the tone was certain.

He turned back to her. Her eyes were wide, and her face was filled with color. Andrew swallowed, tried to focus his reeling mind. The words, when they came, were barely more than breath. "I believe you."

Something settled between them—an accord as fragile and shimmering as spider's silk.

Her voice, when she spoke again, was gentle. "Who is she?"

"My sister, Susannah," he said in a careful tone.

"I'm sorry."

He lifted a hand in acknowledgment and took a breath. "Miss Casey—"

"That isn't my name," she interrupted.

He blinked. "I beg your pardon?"

"I'm not Lina Casey. The cloak I was wearing when I was brought here used to be hers. It had her name sewn inside. I was in no shape to argue when I arrived. But I'm not Lina," she said, leaning forward. "My name is Amelia Matthew."

"Very well. Miss Matthew." Andrew rubbed at the back of his neck and blew out a sigh. "I admit I'm not certain what to do next. I've never . . ." He trailed off with a helpless shrug. "I've never imagined anything like this."

"You know I'm not mad. I don't belong here. You have to let me go."

"It's not that easy."

"Why not? You're a doctor. Can't you declare me sane and release me?"

Andrew felt his face flush. "I'm afraid not. There are circumstances beyond my control. If there were some relation we could contact, someone who could legally claim responsibility for you, then it *might* be possible."

She grimaced and glanced to one side. She pressed her lips together with a little shake of her head. "There's no one."

21

One of the younger nurses appeared at Amelia's door the next day, and she wasn't alone. Jonas stood behind her. She'd seen him from a distance several times since his nighttime visit to her cell, but they hadn't had an opportunity to speak.

"Dr. Cavanaugh's been delayed," the woman informed her as she unlocked the cell. "I'm to fetch you to his office."

Amelia exchanged a quick grin with Jonas behind the nurse's back as they followed her. They slowed, allowing her to get some yards ahead of them.

"I told Cavanaugh the truth yesterday," Amelia whispered, watching the nurse's back. "He believes me."

She'd felt odd when she finished telling him the story. Exhausted. Ecstatic. Nerves singing with relief and frustration. She hadn't planned to be quite so forthright, but something about the look on Cavanaugh's face tempted her into throwing the dice. The exhilaration of knowing he believed her had made it hard to fall asleep.

"Do you think he—"

Jonas fell silent as they approached another nurse in the main corridor. This one shot Jonas a poisonous glare. Amelia blinked, startled. Women never looked at him that way.

She waited until the woman was out of earshot. "What did you do?"

"Nothing." The tips of his ears pinkened, and he avoided her eyes. "I needed some information about the nursing schedules."

"So you flirted with her?"

"I may have done a bit more than that."

"And?"

"And she may have walked in on me with one of the other nurses the next day." He caught her look. "The first one didn't know enough."

Amelia didn't have time to reply before they caught up to the nurse guiding them, who was rapping on Cavanaugh's office door. When there was no answer, she swung it open and peered inside.

"Not here," she grumbled. "As if I've nothing better to do than wait." After another minute, she turned to look down the corridor and sighed. "You," she said to Jonas. "Stay with her until the doctor arrives. Mind she doesn't cause any trouble. I can't be spending my whole morning standing here."

The woman left and, hardly able to believe their luck, Amelia drew Jonas into Cavanaugh's office and nudged the door almost closed behind them.

"So, in all this dallying with nurses, what have you found? What are we going to do?"

"I don't know." He frowned. "Does Cavanaugh really believe you?"

"Yes. I'm sure of it. But he says he can't release me."

"The word is he's on thin ice here."

"I almost told him about you." She'd nearly blurted out Jonas's name when Cavanaugh asked if there was someone who could claim her, but she had stopped herself at the last second. Jonas had no legal claim to her, and he'd made his way onto the island under false pretenses. Amelia didn't think Cavanaugh would expose him, but she couldn't be certain. It wasn't worth the risk.

"It's probably best you didn't," Jonas said, rummaging in his pocket. "I have something for you." He pressed something into her hand: a trio of hairpins. "Just in case."

"Perfect," she said. "I'll pick the locks and walk out the front door."

"If it comes to it, that's what we'll do," he said.

Amelia put her arms around him. He hugged her back, his chin resting on top of her head.

Andrew hurried out of ward four, where he'd been called to attend to a nurse with a bite on her arm. He'd been forced to use his chloral dose on the patient who'd inflicted it, leaving her snoring on her cot. The din of the ward faded behind him as he crossed into the main hall and turned toward his office, where Miss Cas—no, Miss Matthew, he corrected himself—should have been waiting.

He'd been up most of the night thinking about her ability and what it might mean. Andrew's hand strayed to the pocket where he'd been carrying Susannah's locket ever since Ned had come to him. Miss Matthew said she couldn't control that aspect of her ability. But Susannah had come once. It could happen again. His heartbeat quickened, and he tried to discipline his mind. His job was to find Julia Weaver. Amelia Matthew might be the key.

His office door was partly open. She was there, then.

Andrew pushed the door open and froze in shock.

She wasn't alone. A tall, dark-haired orderly stood with his arms around her.

Fury swept through him. "What is the meaning of this?"

Miss Matthew pulled back with a gasp of surprise as he entered, and the orderly's face went taut and wary.

"You," Andrew snarled, stepping toward him. "How dare you? You abuse your position. So help me I will—"

"Dr. Cavanaugh." Miss Matthew stepped between them and lifted a placating hand. "Please, it's all right, he only—"

"It is the furthest thing from all right." Andrew kept his eyes on the man. "To take such liberties with a patient—"

"I lied to you yesterday."

Betrayal lanced through him. He glanced at her. "Lied." His voice was flat. "About what, precisely?"

"When I said there was no one who could come and claim me." Miss Matthew indicated the orderly, who crossed to the door. Rather than exiting, however, he eased it closed and leaned against it, his posture relaxed but watchful.

"This is Jonas Vincent."

A different surname. Not married, then. Andrew caught the look that passed between the pale, black-haired man and the petite blond woman—the sort born of long intimacy—and drew the obvious conclusion about the nature of their relationship.

She went on. "I didn't tell you about him because I knew he was here. I wasn't certain I could trust you."

Andrew looked at her. Her voice was calm, though every line of her body radiated tension. "Well," he said, the word clipped. "It seems you'll have to trust me now. Why don't we all sit."

The orderly—Jonas—lifted his hand in a sardonic half wave. "I think I'll stay right where I am. But yes, there are several things we ought to get sorted, since we're all here."

Andrew sat, feeling much like a man who thought he had been walking on solid ground, only to find himself abruptly adrift with no land in sight. "That was the only lie? You weren't lying about everything else?"

Her eyes widened. "No," she said hurriedly. "I swear to you, everything I told you about what I saw was true, as was everything I said about who I am. I just didn't tell you all of it."

He'd already known as much. Very well. He forced himself to relax before he spoke.

"Miss Matthew," he began.

"Please. Call me Amelia."

"I couldn't. The circumstances—"

"Are highly irregular. But I'm not your patient," she pointed out. "Unless you've changed your mind and decided I truly am mad, after all."

Andrew made a noise that might have been a laugh, if he'd been capable of laughing. "No," he said. "I'm beginning to feel I may be slightly insane, but I concede you are not."

"Then," she said, "I am Amelia, and that is Jonas, and we are both pleased to meet you."

Jonas's impatience got the better of him, and pushed away from the door. "Yes. Delighted. Now that we've got that out of the way, let's talk about how we're going to get her out of here."

The doctor sighed and rubbed his forehead, looking suddenly tired. "I can't release her. I would if I could. But there have been several incidents since her arrival, and—"

"And you went around Harcourt to get those two other women moved, and now he's cut you off at the knees," Jonas finished.

Cavanaugh dropped his hand. "Yes," he said shortly.

"What if there were another way?" He watched the doctor as he spoke.

"What other way?" Amelia asked.

Jonas glanced at her. "Do you remember when I said I'd thought of a way, but that it wouldn't work without help?"

"Yes."

He nodded at Cavanaugh, who looked wary. "If he helps, I can make it work."

Amelia straightened in her chair. "What is it?"

"You're going to die."

Jonas drew far more pleasure than he probably should have from their stupefied expressions. Unable to help himself, he grinned.

Cavanaugh began to sputter an objection.

Amelia stopped him with a raised hand. "Explain, please."

"Do you remember Edmond Dantès?"

"From the novel." She raised an eyebrow. "I remember, but I don't especially like the idea of being sewn into a sheet and thrown into the river."

Jonas waved that away. "Dantès is just the inspiration," he said. "We'll alter the details." He looked at Cavanaugh. "You'll declare her dead. They keep a stack of pine coffins in one of the outbuildings."

Cavanaugh finally found his voice. "Edmond Dantès? *The Count of Monte Cristo*? Are you mad?"

Jonas sighed as he leaned against the desk. "Have you ever seen what happens when a patient dies here?" Jonas went on as they both shook their heads. "I have. And I've talked to the other orderlies—it's always done the same way."

"Which is?" Cavanaugh asked.

"The first doctor on the scene—whoever happens to be nearby when a death is discovered—pronounces her dead. They put the body in one of those cheap pine boxes and haul it off to the ferry and back to the city dock. The city morgue takes charge. If there's family, they can claim the corpse. If there isn't, or they can't afford the burial, it goes to the medical school or to Hart's Island."

"What about the examination? The autopsy?"

Jonas scoffed. "What autopsy? No one has time for that here. And the city certainly doesn't have any interest in paying for it. A corpse discovered at breakfast is on the ferry by lunch. Harcourt signs a death certificate and sends it with the body, and that's that."

Amelia looked thoughtful, but Cavanaugh was already shaking his head.

"It's a preposterous idea," he said.

"What's preposterous is a sane woman remaining locked up in this place because no one will take any trouble to get her out," Jonas said, his voice rising. "She can't stay here. Look at her!" He flung a hand toward Amelia.

Cavanaugh's eyes went to Amelia. Jonas could tell from his face that he was really looking at her—at the weary eyes, the face milk-pale beneath fading bruises, collarbones sharp beneath the thin fabric of her dress. He looked for a moment as if he might capitulate. Jonas held his breath, hoping.

But it was in vain.

"I'm sorry," the doctor said, shaking his head. "It's madness to think something like that would work. And the consequences if I'm caught helping you . . . I can't do it."

Jonas slammed his hand down on the desktop, his anger and disappointment nearly choking him. "Damn you. You know she doesn't belong here. If you're too much of a coward to do the right thing, I'll—"

He broke off as someone knocked on the door.

Cavanaugh rose to answer it. The nurse who'd brought them to the office stood outside. "Dr. Cavanaugh," she said, frowning past him at Jonas as he leaned on the desk. "You're wanted in the infirmary. We think it's a broken arm."

"Of course. I'll come at once."

The nurse left, and Cavanaugh ushered them into the hallway. "I'm sorry," he said again, looking everywhere but their eyes. He turned and walked away.

22

The following morning, Amelia found herself again delivered to Cavanaugh's office. To her surprise, Jonas was already there. She shot him a questioning look as Cavanaugh conferred with the nurse, and he shrugged in reply.

Cavanaugh closed the door and turned to face them, looking wan and rumpled. A rusty cot sat folded against the wall, blankets trailing on the floor. He must have stayed on the island overnight, though he looked as if he'd barely slept.

"Why are we here?" Jonas asked. "Have you changed your mind?"

Amelia waited for Cavanaugh to speak. Instead, he looked at her for a long moment, then plucked something—a photograph—from the desk.

"I meant to show you this yesterday, and then . . ." He gestured vaguely in Jonas's direction. He handed Amelia the photograph. "Do you recognize this woman? Have you—either of you," he said, turning to include Jonas, "seen her in the wards?"

Amelia took the photograph, studying the mousy hair and unmemorable features. She thought of the wards full of rows upon rows of identically dressed, gray-capped patients. She could have looked right at this woman and never noted her. "I don't think so." She passed it to Jonas.

Jonas shook his head. "Who is she?"

"Her name is Julia Weaver. Her brother came to me a little over two weeks ago." He told them of Ned Glenn's visit and his belief that his sister was somewhere in the asylum, trapped there by her own husband.

Amelia and Jonas exchanged a somber look. Just like Elizabeth.

"I said I'd help," Cavanaugh went on, his face lined and weary. "At first, I found nothing. But then—" He stopped and rubbed his eyes.

"Then?" Amelia prompted.

"Several days ago, I found this." He reached a hand into his pocket and withdrew a tattered bit of paper. "It was caught in the track of the desk drawer."

He looked away as Amelia and Jonas leaned forward to peer at the scrap.

Julia Weaver's name, and an amount of money. It seemed Ned Glenn must be right. His sister was here. But what—

Amelia frowned, her attention caught by the markings at the bottom.

Jonas saw it before she did. He made a surprised noise and reached for another piece of paper. He took the scrap from Cavanaugh, set it on the paper, and used a pencil to complete the partial letters beneath Julia Weaver's name. A few strokes and it was there: *Elizabeth Miner.*

Cavanaugh looked at the name, then at the two of them, his eyes stunned.

"Who is that? How did you know?" His voice shook.

By the time Amelia finished relaying the story Elizabeth had told her, Cavanaugh had sagged into his chair.

"Another one," he said in a hollow voice. He pressed his palms to his eyes, then dropped them to his lap. "Even after I found Julia's name, I hoped there was some innocent explanation. But there can't be, not if there's another."

"Why stop at two?" Jonas said, his tone thoughtful. "There are plenty of wealthy men with wives they'd like to have out of the way, and I'd bet private asylums are expensive. Admitting patients outside official channels could be a fine money-making scheme for someone here. Or perhaps several someones." He looked back down at the scrap of paper. "Do you have any idea who wrote this?"

"This office previously belonged to Dr. John Blounton," Cavanaugh said. "It seems likely it was he."

"Elizabeth mentioned him," Amelia blurted. "She said he came to speak with her one day, but then . . ." She frowned, remembering what she'd heard about Blounton.

"He's the one who died," Jonas said. "I've heard some of the orderlies mention him. They liked him."

"Yes," Cavanaugh said. "And there were some irregularities surrounding his death."

All three went quiet for a moment.

Amelia reached for the paper, then hesitated. "May I?"

Cavanaugh nodded. He and Jonas leaned forward in anticipation as she picked it up. She rubbed the scrap between her fingers.

Nothing. She shook her head.

Cavanaugh's face fell. "I suppose it was too much to hope it would be that easy."

Amelia straightened at that, and Jonas's eyes fastened on Cavanaugh, suspicion dawning on his face. "Why are you telling us this? What do you want?"

Cavanaugh looked uncertain for a moment, then took a deep breath before meeting Amelia's eyes.

"I thought about it—about your plan. I still don't think it will work. But I'll do it anyway, if you'll agree to help me first."

"You want me to find Julia Weaver," Amelia said.

"Yes."

"What happens if I can't? Or if I refuse?" Amelia asked, still feeling as though the breath had been sucked from her lungs.

Cavanaugh looked uncomfortable but didn't answer.

Jonas shot him a look that could have flayed flesh from bone. "You bastard," he said, his tone disgusted. He turned to Amelia. "The hell with him. We don't need him. I'll come up with something else. You don't have to do this. To have any chance of finding anything, you'd have to go back into the wards. You've already been hurt once."

Jonas gestured to her face, where Amelia knew the fading bruises still jaundiced her skin. "And god only knows what might happen with your gift," Jonas went on. "You can't risk it."

"Can you afford not to?" Cavanaugh's expression was that of a man who has bitten into something indescribably bitter. As though forcing himself to swallow it, he went on. "Jonas already admitted that faking your death won't work without my help. And if he had another way, he'd already have used it."

Amelia's heartbeat thudded in her ears as she looked at the doctor, betrayal sour in her throat. She'd thought him kind. He'd helped Mara and Janey without asking for anything in return.

But they hadn't had anything he wanted. A sound escaped from her throat—half laugh, half sob. It was her bad luck that she did.

She looked at Jonas, hoping he had another answer, but his face was all helpless fury.

Amelia ground her teeth and tried to calm the storm in her head. They needed his help. But he was demanding too much. The idea of staying in this place with no end in sight—she couldn't bear it.

Elizabeth is bearing it. The thought was like cold water. Elizabeth was trapped here. And Julia Weaver. Amelia had a way out, if she chose to take it. Even if she didn't, Jonas would get her out, eventually. But Elizabeth, and Julia, and god only knew how many others, would stay behind. And it would be Amelia's choice.

Amelia's heart felt leaden in her chest.

As she drew breath to speak, to submit to Cavanaugh's terms, she saw a flash of something on his face—a momentary flash of ambivalence, of hesitancy, even as he leaned forward in anticipation of her agreement.

Amelia caught the words before they escaped. She marshalled her swirling thoughts, studying Cavanaugh, wondering how far she could move him.

"A month," she said finally, pushing the words from between numb lips.

"What?" Cavanaugh looked at her.

"I'll give you a month," Amelia said. "I'll help you look for Julia, but whether I find her or not, you'll help me leave after that. And Elizabeth Miner, too."

"I don't know if I can—"

"You named your price," she said, trying to make her voice firm. "This is mine."

There was a long moment. Amelia held her breath and tried not to sag with relief when Cavanaugh's eyes met hers.

"Agreed."

23

Jonas struggled to keep a rein on his temper as they left Cavanaugh's office. He expected the doctor to look smug, pleased by his victory. Instead, Cavanaugh looked slightly sickened by what he'd done. Perversely, it made Jonas angrier.

Beside him, Amelia was silent, seemingly lost in thought.

When they arrived back at her cell, he opened the door, then glanced down the hallway. It was empty. He looked at her. "You didn't have to agree," he said. "I would have thought of something."

"You already thought of the best way," she said as she stepped inside. "This way, we'll get to use it. And in the meantime, maybe I can actually do what he wants and find Julia Weaver. And help Elizabeth. Neither of them deserves to be here, either. I can stand it for a month." She squeezed his arm, and he swung the door closed behind her.

"If we don't find Julia, what's to stop Cavanaugh from going back on his promise?"

Amelia caught her lip between her teeth, frowning slightly. "He gave us his word. I think he'll keep it."

Jonas scowled. "That's a thin branch to cling to."

"I could have misjudged him, but I don't think so." She shrugged. "It's what we have. We'll manage."

A nurse approached, and Jonas was forced to leave without further reply.

Worry gnawed at his gut throughout the rest of his shift and made him fidget on the ferry ride back to the city. He sat in a corner of the club's bustling kitchen that evening, trying to stay out of the way and eating a quick meal before his shift began. Waiters rushed by, carrying trays full of clean glassware for the bar. Their bay rum mingled with the smells wafting from the ovens.

Damn Cavanaugh. He was putting Amelia in danger. And no matter what she said, Jonas didn't trust him. He scraped the last bite of pie from his plate and shoved it aside. This half-baked plan he'd presented—and that Amelia had agreed to, for some reason he couldn't begin to fathom—would fail, and Cavanaugh would use it as an excuse not to help her escape.

"Doors in five," someone called.

Jonas arranged his face into a genial expression, nodded his thanks to the busboy who took his dishes, and made his way to his customary place beside the bar.

He struggled to maintain the mask as the evening wore on. He flirted and joked and made aimless, pleasant conversation, but all the while his mind churned through the problem like a plow through soil, turning up new options and rejecting each when the light revealed some previously unrecognized flaw. There had to be a way he could better their odds.

When his shift ended, Jonas dragged himself back to his apartment and flung himself onto his bed. Too agitated for sleep, he finally glanced at the clock and sighed, then got up to make coffee. He brooded at the table, rereading the telegram from Sidney that had arrived earlier.

There was a bit of good news, at least. Sidney was on his way home. Jonas had never expected to miss him as much as he had. Sidney's quiet, steady presence should have been dull. Instead, it felt safe. He also had a rigorous, logical mind and a surprisingly pragmatic approach to life for someone who lived—with one notable exception—within the constraints of polite society. What would Sidney counsel, if he were here?

Light was just beginning to show through the front window when Jonas thought of the answer.

24

Andrew tried to hide his discomfort as he glanced around the room. The heavy velvet drapes were tied back to let in the noon light, the tall windows cracked in an attempt to clear the previous night's cigar smoke. With its plush furniture and dark wood, it was the sort of room one might expect to find in any wealthy home, except . . . were those nymphs or cherubs in the painting on the far wall? Nymphs, he decided after a closer look. There were some things cherubs certainly would not do.

Two days had passed since the confrontation in Andrew's office. Jonas had stopped by his office the day before, his face stony, to ask Andrew to meet this morning in one of the club's private supper rooms. He said it was so they could be sure of speaking undisturbed, but Andrew suspected Jonas had chosen the venue to make him uncomfortable.

He supposed he deserved it. In truth, he would have been uncomfortable anywhere after what he'd done. Andrew still wasn't certain whether the bargain he'd struck was justified by the circumstances or an unforgivable act of extortion. Either way, he felt he'd had no choice. He needed their help, and he'd done what was necessary to secure it, despite the flush of shame that roiled him every time he recalled Amelia's face when she realized what he was saying. He crushed the feeling with a ruthless fist.

He had to find Julia. Amelia could help. Nothing else could be allowed to matter.

As Jonas rummaged through the bakery box Andrew had brought, Andrew cast another glance at the cavorting figures on the canvas. Whatever his misgivings, he was committed now.

Jonas muttered something around a mouthful of pastry.

"I beg your pardon?" Andrew asked.

Jonas swallowed and spoke again, his voice studiedly neutral. "I said you should sit down. You look like someone's maiden aunt, standing there frowning. We have more important things to talk about than vulgar paintings. Besides," he added in a more practical tone, "if you think that one is bad, you should see some of what's hanging on the third floor."

Andrew's eyes strayed to the ceiling before he could stop them.

Jonas went on. "We need to talk about the rest of the plan."

Andrew wrenched his attention back to the matter at hand. "The plan?"

"Yes. Amelia's given you a month to let you use her like some sort of human dowsing rod."

Andrew drew an irritated breath, but Jonas left him no opening, going on without pause. "You know how I feel about it. But as a purely practical matter, we need to come at this from more than one direction. We still don't know what Amelia's able to do, or what it will cost her. There are far too many patients for her to sort through on her own, and we have no idea how many staff may be involved. I don't want her on that island one minute longer than she has to be, and I don't want to give you any room to imply we haven't held up our end of the deal."

"What are you thinking?" Andrew asked, trying to ignore the insult.

"My first thought was to pay a visit to our wayward husbands."

Though Andrew wouldn't have imagined it was possible, Jonas's expression went even grimmer.

"Given adequate time, I'm sure I could persuade Daniel Miner or Bryce Weaver to cooperate," Jonas continued. "We could have this whole thing unraveled in short order."

"I can think of several problems with that idea," Andrew said.

"As can I," Jonas said. "Even aside from the fact that Daniel Miner isn't in New York any longer. I went to the courthouse before my shift yesterday. It seems he sold some property a few months back—a house. One he had recently inherited from his wife."

"Inherited?"

"Daniel Miner reported his wife missing—the day after 'Anne Fox' arrived at the asylum, in what might be called a fairly extraordinary coincidence. A few weeks later, a woman's body was found in a vacant lot, badly decomposed. He somehow still managed to identify it as that of his wife."

"I don't understand." Andrew tried to follow. "Are you saying the woman in the asylum isn't Elizabeth Miner?"

Jonas shook his head. "No, I'm sure she is. The body was probably a vagrant or a prostitute—god knows corpses are common enough in this city. Probably just a lucky coincidence, from Miner's perspective. It certainly sped up the court proceedings. He had Elizabeth declared dead, and all her property transferred to him. He sold every scrap and decamped within the week for parts unknown. Left some debts behind, too, so I doubt he'd be easy to find."

"So Miner is out of reach. And beating the daylights out of Bryce Weaver might be satisfying, but it carries its own risks, so we'll set that option aside for now. The other possibility is less exciting, but I think it will work." He looked at Andrew. "All asylum admissions are approved by a judge, correct?"

"Yes. Every patient file has a copy of the order inside."

"Then get me a list of names, and I'll go to the courthouse and match patients to their court records. They're public. If there's no record of a particular admission, then perhaps it means I've found someone who's been admitted through unofficial channels."

Andrew frowned. "You said yourself, there are too many patients."

Jonas nodded. "Yes. But it's the most obvious way to search without anyone on the island knowing it's happening. And I'd need to spend some time at the courthouse anyway. We can't say there's not a judge involved in this somewhere."

"If anyone discovers what you're doing—"

"Don't worry about me," Jonas said. "You and Amelia are the ones who have to be careful. I consider every single person on that island to be a danger to her, one way or another." He looked at Andrew, his eyes hard. "If anything happens to Amelia because she's helping you . . ."

Andrew forced himself not to drop his gaze from the larger man's. "I understand."

"And you're going to have to ask some questions yourself," Jonas went on, in an only slightly less weighty tone. "We need to know what really happened to Blounton."

A chill of unease prickled down Andrew's back at the mention of the young doctor.

Jonas continued, saying aloud what Andrew had spent quite a bit of time trying to ignore. "If he knew about Julia and Elizabeth, if that is his handwriting you found, then he was involved some way—he was either part of the plot, or else he discovered it. And if it was the latter, well then, how *convenient*, his dying when he did."

The words, with their matter-of-fact tone, dropped into the room like stones into a pond. They fell through the silence and were swallowed up, leaving the air around them rippled and unquiet.

It was on the tip of Andrew's tongue to apologize for having dragged the pair of them into this mess. Before he could say anything, though, Jonas shoved back his chair and stood.

"That's everything, then. Get me the list as soon as you can. We've a great deal of work to do, and waiting won't make it any easier."

25

Amelia began her search for Julia Weaver the next morning. Just after breakfast, an orderly arrived to bring her to ward seven.

"Doctor's orders," he said as he unlocked the door. Amelia rose without a word and followed him, her stomach churning. She managed a discreet wave to Elizabeth as they passed her cell, regretting the necessity of leaving her friend behind. But it couldn't be helped. And with any luck, Amelia would discover something that could be used to secure the other woman's release.

To Amelia's relief, ward seven was clean and quiet. Perhaps a third of its patients sat in little clumps scattered around the room. Most were sewing, chattering quietly as they worked. As luck would have it, there was a newly hired nurse working her first day in the ward, and Amelia was able to stay within earshot as a more senior nurse advised her about the patients.

"Most of this bunch're lambs," the older nurse said. "You'll not be this lucky most days."

"Aren't there any to be watchful of?"

"None worth worrying over. These are some they let work outside." The older nurse gestured to one woman, who sat slightly apart from her circle, her hands folded in her lap and a look of benign dignity on her face. "That one won't get her hands dirty, though." A snort. "She thinks she's the Princess Louise."

One of the self-styled princess's companions said something to her, and she bobbed her head in a regal nod before resuming her tranquil pose.

"Most of the other patients go along," the nurse went on. "They think it's funny, and it's a sight easier than arguing with her. She tries to banish them sometimes," she added with a chuckle. "That's a nuisance."

The nurses moved on as Amelia made a mental note to tell Cavanaugh there was at least one patient they could cross off their list. There might be any number of women wrongly imprisoned in the asylum, but it was doubtful the reigning British monarch's daughter was among them.

She spent the rest of the day moving among the patients, speaking to as many as she could. Amelia steeled herself to touch several and was far more relieved than disappointed when nothing happened.

Jonas brought her to Cavanaugh's office that afternoon, explaining his plan for aiding the search as they walked. When they arrived, Amelia was relieved to find the atmosphere between the two men was, if not warm, then at least businesslike.

She was relaying what she'd learned that day—including the story of the alleged royal—when they were interrupted by a knock at the door.

It was the young man from the front desk, holding a stack of files and looking harried.

"I've brought the list you requested," he said. "The full patient roster. And I thought I'd file these while I was here." He dropped his chin toward the folders. "Although I can come back later if you'd prefer." He darted a curious look at Jonas and Amelia, the former leaning against the wall, his arms folded, while the latter sat beside Cavanaugh's desk, trying to look sane and inconspicuous.

"Thank you, Winslow." Cavanaugh took the stack. "I'm happy to file these for you so you don't have to make another trip."

"That's much appreciated," Winslow said. "You will remember deaths are filed separately from discharges, I hope?"

"I remember. Deaths in the bottom cabinet, discharges in the top. Thank you for the reminder." Cavanaugh eased the door closed before the young man could go on. The sound of his footsteps faded, leaving the three of them glancing at one another in apprehensive silence. They were all obviously wondering the same thing. The young clerk had appeared to take note of their gathering. Did it mean something, or were they all simply on edge now that they were officially investigating in secret?

Jonas finally pushed away from the wall. "I shouldn't stay. And we'll need to be more careful. If the three of us are in here together too often, someone will notice. I'll come back for you in an hour," he said to Amelia.

Cavanaugh plucked the sheaf of papers from the top of the stack of files and held it out toward Jonas. "The patient list."

"Wait." Amelia intercepted it. She ran a finger along the columns typed on the thin onionskin, using a pencil to strike through the names of the women she'd spoken to that day. She sat back as she finished, the sheer enormity of the task ahead nearly overwhelming her—despite a full day's effort, the pages were barely marked. With a sigh, Amelia handed the altered list to Jonas, who folded it and tucked it into his waistband, his expression as somber as her mood.

"I'll get started tomorrow morning." He strode out, leaving Amelia alone with Cavanaugh for the first time since she'd agreed to help him search.

Avoiding her eyes, Cavanaugh carried the files into the storage room and began to stow them away. "How is ward seven?" he asked after a long moment. "I didn't want to put you into any of the more challenging wards without warning you first. I thought seven might be a good place to start."

"It's not bad." Amelia followed him into the narrow space. He was near enough for her to notice the clean, spicy scent of his aftershave—much pleasanter than the heavy floral cologne he'd worn the day he confronted her in her cell.

"Thank you," he said after another pause. "For agreeing to help."

"You didn't leave me much choice," she said, though there was no heat behind the words.

Cavanaugh flushed and finally raised his eyes to meet hers. "I know. I wanted to say that I—"

He broke off as another knock came from the outer door.

Amelia stayed in the storage room as he went to answer, wondering what he'd been about to say. That he was sorry? That he regretted what he'd done? That, whatever happened, he would help her escape with the time came?

She didn't get the chance to find out. Cavanaugh returned a moment later, his professional mien firmly back in place, to tell her he was needed in the infirmary—a patient with a fever.

"You can stay here while I'm gone, if you like. I shouldn't be long."

Relieved not to have to go back to the wards yet, Amelia agreed. After Cavanaugh left, she looked at the folders. She might as well file them while she waited.

She was halfway through the stack when something at the bottom of a drawer caught her eye. Amelia reached for it. A cuff link. Bloodred enamel, the initials *JB* picked out in swirls of silver. John Blounton. She set it atop the cabinet and rubbed her fingers against her skirt, struck by a phantom chill at the idea of the late doctor standing where she now did.

She was walking in a dead man's footsteps.

26

The following evening, Jonas arrived at the asylum in a black humor, bearing bad news. "There's no way I'm going to be able to check all the names against the files in a month," he told Amelia as they neared Cavanaugh's office. "If I spend every possible hour at the courthouse, I might be able to get through half the list."

"Half?" Amelia echoed. In her dismay, her voice emerged more loudly than she intended, echoing through the corridor. She winced and cast a furtive look around them, relieved to see no one near enough to have heard her outburst. Nonetheless, she lowered her voice and went on, "But you found the sale records for Elizabeth's property in an afternoon."

"I found them in an hour." Jonas rapped on Cavanaugh's door, then opened it without waiting for a reply.

The doctor looked up as they entered.

Jonas flung himself into a chair with a sigh and went on. "This is something completely different. It turns out there are only a handful of records clerks, and there's a constant flood of documents coming down from the courtrooms. They're all supposed to be sorted and filed at once. Wills and lawsuits—anything involving money or property, anything someone would be likely to need again—actually do get filed. That's why it was so easy to find the property records.

"But everything else? It sits in stacks, and every once in a while, when a stack gets too tall, someone comes along and shovels it into a pasteboard box. Then the box goes onto a shelf—wherever there's space.

"At least they write the date on the side of the box, so you can tell roughly *when* those records came from," Jonas added. He rubbed his forehead and sighed. "I'm going to have to go through every one of those boxes, sort out the asylum admissions, and mark each name off the list. In theory, the names left when I'm done will be those of our hidden women. Or it might just mean they're in a box I haven't found yet. Getting through half the list is a best-case scenario."

Cavanaugh was frowning. "We need more help."

"Indeed." Jonas gave him a withering look. "Why didn't I think of that? If you have an army of clerks you've neglected to mention, now would be an excellent time."

Cavanaugh didn't reply, though his expression was frosty.

Amelia suppressed a sigh. Jonas always grew snide when he was frustrated, but Cavanaugh didn't know him well enough not to take it personally.

"Well," she said, deliberately stepping into the silence, "it's true there's no one we can trust outside the asylum. But there is someone we can trust inside it."

Both men turned to look at her.

"I'm quite certain Elizabeth will be willing to help search the wards, if we ask," Amelia went on. "I didn't get a chance to tell her what was happening before I left the isolation ward, but she's as involved in this as any of us. More, even."

"Perhaps." Cavanaugh's voice was thoughtful. "But she doesn't have your gift."

Amelia made a derisive noise. "We don't know if *my* having my gift will be any help. Elizabeth is as capable of talking to patients as I am."

Jonas looked skeptical. "The more people we involve, the more likely it is that someone finds out what we're doing."

"I'm willing to trust her discretion," Amelia said. "Elizabeth isn't stupid. She's not going to walk through the halls shouting Julia's name. She'll understand the stakes."

Both men looked unconvinced, and Cavanaugh opened his mouth as if he were about to object.

Amelia spoke first, her voice stony. "Elizabeth has a right to make this choice for herself. Who are you—either of you—to take it away from her?"

27

An unexpected wave of relief swept through Amelia when Elizabeth appeared at the mouth of ward seven after dinner the following evening, an orderly guiding her by the elbow. Amelia had Jonas and Cavanaugh watching over her, but they didn't wake each morning in the wards. They didn't wait for their portion at mealtimes, hoping whatever they were given wouldn't be too spoiled to eat. They weren't dressed in clothes worn thin by institutional soap and countless other bodies. Didn't worry that a careless word spoken to an irritable nurse would earn them a slap—or worse, a needle in the arm and a day lost in drugged slumber. Sympathetic as they were, neither of the men could understand.

Elizabeth did.

Amelia hadn't realized how much that mattered until now. Perhaps help in searching wasn't the only reason she'd been so insistent. She swallowed hard against a sudden thickness in her throat and waved for the other woman to join her.

Elizabeth smiled as she approached. "I'm glad to see you."

"I'm glad to see you, too," Amelia said, making room for Elizabeth to sit. "You're well? Did Dr. Cavanaugh explain what we're doing? Did he show you the photo of Julia Weaver?"

"This morning," Elizabeth said. "Of course I'll help search. That poor woman. To take a mother away from her child like that. I can't imagine what her family must be going through."

"Did he also tell you about . . . ?" Amelia stopped, uncertain. Elizabeth had a right to know exactly what her husband had done, but if Cavanaugh hadn't already broken that bit of news, the middle of the ward might not be the place for it.

"About Daniel?" Elizabeth's expression went grim. "He did. I feel as though I ought to be shocked, but I can't quite manage it. I realized months ago he had no intention of coming back for me." She sighed. "Do you know, the bit that hurt the most was finding out that Daniel sold the house. *My* house. I was born there. Both my parents died there." Her face tightened, and she closed her eyes for a moment.

Amelia put a sympathetic hand over Elizabeth's.

The din of the ward vanished, and her vision went black. Shadows flickered behind her eyes. Amelia gasped, involuntarily tightening her grip on Elizabeth's hand. The shadows became sharper, color flooding them until they were as vivid as life. Two frozen moments, caught in a balance so fragile that it seemed a feather's touch would send them tumbling.

Elizabeth, appearing in a train window as it began to roll away from the platform. She waved to someone, smiling.

Elizabeth, pale and still on an asylum cot, her eyes open and staring at nothing. A hand brushed them closed.

The images seared themselves into Amelia's mind in an instant, and then they were gone. Amelia blinked, and Elizabeth was alive and looking at her anxiously.

"Amelia?"

"I'm all right," Amelia said in a thin, breathless voice. She leaned against the wall, her heart pounding, pressing the heels of her hands to her temples in a vain attempt to quiet the maelstrom growing in her mind.

Much as she wanted to deny it, she could not. She knew what she had just seen.

Two futures. Two possibilities.

And in one of them, Elizabeth would die.

28

Jonas arrived to escort Amelia to Cavanaugh's office only moments later.

"What's wrong?" he asked, frowning as they stepped into the hallway.

Still reeling, Amelia drew breath to tell him what she'd seen, the words jostling one another in their urgency.

Before she could speak, the ward nurse called out to Jonas. Suppressing a look of irritation, he returned to confer with her, leaving Amelia just outside the door. As he bent his head over a file, Amelia's eyes strayed past him—to Elizabeth, still seated on the bench and looking at Amelia with an expression of mild concern. Amelia forced the corners of her mouth up in what she hoped was a reassuring smile as she attempted to corral her thoughts.

They had to get her out of the asylum. Quickly. Perhaps Cavanaugh could do something. But if he couldn't—

Amelia's eyes snapped back to Jonas as he stepped away from the nurse. If Cavanaugh couldn't get Elizabeth released, they could use Jonas's plan to do it.

Relief flooded through her. Just as quickly as it arrived, however, it drained away, and a tiny ripple of apprehension spread through her chest. Jonas had a plan—to free Amelia. He would not be happy about using it for someone else. But surely he would see the necessity. He would agree once she explained. Amelia was almost certain of it.

Almost.

Amelia's heartbeat, which had begun to slow, accelerated again as she acknowledged the little sliver of doubt. It was possible—just possible—that Jonas would refuse. Not because he didn't care if Elizabeth died. But because he wouldn't want to waste—and yes, that was how he would see it—his plan on someone else, not if he could convince himself it was unnecessary.

Jonas rejoined her. "What were you going to say?"

Amelia swallowed, her mind scrambling. "I was about to tell you that I know how we can get Cavanaugh to help with the escape," she said. "Now. Not in a month."

"What?" Jonas's voice was sharp. "How?"

In all their years together, Amelia had never lied to him. Her next words could break something between them she would never be able to repair.

She hesitated for an endless second, then took a breath and forged ahead. "I can tell him that when I saw Elizabeth today," she said carefully, "I had a vision. That if she stays at the asylum, she'll die. That we have to get her out, and that we'll have to use your plan to do it. And then . . ."

"And then when he agrees, we use it to free you instead." Jonas considered for the space of a few steps, then nodded. "It could work. If you can make him believe it."

Amelia knew her resolve would break if she looked at him. She kept her eyes pointed forward and forced her voice to steadiness as she replied. "I can make him believe it."

∽

"You're certain?" Andrew asked, realizing even as he did so that it was a stupid question. Amelia hadn't been still for a moment since arriving in his office, and the air around her fairly radiated tension. He sighed and put a hand to his head. "All right. Then we have to get her out. But before we take such a risk, let me try another way."

"What other way?" Jonas asked, suspicion in his voice.

Andrew explained. Since his confrontation with Harcourt, he'd had taken to using Tyree as a go-between, mixing his proposed discharges in with the other doctor's. Once or twice, it had actually worked. Elizabeth's record at the asylum, unlike Amelia's, was unremarkable. She was a good candidate.

"But if Harcourt or Tyree was involved in bringing her here, they'll know she's been discovered," Jonas said.

"But they won't have any reason to think I've discovered the plot," Andrew said. "All they'll know is that I've run across a patient I judge is fit to be released. And at any rate," he added, "there's no way I'm agreeing to do it your way without at least trying mine."

Jonas looked as if he wanted to press the issue, but he subsided at a gesture from Amelia, who studied Andrew's face for a moment, then nodded.

Andrew took Elizabeth's file to Tyree that afternoon.

The other doctor returned less than an hour later, looking apologetic.

"He refused," Andrew said. "Why?"

Tyree, leaning against the doorjamb of Andrew's office, lifted one shoulder in a half shrug. "He did not say. I presented the case and suggested we discharge her. He skimmed the file and declined. It didn't look to me as though he gave it much consideration, but I did not feel I could argue. We can try again in a few months, if the patient remains stable. Perhaps he'll see reason then."

A few months. If Amelia was right—and Andrew had no reason to doubt her—Elizabeth Miner didn't have a few months.

Andrew realized Tyree was looking at him, and he arranged his face in what he hoped was an unconcerned expression. "Thank you for trying."

Tyree studied him for a moment, then spoke again, his voice careful. "I do not wish to pry, but I feel I must inquire. You seem burdened. Is it this case alone, or is something weighing on you?"

For a moment Andrew wavered. Over the past few weeks, his life had become more complicated than he'd ever imagined. Ned's visit and his search for Julia Weaver. Amelia and her uncanny abilities. Jonas and his deceptions. What a relief it would be to confide it all to someone.

But he couldn't.

Even if Tyree weren't involved in the scheme—and Andrew couldn't believe it of him—the other man hadn't seen the things Andrew had. He would think Andrew was losing his grip on reality. In fact, Andrew realized, that was why he was asking. Tyree had seen one colleague go down a melancholy road, and he was likely afraid Andrew was following in his footsteps.

Andrew forced a smile. "I'll be fine."

"If you're certain." Tyree seemed unconvinced. "But please remember, if you want to talk, I'm just down the hall."

⚭

Amelia examined the interior of the heel of bread, frowning. She dug out a dark speck and studied it more closely. It had legs. Her stomach lurched, and she set the bread on the bench.

"If you're not going to eat that," the woman next to her said, "I'll take it."

Amelia handed it over. She was too anxious to eat anyway. She'd spent the past two days fretting that her deception would be discovered and clinging to Elizabeth's side like a burr, worried to the point of illness that something would happen before they could get her away. Jonas had been unable to prevent a flash of relief from crossing his face when Cavanaugh told them his attempt to get Elizabeth released had failed. Thankfully, Cavanaugh hadn't seemed to notice. The plan was moving forward.

The only one who didn't know was Elizabeth herself. Amelia grimaced. For all her fine words about Elizabeth having the right to make her own decisions, she hadn't been able to bring herself to tell her friend what she'd seen of her future.

The meal finished, the women began to line up two by two for the Promenade. Amelia took her place beside Elizabeth.

"I need to talk to you," Amelia began.

At that moment, Cavanaugh entered the ward, an orderly behind him, and began making his way down the line. He looked nervous.

Amelia's chest tightened. Surely not already. She had thought it would take Jonas another day or so to get ready. Cavanaugh swept his eyes across the line of women. They stopped on Amelia, and he dipped his chin in a tiny nod as he neared.

It was time.

"I'm sorry about this," she whispered to Elizabeth, then drew back a hand and slapped her friend full in the face. "Slut!" Amelia shouted as Elizabeth lifted a hand to her cheek, staring at Amelia in shock. Amelia shoved her, raising her hand as if to deliver another blow. Elizabeth instinctively raised her own hands in defense.

"Here now," Cavanaugh cried, catching her by an arm and pushing her toward the orderly. "We'll have no fighting. Take them both up to isolation while I finish here," he told the man, who hooked his other hand around Amelia's arm and pulled her along. The nurses scowled at them as they left.

The orderly locked them into cells in the isolation wing and departed.

Late that afternoon, Jonas pushed a cart full of chamber pots through the ward, swapping dirty ones for clean. As he replaced Amelia's, he shifted his eyes in her direction, then looked significantly at the bowl in his hands.

The remainder of the afternoon passed at a crawl. Amelia fidgeted in her cell and waited, resolutely avoiding looking at the chamber pot. She forced herself to swallow her dinner. The water in her mug had a familiar bitter tinge.

Amelia couldn't suppress a wry grin—it had also been a laudanum night the last time she and Elizabeth had been brought to isolation after "fighting" in the wards. The awful pain in her face had made her glad enough for the drug that evening. There'd been a death on the ward that night, too—the old woman who called for her cat. Amelia's grin faded, and she shook off a chill. Tonight's outcome would be different.

Had Jonas known the ward was going to be drugged? It would make things easier.

Amelia tipped the mug onto the mattress. She watched as the tainted water soaked into the thin material and waited for the ward to quiet. When the last of the light faded, Amelia slid from the cot. She knelt beside the chamber pot and considered the supplies within.

She hadn't allowed herself to think about it before, but the reality of what she was about to do settled in her stomach like a rock. In freeing Elizabeth, Amelia was giving up her own best chance at escape.

Unless.

Amelia's breathing went ragged. It wasn't too late. She'd never gotten the chance to tell Elizabeth what they were planning. There was nothing stopping her from using the supplies for herself, just as she'd allowed Jonas to believe she would. Cavanaugh would be furious, but once it was done, he would probably play along.

And Jonas would never have to know she'd lied to him.

Amelia had the keys to her freedom at her fingertips. Longing surged through her. Perhaps there was time. Amelia could leave now, and if they could somehow get Elizabeth out soon after. . . .

Amelia shook her head, disgusted with herself. She knew what she had seen and what it meant. She could leave.

The price was Elizabeth's life.

Still, the yearning was there, sly and seductive. Shame stabbed through her, bitter as gall in her throat. Who was she, to even consider trading another woman's life—her friend's life—for her own freedom?

Amelia buried her face in her hands and crouched, shaking, in a pale beam of moonlight streaming through the window across the hall, childish anger at the unfairness welling in her chest until she thought it might choke her. In that moment, she hated them all. Elizabeth, for her need. Jonas and Cavanaugh, for forcing her to choose between betrayals. Herself, for her susceptibility to temptation.

And, most of all, her damned, damning, unwanted, unasked-for gift, for bringing her to such a pass and ripping away the fiction of her own righteousness.

Uncounted minutes passed. Finally, Amelia dragged in a shuddering breath and lifted the lid from the pot, her decision made.

29

Andrew loitered in the hallway, holding a stack of files, near enough to the entrance to the ward that anyone coming out would be sure to see him.

His heart thumped against his ribs. His sweating palms left damp, softened impressions in the margins of the case notes he was pretending to read. Every instinct screamed that this was a mistake. It was never going to work.

Andrew had always believed Jonas's plan to free Amelia would fail, even as he agreed to help them make the attempt. He had always accepted that they would get caught and he would lose his job for his role in the scheme. But at least under the terms of the initial bargain, they wouldn't have tried it until after they found Julia Weaver. Losing his job wouldn't have mattered—would have been worth it, even.

But now everything would be ruined. They'd be caught trying to free Elizabeth. Andrew and Jonas would be fired. Andrew would have to tell Ned that Julia was here but that there was no way to get to her. And Amelia would be trapped. It would all be for nothing.

Why, *why* had he agreed to do this?

Andrew struggled to maintain his composure as he waited for someone to raise the alarm. He flicked his eyes at the door, then dragged them away, trying to calm himself. What was taking so long? The breakfast service should have started by now. If no one—

A muffled shriek rang out from behind the metal door. Andrew started at the sound, and one of the folders began to slide out of the stack. He fumbled to catch it before it hit the floor and looked up as the heavy door to the ward all but burst open. A white-faced, pale-haired orderly hurtled out into the hallway. The man caught sight of Andrew.

"Doctor! Come quick!"

Andrew swallowed. "What's happened?"

"There's blood everywhere, Polly won't stop screaming. . . . She's got to be dead."

"Who?"

"One of the patients, she's—" The orderly stopped, looking ill. "I don't know, I only took the one look and then ran to get someone. You have to come!"

Andrew turned toward his office, feeling like the world's worst actor. "Let me put these down and get my medical bag."

The orderly's face was grim. "You won't need it."

He led Andrew to the mouth of the ward and all but shoved him through. He did not follow.

"I'm not going back in there." He turned and walked away.

Andrew watched him go and tried to prepare himself. What on earth could have provoked such a reaction? He'd asked for the particulars of the plan, but Jonas refused to tell him.

"It's better if you don't know," he'd said. "Just make sure you're near the ward tomorrow morning."

Andrew peered down the hallway. A nurse leaned against the wall across from an open cell door, her hands over her face, her shoulders shaking. She must have been the one who'd screamed. She'd stopped, but the entire hall still felt as if it were hanging over the edge of some terrible cliff, as though a tiny shove could tip the whole place into hysteria.

Andrew straightened his spine and started toward her. Some of the patients stood at their doors, watching, and he tried to project an air of calm and reassurance as he passed. He was certain he was failing miserably. Even from halfway down the hall, the mingled odors of blood and waste were apparent. Andrew swallowed hard.

As he approached the open door, his racing mind snagged on a sickening possibility. They could have betrayed him. Neither Amelia nor Jonas had wanted to make the bargain in the first place. He'd coerced them into the agreement. Would they really balk at breaking it?

Andrew nearly stumbled, cold with dread. Possibility hardened into certainty in his mind, growing stronger with every step. Hadn't there been a playacting quality to Amelia's plea? And Jonas had agreed far too easily. The promised month had barely begun, and they'd tricked Andrew into going along with an escape attempt. Amelia was lying in the cell ahead, playing the corpse, leaving it to him to decide in the moment whether to expose the ruse or go along with it and lose her aid in searching.

They had called his bluff.

A flash of movement caught his eye from the cell on his right. A dissonant jolt tore through him as Amelia stepped into view. Andrew's steps stuttered as his eyes met hers, and he felt his expression begin to slide toward confusion. Amelia motioned him onward with a sharp jerk of her head, her own face unreadable.

Andrew forced his numb legs to keep moving, trying to marshal his thoughts in the wake of their aborted riot. As he drew even with the still-sobbing nurse, he turned.

His mouth fell open in horror.

Elizabeth Miner lay half on her side, her head tipped back to show a ridged gash across one side of her throat. Blood spattered the cell and sheeted down her chest and onto the floor. One breast was bared by a rip in the neckline of her dress, and dried blood coated it, crusting over the nipple.

A glint on the floor beneath her outstretched hand—also blood-covered, he noted from what seemed a great distance, appeared to be a jagged shard of . . . something. Metal, perhaps? The copper smell of blood was so heavy it coated the back of his throat as he breathed.

"My god." His voice was strangled. He coughed and tried again. "I . . ."

Andrew stepped into the cell, avoiding the sticky puddle of blood only now drying to black around the edges. He felt like an automaton, his movements jerky and unnatural.

He crouched and reached for the wrist dangling off the cot, half expecting it to be cold and stiff. He bit back an exclamation as he found the pulse, strong and steady. The rush of relief was so profound the room tilted around him for an instant before he collected himself. He lifted the limp hand and laid it gently on the cot. His own hand, he noticed, had a pronounced tremor.

Andrew leaned forward, pretending to examine the gory "wound" in her throat. At this near a distance he could see it was false. But from a few paces away it would look—had looked—unnervingly real. Andrew closed his eyes for a moment and tried to orient himself. He knew what he was meant to do next; he just needed to make himself do it. He stood.

"That's done, then. I suppose there are reports to be made?" He directed this to the nurse. Her face was pale and tear-stained, though at least she'd stopped sobbing. He softened his tone. "Nurse? Polly—is that your name?"

She started and blushed. "Yes, sir."

"I don't know the procedure for an incident such as this."

"Oh! Yes, sir. Dr. Harcourt. He'll . . ." She stopped.

"Why don't you go and see if you can find him, then get yourself a cup of tea? Wash your face," Andrew said. "And if you happen to pass an orderly on your way, send him to me as well, if you please." Jonas was meant to be waiting to help with the removal, so Andrew wouldn't have to find a way to keep the other orderlies away from Elizabeth's "corpse."

She departed, and moments later, Jonas appeared in the doorway. His face went white as he took in the scene, and he shot a furious look toward Amelia's door.

Andrew had only an instant to wonder at his reaction before Harcourt came rushing in behind him.

"Dear god," the superintendent said with a gasp, coughing and holding the back of his hand to his nose.

Andrew stepped forward, partially blocking Harcourt's view. "Yes. It's a messy one." He tried to sound calm. Here was where it would all fall apart. "Without family, I believe. I'm told you'll handle the paperwork?" His voice was brusque.

"Yes." Harcourt backed away. "I'll let the ferryman know they'll need to leave room. Excuse me."

To Andrew's amazement, the superintendent strode away without another look. God in heaven, it was working. Andrew's shoulders sagged.

Jonas's face was hard, and his eyes glittered as he stepped into the cell. "Did you have anything to do with this?" He searched Andrew's face and must have read his confusion. "Damn her," he muttered. He bent and peered beneath the cot.

"What are you doing?" Andrew hissed.

"Making sure there's nothing in the cell that shouldn't be," Jonas said in a low voice, checking the door. "Amelia knew what to do, but if . . ." He leaned over Elizabeth, scanning the mattress. "We're all right. She's hidden it all in her dress. Just make certain nothing falls out when we move her. Let's get her wrapped before anyone else comes." He nodded at Andrew, and they tucked the ends of the blanket around Elizabeth's still form.

Andrew stepped out of the cell as a second orderly appeared, carrying a stretcher under his arm. Andrew stood in the hallway as the new man and Jonas lifted the shapeless gray bundle from the ruined mattress, Jonas with quiet efficiency and the other man with muttered complaints about the mess, the smell, and the indignity of being asked to do such work. Moments later, they carried Elizabeth's supposed corpse past him and out of the ward.

Andrew leaned against the wall, his legs going weak with relief. He'd done what he could. The rest was out of his hands.

∽

Jonas carried his end of the stretcher in grim silence, unable to remember the last time he'd been so furious. Amelia had thrown away his perfect plan on some near-stranger. And she'd deceived him to do it. If he'd been asked, he would have sworn there was no way she could have managed it. He would have said he knew her too well for it to ever work.

Showed what he knew.

Half a dozen little inconsistencies made sense now. Her hesitancy, her tension. He'd thought she was feeling guilty for double-crossing Cavanaugh. Jonas snorted, feeling like a fool.

How was he going to get her out now? They couldn't pull this same stunt again. No, Amelia was trapped here until he came up with something else, and he had no idea what the something else might be. He ground his teeth.

Fortunately, Russo didn't notice his mood. The pock-faced orderly kept up a steady stream of grumbling that required only the occasional grunt of acknowledgment from Jonas. The man had a remarkable aversion to doing his job.

They reached the stairs. Without warning, Russo stopped to adjust his grip. The stretcher tilted and lurched.

"Be careful," Jonas snapped. "That's all we need, for this mess to fall off and go rolling down to the bottom. I'm not cleaning it up if that happens."

The other man rolled his eyes, but he did move more carefully.

Elizabeth remained perfectly still throughout the exchange. Jonas felt a flicker of grudging admiration for the woman. For a complete amateur, she was playing her part well.

He blinked in the relative brightness as they stepped outside. The wagon was already waiting, the open coffin sitting on the bed. As they neared Jonas caught a whiff of pinewood, clean and welcome and almost enough to overwhelm the faint stench coming from the wrapped bundle on the stretcher.

He and Russo slid the stretcher onto the wagon alongside the coffin and climbed up.

Jonas took hold of the blanket wrapped around Elizabeth's shoulders and nodded for Russo to take her feet.

"Easier to lift the stretcher and tip it. Body'll roll right in," Russo said. "Don't have to touch it again that way."

By damn, the man was lazy. Elizabeth would roll right in, true enough, but she would land on her face in the hard wooden box. There was no way she was that good an actress. And tipping her might dislodge the things she'd concealed in her dress. They couldn't risk it.

"Have some respect," Jonas barked. "On three."

To his relief, Russo made a sour face but complied, then climbed down to remove the stretcher. Jonas lifted the lid halfway into place. He hesitated, then, making sure no one was looking, he reached inside and twitched the flap of blanket away from Elizabeth's still face. Relief flashed across her face before her expression smoothed again. He scraped the lid into place and jumped back down onto the gravel. Jonas thumped a fist against the wagon's side.

"Good to go," he called to the driver. The wagon lurched forward, and Jonas watched in bitter defeat as his perfect plan rolled toward the river, carrying the wrong woman to freedom.

30

Amelia fidgeted in her cell, dreading Jonas's return. His face as he carried the stretcher past her cell had been livid. Perhaps half an hour passed before he appeared at the door and extracted her from the cell.

"Jonas, I—" she said.

"Don't." His voice was black and unyielding as cast iron.

She went quiet, guilt forming a hard lump in her chest.

When they reached Cavanaugh's office, he rounded on her the instant the door was closed behind them.

"Why?"

"I'm sorry," she said. "I had to. Elizabeth is my friend, and she was going to die. I had to get her out, and I couldn't be completely sure—"

Amelia glanced at Cavanaugh. He'd risen at their entrance and now stood behind his desk, looking between them with narrowed eyes. Amelia grimaced. He might not understand exactly what had happened, but he knew there was something here he wasn't privy to.

Jonas followed her gaze, then closed his teeth on whatever he had been about to say and stepped back.

Cavanaugh continued to regard them for a long moment. Finally, he shook his head. "Whatever it is, it's between the two of you. I don't want to know. But could one of you please, for the love of god, explain to me how you did that? What was all that blood?"

Amelia looked at Jonas. "Didn't you tell him what you were going to do?"

"Not in any detail," he said, the words clipped. "I wanted his reactions to be as authentic as possible."

"But. Oh. That must have been terribly distressing." Amelia fought a sudden, highly inappropriate urge to laugh.

It must have shown on her face, since both men glared at her.

"It was, in fact," Cavanaugh said with exaggerated patience. "Please tell me how you did it."

Amelia glanced at Jonas, who still seemed to be barely holding himself in check. His jaw was tight as he turned away and waved a hand at her to go ahead.

"It was easy enough. We have a friend who does costumes for stage shows. He's very good. He got Jonas the supplies—the sharpened metal, wax to mold the wound, a little spirit gum to hold it in place. The blood was mostly real—it's hard to fake the smell. It was cow's blood, I assume." She looked at Jonas, who nodded once. "If you mix it with glycerin and carmine, it keeps its color and stays liquid longer. I picked the locks with a hairpin, explained everything to Elizabeth, then helped her get in position. All she had to do was hold still until someone found her."

"And now they have," Jonas said. His face was bleak. "We'll need a new plan for you."

"What was your second-best idea?" Amelia asked. "What were you planning on doing if we hadn't had help?"

He looked sour. "I was thinking of sneaking you out the next time one of those big charity groups came in. I thought if I could get you the right clothes, you could mix with them in the hallway and leave the island when they did."

Cavanaugh's face was horrified. "But that would never work."

"That's why I didn't propose it," Jonas said in an acid tone.

"Well, we've got some time," Amelia said.

Jonas pinned her with a look. "Twenty-two days."

"But if you haven't come up with another plan—" Cavanaugh began.

"Oh, I'll have one by then," Jonas said, a warning in his voice. "Twenty-two days from now, we're leaving. And if your help is still worth anything, I expect you to give it without complaint."

Jonas went on when they looked at him. "It's not going to do your reputation here any good, having a patient turn suicide two days after you recommended she be released."

It was Cavanaugh's turn to look sour. "No. I suppose it couldn't be helped. Although if I'd known exactly what you were planning, I might have—" He cut himself off and looked away.

"What's done is done," Amelia said. She took a breath, eager to move on, yet dreading the topic she was about to introduce. "For now, I think you should transfer me to ward five."

"The incurables? Are you sure?" Cavanaugh asked.

Jonas didn't speak, though he looked no more enthused than the doctor.

"I'm as sure as I can be that Julia isn't in ward seven," Amelia said with a grimace. "I'm going to have to search five eventually, and I'd just as soon get it out of the way."

31

Jonas woke the following morning to the familiar sound of water running in the washroom. It took him a few drowsy, contented seconds to remember it wasn't Amelia in the other room.

A jumbled wave of emotions swept over him. He lay staring at the ceiling as he tried to sort through them. Anger, obviously. Frustration and disappointment. A not-insignificant degree of embarrassment—he was supposed to be the brilliant one, but Amelia had managed to trick him with ease. A measure of affront that she had believed it necessary.

And down, deep down at his core, a whisper of chagrin that it might have been justified.

Jonas rubbed a hand over his face, appalled by the realization. Angry as he was with her, Amelia might have saved him from a choice that would have made a monster of him.

The sound of the water stopped. In the silence, Jonas blew out a breath. There would be time enough to consider that thought later.

He rose and dressed, emerging from his bedroom to find Elizabeth Miner sitting at the table, flipping the pages of a magazine.

"Did I wake you?"

Jonas shrugged. He'd worked two full shifts, switching with one of the other orderlies so he could be on duty to both deliver the supplies for their masquerade and help with the removal of Elizabeth's "corpse" once it was complete. He'd been looking forward to sleeping in this morning, with Amelia in her own room doing the same.

"It's fine. It means we should be able to get you on an early train, if you're ready."

They'd talked it through the night before. Elizabeth had been remarkably self-possessed for someone who'd been told only hours before that she would die if she didn't immediately agree to a chancy, frightening escape attempt requiring her to unearth enough innate acting ability to fool trained medical personnel into believing her dead. Not to mention taking a ferry ride trapped in a coffin with the vague assurance that someone she'd never met would be there to rescue her on the other end.

The woman had moxie. Jonas would give her that much.

By the time he'd gotten back to the apartment, Elizabeth had already worked out the next step on her own. Everyone she'd ever known believed her dead. Turning up alive in the city would create an uproar—one that might well reach the ears of whoever was running this plot. They had to get her away as soon as possible. Elizabeth had a childhood friend in Chicago, someone her husband hadn't known, so it was probable he hadn't bothered to convey the news of her supposed death. Elizabeth claimed the friend would help her. Jonas detected a hint of uncertainty in her voice, but he didn't care enough to pry.

"I'm ready." She stood and smoothed the skirt of the ill-fitting brown dress she wore.

Tommy had gotten it for her. Jonas had asked him to help, and he'd performed admirably. According to Elizabeth, he barely blinked when he wrenched the lid from the coffin to find a blood-spattered stranger peering up at him. He brought her back to the apartment so she could tidy herself up, and—since she left the asylum with quite literally nothing but the ragged, filthy clothes on her back—went back out to find her something clean to wear.

It had probably been bought with his own money. Jonas grimaced. He'd have to pay the man back. He lifted the cashbox from its hidden shelf behind the icebox and examined its contents. They'd also need money for Elizabeth's train ticket. And whatever supplies Jonas required for Amelia's eventual escape. *And* the rent was due—a bit past due now, in fact. He'd been ducking Sabine for the past several days.

Jonas pulled the thin stack of bills from the box and fanned through it. His orderly's pay, extra shifts notwithstanding, didn't come near to filling the void in their finances left by Amelia's absence and his own recent patchwork schedule.

A few silver coins slid across the bottom of the box. He scraped those up as well—they'd need fares for the streetcar, and perhaps something to eat along the way. He placed the empty box back on the shelf with a resigned sigh. "Let's go."

Dawn was a pale gray smear in the east as they left the apartment. They were silent as they walked down the sidewalk beneath flickering streetlights. The streets were quiet, though not deserted.

A loutish-looking fellow eyed them from the mouth of an alley. Jonas gave the man a quick sideways glare, and he shrank back into the darkness, convinced to try his luck elsewhere. Jonas and Elizabeth paused at a corner as a milk wagon rattled by, crates of empty glass bottles tinkling as the wheels rolled over the cobblestones.

"Amelia said you were the one who planned the escape," Elizabeth said as they crossed the street near the park.

Jonas grunted his assent, wondering if the thing Amelia had described seeing on the footpath was still there. He suppressed a shudder. Amelia's description of the shade, with its reaching hand and eager face, had been enough to make him vow never to go anywhere near that spot.

"How did you come up with such an idea?"

The words were slightly breathless. Jonas looked down. Elizabeth trotted along beside him, trying to keep up with his long strides. He slowed, and she flashed him an appreciative smile as she asked, "How did you know what to do?"

Jonas felt himself thawing in the face of her determined good nature. None of this was Elizabeth's fault. It was unfair to blame her. "We have a friend who does costumes for a theater troupe," he said. "We ran with the same gang for a while several years ago. He's a genius with things like that—he can paint an entirely new face on you if you need one. I asked him what to do, and he got me the supplies."

They climbed aboard the northbound streetcar at Broadway. This early in the morning, it was all but empty. Fifteen minutes later, they stepped off less than a block from Grand Central Depot.

In contrast to the streetcar, the depot was bustling. Jonas led Elizabeth across the shining marble floor and over to the ticket counter.

A clerk looked up at their approach. "How may I help you?"

"The lady is headed to Chicago," Jonas said.

"Alone?" He peered at Elizabeth. "You'll want at least second-class," the man said, "for a lady traveling unaccompanied. Wouldn't do to put her in third with all the trash." He eyed Jonas as if he expected him to argue.

"How much?" Jonas asked.

"That will be twenty-three dollars."

Gritting his teeth, Jonas peeled off a large portion of the stack of bills and handed it to the man, who handed over a wide yellow ticket in return.

"Train leaves in half an hour," he said. "Second-class waiting room is that way." He pointed.

In the waiting room, Jonas bought coffee and a pair of sweet rolls. By the time they finished, the train was boarding.

Elizabeth gave him an unsteady smile as he helped her up the steps. "I suppose this is it."

Jonas wanted to say something encouraging. This would be well beyond anything she'd been prepared for. He plucked the remainder of the bills from the wallet and handed them to her. "Here. You'll need to eat on the train, and something to see you to your friend's house."

Elizabeth blinked, then took the money with a nod. "There aren't words for what you've done," she said, a catch in her voice. She folded the bills carefully into a pocket. "You and Amelia both. Thank you."

The whistle blew again, and the train began to move. Elizabeth allowed the conductor to take her arm, and a moment later she appeared in one of the windows, waving.

Jonas raised one hand in farewell and jingled the coins left in his pocket with the other. He watched as the train pulled away, not precisely sorry to have helped her but unable to avoid counting the cost.

32

After the concentrated terror surrounding Elizabeth's escape, Andrew was almost relieved to wake the following morning to the mere constant, buzzing anxiety of the previous weeks. Julia Weaver remained hidden from them, her captor remained unidentified, and the date of Amelia's own departure remained nonnegotiable.

It felt positively manageable.

Andrew answered a knock at his office door that evening to find Jonas standing in the hallway.

"What's that?" Andrew asked, nodding at the bundle Jonas held under one arm.

"Boy's clothes in Amelia's size, and some theatrical makeup," Jonas said, thrusting it at him.

Andrew must have looked skeptical, because Jonas's tone hardened. "She's done it before. I don't know that we'll use them, but better to have them than not. I'm trying to create some options. Just stow them for me."

Andrew accepted the clothes, despite his doubts about their utility. Even as slight and fine-boned as she was, he had a hard time imagining anyone ever mistaking Amelia for a boy. Beneath the ragged mop of hair, her face was distinctly feminine. Her eyes, especially. And her mouth was— He cut himself off, suddenly uncomfortable.

Andrew hid the bundle in the storage room and left his office, headed for the infirmary, where he had little enough time to think about things best left unconsidered. Six patients—all from the same ward as the woman earlier in the week—had come down with some sort of ague. Three were quite ill.

Another eight sickened the following day, and Andrew spent a sleepless night tending to them.

When he stumbled back to his office the next morning, he found a thick envelope from the coroner's office waiting on his desk—the copy of Blounton's autopsy results he had requested. He paged through them wearily, but they told him nothing he hadn't already known.

The body had been spotted by a passing boat some two hundred yards north of the asylum dock, which meant it had gone into the water near the north end of the island. *Depressed fractures in the area of the suture of the occipital and parietal bones*, Andrew read, rubbing the area at the back of his own head. *Water in the lungs. Cause of death: drowning.*

Perhaps Blounton slipped and hit his head on the seawall as he went in. Or perhaps he'd been attacked. Based on the report, there was no way to know. Andrew sighed and tossed the report in a drawer, just as Jonas knocked at his door again. Amelia was at his side, her face pale and strained.

Alarmed, Andrew swung the door wide and ushered them inside.

"She can't stay in five," Jonas muttered to Andrew he passed.

Amelia paced the office like a tiger in a too-small cage as she relayed the things she'd seen when she touched the women in the incurables ward. A harrowing childbirth. A fire in a crowded tenement. Several near strangulations. Beatings at the hands of mothers, fathers, strangers, lovers. Her voice was strained, her face pale as she ticked off their names.

Andrew shot Jonas a horrified look over her head and hurriedly wrote out a transfer to ward four. Jonas crouched beside her chair, speaking in a low, gentle voice. Whatever friction there had been between them seemed to have evaporated.

"They've all been like that?" Andrew asked.

Amelia nodded, her eyes tired.

"But you don't get a vision every time you touch someone?"

"No. Thank god." She shuddered.

"And these are definitely memories, not futures?"

Amelia nodded again, frowning slightly. "They feel different. More like with Mara. I don't know how to explain it, but I'm sure these are things that have already happened."

Jonas looked thoughtful. "I think I understand what's happening. Your power changed when you nearly died, and now death is what you're seeing in others. All these memories you're seeing, they're times when someone almost died. If someone hasn't had such an experience, you don't see anything when you touch them. And those flashes of the future you're getting, they're happening when you touch people who are at risk of death—Mrs. Franklin, Elizabeth. When they're in the valley of the shadow, if you will."

They looked at him.

Jonas waved a hand. "Yes, I know. That was overly dramatic. But accurate, nonetheless. That means—"

"It means there's no point to my going around trying to read people," Amelia said. She laughed, and the hollow despair in it made Andrew's heart twist. "I've been making myself see all those horrible things for no good reason."

There was an appalled silence in the room. Guilt stabbed at Andrew's chest. He'd kept her here. He was responsible for what she was enduring. And it seemed it was for nothing.

"We're going to have to try another way," Jonas said finally. He looked at Andrew. "That scrap of paper you found in the desk. Do you have it?"

Andrew blinked at the change in subject. "It's in my rooms at the boardinghouse." Hidden in the middle of a book on diseases of the kidney, in fact, and buried in a box of similar tomes. He'd initially kept it in his shaving case but found himself imagining outlandish scenarios in which it was discovered—by whom was unclear, even in his own mind. He'd moved it in the middle of the night during a fit of paranoia. In the light of day, the precaution seemed foolish.

But he hadn't moved it back.

"Could you bring it with you in the morning?"

"Why?"

Jonas gestured to Amelia. "I want both of us to have another look at the handwriting before we start searching the doctors' apartments."

Andrew gaped at him. "You cannot be serious."

"It's the obvious next step," Amelia said. "We need proof. Letters, records of payments—anything that proves someone here knows about Julia or Elizabeth."

This was madness. "You'll be caught," Andrew protested. "Surely there's another way."

Jonas snorted. "I suppose one of us could stand in the Octagon and shout accusations. Anyone who looks confused probably isn't involved."

"We could go to the police," Andrew said. "Or the press."

"With what?" Amelia's voice had steadied. "We think there may be more women hidden, but we're certain of only two. We haven't found Julia, and as far as anyone knows, Elizabeth is dead. We have a suicide, a psychic, and a scrap of paper. That's not proof of anything. There's no reason for anyone to believe us. This is the only way. And we won't get caught."

Andrew had the distinct impression she was now avoiding his eyes.

"We're not precisely amateurs," Amelia concluded.

33

Jonas had forgiven her, and ward four was almost pleasant after her brief sojourn in ward five. Nevertheless, Amelia rose the following morning with a churning stomach and a sullen headache prodding behind her eyes. Their years on the street had left them with a great many unorthodox skills, but it had been a long time since she and Jonas tested their housebreaking prowess.

The stakes were unutterably high. Disguise or no, Jonas would never be able to sneak her away from the asylum later if they got caught breaking into the doctors' apartments. He'd be fired—or jailed. And they'd toss Amelia in isolation and put a nurse in front of the door.

She pushed her breakfast aside—one of the other women snatched up the bowl before it stopped moving—and waited for someone to bring her to Cavanaugh's office.

Midmorning, however, there was a flurry of activity. The patients were lined up, and nurses began dividing them into groups. Amelia was waiting her turn when Jonas appeared near the door. He conferred with a nurse, then beckoned to her. Amelia followed him into the hallway and stepped into chaos.

"It's the fever," he explained as they walked. "Another dozen patients came down with it overnight. Too many for the infirmary. They're turning ward four into a quarantine unit, trying to keep it from spreading further."

As they maneuvered through the hall, harried nurses rushed past. Carts piled with linens sat outside the wards while strings of orderlies carried folded cots through the hallways, looking like ants hauling grains of rice.

If the second floor was pandemonium, the third was eerily quiet, which allowed the sound of a muttered curse to filter toward them from the hallway ahead. Amelia and Jonas glanced at each other, their steps slowing as they rounded a corner. Klafft's assistant, Connolly, stood outside the door to the doctor's apartment, struggling to maintain his hold on a large, unwieldy carton as he fumbled with the key. His burden began to tilt to one side, a series of muffled clinks sounding from within. Connolly dropped the key with another oath and grabbed at the box, raising one knee beneath it. This done, he looked down at the fallen key.

"Hang on," Jonas called as the secretary began to reach for it.

Connolly looked up as they reached him.

"Let me." Jonas bent to retrieve the key, then unlocked the door and swung it open. Amelia had time for a glimpse of gleaming wood and velvet curtains before Connolly brushed past with a mumbled thanks and kicked the door closed behind him.

"I wonder . . ." she said.

Jonas finished the thought in a low voice as they began walking again. "Where Klafft gets his money? I saw it, too. That furniture looked expensive. He wears good-quality suits, and he's paying for a private secretary."

They'd almost reached Cavanaugh's office when Klafft's voice came from behind them. Amelia turned. He and Connolly were stepping out of the apartment and heading for the stairs.

Amelia exchanged a wordless nod with Jonas as the two men disappeared from view. They couldn't ignore the chance to have a look at the good doctor's unaccountably luxurious quarters.

Amelia tried to slow her pounding heart. An air of unreality settled over her as they turned back toward Klafft's apartment, Jonas scanning the hallway in both directions. They were really going to do this. She slid a hairpin from her pocket as they neared the door, her eyes already fastened on the lock.

They were no more than three paces away when two things happened. Perhaps twenty feet ahead, Lawrence's apartment door swung open. And from around the corner just beyond him, a pair of voices approached. One, meek, was unintelligible. The other, strident, was that of Mrs. Brennan.

Lawrence stepped into the corridor and swung the door shut behind him.

He did not lock it.

Amelia plucked at Jonas's sleeve and glided past Klafft's door.

Lawrence passed without looking at them.

The hectoring voice ahead grew louder.

Amelia's hand reached out, as if of its own volition, to turn the knob on Lawrence's door. Then they were inside the apartment, and the door clicked shut at what must have been the same instant Mrs. Brennan rounded the corner.

Amelia pressed her forehead against the wooden panel, hardly daring to breathe, Jonas standing rigid behind her. One heartbeat. Two. Amelia could have sworn she felt when the woman passed by the door.

She and Jonas shared a relieved smile. Amelia turned, then blinked in surprise.

Notebooks. Everywhere, stacks of notebooks. They covered every surface and lined the walls in ragged towers—several of them almost as tall as she. Some were pocket-size booklets of the sort used to hold lists and reminders. Others were sturdy hard-covered journals, their ribbon page markers frayed and faded. One long shelf on the opposite wall was crammed with wide volumes, all dark blue bindings and blank spines. The rooms were full of dust and the musty scent of damp and old paper.

Jonas ducked into the bedroom.

"More of the same," he reported as he emerged.

Amelia lifted the topmost book from one of the stacks. The date inside its cover indicated Lawrence had begun using it some six years before. She fanned through the pages. A half-drafted essay on the efficacy of a solution of cocaine as a cure for melancholy. A list of temperature readings in ward three during the month of July 1888. Patients' names, followed by indecipherable strings of abbreviations and symbols—some sort of personal shorthand. Amelia could make nothing of it.

Jonas held up another book from a stack on the other side of the room. "A description of every meal served at the asylum over the course of a week." He snapped the book shut with a derisive sound. "What in hell does Lawrence think he's accomplishing by recording such rubbish?"

Amelia looked around again and conceded defeat. "This is pointless. Finding anything useful in this mess would be like hunting a needle in a field of haystacks. Blindfolded."

"It isn't as though he's much of a suspect, in any case," Jonas agreed. "Let's move on to Klafft."

Amelia replaced the book on top of the stack and returned to the door. She pressed her ear to the wood and heard nothing, then eased it open an inch and peered out. The hallway was clear. In a moment they had slipped back out of the apartment and closed the door.

Before they could turn, Klafft appeared at the other end of the hallway, walked past them without a glance, unlocked his apartment, and entered, closing the door behind him.

Amelia exchanged a somber glance with Jonas. If they'd gone for Klafft's apartment as they planned, they would have been caught. Their instincts were rusty. It was only the merest coincidence that had saved them. They'd be fools to count on it happening again.

34

Amelia loitered behind Cavanaugh as he and Dr. Lawrence examined Mrs. Lattimore, a querulous-looking woman of about forty. While Cavanaugh took the woman's pulse, Lawrence nodded and scribbled, never looking up from his notebook. He listened with every appearance of interest to the torrent of gibberish coming from her.

What could the elderly doctor possibly be writing? The notebooks in his apartment were full of bizarre details, but they were at least coherent. Mrs. Lattimore mixed words with her nonsense now and again, but nothing was worth recording. Amelia leaned forward, hoping for a glimpse of the pages, then hastily moved back as the woman threw her a dark look. No point in antagonizing her. The patients assigned to ward six tended to be docile, but there were exceptions.

Cavanaugh muttered something soothing, and Mrs. Lattimore subsided. Amelia's eyes settled on his hand as he held the woman's wrist in a gentle grip. His square nails were tidy, as usual, and the shirt cuff was sharp and clean. How did he always manage that, working in this place? She glanced up and caught him studying her face. He looked chagrined as their eyes met, and he shifted his gaze back down to the pocket watch he held. Amelia looked away, then back again. He looked tired. She'd barely seen him since the fever had taken hold. Jonas said he was sleeping in his office, spending almost all his waking hours tending to sick patients. No one had died—yet—but all the staff were on edge.

Warm sunlight filtered through the large windows on the opposite wall, and Amelia stifled a yawn. Cavanaugh wasn't the only one who was tired. Jonas, in particular, was ragged and moody with fatigue. Somehow he was managing to work shifts at both the asylum and the club, all while continuing his search of the courthouse records. Twice, she knew, Cavanaugh had waylaid him in the hallways on the pretense of some task or other and sent him to sleep through part of his shift on the cot in the storage room.

Jonas had yet to come up with a workable replacement plan for Amelia's escape that didn't involve Cavanaugh's aid. If he had, she knew he would have told Cavanaugh he could go to hell with his bargain and taken her away already.

"Faking a death works because it doesn't leave any loose ends," Jonas said. "I might be able to sneak you off the island on one of the supply boats. Or maybe I could hire someone to pick you up along the shore. But they'd know a patient was missing. Harcourt couldn't cover it up—Klafft would bray it from the rooftops if he tried. So there would be a search."

"Someone would talk eventually," Amelia said.

Jonas nodded. "They don't have your real name, but Lina's name would lead them to the club. Legally, whoever you are, they have custody of you. They could bring you back. Maybe we could fight it, but it's not certain. To be absolutely sure, we'd have to change our names and leave the city.

"If you stay, and *if* Cavanaugh follows through on his end, we'll have a better chance. Forging a discharge or even faking a different sort of death may be a better bet. This fever might give us an opening. If he won't help—"

"He will," Amelia said.

"If he won't," Jonas repeated, "we'll have to take our chances without him."

"For the time being, we give him the time we promised," Amelia said. "We keep looking for Julia Weaver."

They were making progress on that front, but it was grindingly slow. Their combined efforts had resulted in some two hundred names struck from the master list of asylum patients. Amelia recalled her sarcastic comment about shouting Julia's name in the wards and fought the urge to do just that. But they had to be careful. Revealing that they knew she was here would alert whoever was responsible. They'd lose any chance of finding her.

The plan to search the doctors' quarters was going no more quickly. Twice, Amelia had a chance to search Tyree's rooms, but something about the lock on his door—some twist or bend—thwarted her hairpin. Jonas reported the same problem. Harcourt did much of his work from his quarters, and thus spent far more time there than any of the other doctors.

And the day after their reckless, failed attempt at Klafft's apartment, the doctor himself fell ill, coughing and shivering in the wards until Harcourt ordered him to his bed. Connolly attended him, hurrying in and out of the apartment fetching whatever Klafft required. They'd get no further opportunity until he was well.

And by then, it was possible they would have—

Amelia snapped to attention as something tickled at the back of her chest. She went still, trying to isolate the source of the sensation. Movement at the corner of her eye. Near the window. Carefully, she turned her head.

There.

Formless and unmistakably *other*, a grayish wisp drifted among the women. It looked like smoke, if smoke could gather itself and choose its direction. It wound around their legs, sinuous as a cat.

The babble of the ward faded as Amelia focused on the thing. It froze as if it felt her attention. Something thrummed inside her when it found her. It roiled toward her, and Amelia's pulse beat faster. The thing tugged at her breastbone, the sensation a milder version of what had happened when she encountered the spirit in the park. Alarm surged through her. If it tried to possess her—

But it was already too late. The thing was on her before she could move, and all her effort turned toward resisting its attempt on her mind.

She must have made a noise, because Cavanaugh turned toward her, the beginnings of concern creasing his face. She ignored him, wholly absorbed by the spirit's touch. It pushed, and she ground her teeth, resisting. It pushed again, harder, and the borders of Amelia's mind trembled.

But they held.

This being—whoever it had been—was far weaker than the shade in the park, with its irresistible need. This was the dying echo of a scream, not the scream itself. A shallow, formless thing. It wanted, it sought, but it had no will, no force.

It could not take her over, not unless she let it. Amelia's fear began to bleed away. She could withstand this. Perhaps she could even control it. She gathered herself, formed the word in her mind, and thought it at the thing: *No.*

It flinched.

Amelia pushed.

It resisted.

Amelia *shoved*, an expulsive little noise escaping her as she did so.

There was a tearing sensation in her mind, and the spirit flew away from her as though hurled by a catapult. It went straight through the window, and to her shock, the pane shattered with its passage, spraying bits of glass onto the lawn below. Several of the women nearby yelped in surprise.

Cavanaugh spun to stare at the window, looking baffled. He turned to her, a question on his face. His eyes went wide as she gave him a shaky nod in response.

Lawrence never looked up from his notes.

35

Twelve days remained in the promised month. Amelia brooded over the encounter with the spirit as she sat beside a window. Yes, she had pushed it away. But she didn't know precisely how she'd done it and wasn't certain she could do it again. It had been weak. What would happen if she encountered something stronger? Something more like Cavanaugh's sister, or the girl in the park? The thought chilled her. Her new abilities weren't fading.

She had to figure out how to control them.

Below, a group of women appeared, carrying tools and baskets. Ward seven, heading out for work in the gardens. Beyond them lay the open ground where other groups went on Promenade.

Amelia straightened, remembering the spirit she'd sensed there weeks before. She hadn't *seen* it, but it was there. She focused on the memory, trying to gauge its strength from the way it had felt. Stronger than the one in the ward, she decided, but not much stronger. It was perfect.

"I need you to move me to ward seven," Amelia murmured to Andrew that evening as he made his way down the row of patients. "There's something I need to do."

He looked as if he were about to ask for an explanation, but the next patient pushed her way forward, complaining about the nurses stealing her jewelry while she slept. While Cavanaugh calmed the woman, Amelia allowed herself to fade back into the throng. He would object to her plan if he knew what she intended to do, and she preferred to ask for forgiveness rather than for permission.

By late the following afternoon, Amelia was digging in the kitchen garden with a group of about twenty other women, under the supervision of a pair of younger nurses. It was warm for May, and the sun was strong enough overhead to dampen her brow as she worked.

Amelia looked up as several orderlies strolled past the group, headed toward the tree where they smoked during their breaks. Jonas was with them. Perfect. He pretended to scan the group, but his attention was on Amelia. She cut her eyes at the nurses. He broke off and turned toward them with a magnetic smile. Both women bloomed like flowers. Amelia smothered a smirk. It never failed.

She waited until one of the nurses glanced back at her charges, then wobbled where she stood and put a hand to her forehead, as if trying to ward off a spell of dizziness. She glanced through her lashes. The nurse was watching, a slight frown on her face. Good. Amelia calculated. A full faint would likely get her taken back inside. That would do her no good. Amelia took a tottering step, bumping into the woman beside her and going to one knee.

"You there." The nurse moved toward her. Jonas broke off his conversation with the other nurse and followed, a quizzical look on his face.

Amelia made as if to stand. Instead, with a well-timed lurch, she toppled toward Jonas, who caught her.

The nurse sighed, annoyed. "I suppose you'd better take her back inside," she said to Jonas.

"Oh. No, please." Amelia let real anxiety bleed into her tone. "It's so much nicer outside. I'm sure it's just the sun. I'm not used to it. If I could sit in the shade for a bit. Perhaps under those trees." Amelia gestured toward the clump of trees some thirty feet away beside the little rise. "I'm sure I'll be fine."

"I can walk her over," Jonas offered. "I'd rather not go back inside, if I can help it. It's my break, and if I go in, I won't get a chance to smoke. I'll be right back," he promised in a voice like a caress, already heading away with Amelia.

The nurse conceded with a flustered smile. "Stay where we can see you, mind," she said to Amelia, not looking at her.

"Of course," Amelia said meekly.

She leaned against Jonas as they made their way toward the trees.

"What are you doing?" he asked in a low voice.

"I need to try something. I can't explain right now. Just keep their attention off me for a bit. If you think you can handle them both." She added the last bit with a wry grin.

"Of course I can," he said in faux affront. "Just be careful, whatever it is you're up to."

Amelia waited until Jonas was back with the group, positioning himself so both nurses—and most of the patients, Amelia noted—were facing him, their backs turned to where Amelia sat.

She waited another moment, then eased herself up and backed into the trees. When they were between her and the others, she turned and scrambled over the crest of the hill, watching behind her all the way, waiting for someone to shout at her to stop. No one did.

On the other side, and certain she was out of sight, Amelia turned, then stopped with a gasp.

Perhaps forty yards away, a stone tower stood on a narrow promontory jutting into the river, some fifty feet tall and stark against the water and sky behind it. Amelia took several hesitant steps forward, chilled by how much the rough gray structure resembled the drawing of the Tower on her Tarot card—and even more, if she were being honest, the one from the nightmare she'd had after her injury. There was a wooden door at the bottom and an enclosed glass cupola at the top. A lighthouse, she realized as she drew nearer, meant to keep boats on the river at night from running aground on the island.

Amelia tore her eyes away from it and surveyed the surrounding area. The grassy swathe was only about thirty feet wide. It gave way to a flat, hewn-stone seawall running level with the ground along the perimeter of the narrow finger of land, dropping on the river side straight down into the water. Feeling gloriously free for the first time in weeks, she walked along the edge and studied the drop, willing a boat to appear below. She would have leapt into it and been away, never mind her pledge to stay.

No boat appeared, and Amelia reluctantly turned her attention to her task, following the wall as it curved around the lighthouse, waiting for the spirit she'd felt during the Promenade to make itself known. Nothing happened, and after a second circuit of the wall, Amelia stood still, frowning.

She didn't have much time; Jonas was good, but all it would take was for one of the nurses to glance at the trees where Amelia was supposed to be resting and see her gone. They'd find her in minutes, and she doubted she'd get outside again.

She strode toward the lighthouse door. A metal plaque was affixed to a stone block beside it.

This is the work
Was done by
John McCarthy
Who built the Light
House from the bottom to the
Top All ye who do pass by may
Pray for his soul when he dies.

"Quaint," she muttered, looking at the name. "John McCarthy. Was it you I felt that day?" It seemed possible some part of a man so eager for prayers might well stay behind to hear them.

Amelia stepped into the center of the path. She couldn't afford to wait. She'd have to try something a bit more direct. "Spirit," she called, feeling foolish. "Come to me." Still, nothing.

Amelia stood listening to the sound of the river lapping against the stone of the seawall and fought the urge to stamp her foot. There had to be a way.

She tried to relax and closed her eyes, attempting to summon the same feeling of will she'd felt when she repelled the spirit in the ward. This time, however, she pulled instead of pushing.

"John," she said, a note of command in her voice. "Come to me."

The itchy, tickling sensation began in her chest before the words were out. Her heartbeat thudding in her ears, Amelia opened her eyes.

It was, as she'd suspected, nothing like the shade in the park. It wavered in the air before her, a dim outline of a human figure only slightly more defined than the wisp she'd shoved away in the ward. There was a suggestion of a man's face, but no single feature she could have described. Amelia held her breath, but the spirit did not move, did not solidify. It waited.

Steeling herself, she inched toward it, half afraid it would collapse as she approached, half afraid it wouldn't. She hesitated with it hovering inches from her skin. Then, her heart pounding, Amelia stepped into the cloud. As the mist touched her, an insistent pressure grew against her mind. She didn't fight it.

A confused jumble of images. A bright flash and a shocking pain in the back of her head.

And then it was gone. Amelia was on her hands and knees, staring at the grass. There was a puddle of vomit in front of her. Everything was sharp and bright, with a silvery air of unreality. Carefully, she eased back onto her heels. The world whirled around her. She lurched forward, afraid she would be sick again. She waited a few seconds, then made another attempt to sit, still shaking and queasy. After a moment, her stomach quieted.

Amelia's throat was as parched as if she'd swallowed sand. She had no sense of how much time had passed. She rubbed at the back of her aching head and squinted at the sky. It couldn't have been more than a few minutes. The sun didn't appear to have moved, and there was no outcry coming from the direction of the asylum; hopefully she hadn't been missed. Filmed with drying sweat, she pushed herself up on trembling legs and regarded the gentle slope up toward the asylum with weary resignation.

Amelia was woozy in truth by the time she staggered back into the shade of the trees. She sank to her knees and leaned against the rough bark of the largest tree. Jonas, who had apparently been keeping watch over the shoulders of the nurses, was beside her a bare moment later.

"Faint," he told her. "I'll take you back inside."

She let herself fall against his shoulder an instant before her feigned swoon became real.

36

Andrew found the pulse in Amelia's wrist with one hand as he clicked open his pocket watch with the other. Still a bit fast, but steadier than it had been an hour before, when a furious, panicked Jonas dragged him from his office to the infirmary, telling him Amelia had intentionally allowed a spirit to overtake her.

She sat in the bed beside them, propped up by pillows and looking pale but unrepentant.

Andrew tucked the watch away. "You shouldn't have done it without letting us know what you were going to do." He held onto her wrist for another moment before letting go.

Jonas scowled. "You shouldn't have done it at all."

A woman several beds away began to cough, a rough hacking sound that brought a nurse over with a cup of water. Murmured voices filtered toward them.

Jonas lowered his own voice. "Anything could have happened."

"I needed to know if I could control it," Amelia said. Her tone was apologetic, but the words themselves, Andrew noticed, were not an apology.

Jonas was not mollified. "You didn't even know if—"

Andrew interrupted. "Perhaps we should move this conversation to my office." He indicated their surroundings. "If you're feeling no further ill effects," he said to Amelia.

"I'm fine, although I am hungry."

Andrew smiled. "I'll see if I can remedy that."

He left them there, still arguing, as he went to arrange the move with the nurse. He made his way to his office, flagging an orderly on the way and sending him to the staff kitchen for a tray of food and a pot of coffee. "Bring an extra portion," he told the man.

Andrew waited, keenly aware of the depth of his own relief that Amelia had not been hurt. Despite agreeing with Jonas that she had been reckless, part of him couldn't help but admire her for it. She kept startling him. He'd never met anyone like her before, and he was coming to doubt he ever would again. Andrew straightened, mindful that his thoughts were treading a dangerous path. This was hardly the time or place for such adolescent infatuation. The circumstances were beyond bizarre. Even if they had not been, there was still Jonas, with his prior claim.

They arrived a moment later. Jonas looked, if anything, more peeved than before. As it turned out, however, his anger had a new target.

"Klafft saw me in the hallway," he said with a scowl. "He wants me to come help him with something." He deposited Amelia inside the door and left.

Amelia took a seat, seeming more amused than anything. "Don't mind him," she said to Andrew. "He doesn't like feeling thwarted. And he doesn't like Dr. Klafft."

"I think," Andrew said carefully, "that he doesn't like you being in danger. I can't blame him for that."

"He's protective. He always has been."

"How long have you been with him?"

"My whole life," Amelia said. "We grew up together—at the Foundling."

"What is that?"

"The Foundling Asylum of the Sisters of Charity. One night a man—my father, perhaps, although there's no way of knowing—walked into the building with a bundle under his arm. He handed it to the sister on watch and walked out without a word. I'm told I was only a few hours old." Amelia might have been speaking of the weather, so little interest did she evince in the circumstances of her birth. "They gave me to Jonas's mother. She was one of the ones who came to give birth at the Foundling and stayed on afterward. They let some of the women do that sometimes, when they had need of more hands," she explained. "She took charge of me. She died about a year later. Jonas remembers her, a bit. He would have been about four by then.

"After she died, they let us stay together. Although it was probably more that no one bothered to separate us," Amelia added. "Boys and girls weren't meant to mix after a certain age, so we were in different buildings. But Jonas found me whenever he could. He always made sure I had enough to eat, that no one was bothering me."

Unmistakable affection—the first emotion he'd seen from her since she began the story—colored her voice. Andrew tried not to react.

"And they kept you both there? They never found families for you?" he asked.

"I'm sure they tried," Amelia said, "but there were so many of us. When they first opened the Foundling, someone left a baby on the doorstep the very first night. In less than three months, they had over a hundred. After two years, they had twenty-five hundred. It got even worse after the Panic began. By the time I came along the next year . . ." She shrugged.

There was a knock at the door, and Andrew moved to answer it, relieving the orderly standing outside of a tray laden with a platter of sandwiches and a steaming coffeepot.

Amelia wasted no time, snatching a sandwich from the plate and tearing into it. Andrew poured coffee into the lone mug, but she waved it away. He sipped at it and pondered her words.

He'd been a child during the financial crisis of 1873, but old enough to realize something bad was happening. Banks failed. Factories laid off workers or cut their wages. Strikes and even riots became commonplace and were often quelled through violent means. His father's business weathered it better than most, but there had been a few tense, straitened years in the household. He shook his head. Despite the wreck his family had become, he couldn't imagine having grown up the way Amelia had. What must it have been like to be so alone?

He didn't realize he'd spoken the last aloud until Amelia contradicted him.

"I've never been alone. I've always had Jonas."

"When did the two of you leave?"

Having devoured the first sandwich, she reached for another. "They put the girls into domestic service at thirteen. Jonas had left the Foundling two years earlier. They were going to send him west."

She looked at Andrew, and he nodded, familiar with the practice. Orphaned children—particularly boys—were often sent to families in the western territories, where cheap labor was always needed.

"He didn't want to go, so he ran away," Amelia said. "I'd been a scullery maid for a week when Jonas came to check on me. I left with him that day." She grinned. "I told one of the other girls we were going to get married. They thought it was very romantic."

Andrew couldn't help but glance at her ringless left hand.

"A long engagement?"

Laughter burst from her. Andrew realized with a jolt that it was the first time he'd heard her express genuine mirth.

"No engagement at all," she said finally. "I've never wanted to marry. And of course Jonas had known for several years by then that he preferred men."

Andrew, in the midst of swallowing a mouthful of coffee, choked and sputtered. When he finally regained his composure, he looked at her. "You mean he's not—that is, I didn't realize he was, ah . . ."

Amelia looked amused. "A fairy? A mollie? Or I suppose perhaps you'd call him an invert?"

Andrew's ears burned, and he knew his face was red. He'd never heard a woman use those terms so casually, without any evident embarrassment. He doubted most of the women of his social set—his former social set, he corrected himself—even knew such words.

The men did, though. By the time he was thirteen, Andrew and his schoolmates knew all about fairies—those mincing, simpering aberrations who played at being women and did unnatural things (none of them knew at that age precisely what those things were) with one another. He'd sniggered with his friends at one of their classmates, a pale, lonely boy whose family finally sent him away somewhere after catching him in some unknown—though much speculated about—transgression with one of their servants.

There had been some brief references to the subject in medical school. A staid, uncomfortable-looking professor spent an hour describing the treatments for suspected deviance in adolescents before moving on. Those experiences, along with gossip and scenes from a few lurid novels, were the sum total of his knowledge of such men. Until now, it seemed.

Andrew groped for the correct response in the face of Amelia's casual revelation. "Yes. Well. The proper scientific term is a matter of some debate. I'm certainly familiar with— That is to say, I'm aware of such things, from a medical perspective. But I admit, I've never actually known anyone who—"

"Yes, you have," she interrupted. "You just don't know it. You'd be shocked if you knew how many very upstanding, very married men come to the club and arrange to be seen disappearing up the stairs with a chorus girl, only to trade her for one of the boys once they're out of sight."

The notion was stunning. Andrew took another sip of coffee as he wondered uncomfortably who among his acquaintance might be hiding such a vice. After a moment, he shook his head, abandoning the very awkward topic in favor of the slightly less awkward one—which he suddenly found much more interesting.

"You don't wish to marry at all? Why not?"

Amelia looked at him as if he were simple. "You can ask such a question, given our current pursuit? Isn't it obvious?" She ticked off points on her fingers as she went on. "A man can have his wife committed, and her protests mean nothing. He can beat her, and as long as it isn't too severe, no one will do anything. He can wear her out with childbearing, then take her children away from her. He can take her money. He can demand total obedience while offering nothing in return." She shook her head. "I want no part of it."

"There are happy marriages," Andrew said weakly.

"Are there?"

Neither of them spoke for a beat.

"What about you?" Amelia asked. "If you're such a believer in the institution, then why haven't you married?"

A demurral rose to his lips, but he couldn't bring himself to voice it. He would be a coward to avoid the subject when she'd been so open about her own life.

"I was engaged, for a time," he admitted. "It came to an end shortly before I moved to New York."

"Did you love her?"

"I thought I did," he said, although he wondered now if that were actually true. Cecilia was pretty. Educated. From a good family. He could admit to himself now that he'd never found her particularly interesting, but at the time, that hadn't seemed like a relevant consideration.

"I was finally established in my career." He toyed with his empty mug. "It seemed the right time to marry, and she seemed the right sort of woman. Our families encouraged it, and I asked her almost at once. She seemed eager enough. In truth, we hardly knew each other. I think she wanted what I represented. Which is only fair, I suppose," he added, "since I wanted the same from her. I'd have gone through with it, even so, if it hadn't been for—"

Andrew caught himself and glanced at Amelia. She was listening, obviously curious. But there was something in her expression that said she wouldn't push further if he chose not to go on. He was tempted to stop. But he'd come this far.

"When my sister died," he said, and it felt like stepping off a cliff and into empty air, "it changed everything. I couldn't bear the falsity of my life, the utter artifice of it, any longer. My family was—is—prominent. Everything any of us ever did was done with an eye toward protecting our position. My engagement was one more piece of that calculation." He shook his head. "Then Susannah died, and it all began to feel like gilding painted over so much rot."

"You were close."

"Very. Our older brother was already ten years old when she was born, and fourteen by the time I came along, so it was always the two of us. Once, when I was small, an older boy pushed me into a pond and stole the toy boat I'd been playing with. Susannah was like a fury. I got my boat back, and Susannah went home with a bloody lip and a torn dress." He smiled at the memory. "My mother despaired of her."

He sobered as he continued. "I was home from college for Christmas when I first realized something was wrong. Susannah was withdrawn. She'd always been outgoing, but now she didn't want to leave the house. By my next visit, she wouldn't even leave her room. She'd have times when she was better, but they never lasted, and she was never as she had been before. My parents put it about that she was in delicate health.

"By the time I returned to Philadelphia for medical school, the Susannah I'd grown up with seemed to be gone. She refused to bathe. She'd begun talking to herself—at least, that's what we thought at first. Later, it became clear she was hearing voices. Sometimes she had screaming arguments with empty air."

He stopped, lost in the memory for a moment, before he shook himself and continued.

"My parents engaged a nurse, and they paid all the servants well to keep the truth of her condition private, but eventually she became too unruly to handle. My father found a private asylum away from the city."

Andrew stopped again, struggling against the wave of guilt that always threatened to swamp him when he thought of those years. He'd been absorbed in his own life. And, he could admit now, he had been embarrassed by his sister.

"I wrote to her occasionally," he said, avoiding Amelia's eyes. "I visited her once. She begged every year to come home for our birthdays. We were both born in July, and when we were children, we always had our party on the Fourth before going to watch the city fireworks. She was doing well, and so the summer after I finished medical school, our parents agreed to bring her home for the week.

"She behaved almost normally, but there was a frailty to it. A sense that she was playing a part and straining to do it. The night before she was meant to go back, Susannah came to me. She said she couldn't bear to return to the asylum and begged me to intervene with our parents. I refused. I told her I didn't think she was well enough to come home."

Andrew would remember everything about that moment until his last breath. They stood together, watching the fireworks as they had when they were children. Her hand clasped his as bright streaks blazed over their heads and left their sulfur stench in the night air. A red shell burst as she turned to him with her plea. It lit her face crimson but didn't hide the naked desperation in her eyes, or the despair when he said no.

His memory of the knock at his bedroom door the next morning was no less perfect. It was a family tradition to give the servants the day off, so it was his father who stood there, stunned and hollow-eyed, when Andrew opened the door.

Andrew looked away. "My mother found her the next morning. She'd used a bedsheet." He swallowed hard. "I cut her down, but it was too late. She was gone."

37

Jonas was quiet the next day as he led Amelia through the hallway. Still upset, it seemed, about the risk she'd taken the day before.

She broke the silence as they stepped into the main hall. "When we get to Andrew's office, I think we should—"

Jonas was looking at her with a quizzical expression.

"What?"

"It's 'Andrew' now, is it?"

The observation brought Amelia up short. She had made no conscious decision to use his given name. She hadn't even realized she'd done it. Perhaps it was because he'd blushed—much to her amusement—at the revelation of Jonas's romantic inclinations. Or because he'd seemed to listen so intently as she spoke. That was a rare enough quality in a man, in her experience.

Or perhaps it was because she recognized what he'd given her when he trusted her with the story of his sister. Her death obviously grieved him deeply, and the wound wasn't a clean one. It wasn't his fault, but he felt guilty nonetheless. The story went some way toward explaining why he'd been so desperate to gain Amelia's aid in the search for Julia Weaver. He was trying to atone.

Whatever it was, he was real to her now. He wasn't Cavanaugh, the doctor who stood between her and freedom. He was Andrew. He yearned for something, and he believed she could help him have it.

And she found that she wanted to.

Amelia blinked at this new realization, unsure how she felt about it. She followed Jonas down the hallway, suddenly reluctant to arrive at their destination.

They were down the hall from the office—*Andrew's office*, Amelia thought to herself, testing the words—when a nurse called out for Jonas's help with the patient she was escorting, who had begun to struggle out of her grip.

"Go on ahead," Jonas said. "I'll be there after I take care of this."

Amelia stood alone in the hallway, trying to ignore this unexpected bout of nerves. She took a deep breath, set her face to pleasant neutrality, and strode through the door.

Andrew looked up as she entered, and his hesitant smile of greeting set off a round of moths fluttering in her chest. She swatted them down. This was ridiculous. She was not a schoolgirl. Perhaps they were friends now. But there was no need to make it more than it was.

"Jonas had to help with something." She gestured at the open door, through which the patient's fading howls echoed. "He'll be here soon."

She took her seat, and though neither of them said anything, the unexpected intimacy of the previous day's conversation continued to hang in the air between them, as palpable as smoke.

They both started when Jonas appeared in the doorway, slightly out of breath. He closed the door behind him and leaned against the wall. "Well, what's the plan? Are we going to get back to searching the asylum, or are we going to take another jaunt out to the lighthouse to—"

Andrew's voice was sharp. "The lighthouse?" He leaned forward, his face strangely intense. "Tell me exactly what happened."

Amelia glanced at Jonas, who looked as puzzled as she felt, then recounted the episode, step by step. "And then it was like something slammed into the back of my head, and he was gone."

"A blow to the back of the head. Out by the lighthouse." Andrew was pale. "Amelia." His voice shook. "I don't think you summoned John McCarthy. I think you summoned John Blounton."

"What?" Jonas's voice was sharp. "You said Blounton drowned."

"He did," Andrew said. "There was water in his lungs. But there was also damage to the back of his skull. The autopsy report speculated that he hit his head on something—possibly a rock—when he fell in. And based on where his body was found, they determined he'd gone into the water near the north end of the island. Near the lighthouse."

"You never said anything about that." Jonas's voice was outraged.

"I didn't have any idea it mattered."

"I couldn't tell exactly what happened to him—whether someone hit him, or whether he fell," Amelia said. "I'm not sure he knew. But there wasn't much of him out there. He was . . . 'thin' is the best way I can describe it." She frowned as a thought struck her, then stood and walked into the storage room.

"What are you doing?" Jonas followed her to the doorway.

"Looking for something." She tried to remember where she'd put the cuff link she'd found in the drawer. She spied a flash of red atop one of the cluttered cabinets. She held it up. "I think this belonged to Blounton. Maybe I can use it to bring him through more strongly."

Jonas peered at it, then at her. He continued to look at her for a long moment, then sighed in resignation, his shoulders dropping. "Will you listen if I tell you I think this is a bad idea, or will you just wait until I'm not here and try it without me?"

Amelia grimaced. "I don't particularly want to try it at all. But it seems likely Blounton knew more than we do about what's going on here. We can't afford to ignore that. We're not spoiled for choices."

With another sigh, Jonas stepped aside and waved her ahead of him into the office.

Amelia resettled herself on the chair and tried to relax. Both men hovered, their anxiety thick in the air, and she frowned at them until they stepped back. Jonas took up a position against the wall, while Andrew leaned against the edge of his desk.

Amelia evened her breathing and closed her eyes, rolling the cuff link between her fingers, feeling the raised silver swirls of the letters and the smooth enamel beneath them. She tried to re-create the tone she'd used the day before and called the dead man's name—his full name, this time. "John Blounton," she said, her throat dry. "Come to me."

If he formed, she didn't see it. Her eyes were still closed when the itch began in her chest. She took a breath, and he was there, flickering against the borders of her mind. Amelia fought the urge to shove him away and instead leaned into the feeling. The shade began to slide through the barrier. She rode the panic and allowed it, feeling herself being pushed aside, as if a thick glass wall was between them—her side growing smaller, his larger, as he came on. And then it stopped. She'd been right. There wasn't enough of him to take her over. Amelia was still there, behind the glass. She reached out and felt Blounton's confusion, his lack of self. Words, not her own, slid from her lips, slurred and indistinct.

"Wss appng." Her voice was lower, huskier. His, layered over hers.

"John?" Jonas's voice sounded as though it came from a great distance. "John Blounton, is that you?"

"Y'ssss," they sighed together.

"The women on the list, John. Who brought them to the asylum? Who is doing this?"

Blounton groped for the words as Amelia tried to understand, tried to help him push them out. "F'nd 'mm. S'mny." A ragged gasp. Angry. "Bas'ard. S' th' one." An enormous effort. "Finds 'em a'th'lub. Mmmmhm. 'S all 'ranged. Ussng 'onn lee."

They tried to say more, but the effort was too much. The part of them that was Blounton fell apart like mist in the sun, and Amelia was wholly herself again, alone in her mind, shaking and dizzy. She slumped to one side and took a shuddering breath.

⁓

"So it didn't work, even with the cuff link?" Sidney asked. He gestured for their waiter to pour the wine.

Jonas sat across from him in a semiprivate dining room at the Union League Club, one of the city's most exclusive gentlemen's social clubs. As they'd passed through the main lounge on the way to their table, Sidney had quietly pointed out several millionaires and a brace of government officials. Jonas had also seen a half dozen men he recognized as regulars at Sabine's, although none of them were personal clients of his. If they had been, he would never have acknowledged it, discretion being one of the many keys to his success over the past few years.

Jonas waited until the officious-looking server had stepped back before responding.

"Not really. The voice was so muddled, none of us knew what he was trying to say. Amelia rested for a bit and tried again, but she couldn't get him back. She thinks there's not enough of him left."

Sidney shuddered. "So you're going to go back to searching the way you were before?"

Jonas nodded.

"And you're certain there's nothing I can do to help?"

"If Cavanaugh reneges on his side of the agreement, we may wind up needing your skills. But for now, there's nothing."

"What are you thinking about how to get her out?"

"Ironically, solving this mystery actually might wind up being the easiest way," Jonas said. "If we can find Julia Weaver—or any other hidden women—and proof of whoever is responsible, we could claim Amelia was one of the victims and get her released that way."

"And if you don't?"

Jonas shrugged. "I still don't know for sure. The fever's spread seems to be under control, and no one's died of it, so trying that seems like a bad idea. I may be back to trying to sneak her off the island." Jonas took a sip of the rich red wine. "There's another ladies' charity group coming in, a big one. It's not a great idea, but I'm running out of time. I went to see Charley today about getting the right sort of clothes."

He set down the glass and picked up his fork, spearing a bite of tender beef. "He didn't have anything on hand that would fit Amelia, so he's going to have to find the right kind of dress and cut it down. He says he'll have it next week. Either way, it won't go on much longer. Ten more days until Amelia's fulfilled her end of the bargain. If Cavanaugh balks, or if there doesn't seem to be a better solution, the ladies will be there three days after that. I'll make it work."

Sidney was quiet for a moment. "What about afterward? Have you thought any more about what we discussed?"

"Some." Jonas looked at his plate, then up at the other man. "I can't make any decisions until all this is over. But it's appealing. I've been borrowing books from the doctors' library at the asylum. Psychology is fascinating. Although," he said, "some of it is clearly rubbish. Did you know there's actually a theory that the color of one's hair correlates with one's likelihood of becoming insane? I read it in Tuke's *Dictionary of Psychological Medicine*. It's interesting that—" He broke off, realizing Sidney was suppressing a smile. "I'm rambling. I'm sorry."

Sidney shook his head. "Don't be. It's fun to see you so excited about something. There are thousands of books in the university library, about every conceivable subject, and they'll all be available to you if you decide to enroll."

Jonas looked around the room, all dark, polished wood and Tiffany glass. His years at Sabine's had made him familiar with the habits of New York's wealthier citizenry, but spending time with Sidney gave him a far more intimate perspective. Sidney's grandfather had been a founding member of the Union League Club, so Sidney had been destined for membership from birth. His rarified pedigree—and ready access to large sums of money—gave him an expansive view of what was possible.

"It's not that easy," Jonas said finally.

"It could be, if you'd let me—"

Jonas was already shaking his head. "I won't take your money. Not for that."

Dinners and gifts were one thing. He'd even been willing—all right, somewhat more than willing—to let Sidney take him to Paris. But there was something about accepting an allowance, letting Sidney pull strings to get Jonas admitted to a college course or pay his tuition, that felt wrong. Perhaps he was being irrational. It would make things easier, god knew. But he'd stopped taking Sidney's money after their third night together. Their relationship was not about money, and for the first time in his life, Jonas liked it that way. Amelia would call him ten kinds of a fool if she knew.

"Very well," Sidney said. "The offer is there, if you change your mind. And if there's anything I can do to help with the current situation, please ask."

"I will." There was no one nearby, but Jonas lowered his voice anyway. "Just having you back on this side of the ocean helps. I missed you."

"I missed you, too. I'm sorry you couldn't go with me this time, but we'll have other chances."

If they had been alone, he would have put a hand over the other man's, but of course that wasn't possible here. Jonas sighed and pushed back his chair. "I have to go. I'm due at the club at ten, and Sabine's already unhappy with me after these last few weeks."

Sidney stood, too. "She'll be happier with you when I rent one of the rooms for the night."

Jonas raised an eyebrow. "The whole night?"

"Don't worry," Sidney said, his voice pitched for Jonas's ears alone. "I'll let you sleep a little."

They walked to the curb, where they stood a careful distance apart, waiting their turn for a cab. Jonas glanced down the block, and his eyes snagged on a pair of figures moving toward them. It was Klafft, with Connolly trailing behind, scribbling on a stack of papers.

Jonas tensed. Being seen standing outside one of the most exclusive clubs in the city—in expensive evening attire, no less—was not in keeping with his pose as a lowly orderly. A cab pulled to a stop before them, and he hastened aboard, trying to keep his face turned away from the duo on the sidewalk.

Jonas kept his eyes forward as the driver pulled away, uncertain if he'd been seen and unwilling to do anything to draw attention to himself. Halfway down the block, however, he risked a glance out the window.

Connolly had stopped and was turned toward their retreating cab, but Jonas couldn't make out the expression on his face. Klafft was standing outside the door Jonas and Sidney had just exited. As Jonas watched, Connolly turned and hurried to hold the door for his employer, then followed him inside.

"Klafft is a member of the Union League Club?"

"He is," Sidney replied, "although I don't know him personally."

Jonas settled back into his seat, wondering where an asylum physician got the money to mingle with society's elite. He grimaced. If either man recognized him, they were probably wondering the same of him.

38

Jonas seemed pensive the next day as he walked beside her to Andrew's office.

"Amelia?" There was a tentative note in his voice.

She turned to him, her eyebrows raised.

"Have you— Have you ever thought about what it would be like to do something else? To leave the club, I mean?"

She gaped at him. "Why would I? Working at the club is perfect for us. Assuming Sabine will have me back, once I'm out of here."

He was about to reply when one of the ward doors opened and Klafft emerged. Jonas stiffened, a look of guarded alarm on his face. He relaxed once the doctor was out of earshot and looked at her.

"Now that he's on the mend, we really need to try for his apartment again. I saw him with Connolly at the Union League Club last night. If Klafft can afford the fees there, he's got far more money than he's making here."

Amelia frowned. "What were you doing at the Union League Club?"

Jonas glanced away and began walking again. His voice became studiedly nonchalant. "Having dinner with Sidney."

Amelia stumbled. Jonas caught her elbow.

"I thought he was in Europe."

"He's back." His next sentence stunned her. "When all of this is over, I want you to meet him."

Amelia was saved from having to think of a reply by their arrival at Andrew's office.

The doctor was inside, and Jonas outlined their suspicions about Klafft as Amelia sat mulling over Jonas's casual declaration. When he'd told her Sidney had left, she'd assumed it meant their affair was at an end. Clearly, she'd been wrong. His talk of leaving the club—that had to be Sidney's influence. Jonas would never have suggested it, never even considered it, before Sidney came along. And wanting them to meet? He'd never proposed such a thing before. At least she still had a little time before she had to actually do it.

With a pang of bleak amusement at the idea of her current predicament saving her from a tedious social engagement, Amelia wrenched her attention away from Jonas's romantic foibles and back to the matter at hand: Klafft and his suspicious wealth.

"I agree it's suggestive," Andrew was saying, "but it doesn't mean he's involved. He could have some other source of income—family money or the like."

"I'm just saying, he bears watching," Jonas replied. "It's clear he doesn't think much of women, and it isn't so great a stretch to imagine him being part of the scheme. Remember, Elizabeth said he was the first to examine her after she arrived. He's exactly—"

Jonas broke off at the sound of footsteps in the hallway and plucked a sheet of paper from Andrew's desk. He pretended to read it as Tyree appeared in the doorway, his coat thrown over one arm and carrying a valise. It was meant to be his weekend at liberty, although Amelia had assumed he would stay on the island with so many patients ill. It seemed she had guessed incorrectly. Perhaps while he was gone she would get another chance at that dratted lock.

"Headed out for the weekend?" Andrew asked.

"Indeed," Tyree said, shifting his coat from his right arm to his left to shake the hand Andrew offered. A muffled jangle came from the pocket. His keys.

Amelia straightened and caught Jonas's eye. He'd heard it, too. Amelia leaned forward, wondering if she dared make a try for them.

"I meant to ask you," Andrew said to Tyree suddenly, and somehow Amelia was certain he'd known what she was thinking. He was making a credible effort at sounding as if he had just remembered something. "There's a woman in three whose case I'd like your opinion of. I don't want to make you miss the ferry," he went on, "but if you can spare a moment before you go, I would appreciate it."

Tyree set the valise on a corner of the desk. He laid the coat across it.

Amelia was careful not to look at it as Tyree pulled his watch from his vest pocket and clicked open the cover.

"I have precisely forty minutes before the next ferry," he said.

"Fifteen minutes, at most," Andrew assured him, looking at Amelia as he said it. "Just down the hall, a quick look, and right back here for your things. Mr. Vincent," he said, turning to Jonas, "would you mind remaining here with Miss Casey until I return?"

"Of course, Doctor," Jonas said.

"Well, then." Tyree tucked his watch away and gestured to the doorway. "Lead on."

The moment the two men were out of the room, Amelia plunged her hand into the pocket of the coat and withdrew a heavy ring of keys. By the time Andrew and Tyree disappeared around the corner, she and Jonas were at Tyree's door. The hallway was empty in both directions.

"Hurry," Jonas said. "I'll keep lookout this time and give you a knock at twelve minutes. Tap when you're ready to come out, and I'll open the door if it's clear."

Amelia's hands shook only a little as she tried the keys one after another. The third slid into the lock, and it clicked open. She was inside in a flash.

Twelve minutes—less now—until the keys had to be back in Tyree's pocket. Not time enough to search the whole place. Amelia wasted a second on indecision before turning toward the boxes beside the wall. Andrew had mentioned Tyree was storing Blounton's belongings. The scrap of paper bearing Julia's name might have been left behind when the killer removed Blounton's notes, but it was also possible Tyree had left it behind while cleaning out the desk after Blounton's death. If the rest of the page was still with Blounton's things, it might contain the solution.

Amelia knelt beside the boxes and glanced at the knots tied in the string—simple enough to re-create—then opened the first box and scrabbled through its contents.

Books. A bundle of letters addressed to "John" and signed "Mother." A half-finished reply. The handwriting matched that on the scrap Andrew had found. Definitely written by Blounton, then. There was also a small black notebook, mostly blank. A few telegrams. A note from Tyree, suggesting a time and place for dinner in the city.

Amelia turned to the second parcel. Along with Blounton's medical bag, it held a small shaving kit—Blounton must have stayed overnight on the island as Andrew sometimes did. There was also a wrinkled shirt and collar and a single cuff link—the mate to the one she'd found in Andrew's office and used to summon the man—in a little padded box.

Nothing else. Amelia sat back on her heels with a muttered oath as Jonas rapped on the door. The twelve minutes were gone. She'd guessed wrong, and now there was no time to search elsewhere. She retied the boxes and hurried to the door. Jonas opened it at her tap, and she slid back into the hallway. They hurried back to Andrew's office, where she stuffed the keys back into the coat pocket and resumed her seat.

The doctors returned no more than a minute later. His workweek done, Tyree bade Andrew farewell with a smile, his keys jingling in his pocket as he strode away.

Andrew looked between them as the other doctor vanished around the corner.

Amelia shook her head. "Not enough time for a full search. There was nothing helpful in Blounton's boxes."

Andrew slumped against the doorway, disappointment on his face.

Jonas sighed. "I should get back to the wards. I've got two hours left in my shift."

"Hold on," Amelia said, reaching for a pencil and paper. "I've got some more names we can cross off the list."

The lead of the pencil snapped at the first stroke.

"There should be another in the desk," Andrew said from his place by the door.

Amelia slid open the center drawer. The familiar photo of Julia was there. But beside it was another, one Amelia hadn't seen before. Julia, plain and solid, sat on a bench, one arm wrapped around a pretty little girl with golden curls.

Something restless moved at the back of Amelia's mind as she looked at them. "What's this?"

Jonas leaned over to look as Andrew walked toward them.

"Ned gave me that one along with the other photograph."

"You never showed it to us." She focused on the little girl's face, then traced it with a finger.

"I didn't think it was much use, since you can't really see Julia's face."

"This is her daughter?"

"Yes," Andrew said. "Catherine. Although I believe the family calls her Kitty."

Kitty.

The word slammed into Amelia's mind like a mallet, and the restless thing slipped its bonds.

My cat. She'll wonder where I've gone, my sweet little kitty.

Amelia's blood froze in her veins. The world dwindled to a single, brilliant point of light. It pulsed in time with her thundering heartbeat, and each blinding, infinite flash loosed another revelation.

A woman in a dream, following a yellow cat through a field of flowers.

A woman in a cell, weeping, a stuffed cat at her feet.

A visitor in the night, and a gray-wrapped corpse carried away with the dawn.

My Cat. She'll wonder where I've gone, my sweet little Kitty.

Amelia mouthed the words through numb lips as their import seared through her: They'd failed before they had ever begun.

Julia Weaver was dead.

39

Andrew looked over in time to watch the blood drain from Amelia's face. She swayed in the chair. He put out a hand to steady her and found she was trembling.

"Amelia?"

She tore away from his touch and leapt for the door, wrenching it open, as if desperate to escape from the room. She strode down the hallway, her breath coming in loud gasps. He went after her and found he could only barely keep up, despite the difference in their heights.

"Amelia, wait," he said, reaching for her arm.

She rounded on him, her eyes blazing. "Julia Weaver is dead," she spat.

"What?" he said, as stunned as if he'd run into a wall.

There was movement at the corner of his eye. Jonas. He'd forgotten the other man was there. Jonas glanced at the fortunately empty hallway, then took them each by an elbow and, with a jerk of his head, directed them back toward Andrew's office.

A torrent of words poured from Amelia's mouth as they went, low and intense. Andrew's head buzzed as he tried to keep hold of the thread. Her dreams. A stuffed toy. Footsteps in the hallway and a floating specter and the sound of a cell door opening in the middle of the night. Every word was a knife.

He'd failed. She was dead. He would have to tell Ned that his sister was gone.

"We were never going to find her," Amelia finished in a bitter tone as they reached the office. "She was in the cell next to mine that night, but she's bones on Hart Island by now."

Jonas nudged them inside. "Both of you, sit. Wait here. I'll be right back." He closed the door.

Numbly grateful for the other man's presence of mind, Andrew did as he instructed.

Some silent, endless time later, Jonas returned. "I don't think anyone heard anything. But you can't go around doing that," he said to Amelia. She looked up at him, her eyes hollow. He lifted the hem of his tunic to retrieve a silver flask from his waistband. "Here."

"Where did you get that?" Andrew asked.

"From Russo," Jonas replied as he unscrewed the cap. "The orderly with the scarred face. He keeps it in his locker and takes nips when he thinks no one's watching. He thinks he's sly, but everyone knows."

He passed the flask to Amelia, who tilted it up and swallowed, then coughed and sputtered. She passed it back, her eyes watering. She wiped them with the backs of her hands.

Jonas took a swig, then eyed the flask with what looked like admiration. "Russo likes the good stuff," he said, sounding impressed. "I'd have nicked it sooner if I'd had any idea." He offered it to Andrew, who shook his head, still feeling as sluggish as if he were moving across the bottom of the ocean. Liquor was the last thing he needed.

Jonas took another swallow and looked at Amelia appraisingly, then passed the flask back to her. "One more, I think. Just a little one."

She obeyed. Color began to return to her cheeks, and something in her shoulders relaxed.

"Good." Jonas capped the flask. His face was grim, but his tone was matter-of-fact. "We have to decide how to proceed. We know Julia is dead, was deliberately murdered. Seems likely Blounton was, too. Which points to another probability. Elizabeth Miner looks like an anomaly. If Julia was the norm, then perhaps there's a reason we haven't found anyone else."

"My god," Andrew whispered, as cold understanding swept over him. "There's no telling how many women could have been killed here."

There was an instant's silence before Amelia lurched to her feet with a sound like a snarl. "The thing I saw that night outside Julia's cell. It was him. It must have been. He stood in the doorway and looked at me. He killed Julia right in front of me, and I didn't even know what I was seeing."

"Still no idea who it was, I suppose?" Jonas asked.

She shook her head.

Andrew spoke. "What about the next morning?"

They looked at him as he went on, the threads of the thought coming together. "We made certain I was going to be the one to find you after your 'death,'" he said. "Would our murderer allow someone else to find his victims? What if someone noticed something amiss? Who did you see outside Julia's cell?"

Amelia closed her eyes and fisted her hands at her temples as if she could tear the knowledge from her head by brute force. Then she dropped her hands to her sides and shook her head. "Nurses. Orderlies, but I don't remember who. I didn't know to pay attention, obviously, and I'd had the laudanum that night, too. I don't remember a doctor, but that's not to say one of them wasn't there."

They went quiet again, each of them lost in thought.

"The dead," Jonas said abruptly.

Andrew blinked at him, uncomprehending.

"The records," he explained. "If we're right that the women we're looking for are dead, then I'm wasting my time looking for court records on current patients. Get me a list of the women who've died in the last few years, along with the dates they arrived at the asylum. It should narrow the search enough to make it manageable."

"What if," Amelia said, the words coming slowly, "we could get more than their names? Julia died here. What if she hasn't left? What if she can tell us who killed her?"

"Do you really think you can speak to her?" Andrew asked. "Have you seen any indication she's still here?"

"Not unless the wisp in ward six was her, and I didn't get any sense of that when it touched me, but it's worth a try."

"Not tonight," Jonas said. "You've already had a shock and a couple of belts of whiskey. Those don't seem like helpful circumstances. Besides that, I don't want you trying this again without me here, and I have to be at the club in less than two hours. It can wait until tomorrow."

Amelia pressed her lips together. "Fine."

∽

Amelia lay awake late into the night, despite her utter exhaustion. When she did finally sleep, her dreams were heavy and incoherent. She woke to a sense of wrongness, confused for a long moment, before the events of the previous evening rushed back to her.

The next day crawled past. A nurse came for her just after dinner. Amelia trailed behind her, her footsteps leaden. She almost failed to notice the odd trio standing outside the main office, speaking in hushed voices. It wasn't until they had drawn almost abreast of the men and she heard a snippet of their conversation—"have to be at the docks when the next one arrives, or we won't be able to make certain"—that she focused on their faces: Russo, the cratered skin of his cheeks flushing as he spoke; Connolly, looking harassed as usual; and Harcourt himself.

Amelia and her escort passed out of hearing before the sentence was complete, but it didn't matter. Amelia had heard enough.

Connolly worked for Klafft, who had far more money than he ought to. Russo drank expensive liquor on an orderly's salary. She hadn't expected Harcourt himself to be at the center of the plot, but it seemed obvious now that he was. Russo and Connolly could pose as ambulance drivers and bring the women to the island. Klafft and Harcourt could falsify the paperwork to admit them and cover each other's tracks. Even the well-known enmity between them would deflect suspicion.

And any of the four could do the killing.

By the time they reached Andrew's office, Amelia was certain she was right. She told him at once.

He nodded slowly as she finished, his elbows on his desk. "It makes sense." Andrew rubbed his forehead with both hands. He looked as though he hadn't slept at all. His eyes were red-rimmed, and his voice had an edge of despair. "But I have no idea how to prove it."

"There must be a way," Amelia said. "Maybe Jonas will have an idea. In the meantime, we need to get that list for him—the patients who've died."

They worked side by side in silence for more than an hour, growing ever grimmer as they copied names and dates from the file drawer in the storage room. They filled three pages with the names of women—some had died only weeks after their admission, some years later.

When they were finished, Amelia ran a finger over one name, feeling the depressions left by the nib of the pen. Sarah Talbot. That had been the name given to the woman who'd died in the cell beside her own, the woman who was actually Julia Weaver. Her record said her heart had given out. Amelia shuddered, imagining how it might have really happened. In a laudanum-induced sleep, Julia could have died without a struggle. Or she could have woken—perhaps not enough to fight her attacker, but enough to know what was happening, to feel terror at the approach of the relentless dark.

When Jonas arrived, she handed him the list and recounted the conversation she'd overheard earlier.

"You could be right," he said, his tone guarded. "Maybe Julia will be able to tell us something."

Amelia did everything she could think of. She tried variations of Julia's name. She wrote it on a sheet of paper and called her as she formed the letters. She cajoled and ordered and pleaded.

Julia did not come.

At last Amelia sat back, defeated. "I don't think she's here."

Andrew, who had been silent throughout the attempt, finally spoke. "Maybe if I can get something of hers from Ned—something like Blounton's cuff link, that could help."

"No," Jonas said. His voice was gentle, but there was no give in it.

Amelia looked at him, and his eyes bored through her.

"This has gone on long enough," Jonas continued. "I thought about it all night. You promised to stay one month or until you found Julia. You found her. It's over. There's no point to your being here any longer."

"No point?" Amelia cried. "Russo said, 'When the next one arrives.' They're going to keep doing it. They're going to keep killing women, and they're going to get away with it."

"And I'm sorry for it," Jonas said. "But I'm not willing to risk your life to stop them. Don't you understand? This was dangerous enough when we thought these women were being imprisoned. But these men, they're cold-blooded murderers. We've been lucky so far. But if you keep pushing this, you'll be caught. They. Will. Kill. You." He spat the last four words like bullets.

Amelia shook her head, unable to speak, and glanced at Andrew. Jonas was right. She knew it, but it didn't matter. She couldn't leave, not yet. Not like this.

Jonas's face tightened as he looked at her, and he wheeled toward Andrew, who took a step back. "You agreed to the terms. She's more than fulfilled them. Help me get her out."

Andrew licked his lips, and his eyes darted toward Amelia before coming back to Jonas. "A week," he said finally, his voice hoarse. "Please. Just give me this one last week, and then I'll help."

"I knew it," Jonas said, contempt curdling the words. "I knew your word was no good."

Amelia sucked in a breath. "That's not fair."

Jonas's eyes snapped back to hers. "I don't give a damn about fair. I want you safe. I want you out of this. I want him to do what he said he would."

"Please," Andrew said again. "We can find proof. We can end this."

"How far are you willing to go?" Jonas asked. "What will you do if Julia won't come? If the names on this list don't lead anywhere?"

"I don't know. I'll think of something. I have to stop them. *I have to.* They killed Susannah. I can't let them—" Andrew stopped, his face going white as he heard his own words.

Amelia held her breath.

The room was still and heavy as the air before a storm.

Jonas's jaw tightened, and his eyes narrowed. His voice was icy when he finally spoke. "Your sister is dead. I'm sorry for that, but it doesn't mean I'm going to let you kill mine."

He strode from the room, slamming the door behind him.

Amelia sat frozen as Andrew staggered to the other chair and flung himself into it, burying his face in his shaking hands.

The last of the light faded as the minutes ticked past. Amelia turned up the lamp until it sent shadows flickering over the walls.

"I'm sorry," she said softly. "He shouldn't have said that."

"But he's right." Andrew didn't look at her. "You should leave. I'll find him later and tell him I'll help. Whatever he thinks we should do." He went on before she could speak, before she could protest that she'd refused Jonas before Andrew had. "It's not safe for you here. I don't have any right to ask you to risk yourself that way. If I don't help you leave and something happens to you, I'll never forgive myself. I already—"

Andrew raised his head then, and the devastation on his face made Amelia's heart ache. She saw now just how deep his guilt over Susannah's death ran and what their search for Julia Weaver had meant to him. Some part of him had truly believed, at his core, that if he found Julia, it would save his sister. It was irrational. It was impossible. He knew it. But something in him had clung to it all the same. And now that same something screamed that he had failed her. He had let her die. Again.

He would never be free of it.

Amelia wanted to cry. None of it was his fault, but there was nothing she could say or do to convince him of it.

Except perhaps there was.

Ice slid down Amelia's spine. She could bring his sister to him, let him speak to her one last time. She could give him that much. If she could bear to do it.

Her throat went dry. Before she could think the better of it, she stood and dragged her own chair around the desk to face his. She sat in front of him, so close their knees nearly touched.

"Do you have something of Susannah's I can use?"

Raw yearning blazed from him as he realized what she was offering. In that moment, Amelia knew there was no turning back.

Andrew nodded once, a jerky movement, then reached into his pocket with a shaking hand and withdrew something small and shining. A silver locket. He held it out to her. The delicate filigree on the locket's face sparkled in the lamplight.

Amelia tried to swallow and found she could not. Her heart thrummed in her ears.

He caught her hesitation. "You don't . . . you don't have to do this."

"I want to," she said, meeting his eyes.

It wasn't true. And yet it was. Anything to drive that stricken expression from his face.

Amelia forced herself to relax and reached for the necklace. The tips of her fingers tingled as they brushed against Andrew's. The moths fluttered in her chest again. She swatted them down, took a breath, and gathered the chain, looping it around her hand. She laced her fingers through Andrew's, pressing the locket between their palms.

"Are you ready?" Amelia asked.

He swallowed and nodded, his eyes roving over her face.

"Susannah Cavanaugh," Amelia murmured. "Come to me."

The itch began in her chest almost immediately. She focused on it. The pressure grew. She leaned into it, took a long, slow breath, and opened her eyes. The woman was there, more vivid than she'd been that day in the cell. Susannah Cavanaugh stood behind her brother, her face eager. She was pretty, with a fresh, vital look and a hint of mischief around her mouth. There was something of Andrew in her features.

Amelia didn't see her move, but there was the sensation of something cold sliding beneath her skin like a hand into a glove. Amelia closed her eyes again and had time to think only that Susannah was so much stronger than Blounton.

∽

Andrew saw when it happened. Amelia looked past him, her eyes widening. He fought the urge to turn, keeping his attention on Amelia. Her eyes closed, something rippled across her face, and the very planes of her face changed, became subtly different. And then Susannah was looking out at him from behind Amelia's eyes.

Andrew's breath caught in his throat. It was the Susannah of his youth, clear-eyed and lucid. Not the Susannah of her final years, with her fragile moods and volcanic anger. Not even the Susannah of several weeks ago, in Amelia's cell. She looked around the office, just as she had that day. But this time, something in her shoulders relaxed.

Her eyes settled on his face. She beamed at him, and his hands tightened on hers until his knuckles whitened.

Susannah's smile, on Amelia's face.

"Jamie."

Susannah's voice.

Grief and joy overwhelmed him. He managed to bite back a sob but didn't try to stop the tears. They streamed down his face as he smiled back at her, and she reached to wipe them away with her fingers.

"Susannah, I'm so sorry," he managed to choke out. "I should have listened to you. I should have done something, I—"

She shook her head. "No. None of that. It doesn't matter now. And there was nothing you could have done. I couldn't bear it any longer. There was too much. The voices were there in my head, all the time, and I had to make them stop. And I couldn't go back to that place."

He started to speak, but she went on before he could.

"And that wasn't your fault, either. You couldn't have known what it was like."

"I should have. I would have if I'd been a better brother—"

"Oh, Jamie, you were the best thing—the only thing I hated to leave. Never doubt that."

Andrew bowed his head, the lump in his throat too large to permit words to pass. He looked back up at her—at Susannah—and swallowed hard. "I miss you. I'll miss you forever."

"I know. But part of me had already gone, even before I left."

He nodded, mute.

She looked down at their entwined fingers. "I can feel her, you know, this body I'm in," Susannah said. "I can feel some of what she feels. If I concentrate, I think I can almost . . ." Her expression went distant for a moment. She smiled slightly as she came back, her eyes shining with some new emotion. "Oh, Jamie." She reached out and stroked the hair back from his face. "Be happy. There's so much here for you, so many possibilities—things I never would have had." She looked wistful. "I wish I could stay to see it. But I can't, can I?"

"No." Andrew was barely able to get the words out. "You can't."

"It's all right. I think I can go on now. I think I was waiting." Her voice grew fainter. "I had to stay so I could tell you. So proud of you. Love you. More than anything."

40

They were careful with each other the following evening. A door had opened between Amelia and Andrew, and it felt as if neither of them was certain whether to close it or step through.

"There's a woman in four you should talk to," Amelia said when she arrived in his office. "The nurses were talking about her. She's been saying her father will come take her home if they send for him. She's probably not one of ours, but it's worth—"

Amelia broke off and sank back into the chair as footsteps approached. Harcourt leaned around the doorway. He spared her a glance, then turned his attention to Andrew.

"Dr. Cavanaugh, I'm glad you're still here." His tone was polite without being warm. "I wonder if I might beg a favor. I have plans in the city I would hate to cancel, but with Dr. Tyree away and Dr. Klafft still not entirely recovered, we'll be understaffed while I'm gone. Would you be willing to stay a bit later this evening?" He pulled out a handkerchief and muffled a sneeze.

"Are you certain?" Andrew asked. "You seem a bit under the weather yourself."

"Merely a touch of cold."

Andrew sensed Amelia's eyes boring into his back. "Of course." He gestured to the cot still folded against the wall. "It's no trouble for me to stay."

"Oh, you won't have to stay overnight," Harcourt said. "I don't plan to be very late."

"Well, then, certainly, I'll stay," Andrew said.

"Wonderful." A genuine smile stole across Harcourt's face. "Thank you."

Amelia spoke as soon as Harcourt was out of earshot. "I'm going to search his apartment while he's gone." She went on, even as Andrew opened his mouth to object, "It's the only chance we're likely to get. The last chance to find something that could tie him to the deaths."

Andrew considered arguing, but her expression said it would be wasted breath.

Thirty minutes later, Harcourt passed the office door again, flushed, but wearing evening dress and a determined expression of his own.

∞

They waited in silence for the hall to empty. Andrew fidgeted in his chair, and Amelia reached across the desk to give his hand an encouraging squeeze. He raised his head to look at her, and something swelled in her chest as their eyes met. After a long moment, Amelia pulled back and stood.

"It's time."

Andrew nodded, his mouth tight.

Amelia could still feel the warmth of his hand on her palm as she approached Harcourt's apartment. She gave herself a mental shake. She had to focus.

She pulled a hairpin from her pocket and checked the hallway. Clear in both directions. She had the lock open in seconds. Her hand on the knob, she glanced back long enough to see Andrew watching her from his office before she opened the door and stepped through, closing it behind her with a gentle click.

The fading light from the west-facing windows lit the space just enough to make a lamp unnecessary. She stood in a wide room that appeared to be a combination of private study and parlor. On one side was a desk piled high with papers, one small cabinet, and a bookshelf.

On the other, a small, round cabinet sat between a pair of comfortable-looking chairs with matching ottomans. Harcourt's bedroom was visible through the open door behind them.

Amelia took a moment to relock the apartment door. There was no reason to think she would be disturbed, but the sound of a key in the lock would give her a few extra seconds if she was wrong. She took a breath and set to work with all the frustrated energy she'd been unable to expend on the other apartments.

First, the desk. Files upon files. She skimmed them all, but they looked no different than any of the hundreds of patient files she'd seen over the past weeks. There was a stack of admissions documents, none with a date earlier than a month before, and a smaller stack of discharges. None of it was suspicious. She went through all the drawers, looking for hidden compartments, but found nothing.

She turned to the cabinet. It was low, fitted with brass hardware and glass knobs. The left side held supplies—pens, blotters, empty files, blank notepads. The right side was locked. Out came the trusty hairpin, and within a minute she had it open. Amelia blinked at the selection of bottles. Whiskey, cognac, brandy. A double row of wines. All of them expensive, equivalent at least to the best served at the club. A tell, just as with Russo.

She moved on to the bookshelf. Fortunately, Harcourt did not appear to be a voracious reader. Amelia flipped through each volume and checked the backs of the shelves for hidden panels.

She turned to the chairs, though she doubted he would hide anything in that part of the room; no point in keeping one's secrets where any casual guest might happen across them. She was thorough, however, hunting for hidden pockets and checking under cushions. The cabinet between the chairs held a tray of glassware and an empty decanter.

Satisfied she'd missed nothing in the front room, Amelia hurried into the bedroom. She searched the washroom first, finding only the usual assortment of grooming aids and personal items. In an alcove on the back wall was a ladder, similar to the one in the file room beside Andrew's office. She turned her attention to Harcourt's bedroom, the most likely place—indeed the only place remaining—where there might be something worth finding.

Amelia began with the wardrobe. She put a hand into each shoe sitting at the bottom and checked the pockets of all the garments. Nothing except a few crumpled bits of paper. She put them in her pocket. The drawer of the bedside table was similarly unrewarding: tissues, throat drops, a pair of reading glasses missing an arm. She went through the dresser drawers and ran her hands behind the mirror.

She felt behind the headboard and beneath the mattress. She swiped an arm through the narrow space under the bed, scratching her arm on the jagged bottom of a protruding bed spring but finding only dust. Frustrated, Amelia sat back on her heels, her roving gaze scanning the room before coming back to the bed.

The headboard and footboard were solid panels all the way to the floor. The mattress sat low, the space under it no more than a foot high. Nothing very large could fit under there, and she hadn't felt anything. But there was nowhere left to look, short of slitting open the mattress itself. She bent to peer into the dark space.

A shallow metal strongbox sat exactly beneath the center of the bed, just past the reach of her bent arm. Amelia laid down flat on the floor and reached in, taking care this time to avoid the points of the twisted steel springs stippling the underside. Pressing her shoulder hard against the side panel, she was able to hook the tip of one finger around part of the latch. Slowly, she urged it toward her until she could get her hand and wrist around one corner. With a grunt of effort, she dragged it from beneath the bed. It was heavier than she'd anticipated. It also had a stout lock, considerably sturdier than the ones on either the apartment door or the liquor cabinet. She studied it, then spent several precious minutes working on it before it clicked open in her hand.

Amelia's chest buzzed with anticipation as she lifted the lid. She went still, her heartbeat pounding in her ears. Money. More than she'd ever seen in one place in her life, even on the club's busiest nights. Stacks of bills five inches deep, bound and not, wrinkled and crisply new, all denominations. She began to count it but gave up after a few minutes. There were thousands of dollars here.

Got you, she thought.

41

Andrew waited for the better part of an hour. He tried to ignore the acid churning in his gut and pretended to scribble notes on the paper in front of him. Every few minutes, he scanned the hallway and aimed what he hoped looked like a casual glance at Harcourt's door. He'd just completed his most recent check and taken one step back toward his chair when a hacking cough echoed through the hallway.

He froze. Probably an orderly. *Please let it be an orderly.* Or Klafft, out of his room for some reason. With a deliberate movement, Andrew pivoted on his heel and stepped into the doorway again. He clutched the doorjamb as a wave of horror swept over him. Harcourt, his face hectic and his normally smooth hair disarranged, stood at the top of the stairs. The older man was halfway to his office before Andrew tore himself from his stupor and stepped out to meet him. Harcourt didn't pause, forcing Andrew to walk along beside him.

"Dr. Harcourt. I didn't expect you back so soon. I hope nothing is the matter?" Andrew thought his voice sounded almost normal.

They stopped outside the apartment. Harcourt fumbled in his pocket for the key. He paused to muffle a mighty sneeze with his handkerchief, then answered.

"A change of plans, I'm afraid. I've got a splitting headache. I'm sure it's nothing. But I do find myself rather fatigued. I thought it prudent to come back early and try to get a good night's sleep."

Andrew raised his voice as much as he dared, praying Amelia could hear him. "Yes, I'm certain that will help. So sorry to hear you're not well. But I'm sure it's for the best that you've come back early." He aimed the last four words directly at the wooden panel. What would he say if Harcourt found the door unlocked?

Harcourt looked at him strangely. "I'm afraid I must excuse myself. I have some work I really must get to, then I am going to retire. Thank you for staying," he continued, "but please do feel free to go home, if you like. You've missed the seven o'clock, but you'll be able to catch the eight."

"Ah, well, I have a bit more work myself. I'll be here a while yet."

Paralyzed, Andrew watched as Harcourt unlocked the door and walked inside.

42

Jonas slid the last of the boxes back into place and stretched. He grunted as half the joints in his upper body crackled. He'd traded away the day shift he'd been assigned at the asylum and been waiting on the courthouse steps when it opened that morning. It would be closing soon, and he'd spent every moment in between hunched over a rickety table in a cramped room, sorting through mountains of paperwork until his eyes ached.

It was as close as he was willing to come to apologizing for what he'd said to Cavanaugh the night before. It hadn't been incorrect, but it had been unkind.

Jonas settled back into the too-small chair and pulled his notepad closer. One of the clerks fussed with a box on the shelf behind him. He scanned his list and began to write down the names not scored out by black lines. Eight names. Eight women in the past three years who, as far as he could determine, had never been admitted to the asylum but had died there nonetheless.

Jonas shoved his chair back and stood, startling a little squeak from the clerk. Jonas ripped the list from the pad and stuffed it into his pocket. He scraped the remainder of his things into his bag and strode out of the courthouse, where he stood on the steps, blinking in the late-afternoon sun. The day was unseasonably warm for May, but the heavy air couldn't fully drive away the chill his discovery had birthed. But if Amelia was determined to stay on the island, he would do everything in his power to solve this mystery.

Jonas wondered if she even knew why she was doing it. He'd seen the way her face softened when she looked at Cavanaugh. If the circumstances were different—if he hadn't been so damn terrified for her—he would have welcomed it. If Amelia had tender feelings for Cavanaugh, maybe it would make her a little more understanding of his relationship with Sidney.

Jonas shook himself alert. He and Sidney were meant to meet for an early dinner before his shift at the club, but according to the courthouse clock, he had some time yet. A cabdriver hailed him from the street, but Jonas waved him on and started down the sidewalk. Sidney's office wasn't more than a mile away, and the walk would do him good.

Lost in thought, Jonas barely noticed as the city changed around him. The streets nearest the courthouse had been bustling with workers leaving their offices and shops. But the crowds thinned and died away as he crossed into a gritty area dominated by bars and warehouses. In the way of cities, it would give way again in another block to the quiet, elegant street where Sidney worked.

He had just passed the mouth of an alleyway when a footstep scraped on the cobblestones behind him. Jonas tensed, but before he could turn around, something hard prodded him between the shoulder blades.

"Don't move," a nervous voice said.

Chiding himself for his carelessness, Jonas waited for the man to order him to empty his pockets. He didn't bother telling the fellow he had no money; he'd find out for himself in a moment. But instead of a voice demanding his wallet, Jonas heard an unmistakable click as the man drew back the hammer of the pistol pressed to his spine.

He spun with a choked shout. There was a loud crack, and Jonas staggered as a terrible blow struck his arm. He had a fleeting impression of his attacker—a hat pulled low, panicked eyes, and a bizarre plaid handkerchief tied over the lower half of his face like a stagecoach bandit—before his vision grayed at the edges.

The horizon tilted, and the cobblestones rushed up to meet him. The last thing Jonas saw before the world faded was a surprisingly clean hand, the nails neatly trimmed, reaching into his pocket. He was amused by the irony, in a distant, indifferent sort of way. He'd worried for Amelia, but there he was, dying on a city street so a man could have his empty wallet.

43

A melia went still at the sound of muffled voices in the hall. The scrape of the key in the lock, unmistakable even from the next room, made her heart leap into her throat. She thrust the money back into the box and lowered the lid. As she snapped the lock back into place, she hunted in a panic for somewhere to hide. *The wardrobe*—but then imagined coming eye to eye with a startled Harcourt if he should open it. She squelched a hysterical giggle. The washroom was out of the question, but if she could get to the ladder beyond—

Footsteps moved toward the bedroom door.

She was out of time. Amelia flung herself down and, her head to one side and her cheek pressed flat to the floor, slithered into the tiny space beneath the bed. No one larger than she could have fit. Even so, her shoulders hung on the side rail as the footsteps moved closer. She exhaled with a desperate huff and forced her body through the narrow opening, the pointed tips of at least a dozen springs scraping painfully across her upper back and shoulders. She hauled the box into place in front of her as the door opened.

Amelia heard Harcourt enter the room and walk around to the far side of the bed. Shadows leapt across the floor as he lit the lamp. She could not move her head, and she quivered at each footfall on her blind side, each creak of the floorboards. She lay in an agony of suspense, with a paranoid certainty that he somehow knew she was there. Of course he had noticed something out of place in his study, or a drawer not completely shut, or a faint track in the dust on the floor. She would be discovered. Any moment now, a hand would reach into the dark and grab her, would drag her painfully into the lamplight. Instead, silent minutes ticked by.

And then, disaster. Harcourt sat down on the edge of the bed, then lay back with a sigh. The pointed springs dimpling her back stabbed deep. Amelia stifled a scream. Tears leaked from her eyes. She felt a trickle of blood run down the valley of her spine. She squeezed her eyes closed and concentrated on taking short, shallow breaths. Dust tickled her nose and throat. There was no room to lift her cheek from the floor, and the cashbox in front of her upper body meant she couldn't lift a hand from her side to rub the itch away. She fought the urge to sneeze, the knowledge that it would be disastrous only sharpening the need. She lay beneath the bed, hating herself for ever having thought this was a good idea.

After what felt like eons, the crushing weight lifted as Harcourt stood. Amelia had to squelch another sound, this one of relief, as the daggers embedded in her back retracted. The space felt suddenly, blessedly, cavernous. After a time, the lamp went out. She went limp with relief as his footfalls faded, retreating back toward the door.

Her relief was short-lived. The apartment door didn't open. Instead, dim light filtered into the bedroom from the study. She nearly cried. He wasn't leaving. He was reading or doing paperwork, and when he finished . . .

Amelia fought her rising panic and tried to think. If it weren't for the damned springs, she could wait it out. She could stay where she was until he fell asleep. She knew she could move out of the room quietly enough to avoid waking him. But the throbbing in her back, the thought of lying there, skewered like a bug, for god only knew how long, rendered that option distinctly unappealing. She thought again of the little closet with its ladder and hatch.

It was a risk. Would it open at all? If it did, how much noise would it make? With only the washroom door between them, there would be little to dampen the sound. Could she even get there without alerting the currently-very-much-awake man in the next room? The door to the study was open. She would have to move past it. What if he saw her? At best their investigation would be ruined. Andrew's complicity would be discovered. He'd be fired. Amelia would be drugged and tossed into a cell. At worst . . .

If Harcourt were involved in the scheme—and everything she'd seen said he was—there was no limit to what he might be capable of. Julia knew. John Blounton might have found out. She thought about the mother taken from her daughter, and about the young doctor, his poor head smashed and his body in the river. Amelia shuddered, imagining what might happen if she were found, and the movement sent a fresh shiver of pain through her back. Then, with a careful breath, she began to slide from her hiding place.

44

Andrew held his breath as the minutes crept past. How could Amelia have possibly avoided being found? But if she had been caught, there would have been some sort of outcry. Should he knock on the door? Attempt to lure Harcourt from his apartment?

Just as he made up his mind to feign some sort of emergency and call for Harcourt's aid, a muffled thump came from the records room. Andrew nearly jumped out of his skin; then he waited, uncertain. A series of thuds decided him. He closed his office door, then eased open the door to the records room and peered inside. The noises resumed, louder now. Dust drifted down from the access panel in the ceiling.

He climbed the ladder and reached up to push against the panel. It resisted, and then it swung up a few inches with a screech he felt in his teeth. A dirty pair of hands appeared, clutching the edge. There was a grunt, and another screech, and Amelia knelt, looking down at him, her hair wild and her face streaked with grime. He stared at her, then broke into stunned laughter.

She smiled. "Help a lady down?"

She reached out a hand. He took it, and something passed between them at the touch. They gazed at each other for a long moment. Amelia flushed, then seemed to shake herself alert and began to climb down.

He gasped when he saw the back of her dress. "You're bleeding!"

She reached the bottom of the ladder and turned with a grimace. "I know. I had a terrible time making sure I wasn't leaving a trail through the apartment as I left. Is it bad?"

He leaned forward, peering at the holes in her rough asylum dress. "Bad enough. Some of these look deep. You need to let me clean them. What happened?" He led her through to the office and reached for his medical bag, rummaging for gauze and disinfectant as she explained.

"I shouldn't have let you take such a risk," he said.

She scoffed. "You couldn't have stopped me. And besides, think of what we've found. Unless he has a damned good explanation for all that money, it proves Harcourt is involved."

She reached up to smooth her hair, running her fingers through the strands. They curled around her face, brushing along her jawline. Andrew forced himself to look away.

"It seems likely." He stopped, gauze in hand. "Now, you'll need to . . ." He motioned awkwardly to her shirtwaist. He cleared his throat. "I can't clean those wounds until . . ."

"Oh." She went still. Then, slowly, she turned her back to him and began to undo the buttons down the front of her dress.

Andrew held his breath as she opened it to the waist, then pulled her arms from the sleeves and pushed it partway down. She hesitated, then slid her torn shift off her shoulders. Bare from the hips up, she kept her back to him as she glanced over one shoulder.

"Is . . . is that enough?"

He forced himself to meet her eyes, to keep his voice matter-of-fact. He was a doctor tending to a patient, nothing more. "Yes."

She dropped her gaze and stood silently, her head tipped down, tendrils of hair trailing over the slender column of her neck. Below the delicate line of her shoulders, Amelia's back was ravaged, the pale skin marred by scrapes and punctures, some still oozing blood. Something clenched inside Andrew, fierce and protective, at the sight.

He cleared his throat again and tipped the disinfectant onto the gauze pad. "This will sting."

She closed her eyes. Her breath whistled through gritted teeth as the caustic liquid touched the raw flesh. Her head came up, and the line of her jaw hardened. He worked as quickly as he could, gently cleaning the wounds and wiping smears of drying blood from her skin. When he'd finished, he capped the bottle and set it down.

"There." He didn't step away, and she made no move to cover herself. The silence stretched, heavier with each passing moment.

Andrew watched the rise and fall of her back as she breathed. Without even deciding to do it, he reached forward and trailed one finger down the nape of her neck and along the crest of one shoulder. Her skin was warm and vital beneath his own.

She gasped at the touch and went still. Her head tipped forward. He stepped toward her, feeling as though he were in a dream.

The rap of knuckles on the office door sounded as loud as a gunshot.

They leapt apart. Amelia grabbed at her dress and pressed it against her chest. She looked at him, her cheeks flushed.

Hardly any more composed, Andrew put a shaking finger to his lips, then he called out, "What is it?"

A voice replied through the closed door. "There's a man on the telephone for you, Dr. Cavanaugh. He says it's important. He says he won't leave a message, that he must speak directly to you."

After a pause, Andrew replied, "Very well. I'll be along in a moment."

⁓

Andrew turned back to her after dismissing the messenger, but Amelia didn't give him an opportunity to speak. She held up her dress with one arm and retreated into the storage room. She heard him leave as she shrugged back into the top of her dress and buttoned the bodice with trembling fingers.

Her blood was still singing in her veins. Amelia caught herself staring at the folded cot beside the wall and wrenched her eyes away from it as heat flooded her face. She pressed her palms to her cheeks and tried to ignore the other, lower heat blooming in her body.

Her back stung. She focused on it, thankful for the distraction. She wished there was a mirror. She must look a fright. Amelia combed her hair with her fingers, then realized what she was doing and, irritated with herself, forced her hands to her sides.

Amelia took a deep breath and tried to steady herself. Andrew would be back soon, and she must behave normally. She would not let what had just happened affect her. And, she told herself, nothing had actually happened. And nothing would have happened. If that knock on the door had not come, it was not as though they would have—

Amelia yanked her eyes away from the cot again as she heard the office door open. She steeled herself and stepped from the storage room, her head down, pretending to fuss with the buttons.

"Amelia."

She looked up at his tone—more serious than she'd ever heard him. His face was solemn.

Dread thudded into the bottom of her stomach like a lead weight. "What is it?"

"It's Jonas."

45

S hot," Amelia repeated. Her voice was flat, and her face had gone white. Andrew strode past her into the storage room and flung open the drawer where he'd hidden the clothes Jonas had brought. He turned and thrust the garments into her hands.

"Put these on. Hurry."

She didn't move, staring at the clothing as if unable to comprehend its purpose.

He took her by the elbow and tugged her toward the storage room. "You have to change. We're leaving. Now."

Andrew had made up his mind even as he turned away from the telephone. The voice on the other end hadn't given him a great deal of information, but if the situation was as dire as it seemed, there was a real chance Jonas would die. Andrew knew all too well how it felt not to get the chance to say goodbye. Amelia had delivered him from it. He would move the heavens to keep her from knowing such regret.

She looked at him, her expression lost. "Leaving? But what about—"

He was still holding her elbow, and now he shook it. "There's no time. If you want to see Jonas before—" He cut himself off, but understanding filled her face, followed by dread. She pulled away from him and hurried into the storage room.

As he waited for Amelia to emerge, Andrew donned his own coat and picked up his hat, resolutely ignoring the frantic voice clamoring at the back of his mind. There were a dozen different ways the next quarter of an hour could go wrong. Even if her disguise was convincing—and he had his doubts about that—there weren't supposed to be any adolescent boys in the asylum. If they were seen, they would need an explanation.

And if they managed to make it off the island, he'd be left with an even larger problem: Amelia's absence would be discovered. The fever had delayed the reconciliation, but sometime soon—within the next two days, at most—there would be a head count. A missing patient would cause an uproar.

Andrew turned as the storage room door creaked, and his jaw dropped.

If he hadn't known it was Amelia standing before him, he would never have guessed. His eyes jumped from feature to feature, unable to take in the whole of the transformation at once. Corded trousers hung in a straight line from her waist to her ankles. In concert with her worn, patched shirt and lumpy jacket, no trace of her figure was visible. Heavy shoes gave her the oversize feet of a boy not yet come into his full growth.

But it was her face that was most arresting. She'd parted her ragged hair and slicked it down behind her ears, somehow making them look as though they stuck out from her head, though he'd never noticed any such tendency before. She'd done something to her eyebrows to make them thicker and straighter. Her smooth complexion was now roughened and bumpy. On the whole, she looked slightly dirty and wholly unfeminine. She twisted a cap in her hands beneath his wide-eyed stare, then put it on and tugged the brim down so it shadowed her eyes.

Andrew cleared his throat. "Come on."

He poked his head into the hallway and looked in both directions. Empty. He beckoned to Amelia, and she slipped past him into the corridor, headed for the stairs with a boyish saunter. She really had done this before.

He was about to step after her when he pulled up short. He had forgotten his medical bag. He ducked back in for it and was in the doorway again when the unmistakable sound of Mrs. Brennan's voice came from around the corner behind him.

It was a curious sensation, feeling his heart both leap into his throat and sink into his feet in the same instant.

Amelia heard it, too, freezing where she stood and looking back at him with a desperate expression.

He made a sharp shooing motion. She scurried for the stairs. Andrew turned away from her as Mrs. Brennan rounded the corner. She slowed, scowling as she saw him.

"Ah, Mrs. Brennan," Andrew said, his mind racing. "I was coming to look for you. I'm leaving for the evening, but I have several assignments I'll need you to complete before I arrive tomorrow."

Her eyebrows shot up. Since Harcourt had scolded him for his treatment of her, Andrew had avoided the nursing matron as much as possible, and he certainly hadn't presumed to give her orders. Well, in for a penny, in for a pound, as they said. His heart thudding, with no time to compose a suitable list of tasks, Andrew rapped out a random list of demands as quickly as he could think of them, using the most peremptory, entitled tone he could muster.

Mrs. Brennan's face was a thundercloud when he finished. She stood staring at him, breathing heavily. Andrew half expected her to box his ears for his effrontery.

Before she could move, he snapped, "Well? You've a great deal to do. Best be about it."

She flushed a dark red, and her mouth worked as if she would make some reply. Andrew drew himself up and gave her his most contemptuous look. She glared at him, thenspun on her heel and stomped back the way she'd come, muttering under her breath.

Andrew sagged against the doorframe, limp with relief. Good god, had he really just ordered the asylum's nursing matron to complete an inventory of the bedpans in the infirmary? No doubt she would complain to Harcourt at the first opportunity. He grimaced. It was a problem for later.

He hurried to catch up to Amelia, expecting she would be already out the front door. To his horror, however, she stood outside the main office, face-to-face with Winslow in the otherwise empty hall. The young clerk had seized her by the arm, and she stood slumped, her face angled toward the floor, as he harangued her.

"You certainly never signed in at the office! We do not allow visitors to simply wander about. You will tell me what you are doing here at once, boy, or—"

Andrew eased closer, desperately trying to decide what to do. He could claim Amelia had come to bring him a message, but that would connect Andrew to the unknown "boy" in Winslow's mind. That outcome seemed better avoided. Besides, after his encounter with Mrs. Brennan, Andrew was not certain he was up to further adventures in verbal improvisation. He had to do something, however. Winslow was angry and inattentive, but at any moment he might see through Amelia's disguise. Everything would be ruined.

Sweat prickled beneath Andrew's arms. His chest felt as though it were in a vise. Winslow still hadn't seen him, absorbed as he was in ferreting out how this breach of procedure had occurred. Andrew was two long steps behind the young man when Amelia's eyes flickered up from the floor and met his over Winslow's shoulder.

Winslow caught the movement and began to turn.

Quick as a flash, Andrew covered the distance between them and, without stopping to think, snaked his right arm around the younger man's throat. Even in his haste, Andrew was careful to keep his arm bent in a V and the elbow pointed down as he locked the hold with his left hand over his right fist. Getting it wrong could kill the young man, which was the last thing he wanted.

Taken utterly by surprise, Winslow barely had time to struggle. He flailed for only a moment before he began to go limp. Andrew eased him to the floor, already reaching into his own jacket pocket. His heart raced. They had only seconds before Winslow would begin to wake. Where was it? His hand closed over the hard rubber tube containing the syringe of chloral hydrate.

"What did you do?" Amelia's voice was full of horrified awe.

Kneeling over Winslow, Andrew glanced up at her astonished face. "That hold compresses the carotid arteries without crushing the windpipe." He looked down and flipped the cap off the tube. Shook the syringe into his hand. "It interrupts the blood flow to the brain, causing the victim to rapidly lose consciousness. It's dangerous, though. If you hold it too long, it can be fatal."

Winslow, however, was already beginning to stir. Andrew located a vein at the back of his neck and plunged the needle in. The syringe contained enough chloral hydrate to knock out the largest patient in the asylum in the midst of a violent episode, so he injected only a third of the dose.

Andrew dropped the syringe back into the tube and returned it to his pocket. He glanced around. They were still alone. He sagged in relief. But they weren't free yet. He grabbed Winslow beneath the arms and began to drag him behind his desk. Amelia took his ankles.

"How did you know how to do that?" she asked, panting slightly.

They curled the young man's limp form where he wouldn't be visible from the hallway.

"I'm a doctor." Andrew flashed her a quick smile. "Also, I used to wrestle in college. Young men that age try all sorts of stupid things. That one happens to be useful."

"You'll have to show Jonas how to do it," Amelia said. "He'll . . ." Her face went tight as she remembered. "We have to go."

They hurried out the front door without further incident.

They were halfway to the ferry when Andrew's misgivings began to get the better of him. He'd done the choke correctly. Winslow had been breathing easily and beginning to regain consciousness when Andrew injected him. And based on his weight, the chloral dose he'd taken shouldn't cause any problems. He would wake confused and groggy, perhaps even without much memory of what had occurred.

But out of sight as he was, it was possible no one would find him for hours. It was also possible that the combination of the hold and the drug could have some unanticipated effect. If it did, if Winslow were seriously harmed, it would be Andrew's fault. He liked the young clerk. Wouldn't it be better if Andrew were to "find" him on his way out for the evening and try to rouse him? He could monitor his condition and perhaps even plant the suggestion that Winslow had merely fainted—perhaps he was coming down, like Harcourt, with a trailing case of the fever that had so ravaged the asylum.

Andrew skidded to a stop under the branches of the oak tree as the ferry's warning whistle pierced the air. He shouldn't let the ferryman see them together, either. It would be safest for Amelia to go alone from here. He explained as quickly as he could, and Amelia nodded as if she understood, though in her haste to be away he wasn't certain she was hearing everything he said.

Andrew squeezed her hand once in farewell and remained in the shadows as Amelia picked her way down the remainder of the path to the dock, never looking back. He held his breath as she stepped onto the ferry. Surely the ferryman would question a lone boy boarding from the asylum dock. But whether he was eager to keep to his schedule or merely counted his passenger's business as none of his own, the man said nothing, casting off at once and turning the craft for shore.

Andrew watched until Amelia's silhouette disappeared into the darkness. He'd done it. She was free. He turned and started back toward the dark bulk of the asylum, knowing his own task was now far more difficult—and far more urgent. Despite his precautions, Amelia's absence *would* be discovered, and it would likely be traced to him. She was known to be one of his patients.

Andrew was almost out of time. He had, at most, a few days to expose the truth of what was happening at the asylum. And now he would have to do it alone.

46

The city docks bustled with activity despite the hour. Amelia took a deep breath, dizzy at her first sight of the world outside the island in months. The air around her was close with the scents of smoke and sweat and river mud. She still felt as though she were in a vivid dream, expecting any moment to wake in her cell and find that the last hour had never happened.

She stepped off the ferry and strode into the crowd, shouldering her way through without apology. She was nearing the sidewalk when a hand reached out and took a firm hold on her elbow. Amelia whipped her head around and looked up into the face of a young man for a confused instant before fury bloomed in her chest.

She yanked away. "Let go of me this—"

"Miss Matthew?" he interrupted, some uncertainty on his face. "I was told to expect—you are Miss Amelia Matthew, are you not?" He went on at her guarded nod. "I've been sent to fetch you. Please, come with me."

"Who are you?" she demanded, as he urged her toward a cab waiting at the curb. "I'm not getting in there." She tried to pull away. "Bellevue is only a few blocks from here. It will be faster to walk."

"Mr. Vincent isn't at Bellevue. Didn't Dr. Cavanaugh give you the message? I know Mr. White told him—"

"Who?"

"Mr. White," he repeated. She must have looked confused. "Mr. Sidney White? I believe he is a friend of your brother's? I heard him tell Dr. Cavanaugh I would be waiting for you. Did he not relay the message?"

He may have done. But with the shock of hearing that Jonas had been shot, and the subsequent drama of her escape, it was entirely possible she'd missed some details.

It didn't matter now.

They reached the cab, and Amelia allowed the man to hand her in. He said something to the driver and climbed in after her. As the door swung closed behind him, the air of unreality vanished, and Amelia was abruptly aware of being alone in a cab with a strange man, who'd just ordered the driver to take them . . . somewhere.

She took a deep breath and tried to focus.

"Who are you?" she asked again. "Where is Jonas?"

"My name is David Morris." He settled back into his seat. "I am Mr. White's law clerk and assistant. I was told to meet you at the dock and bring you to Mr. Vincent."

She looked him over. He was perhaps twenty-five, with dark hair and patchy side whiskers. He wore a sedate but well-cut suit, although it was rumpled. Dried blood stained the cuffs of his shirt.

Amelia swallowed. "I don't understand. What happened? How did Sidney get involved? I thought Jonas was shot?"

"It happened not far from our offices. Mr. White and I heard the shot, in fact, and went outside to see what had happened. The authorities arrived quickly, but the perpetrators were already gone. I'm given to understand no one saw anything, even though it's such a busy street, you wouldn't think it possible. I don't know what this city is coming to. Gunfire in broad daylight, and—"

"Jonas?" Amelia prodded.

"Oh. Pardon me. When he realized it was Mr. Vincent who had been injured, Mr. White stepped in. Several bystanders had already come to his aid, and one of them put a tourniquet on, but—"

"A tourniquet?"

"Yes. Apparently the shot hit Mr. Vincent in the upper arm, and he was bleeding quite heavily. Mr. White knew he would need further attention, so he made the arrangements and sent me to fetch you."

"What arrangements? Where is he? Which hospital, if not Bellevue?"

"Mr. Vincent isn't in a hospital," Morris said, as if speaking to a child. "Mr. White wanted to make sure his care was of the highest quality, and hospitals," he said with a little grimace of distaste, "are nothing but pits of infection. Mr. White sent for his own physician. And he wanted Mr. Vincent to have more comfortable surroundings."

"How is he?"

The young man did not immediately answer, and Amelia's heart stuttered.

"The doctor had only just arrived when I left to fetch you."

"Was he awake?"

"No."

At this, Amelia fell silent. The blocks passed as they rode north. The electric streetlights in this part of town were brighter than the more familiar gas. Their harsh white light threw dark shadows over the faces of the people on the sidewalk, hollowing their eyes into the empty sockets of skulls. She turned away from the window and scrubbed at the makeup on her face. The drive was taking too long. If Jonas were at Bellevue, she would be with him by now. Damn Sidney and his high-handedness. It was so typical of men like him to—

The cab jerked to a stop. Morris glanced out.

"We're here."

He stepped down and offered a hand up to Amelia.

She climbed down and gaped in confusion at the massive limestone before her.

The twelve-story Hotel Savoy had opened less than a year before to great fanfare. Amelia had not been inside, but one of the club's wealthier patrons had rented the ballroom for his daughter's society debut. He'd pretended to complain about the expense, but they all saw how much he relished describing the colored marble columns, the intricately painted ceilings, and the silk carpets.

Morris took her elbow and led her up the steps to the heavy bronze-covered doors. A pair of doormen, wearing striped coats dripping with gold braid, eyed her as she approached, but they swung the doors open on noiseless hinges at a nod from Morris.

"The firm retains a suite here for important guests, or for when one of the partners visits from another branch," Morris explained. "It's empty at the moment, and near the physician's office, so Mr. White had Mr. Vincent brought here."

Worried as she was, Amelia still found herself wide-eyed and curious as Morris guided her through the lobby. Electric lights shone down from fixtures of filigreed silver, many dotted with gemstones. Amelia attracted no few stares herself, in her ragged urchin's garb. She eyed the steam-powered elevator with mistrust but stepped in, too proud to admit this was the first time she'd ever ridden in such a contraption. The operator nodded to Morris as he closed the door and began the ascent. Amelia's stomach dropped as the car rose, and she thought perhaps she preferred stairs, though this was doubtless faster. After what felt like an endless ride, the car slid to a stop. The doors opened to reveal a lushly carpeted hall.

Morris gestured for her to step out ahead of him and led her to a wide, polished door. He fumbled with a key and opened it. Amelia stepped into a foyer larger than her apartment. A young man appeared at the other end. It took Amelia a moment to realize it was Sidney. He was in his shirtsleeves. His cuffs were bloodier than Morris's.

Amelia darted toward him. "What happened? Where is he? Why did you—"

Sidney put a hand on her arm. She shook it off and all but pounced on him in her anxiety. He gave her a level look and turned to the clerk.

"Thank you for your help this evening, Morris. You handled everything beautifully, as usual."

"Will you need me for anything else, sir?"

"No, thank you. You may go."

"Very well. Good night." The man nodded at Amelia and withdrew, closing the door softly behind him.

As the latch clicked closed, Sidney slumped, and the careful neutrality of his face cracked to reveal the worry beneath. He turned and walked into an enormous sitting room, Amelia close on his heels.

"He's in there." Sidney gestured to a closed door on the far wall, one of a pair. "You may as well wait out here. The doctor tossed me out. I doubt he'll let you stay."

She cast a frustrated look at the closed door, then turned back to the man. "What happened?"

"I don't know precisely. It was already over when I got there. Apparently someone tried to rob him on the street near my office." He sat down on the end of an enormous velvet couch and rested his head in his hands.

"How bad is it?"

He hesitated, then looked up at her. "I don't know. It's his right arm, so one would think it shouldn't be so dangerous. But there was so much blood. Someone had tied on a tourniquet, or perhaps he did it himself somehow. When I saw him, I thought—" Sidney stopped to gather himself. "I had him brought here. Then I sent Morris to fetch you."

Amelia shucked off the boy's cap and jacket and perched on the edge of the couch. "Does he know? Morris? About you and—"

"No."

They sat, waiting.

Amelia finally broke the awkward silence. "Thank you for taking care of him."

"Of course I did." His voice was tight.

The silence descended again, as strained as before.

They both leapt up as the bedroom door opened. A silver-haired man stepped out, rolling down the cuffs of his shirt.

"How is he?" Sidney asked.

Amelia didn't stay to hear the answer. She brushed past both men and into the room.

Jonas lay unconscious on the wide bed, the linens as snowy white as the bandage on his arm and only barely whiter than his skin. He was so dreadfully pale.

She sat down on the edge of the bed by his uninjured side and took his limp hand in both of her own.

The doctor spoke from the doorway. "You're the sister, I take it?"

"Yes." She ignored the skeptical note in his voice. "He'll be all right, won't he?"

"He's alive, for now," the physician said. "I've stitched him up. The bleeding's stopped, but he's lost as much blood as a man can and still have any chance of surviving. Bullet went right through, but it tore the muscle and nicked the big vein in his arm. Damned good thing someone got that tourniquet on when they did, or he'd never have made it this long. But it's too bad they couldn't have used a clean cloth while they were at it. I've disinfected it as well as I could, but the bullet pushed bits of his coat and shirt into the wound, and with that dirty cloth over it. . . ."

"He's strong," Amelia said.

"He *was* strong," the doctor corrected. "If he hadn't lost so much blood, I'd say he'd have a good chance of throwing off any infection. As it is, we'll have to wait and see."

"But he might not get an infection at all," she argued, furious with the man for his matter-of-fact tone.

"You didn't see that filthy rag on his arm." At her stricken look, he softened. "You'll need to be prepared," he said gently.

He turned to Sidney, who stood behind him. "I'll come back in the morning. He's unlikely to wake, but if he does, he'll be in pain." He handed over a small bottle. "He needs to be kept still or he'll tear that vein open again. If he does, he won't last long enough to get it closed a second time. You can give him three drops of this in a bit of water every six hours. No more than that, mind you." He looked between Sidney and Amelia until they both nodded. "He's lost too much blood to tolerate a heavier dose."

He focused on Sidney again. "He'll be staying here? He shouldn't be moved in his condition."

"Yes," Sidney said. "He'll be staying here as long as he needs. Thank you for coming so quickly. Please send your bill to my attention. I'll handle it personally."

They stepped out of the doorway, and their voices faded as Sidney, presumably, showed the doctor to the door. The room went quiet, the ticking of the clock on the wall the only sound.

Amelia sat beside Jonas, her stomach knotted and her eyes locked on his still face. The doctor was wrong. He didn't know Jonas, didn't know how hard he was capable of fighting. She did. He would be all right. She tightened her grip on his hand. He had to be.

Sidney returned, drew a chair to the other side of the bed, and sat down across from her. He didn't speak.

Amelia studied him from the corner of her eye. She'd seen him from a distance at the club several times, but this was the first chance she'd had to take his measure up close.

He was utterly ordinary.

He was of moderate height and slight build. His hair was an indeterminate color, neither blond nor brown. His features were regular, but neither particularly handsome nor interesting.

She caught him looking at her and had the distinct impression that he was evaluating her, even as she evaluated him. She fixed her eyes back on Jonas.

"Thank you for looking after him," Amelia said again. "But you don't have to stay."

Something flickered behind Sidney's eyes as he looked at her. A muscle in his jaw twitched, as if he were biting down on what he'd intended to say. "How thoughtful. But I believe I will stay." His tone was carefully neutral.

The clock ticked. Five seconds. Ten.

Amelia tried again. "Really, it's not necessary for you—"

Sidney sat abruptly forward, his mild demeanor going fierce. "Are you truly that selfish?"

Amelia's jaw dropped.

"It took me a while to realize," he went on. "Jonas was very smooth about why you and I hadn't met. But I finally understood. You didn't want to meet me. You hated the very idea of me. The idea that there could be something in Jonas's life that wasn't you. Are you so desperate to keep him to yourself that you can't even let me share this?"

Amelia sucked in a quick breath. "How dare you? You don't know anything about me." The words were a hiss.

"I know more than you think." Sidney's voice was no louder than hers but just as intense. "He's spent his whole life taking care of you, and you've let him. Did it never occur to you that he deserves more?"

"I knew it," she said, half rising. "I knew you were the one putting those ideas in his head."

"What ideas? That he could do more with his life than flirt and toss drunks into the street?"

"We like working at the club, and—"

"'We'?" Sidney's tone was incredulous. "You haven't been there in months. Do you have any idea what it's been like for him? He's worn himself ragged trying to solve this puzzle and get you out. He's about an inch away from getting fired from the club and evicted from your apartment, and—" Sidney stopped, evidently noticing her surprise. "He didn't tell you."

All Amelia could do was shake her head.

"Of course he didn't." Sidney sighed, and the anger seemed to drain out of him. He leaned back in his chair, his distress and fear visible once again. He looked to Jonas, and his face softened. "He's brilliant and charismatic, and he could do anything he wanted. But he's never been free to try, because he's made looking after you his whole world. I wanted to show him more of it."

"Like Paris?" Amelia asked. She meant to make the words sharp, but the rapid-fire shocks of the past few minutes—the past few hours, really—seemed to be catching up to her. She sank back into her chair, abruptly too tired and numb to summon further anger.

"Yes," Sidney said. "Like Paris. I invited him to go with me. It was only a few weeks. I thought he would enjoy it, and I wanted to spend some time with him away from New York, somewhere we wouldn't have to be so careful. It's hard, you know, to have to hide from everyone all the time."

Amelia could think of nothing to say to that, and they lapsed into heavy silence. She fidgeted in her chair. The back of her shirt felt damp. Some of the clotted wounds on her back must have opened again. Jonas didn't stir.

Sidney surprised her by standing and leaving the room, returning with two glasses. He handed her one and sat back down.

Amelia sniffed at the contents. Brandy. She swallowed half of it in a gulp. The warmth pooled in her belly.

"I don't want to take him away from you," Sidney said in a subdued tone. "I wouldn't, even if I could. You're his family. I understand that. But we both heard what the doctor said." His voice hardened. "I'm not leaving him."

47

Hours passed. Sidney called down for a pot of coffee, and the two of them sat without speaking. At first, the atmosphere was distinctly uncomfortable, punctuated by sharp, restrained glances and tightened lips. But it was impossible to maintain the tension as the night wore on. Amelia tilted her head back against the chair and lapsed into the kind of fuzzy, disjointed thoughts that come with extraordinary fatigue. The things Sidney had said flitted through her mind, but she refused to let them linger. They weren't worth considering. He was wrong.

It was well after midnight when Jonas stirred. Amelia, drowsing on the chair by the bed, jerked awake at the movement. Sidney leaned forward.

"Jonas, I'm here," she said. "Don't try to move."

"'Melia," he mumbled, his eyes still closed.

She leaned in and put her hand to his forehead, relieved to find it cool and dry. "Could you take some water, some broth?"

He made a weak pushing gesture with his uninjured arm, then dropped it back to the bed as if the movement had been too much.

"Mmm 'ockt."

"What?" she said, mystified.

"M' pocket," he tried again. "List. Names."

Understanding dawned. "You made a list? You think you found some of the women?"

He made a sound that might have been agreement.

"That doesn't matter now."

He grunted, frowning, and shifted on the mattress.

"Stay still," she soothed. "I'll look, I promise. But you need to rest. Sidney's here," she said after a moment, looking up at him.

Something that might have been a smile flickered across Jonas's mouth before fading away. Amelia stood and stepped back as Sidney slid into the chair she'd vacated and took Jonas's hand.

"Where are his clothes?" she asked. "The ones he was wearing when you found him?"

Sidney gestured into the other room without turning from Jonas. "In a sack beside the table." He seemed to forget she was there as soon as he'd stopped speaking.

Amelia went into the other room. The sack was where he'd indicated, and Jonas's bag sat beside it. Amelia sat and pulled each item from the sack in turn. Already sober, she went positively grim. The shirt was stiff with dried blood. The sleeve and front of the thicker jacket he'd been wearing were mostly saturated and still wet in places. Her heart lurched. How much blood could be left in Jonas's body, with this much soaking his clothes?

She steadied herself with a breath and felt through all the pockets. There was no list. She frowned. Perhaps he'd put it in the bag. She spread the contents out on the table. His pocketknife; his watch, the face cracked—it must have happened when he fell; a few coins; a magazine folded in half; his wallet, stuffed with notes and reminders; a single ragged calling card, the name illegible; a blank notepad; a stubby pencil with the marks of his teeth.

She felt through the clothes again, making sure she hadn't missed something. She looked at all the papers again, then scrutinized the magazine. Perhaps he'd written in the margins? She teased apart the pages, looking for Jonas's familiar scrawl. Nothing. She stuffed the ruined clothing back into the sack, then sat back on her heels.

There was a soft knock at the door, and Sidney came out of the bedroom. "I called for broth, and more coffee."

He opened the door to a uniformed waiter, who swiftly stepped inside and deposited the tray on a table. Sidney handed him what must have been a sizable tip, judging from the way the man's eyes widened, and closed the door behind him.

Sidney picked up the pot of broth. "Help yourself if you'd like the coffee," he said over his shoulder as he went back to Jonas.

Amelia poured herself a cup and sat, brooding, until he came back out.

"He took most of the broth. I gave him the three drops of laudanum the doctor allowed. He's out again." Sidney sat down opposite Amelia. "The list. Did you find it?"

"No. It's not here."

He looked at the things spread across the tabletop and frowned. "But his watch and wallet are. If it was a robbery, the thief would have taken those."

"Yes. He would have."

"It wasn't a robbery, then."

"No. Someone knows."

48

Breakfast was being served when Andrew checked Winslow's pulse one final time, then stood and patted the sleeping clerk on the shoulder.

"Call me when he wakes—I'd guess it will be a few hours longer," he told the nurse as he exited the infirmary. "He doesn't have a fever. It could just be a case of overwork. I believe once he's had some rest, he'll be fine."

The main hall had still been deserted when Andrew returned after seeing Amelia onto the ferry. He'd mounted the stairs to the second floor, halfway expecting to see a panicked scrum of people outside the main office. But there had been no one. Winslow had been curled like a comma and snoring peacefully behind the desk, precisely where they'd left him. Andrew had checked his pulse—strong and steady—and tried to decide how to handle the next bit. He'd settled on stepping into the hallway and shouting for help.

The nurse and a trio of orderlies who'd arrived moments later found Andrew kneeling beside the unconscious Winslow, slapping the young man's cheeks and loosening his collar.

"He's fainted." Andrew hadn't had to try to look anxious. "Help me get him up to the infirmary."

By the time they'd hauled the young man to the infirmary and laid him on a cot, he'd begun to come around. Andrew had shooed the rest of the staff away in case the clerk began relating the story of the strange young man he'd accosted in the halls just before someone assaulted him. Fortunately, Winslow had seemed more drowsy and confused than anything else.

"I'm going to give you a small dose of chloral to help you rest," Andrew had told him, squirting a pair of drops into a glass of water. That amount wouldn't have any additional effect, but it would cover up the administration of the earlier dose and explain why the clerk was sleeping. "It might give you strange dreams," he'd added. Hopefully, if Winslow remembered anything when he woke, he would put it down to the drug. Winslow had drunk the water without complaint and was asleep again before Andrew set down the empty glass.

Andrew had checked on him throughout the night, taking his pulse and avoiding the basilisk stare of Mrs. Brennan, who stood over a white-faced nurse as she counted bedpans.

Now, certain that Winslow would be fine, Andrew made his way back to his office, then closed the door behind him and sank into his chair. He massaged his face with his hands, still unable to quite believe what he'd done. He'd assaulted a colleague. Amelia was off the island without any plausible cover story. His own role in both incidents could be revealed at any moment.

He sat up straighter at the thought. He had work to do before that happened. He pushed himself to his feet, wrinkling his nose at the rank smell of dried fear-sweat wafting from his clothes. Andrew unbuttoned his shirt as he walked into the storage room and opened the drawer for a fresh one. Amelia's asylum dress was wadded up inside, the rips and bloodstains visible. He'd have to get rid of it.

He slid his arms into the new shirt, wondering how Jonas was faring and regretting anew not being able to go with Amelia. He frowned, realizing he didn't know where she was. The man who called him yesterday evening—had it been only yesterday?—had said someone would meet Amelia at the docks, but Andrew hadn't thought to ask where Jonas was. He set the matter aside; she would send word eventually.

He pulled open the "deaths" drawer. The answers were here. He just had to find them. Now.

49

Amelia and Sidney maintained their unspoken détente throughout the morning. Along with lunch, the bellman brought a basket, which Sidney handed to Amelia. Inside was a complete change of women's clothing, including shoes.

"I thought you might like to bathe and dress." Sidney indicated the door to the suite's bathroom.

Amelia was not certain which idea she disliked more—accepting the gift, or continuing to wear her grimy boy's attire. "Thank you."

Her qualms disappeared once she was in the bathroom, with its large enameled tub and hot water on tap. The shirt stuck to the clotted wounds on her back, and Amelia gingerly peeled it away with a series of little tearing sounds. She kicked the clothes into the corner, stepped into the tub, and sighed as she sank into the warm water. She scrubbed the remnants of the makeup from her face, then took a breath and submerged to wash her filthy hair.

Twenty minutes later, clean and dressed, she emerged from the bathroom feeling more like herself than she had in months, despite her fatigue and worry.

Amelia spent the rest of the day sitting beside Jonas as he slept. She was alert to every change in his breathing, every twitch of his face. He felt warm, but the doctor, when he came, said it was normal. To be expected.

"He's not to the crisis yet. When he's hot and dry to the touch. When his breathing goes shallow and fast, or he wakes up out of his head. When that happens—"

"You don't know it will happen. It might not," she insisted.

The doctor ignored the interruption. "Keep giving him water or broth as he'll take it, and keep him still. Use the drops I left for him." He paused. "And if you have other family, you should send for them."

He said the last kindly. Amelia hated him for it.

Sidney dozed on the sofa. Asleep, he looked like a boy.

He woke when the bellman brought dinner, and, hungry and stiff, Amelia watched from the bedroom door as he sank into the chair beside the bed. Sidney leaned forward and stroked a lock of hair off Jonas's still face. There was such tenderness in the touch. Amelia understood with a sudden, bittersweet clarity that Jonas—the only person who had ever been entirely hers—was no longer hers alone.

Sidney shook her awake sometime after midnight, his face white with terror. "He's burning up." He didn't wait for her.

Amelia flung back the blanket and hurried after him.

One look at Jonas, and dread flooded through her. He looked ghastly. His dry lips were cracked. Heat radiated from him. She put her hand to his cheek, closed her eyes, and swallowed a sob. He mumbled and twitched. A damp cloth fell from his forehead. Sidney reached past her to pick it up. She watched, numb, as he dipped it into a basin, wrung it out, and replaced it. Jonas stilled for a moment before the muttering and tossing started again.

"I had them bring up some ice." Sidney's voice was listless. "I don't think it's helping."

The doctor came after what seemed like hours. He took one look and sighed in resignation. He unwrapped the bandage on Jonas's arm. The wound was angry and inflamed. Red streaks ran up toward the shoulder and down past the elbow.

He looked at Amelia. "That arm is poisoning him. I'd take it off, if I thought there was any chance he'd survive the surgery." His gaze widened to take in Sidney, standing in the doorway, his face under rigid control. "There's nothing I can do."

"Can't you clean it again? Do something to kill some of the infection?" Amelia heard the desperate note in her own voice.

"It's in his blood. I've seen men survive blood poisoning, but . . ." He looked away. "The longer he holds on, the better his chances. I'll come back this evening if— Well, you let me know. Watch the streaks," he advised. "When they've grown past the shoulder, if you have much laudanum left, it might be kinder to give him all of it."

The doctor showed himself out. Sidney and Amelia stared hollow-eyed at each other in the thunderous silence he left in his wake.

The hours passed. Jonas's fever climbed. Sidney sent for more ice. They wrapped it in cloths and packed it beneath Jonas's arms, behind his neck, in the hollows of his knees. They trickled cold water into his mouth.

Amelia sat with Jonas's hand clasped in both of hers. Each time his chest fell, she willed it to rise again. She watched the red streaks on his arm and thought she could see them growing.

She and Sidney moved in concert and spoke to each other in quiet monosyllables, as if afraid their voices would draw the attention of the shadow hovering over them. When Jonas began to shudder with chills, they called for warming pans and piled the bed high with blankets. Still his teeth chattered and his body shook. They worried his thrashing would tire him further, worried it would tear open the wound and they would watch him bleed to death before the fever could kill him.

At some point during those several desperate, uncounted hours, Amelia's bladder finally forced her from the room. She returned to find Sidney lying on the bed, around Jonas and holding him still with one arm over his chest. Jonas quieted at the contact, and after that, they took turns, trading off an hour at a time in silent agreement, neither wishing to relinquish their place by Jonas's side but each tacitly acknowledging the other's right.

Jonas did not wake.

The sun sank low in the sky. Sunday dawned. Drew bright. Waned.

They kept their vigil. Amelia must have eaten, must have attended to her body's needs, but none of it mattered. Nothing mattered except trying not to drown in the swelling fear she felt at Jonas's every rasping breath.

That night, his breathing grew shallow and fast, and Amelia's terror began to slip free of its moorings. Neither she nor Sidney dared leave the room. While one huddled with Jonas on the bed, the other moved only as far as the chair beside it. Sidney sat with his elbows on his knees, his face buried in his hands. When it was Amelia's turn, she curled miserably with her feet tucked beneath her and her eyes fastened on Jonas's face. They waited. It was the longest night of her life—longer than any she'd spent in the asylum, longer than any night on the streets after they'd left the Foundling.

The doctor came at dawn. He examined Jonas, then sat with his back to the window at the sitting room table, where Jonas's things still lay scattered. Amelia toyed with the pencil stub, her fingers running over the divots Jonas's teeth had made in the wood. She watched the doctor's lips move, but the words didn't seem to reach her until long after he'd spoken them. She understood well enough, nonetheless. He could offer them no hope. Sometime within the next few hours, the fever would burn away the last of Jonas's strength, and his life would gutter out like a candle flame.

Amelia stayed where she was as Sidney showed the doctor out and went back to Jonas. The early-morning sun shone through the thin curtain, casting a ray of pale light across the table. Jonas would die. No matter how many times she repeated the words to herself, they refused to become real. Jonas would die. She would be alone. In the whole of her life, Amelia had never been alone. There had always been Jonas. She had never imagined there would not be Jonas.

She recalled Sidney's accusations. That Jonas spent his life taking care of her. That he could have had more. That he had deserved more. It was all true. She *was* that selfish. She had let him spend his life—literally, now—taking care of her. It had never occurred to her that he would do—that he might even want to do—anything else. And now he would die. Because he'd been trying to help her.

And he had. Amelia made a noise somewhere between a laugh and a sob as this final irony struck her: Jonas had been trying to find a way to free her. He'd gotten shot, and now she was free.

All it had cost was his life.

It was far, far too much. She wasn't worth it. Had never been, could never be, worth this sacrifice. She'd dragged him into helping her search for the murderer, believing his brilliance, his daring, were hers to use. And he'd agreed, for her. He'd made the plans, done the work, taken the risks, all for her. And he might have done it. He'd found the names, after all. That might have been enough to unravel the whole thing. And then he'd been shot and the list taken. Now even that accomplishment would be denied to him.

Amelia laid her head on the table, expecting the tears to come. But it was as though they'd frozen inside her chest.

Numb, she watched as the sliver of light coming through the window moved toward her. It fell across Jonas's notepad, turning the impressions in the paper into swirling canyons.

Impressions in the paper.

Amelia blinked and dragged herself upright. Her hand trembled as she drew the pad nearer. She tilted it until the light skipped across it again, throwing the loops and lines into relief. Yes, those were letters.

She stared at the page, trying to render it readable, but the letters were too faint, too abstract. Amelia groped for the pencil. Carefully, so carefully, she scrubbed the side of the lead against the indentations.

These were names.

This was the list.

50

Andrew pushed back from his desk shortly before seven o'clock in the morning and kneaded at his eyes with his knuckles. After so many hours, the light from the lamp felt like sandpaper on his corneas. He hadn't been this exhausted since medical school—and he'd been ten years younger then. There also hadn't been a murderer treading on his heels.

He shook himself and went to the door, hoping to flag down a passing orderly to request more coffee. He had barely left the room in the past forty-eight hours. Aside from checking on Winslow and a few visits to the washroom, he'd spent every moment poring over files, making—and discarding—lists of possible victims. He ran a hand over his bristly cheeks and tried not to dwell on the fact that he hadn't accomplished anything. There were still a few hours. The next file could be the one he needed.

There were no orderlies in the hallway, but to his surprise, Dr. Harcourt stepped out of his apartment. He was dressed but had the wan and befuddled look of a man who had been ill and was not yet quite mended. His gaze sharpened as he found Andrew, and Andrew was abruptly aware that the fresh shirt he'd put on two days earlier was no longer necessarily a better choice than the one he'd taken off.

"Here overnight, I take it?" Harcourt approached, holding a messy stack of loose papers in one hand.

"Ah, I've been working on a project," Andrew said. "The time got away from me." He paused. "If you don't mind my saying, you don't really seem well enough to be up and around yet."

Harcourt shook his head. "I'm not. But I need to get these down to Winslow's desk."

"I'll take them for you, if you like," Andrew offered. "I was on my way down, and it will save you the stairs at least."

Harcourt readily handed over the stack and disappeared back into his quarters.

Andrew turned for the stairs, glancing down at the papers as he did. *Certificate of Discharge*, read the bold print at the top. He slowed as he flipped through the sheaf. These were discharge orders, all of them. Harcourt had filled out the blanks on the preprinted forms with the patients' names and dates of release, but his usually copperplate handwriting was shaky and spotted with inkblots. His signature was far less elaborate than usual.

Andrew slowed as a thought struck him. If he could get hold of a blank discharge form, with a little practice, he could replicate Harcourt's signature. Carolina Casey could be recorded as having been discharged, and one threat would be neutralized. He'd never seen a blank form, but he'd never had any reason to go looking for one, either. Surely they were somewhere in the main office.

He picked up his pace.

Andrew rounded the corner into the main office and pulled up short. Winslow was at his desk.

"You're here." His tone was rather more dismayed than was appropriate, so he tried again. "I thought you were going to take another day off."

"I was, but I felt perfectly well by last night," the young man replied with a smile. "I don't know what was wrong with me, but whatever it was, it's gone now. I came in early to get started on the reconciliation." He gestured to a neat stack of papers on the corner of the desk. The reconciliation list—all the current patients and the wards to which they'd most recently been assigned.

A weight appeared in Andrew's gut. He had even less time than he'd thought. He resisted the impulse to snatch the list and run.

"I need . . . ah." Winslow peered at the papers beneath Andrew's arm. "Are those the week's discharge forms?"

It would hardly be reasonable to say no. Or for him to refuse to hand them over.

"Yes," Andrew said, after an instant's hesitation.

"Excellent." Winslow reached for them. "That's the last thing I needed." He took the stack from Andrew's nerveless fingers and sat.

Andrew turned with a jerky movement and left the office. There had to be a way to delay the count. Perhaps if the list were lost. Or destroyed.

Andrew hurried down to the staff kitchen, his brain fizzing with fatigue and panic. He filled a pair of coffee cups to the brim with the asylum's dark, bitter brew. It was only barely warm, but it would do for his purposes. He would tip one onto the forms when he set it down. Terribly sorry, how clumsy!

He carried the cups back up the stairs, walking slowly, trying not to spill their contents before he was ready. He took a breath and stepped into the office.

The stack was gone.

Andrew's eyes darted around the room. There, on the counter beside Winslow, who'd bent and was now pulling open a drawer.

Andrew strode toward him, one hand already extending a cup, the trembling liquid held in check by its own surface tension.

The shrill clamor of the telephone's bell split the air, and with a violent start of surprise, Andrew sloshed a good measure of lukewarm coffee from both cups. It soaked into his shirt cuffs and splashed the floor.

"Oh dear." Winslow straightened. "Are you—"

"I'm fine," Andrew snapped the telephone continued to shriek.

Winslow hurried past him to answer it while Andrew surveyed the wreck of his plan. He was tempted to dash the remnants in the cups over the papers just on principle, but as he surveyed the scene, the tabs in the drawer caught his eye.

He'd found the blank forms.

Andrew glanced back at Winslow, who was shouting into the telephone, "I'm sorry, I can't hear you, I'm afraid the connection is too poor!"

Andrew moved to set the cups down. Perhaps he could get one of the forms before— But no, Winslow had already disconnected and turned back to him.

The clerk brushed past him and reached into the drawer.

It was on the tip of Andrew's tongue to ask for one of the discharge forms, to claim he'd just remembered Harcourt had asked him to bring up another. He managed to bite back the request. Winslow might remember it later, might mention it to Harcourt and set the man thinking. Better to come back for it later, now that he knew where they were.

Winslow extracted a black-bordered form and stood. "Don't worry about the coffee. I'll get an orderly to clean it up. If you're headed back up soon, it would be a help to me if you could drop this off with Dr. Harcourt?" He proffered the sheet.

"Certainly," Andrew said through gritted teeth. He glanced down. Across the top in heavy black letters were the words "Certification of Death."

He stiffened. "There was a death?"

"Yes. A woman in four, last night. They found her this morning."

Four. The sound of the word brought the world to a halt. The coffee, the form, all of it vanished from Andrew's mind.

He stepped into the hallway as his mind replayed the conversation he'd had with Amelia. A woman in ward four, she'd said. Asking someone to send for her father, protesting that she didn't belong at the asylum. The paper shook in his hand. He'd forgotten. In all the chaos, the search of Harcourt's rooms, the news about Jonas, his own frantic combing of the files. He'd just . . . forgotten about her until this very moment. Horror washed over him in a hot, sickening flood. He should have gone to examine her that evening. He could have gone at any point in the last two days. Another woman was dead, because Andrew hadn't bothered—had forgotten—to save her.

51

I 'm sorry." The operator's voice was polite. "The connection failed again. I would recommend trying the call a bit later."

Amelia muttered something profane, ignoring the woman's shocked intake of breath. She disconnected from her third attempt to reach the asylum and rubbed her eyes as she turned to go back to Jonas.

The curtains were drawn in the bedroom. The only light came from a single lamp in the corner. The room stank of despair and illness. Jonas lay gray and wasted on the bed, the sheets damp and wilted beneath him from the ice that melted as they'd tried to cool his fevered skin. Sidney lay beside him, his face buried in the hollow of Jonas's neck. He raised his head as she entered.

Amelia met his gaze. The anguish in his eyes was unmistakable, and the numbness that had surrounded her like a fog since the doctor's pronouncement began to dissipate. She sank into the chair beside the bed.

"I don't think it will be much longer." Sidney's voice was barely audible. He pushed himself up and swung his feet over the side of the bed.

Grief was a sudden, stabbing presence in Amelia's chest. When she finally spoke, her voice was hesitant and thin. "Would you . . . I'm not . . . I'm not trying to keep you from him, I swear, but would you leave us for a bit? Please?" She looked up at him. "I need to—" She swallowed hard, unable to continue.

Sidney hesitated. "I want to be here. When he . . ."

Amelia closed her eyes and nodded, her lips pressed together. She'd tried to keep Jonas's life all for herself. She couldn't do the same with his death.

Sidney left them, and Amelia was alone with Jonas for the last time.

Her heart thudded, the beats painful, as she leaned forward and took his hot, limp hand in both of her own. She found herself clinging to it as though she could stop him from being swept away, could hold back the tide carrying the life from his body with the force of her will. It should be possible. He'd given her so much of himself. Surely she should be able to give it back, pour some of that strength and that love back into him.

A tight band squeezed Amelia's chest, and when she tried to breathe, all she could manage was a series of gasps. A great wave of dizziness swept over her.

This could not be. It was wrong. Obscene. How could someone as vital, as alive, as Jonas possibly die? How was it possible that he would no longer exist? How was it possible that the world would go on without him in it? There were people outside, at this moment, who didn't know, who would never understand, how profoundly everything was about to change. How much worse it would be. Amelia wanted to fling the windows open and scream it until they understood. Until they all hurt as badly as she did.

Instead, she slid to her knees beside the bed and pressed her forehead against Jonas's arm. She made a noise, a strangled howl, only partly muffled by the mattress, as agony overwhelmed her. Great choking sobs racked her body. There were words, or parts of them, mixed in, as Amelia tried to tell Jonas how much she loved him. How much she would miss him. How she didn't know what she would do without him. That she had never understood, had never appreciated, everything he was to her. That she understood it now, at the end, when it was too late. That the thought of living without him terrified her. That she wasn't even certain she wanted to.

She wept until her throat burned and her stomach muscles ached, until the sheet beneath her face was soaked with tears, until every breath was nothing but a gasping whistle, an endless series of shudders and heaves. When the tears finally began to taper off, she knelt, drained and wan, her face still pressed to Jonas's arm, his hand still clenched between her own. She tried to think if there were things she still needed to say to him, then gave up. There were thousands of things. And he would never hear them.

Amelia pushed herself to her feet and stumbled into the sitting room. Sidney waited on the sofa, but she avoided his eyes as she went into the bathroom and closed the door behind her. She washed her face and bathed her swollen eyes. She felt battered by the wave of grief and by the grim knowledge that it was only the first of many. She would have years, decades, in which to mourn.

She stepped back into the sitting room as the clock chimed the half hour, and she glanced at it, suddenly aware of time in a way she hadn't been over the past two days, when the only measure of its passage had been the spaces between Jonas's rasping breaths.

It was Monday. The asylum would be stirring. The reconciliation would happen soon. The patients would line up and be counted. Carolina Casey wouldn't be there. They might think it was a mistake at first, but they'd look again, and they would know she was gone. They would know she'd had help. Suspicion was bound to fall on Andrew. He would be ruined.

But that wasn't the worst risk he faced. A chill settled over Amelia as the thought struck her. Andrew being forced from the island might be for the best. He wouldn't stop searching for the killer, even without Amelia there to help him. Blounton had gone looking alone, and Blounton had died. Amelia imagined Andrew floating in the river, his sightless eyes turned to the sky.

She would have said she had no further capacity for strong emotion, but fury roiled through her at that thought. It swelled until it shoved her fear and her grief into a far corner of her mind and trapped them there, faint and distant things she could set aside until later.

She would lose Jonas and Andrew both, along with any chance of punishing the one who took them away from her.

Amelia's fists clenched around handfuls of her skirt, and the paper in her pocket crackled. The list. Those names were the key. They had to be. She had to get them to Andrew, and she had to do it now.

Amelia glanced at the telephone. She could try calling again. Or she could ring for a bellman. He could send someone with a message. But no. There were too many ways that could go wrong. This wasn't something she could entrust to a stranger. She would have to do it herself.

She fought down a surge of nausea at the prospect.

If she were caught . . . She shuddered. She must not be caught.

Amelia went back into the bedroom and confided her plan to Sidney in a low voice.

He frowned. "You think it will work?"

"It has to."

"And you're certain you have to go now," he said, his eyes searching her face. He glanced back down at Jonas. "I don't think he'll—"

She followed his gaze. "I know what it means." Her voice roughened as she went on. "But it's the only way. I have to do it." Sidney said nothing as Amelia leaned down to press a final kiss on Jonas's scorching brow. "Goodbye," she whispered as she pulled away.

52

Andrew had no memory of leaving the second floor, but at a sound he looked up and found himself standing in the third-floor hallway near Harcourt's apartment. The door opened, and Russo stepped out. The man's hand moved toward his pocket, and Andrew saw a thick fold of bills before he tucked it away. Andrew's own hand tightened into a fist, crushing the paper he'd been asked to deliver.

Red washed over his vision.

Russo flashed him a careless smile and turned toward the stairs. Andrew managed to stop himself from grabbing him as he passed and flinging him to the ground. It was a near thing. He imagined smashing the man's head against the floor until he confessed, beating him bloody until he admitted the exact number of women he'd helped kill, exactly how much money he'd taken to do it.

Instead, at a flicker of movement inside the apartment, Andrew turned and caught the closing door on the flat of his palm. He slammed it open and strode through.

Harcourt stumbled back as Andrew flung the crumpled paper in his face. "What is the meaning of this? Dr. Cavanaugh, I—"

Andrew was beyond caring, beyond reason.

"How many?"

"I beg your pardon? I—"

"How many women have you killed here? I know of two, but how many more were there?"

Harcourt gaped at him.

"What was her name? The woman from four? Was she already slated to die, or was it only because you feared we were about to expose you?"

Harcourt found his voice. "Cavanaugh, you are—"

"Don't bother denying it." Andrew advanced on the older man. "I saw. I saw just now, Russo with his cut of the money. Murder must be a lucrative business, if you can pay your associates and still have those thousands in that box beneath your bed."

Harcourt's eyes widened. He glanced toward the bedroom and then back at Andrew, his face flushing a dull red. "How do you know about—"

"It doesn't matter how," Andrew said through gritted teeth. "I know. And I know what you did to earn it. Murderer," he spat. "You're finished. I—"

"Dr. Cavanaugh!"

Andrew went silent, seething.

"How dare you barge into my rooms and accuse me of—" Harcourt stopped. "Well, I don't know precisely what it is you are accusing me of. Murdering my patients?"

Andrew opened his mouth to speak, furious, but Harcourt held up one hand, palm out.

"No." His voice was stone. "I have allowed you far too much leeway, but it ends now. I have countenanced your unorthodox methods. I have tolerated your interference with other members of the staff. Clearly, I made a mistake in inviting you here. You will leave the island at once, or I will have you removed."

"You won't get rid of me that easily." Andrew shook with anger. "I know what's happening. I'll go to the press. To the board of governors. I'll make them listen. You've gotten away with it until now, but no longer. No more women will die so you can make yourself rich. The woman last night was the last."

Harcourt stood, cold fury in every line of his body. One of his hands shot out and closed on Andrew's biceps like a vise.

"Come with me." His voice brooked no opposition.

He strode out of the room and down the hallway, hauling Andrew along by the arm. Andrew made a halfhearted effort to pull away, then subsided as Harcourt's grip tightened. He seemed to have recovered his strength in the face of Andrew's accusation.

Andrew assumed the older man meant to drag him bodily to the ferry and throw him off the island. It didn't matter; it wouldn't change his next steps.

To his surprise, Harcourt jerked him to a stop outside ward four, where two orderlies were bringing out a stretcher bearing a shrouded form.

"One moment, please," Harcourt told them in a voice coated with ice. He gave Andrew a rough shove. "Go on. Please. Have a look at my supposed victim."

Steeling himself, Andrew lifted a flap of rough gray blanket away from the still face. He blinked and tried to reconcile his expectations with the wizened reality before him.

She was ancient.

Her face was seamed and spotted with age, her mouth sunken and wrinkled. The papery skin of her neck was as wrinkled as crepe. Thin wisps of white hair clung to her scalp. Her father, whoever he was, had obviously been dead for decades.

He didn't realize he'd said some part of the last aloud until Harcourt spoke from behind him.

"Yes, the nurses did report she'd been asking for him these past few days. It's common in such situations. This is Mrs. Ina Tierney, aged eighty-seven. She's been with us since her mind began to fail several years ago. A widow with no living family. This is the woman—*one* of the women, I should say—you accuse me of murdering for gain?"

Andrew was unable to speak. Harcourt reached past him and covered the woman's face, then nodded to the orderlies. "You may proceed."

Harcourt turned to Andrew as the orderlies departed and lowered his voice until it was barely more than a growl. "Are you satisfied? There have been no murders. I cannot think how you even imagined such a thing. There is not one shred of evidence for these *insane* allegations, and if you persist in making them, you will be met with a slander charge.

"As for the money in my quarters, it is none of your business. I could have you arrested for trespassing, since there is only one way you could know of it. But I have no wish to be further involved with you. You are finished here. You will turn your work over to one of the other doctors and remove yourself from these premises. I do not expect to set eyes on you again. And if even a whiff of these ridiculous allegations surfaces"—Harcourt stepped closer and lowered his voice—"I will make it my business to ruin you. You will not work in New York—or anywhere else—ever again."

53

L ot's wife looked back. Amelia would not. Her whole being was focused on what lay before her.

The air was unpleasantly sticky for May, with a still, oppressive quality that hinted at coming storms. The list, with the six names she'd been able to decipher, sat folded in her handbag as she stood outside the hotel. The doorman flagged a cab for her, and she climbed aboard almost before it had come to a stop.

"I'm headed to the Twenty-Sixth Street dock, but I have to make a stop first."

"Whatever you say, miss." The driver looked less sanguine, though, when she directed him to a seamy section of Willett Street on the Lower East Side.

"Don't worry," Amelia said as she alighted from the cab outside a row of saloons. "They know me here."

She took the alley staircase to the second floor, then pounded on the door, hoping Charley was in. If he'd done a show the night before and gone out carousing afterward, there was no telling where he might have ended up. She waited for a count of five, then resumed hammering at the door with the side of her fist. She sighed with relief when an irritated voice came from the other side.

"Do you know what fucking time it is? You'd better have one hell of a good—" The door swung open, and Charley stood scowling at her. "Mellie." The frown turned into a bemused look of welcome. "Long time."

"Hi, Charley. It's good to see you, too."

He stepped back as she pushed past him into the apartment. It was surprisingly clean, although the tang of smoke and sour beer from the saloon below seeped up through the cracks in the floor.

"I need to look like an entirely different person. I can give you twenty minutes. And don't call me Mellie," she added as the door swung closed behind her. "You know I hate it."

Fifteen minutes later, Amelia stepped back onto the sidewalk. She was now a well-rounded, thin-lipped woman with a head full of dark curls peeping from beneath a modestly stylish hat. Its brim tilted to cast a shadow over the last of the yellowing bruises on her face, to which Charley had also expertly applied a layer of stage makeup. The dress she wore was precisely the sort a well-bred, serious-minded woman would wear to visit a charitable institution. It hid the heeled boots that added three inches to her height.

The driver watched idly as she approached, his face devoid of recognition.

"We can go now," she said.

He blinked and peered down at her from his perch. A slow smile spread over his face, and he shook his head. "I'd have never known you, miss."

"That's the idea," she said. "To the docks now, please, as quickly as you can."

By the time they arrived, there was a line of low, black clouds on the far horizon. The river had a smooth, sullen look. It hunkered between its banks as if held down by the heavy air.

Amelia's scalp prickled with sweat beneath the wig, and the padded corset made her torso feel as though it were wrapped in several heavy quilts. She tried to ignore it, but she was flushed and perspiring by the time they reached the island.

"Looks like a storm," the ferryman said as she disembarked. "Maybe we'll get some rain, break this heat."

"That would be welcome." Amelia dabbed at her forehead with a handkerchief, trying not to ruin the carefully applied makeup.

She picked her way along the graveled path to the asylum—the heeled shoes were a disadvantage in such terrain—and walked into the Octagon with her nerves strung tight, prepared to smile and beg assistance from the first person she saw. Miss Matthew wouldn't know her way around, would expect to be shown to Dr. Cavanaugh's office. The edges of her smile melted when the first person she saw was Mrs. Brennan.

The nursing matron fixed her with a baleful look, and Amelia's voice came out thin and breathless. "Ah. Hello. I'm here for an interview with Dr. Cavanaugh."

Mrs. Brennan's habitual scowl deepened at Andrew's name, and she jerked her head toward the stairs. "Tell them at the main office. Second floor." The nurse clumped away without giving Amelia another look.

Amelia released a breath. At least her disguise seemed to be working.

She turned for the stairs, her anxiety mounting as she neared her destination.

Winslow sat behind the front desk, seeming no worse for wear after his ordeal of the other night. Amelia's stomach gave a queasy lurch when he looked at her. He wouldn't recognize her. He couldn't possibly. She looked nothing like the dirty boy he'd seen two days before. Amelia lifted her chin and flashed him her most charming smile.

He blinked and smiled back. "Good morning, miss. May I be of assistance?"

She offered her hand. "I am Miss Matthew. I have an appointment with Dr. Andrew Cavanaugh."

Something flashed across his face.

Amelia tensed. Surely Andrew couldn't have been discovered already.

"May I ask the nature of that appointment? Dr. Cavanaugh didn't mention he was expecting you."

"I'm interviewing to be his new assistant." She'd come up with the excuse in the cab. Klafft had a personal assistant. Why not Andrew?

Winslow looked confounded for a moment, then recovered enough to stand. "This way, please."

Andrew's door was half-open. Winslow knocked on the jamb as he poked his head inside. "Dr. Cavanaugh. Your appointment is here."

There was a confused pause from within.

Amelia tensed. She couldn't let him say he had no appointment. She stepped around Winslow and into Andrew's line of sight.

Andrew rose from behind the desk, a puzzled crease in his forehead.

"Dr. Cavanaugh, so lovely to see you again." She stepped into his office and extended her hand. His eyes widened, and his jaw dropped. "I'm so sorry I'm late," she went on, before he could give away the ruse. He continued to stand there with his mouth hanging open. "For my interview. For the secretarial position."

He shook himself. "Ah. Yes. Miss . . ."

"Matthew," she supplied.

"Miss Matthew. Of course." His voice was hearty and overloud. The whites showed around the edges of his eyes. He took the hand she offered and held it beat too long, as if he couldn't remember what he was supposed to be doing.

The touch kindled a warmth in Amelia's chest, wholly inappropriate to the moment. She'd had no time to dwell on what had happened between them the last time she was in this office, but now she felt her cheeks warming as his eyes roved over her face.

She gave his fingers a squeeze, and he started as though it were an electrical shock, tearing his gaze from hers.

He cleared his throat and stepped back. "Thank you, Winslow."

The instant after the door closed behind the clerk, Andrew whispered, "Amelia, my god." He took her in as if he were certain she was a mirage. "What are you doing here? Is Jonas—" He stopped, evidently seeing something in her face.

"He was alive when I left him," she said, not trusting herself with more. "His . . . Someone is with him." She went on before he could press her further. There was a stack of books sitting beside a box on his desk. "What's this?"

He grimaced as he gestured for her to sit. "I've ruined everything." He outlined the morning's events. "I'm so sorry," he said as he concluded. "I'm finished here at the asylum."

Amelia reached into her bag for the list. "Then we don't have any time to waste."

She explained her discovery, then called out the names as Andrew found their files. Within a few minutes, they had all six lying open on the desk.

They spotted it at the same time.

"The handwriting on the commitment orders," Amelia said.

"The same person wrote each of them." Andrew confirmed. "I would never have noticed while they were all mixed in with the others, but once you see them together, it's unmistakable." He disappeared into the storage room and returned a moment later holding another file. "One of the discharges, for comparison."

The writing was different.

Andrew looked at the six files on the desk, then back at the storage room. Amelia followed his gaze.

"I wonder how many more there are," she said.

"Only one way to know." Andrew's voice was grim.

Half an hour's work resulted in eleven more files stacked on the desk. They looked at each other for a moment, somber, before Amelia plucked a clean sheet of paper from the tray on Andrew's desk and began writing, looking between the files and the page as she went.

"What are you doing?" Andrew asked.

"I want to see the complete list, and I want to look at the dates." Amelia sat back when she was done, pointing at the first name on the new list. "There. That's the earliest of the bunch."

Andrew peered over her shoulder. "Five years ago. Harcourt wasn't here then. So he may well not be involved after all. But thanks to me, he won't listen if we go to him." Andrew dropped into his chair and pinched the bridge of his nose. "What are we going to do?"

Amelia stared at the list until the black lines blurred before her eyes, then blinked and turned away. "I don't know."

54

He was so thirsty. Jonas tried to open his eyes, but his eyelids were made of lead. He licked his lips. His tongue was cotton, his throat full of sand. He coughed. It hurt. Everything hurt.

There was a strangled gasp from beside him, and he tried to look. Turning his head proved too much, but he did manage to force his eyes open.

Sidney. Sidney was there. Jonas tried to smile.

Sidney reached out a hand and cupped his cheek. Something swept over his face, a look of joy so profound Jonas wondered with a faint sort of puzzlement what could possibly have caused it.

"The fever," Sidney said, awe in his tone. "It's broken." His voice cracked on the last word.

Oh. He'd been ill. That explained why he was so tired. He tried to ask for a drink. The word came out covered in rust and barely a whisper.

Sidney leapt to his feet and disappeared, returning with a glass. Jonas's eyes fastened on it.

He couldn't sit up, but Sidney put a hand behind his head and helped him upright enough to put the glass to his lips. The lukewarm liquid trickling into his mouth was the finest thing he'd ever tasted. After a few swallows, Jonas lay back, exhausted.

Sidney said something, but sleep was already pulling him back under.

Shouting roused him to a sort of semiliquid awareness. Sidney was gone, but his voice, the words tumbling over one another in a sort of laughing-sobbing rush, drifted from the other room. "Amelia! Can you hear me? Are you there? He's awake. The fever is gone!"

There was more. Jonas tried to listen, but the fog rolled back over him and carried him away again.

55

Amelia picked up the list and stood. "I'm going to check these against the admissions ledger. It probably won't do any good, but I can't think of anything else to try. Perhaps it will tell us something."

Andrew nodded without looking at her.

Dr. Lawrence appeared at the top of the steps just as Amelia stepped into the hallway, and as if her body had made the decision without her, she turned in his direction. The faint outline of an idea began to form.

He looked up as she approached, his apartment door ajar.

"Dr. Lawrence, I—" She stopped as he blinked at her in complete confusion. She nearly smacked herself on the forehead. He had no idea who the strange woman speaking to him was. "I'm Dr. Cavanaugh's new assistant," she said, hoping he had not heard about Andrew's firing. "I—that is, Dr. Cavanaugh has a question about your notebooks."

"My notebooks?"

"Yes. I know you record a great deal of information about the patients. Do you keep notes on those who die?"

"Yes, of course."

A faint tendril of hope sprouted in her chest. "Do you happen to record details of the discoveries? Specifically, can you identify which of the doctors officially pronounced each death?"

"Certainly. I keep track in case I have questions later."

Amelia struggled to keep her tone level as her heart began to beat faster. "Might Dr. Cavanaugh and I be allowed to go through your notebooks to compile those details?"

Dr. Lawrence looked pleased. "You're welcome to any of my notes. That's precisely why I've kept them. But," he went on, "if it's specifically deaths you're interested in, there's no need for the notebooks. You can check the ledgers."

"I beg your pardon?"

"My notebooks are daily records of my observations," he said, "but I keep a separate log of each patient's admission and eventual outcome."

He moved into the apartment, and Amelia watched through the open door, barely breathing, as he crossed to the shelf of bound volumes she'd noticed—and ignored—during the aborted search of his quarters. He pulled two of the thick books from the end of the row and returned to the door.

"Back when I first arrived here at the asylum," he explained, "records were practically nonexistent. No reliable account of who was even here at any given time, or when they left." He shook his head. "I began keeping my own lists then, and I never got out of the habit. These should cover the last five years or so."

Amelia's hands shook as she accepted the books. "Thank you."

She turned toward Andrew's office, but before she'd taken more than a step, Winslow called out to her from the stairs. He smiled at her as he neared.

"Miss Matthew. There's a gentleman on the telephone for you." He lowered his voice. "I offered to take a message, but he was most insistent on speaking directly to you. I do hope nothing is wrong."

Spikes of ice pierced her chest. Only Sidney knew she was here. And there was only one thing he could be calling to tell her. She almost refused to go. Almost. Feeling as though she were drowning, Amelia turned to follow the young man down the stairs, the books clutched to her chest as though they were the only thing keeping her afloat in a raging sea.

She set them carefully on the counter beside the telephone and lifted the receiver with a shaking hand.

"Hello?" Her voice sounded like a stranger's.

A wash of static came over the line as Sidney spoke. "Amelia! Can . . . hear me? . . . you there?"

He was crying. That much was clear.

"Yes," she said in that same foreign, leaden tone, already knowing what came next and hating him for forcing it on her now.

"He's . . . gone. He just . . . and then he . . ." The line faded out, and with a little click, the connection failed entirely. But she had heard enough.

Jonas was dead.

It was as though the earth heaved beneath her feet. As though the very air itself might crush her. Amelia replaced the receiver and put her shaking hands flat on the counter in front of her, forcing herself to breathe. A minute passed. From far in the distance, a towering wave of grief threatened. But she could not allow it to swamp her. Not yet.

She swallowed hard and turned to the books as she pulled the list from her pocket. She spread it on the counter with icy, tingling hands and opened the first book. She turned the pages, running a finger along the faint, spidery script, until she found the first name on her list. Maryanne Everts was admitted to the asylum in May 1887, aged forty-three. She died—ostensibly of heart failure—three months later.

The page swam before Amelia's eyes as she read the name of the attending physician. Her own heart began to beat a pounding rhythm in her ears, and she sucked in a desperate breath. They had to be certain. She found the next woman: Susan Degrette—apoplexy. And there was the name again.

Amelia made her way through the rest of the list. She was shaking as she finished. The room spun around her.

Seventeen names.

Seventeen deaths.

All confirmed by William Tyree.

56

Amelia burst through the door, a stack of books clutched to her chest. "It's Tyree." Her face was pale. Andrew could see her trembling from across the room.

"Dr. Tyree was the physician who examined all the women on the list when they died," she said. She explained about seeing Dr. Lawrence, her idea about his notes, about the listings.

Andrew felt the blood drain from his own face. "We have to—"

"Cavanaugh? Are you there?" A voice echoed from the hallway.

Tyree's voice.

They looked at each other in paralyzed horror for a split second, then turned as one toward the office door, half open after Amelia's frantic entrance and spilling light out into the hallway. Andrew put a hand on her arm and gestured toward the storage room.

She hesitated, then nodded. *Be careful*, she mouthed, moving across the floor. She slipped inside, easing the door not quite closed behind her.

Andrew had no time to do more than take a deep breath before Tyree appeared in the doorway. His face bore an expression quite different from his typical joviality. It was utterly blank, as if a mask had fallen away and revealed the void behind it. Only the eyes were alive. They glittered.

Andrew was able to look away only when Tyree extended a hand, holding the corner of a folded piece of paper between his thumb and forefinger as if it were covered in filth.

"Dr. Tyree?" Andrew was surprised; his voice sounded almost normal.

"I was passing through on the way to my apartment." Tyree's tone matched his face. "Winslow stopped me. He asked if I'd drop this by your office. He seemed to think it might be important."

Tyree twitched the paper open. It was the list of names and dates Amelia had written. Across the top was Andrew's ornate, curling monogram. Little chance of pretending ignorance now. Andrew felt his own face tighten.

"This is your personal stationery, is it not?"

"Yes." Andrew swallowed and reached out to take the sheet.

Tyree let go just before Andrew's fingers closed on it. They both watched as the sheet wafted to the floor, coming to rest with the barest whisper. The moment stretched. Andrew had the sensation of standing on the edge of a precipice, looking down; the slightest sound, the slightest movement, might send him plunging downward.

"Let us dispense with the pretense, Cavanaugh," Tyree said, and Andrew started. "You've obviously been poking into matters better left alone." Tyree bared his teeth in an expression that could have been a smile, had it contained any trace of warmth. "When I said you reminded me of Blounton, I had no idea what an accurate assessment that would turn out to be."

"He did find you out, then? What you were doing here?"

Tyree gave a single nod. "Indeed. He examined the Weaver woman shortly after she arrived. She managed to convince him to listen to her. He mentioned her case to me. I warned him it was folly to believe the things the patients say."

"But she was telling the truth."

Tyree ignored him. "He started looking into things a bit too deeply. I had to take steps."

"You killed him. How? I thought you were in Philadelphia when he died." Andrew's heart pounded.

"I allowed one of my associates to do the actual deed. And I grieved the necessity. I liked him." He looked past Andrew and nodded at the folders lying open on the desk. "That's how he finally discovered me, you know. He recognized my handwriting on the commitment orders. He might not have put it together, except there happened to be a note I'd left him sitting on his desk while he was looking at the files. Bad luck, really."

Tyree shifted his gaze back to Andrew. "I knew at once that he'd figured it out. He tried to pretend nothing was wrong, but he was a terrible actor. All furtive looks and darting eyes. It concerned me. I searched his desk and found his notes. I couldn't allow him to go spreading the story."

He regarded Andrew with what appeared to be genuine regret. "Just as I can't allow you."

The edge of the cliff began to crumble beneath Andrew's feet. He shifted his weight as if to take a step back. And suddenly there was a gun in Tyree's right hand, the stubby black barrel pointed at Andrew's chest. He went still.

Tyree gestured with the gun. "I made a small detour to my apartment before coming here."

"Are you going to shoot me?"

"If I have to. But I'd prefer to use this." In his other hand he held up a syringe, plucked from somewhere among his pockets.

"What is it?" Andrew eyed the needle.

"It's a concoction of my own invention. Morphine, primarily. You'll drift away, and a bit later your heart will stop. It's quite gentle," he added. "I've never seen it cause anyone the slightest discomfort."

Andrew heard himself laugh—a startled, bitter sound. "Your concern is much appreciated. How many times have you used it, that you're so certain of its effect?"

"Quite a few, over the years. A great many men marry unwisely, you know."

"I'd say it's the women who married unwisely," Andrew shot back, contempt overtaking fear for a moment. "They're the ones who end up imprisoned, tormented for months or years before you finally kill them."

Tyree made a disdainful gesture with the hand holding the syringe. "There's no need to be dramatic. I've never set out to torment anyone. And as for killing, I merely do as I've been directed by my clients. For

some of them, out of sight is out of mind. Others desire a more definitive separation."

"Definitive," Andrew repeated, sickened. "That's why Julia Weaver was
dead inside six months, but Elizabeth Miner was still here after a year.
Bryce Weaver paid for the definitive separation."

"And Mr. Miner did not. He was most emphatic on the matter, in fact.
Something to the effect that if his wife wanted him to remain a poor man,
then she could remain here as a poor man's wife. It was carelessness on my
part, I admit. I ought not to have left her alive, regardless of his wishes.
Rather unsettling when you came to me with her file, but fortunately I
was able to prevent it from going further."

"You never took it to Harcourt at all? The story of his refusal . . ."

"A convenient fiction. I couldn't risk his involvement. I would have
gone ahead and removed her after that, but the problem solved itself. It
was kind of you to alert me that I needed to keep an eye on you, however.
And now I believe that's enough discussion." Tyree lifted the syringe and
the gun slightly, in turn. "Choose."

Andrew hesitated. Perhaps he should force Tyree to fire. He might
miss. Even if he didn't, someone might hear the shot and arrive in time
to save him and catch Tyree with the gun in his hand. He was better off
taking the chance.

As if he'd heard these thoughts, Tyree stepped forward and pressed
the gun upward under Andrew's chin. His hand did not tremble. His
voice was quiet and firm.

"Once I've blown your head off, how long do you think it will take
for someone to come? Do you think I'll have time enough to wrap your
hand around the grip? I think I will." He bared his teeth again in that
terrible, toneless smile.

"In fact, I think once I've injected you, I'll go ahead and use this
anyway. It will tell a better story than your sudden, unexplained death. I
heard about your confrontation with Harcourt earlier. You're estranged
from your family. Your fiancée left you. You took a low-status, low-paying
job and couldn't even keep that. Would anyone be shocked that you'd
taken your own life? That I arrived in time to see you do it but was tragi-
cally unable to prevent you?"

He pressed the gun harder into the soft flesh behind Andrew's chin, the barrel against the bottom of his tongue. Andrew thought he could taste the metal.

"I'm offering you the kindness of the needle first. But if you decline, if you force me to do it this way, then I will. And once I've taken care of you, I'll send my associates to tend to Miss Casey." Tyree nodded at Andrew's expression. "Did you think I wouldn't notice what you were about, her always here in your office—she and that Vincent fellow. He's been taken care of, but the girl is a loose end. I myself would dispatch her directly, but young men do have certain . . . appetites. They might enjoy some time with her before they finish things."

Tyree pulled the gun back a fraction and lifted the syringe. "Or you can sit down at your desk and drift away."

Andrew raised his hands in a slow gesture of surrender and stepped back.

57

Amelia stood as rigid as stone. The angle of the door cast a deep shadow, and she forced herself to remain still and silent inside it. As Tyree spoke, it took every ounce of her will not to spring from her hiding place and attack him with her bare hands. He killed Jonas. She clenched her fists around handfuls of her skirt at his casual admission and bit down on her anger.

Terror nearly overwhelmed her when Tyree pressed the gun to Andrew's head. She wanted to close her eyes, wanted to block out what she was about to witness, but she forced herself to keep watching. If they were to have any chance, she had to be prepared.

His threat against her sent a shudder of disgust through her, but she focused on the mention of his *associates*. There were at least two of them, as they'd thought. And they were young. That detail set her mind racing.

It seemed clear Harcourt wasn't involved. If she could get up the storage room ladder and onto the roof, she could find him, convince him to help.

But there was no time. Tyree pressed the gun upward. He'd hear her as she went for the ladder, and she didn't dare do anything to startle him with the gun where it was.

Then, as if he'd heard her thought, Andrew raised his hands and stepped away from Tyree. And away from the gun.

Acting on pure instinct, Amelia stepped forward, pushing the door open a few inches. A hinge creaked. Time stretched. She spent an endless instant watching Tyree's head turn. His eyes met hers and widened in surprise, then narrowed. The barrel of the gun began to swing toward her.

She darted back into the storage room, raised two hands to the door, and slammed it with a crash. She whirled and dashed for the ladder. As she went, she flung her arms wide, yanking files from the shelves and sending an avalanche of boxes and papers cascading to the floor behind her.

Amelia's steps stuttered at the gunshot's crack, but she recovered her stride and flung herself at the ladder. She began to climb, her skirts swirling around her ankles and catching beneath her shoes. One foot—clumsy in the high shoes—slipped off a rung. Her knee slammed into the metal bar, hard enough to make her leg go numb. She caught her fall by the crook of an arm and kept going. She reached the top as she heard the door burst open behind her.

Amelia risked a glance over her shoulder and saw Tyree's stocky form silhouetted in the doorframe, the gun still in his hand. She turned back and reached up toward the trapdoor with shaking hands, panting with fear, expecting to feel the punch of a bullet between her shoulder blades at any moment. Instead, she heard Tyree kicking his way through the debris on the floor, then a muffled curse. She shoved the door open and lunged upward, pulling herself up until she hung by the waist on the edge of the hole, desperately trying to swing her injured leg over the lip.

A hand brushed against her ankle, and she kicked back with her pointed heel. It connected with something, and Tyree let out a pained grunt as Amelia pulled herself up onto the roof.

The dome rose high and dark to her left, and to her right, out over the river, she could see the edge of the approaching front. The low, boiling clouds flickered with lightning and drew nearer with every heartbeat. Amelia ordered herself to run. Her bruised knee buckled at the first step, but she ignored the pain. If she could get to the other door and get it open, she might be able to get into Harcourt's apartment. Perhaps she could—

The pistol cocked behind her, the click flat and loud in the humid air.

The breath rushed from her lungs. Too late. She turned, fighting the urge to cower. Tyree came toward her, his gun leveled. Blood dripped from his nose and coated his teeth, which were set in a snarl.

Jonas was already gone. She wondered if Andrew was dead as well, if his shade was even now waiting for her, standing mute and pale beside his corpse. She didn't think she could bear to see it. But, she thought dully, if she died up here on the roof, she wouldn't have to. Perhaps she would see them both on the other side. Perhaps she could tell them she was sorry.

Tyree drew nearer, and she forced herself not to shrink away.

"I won't let you ruin everything," he said. "Another year, maybe two, and I'll have enough saved to leave this place behind me." He raised the pistol and stretched out his arm.

The air around them hummed, and Amelia closed her eyes.

There was a blinding flash through her eyelids, and a roar of sound engulfed her. She flinched, disoriented, expecting the searing pain of the shot.

But no.

She opened her eyes to see Tyree looking up at the dome. Amelia followed his gaze. The metal spire at the top glowed orange, dying sparks falling from it as it cooled. The air crackled, thick with the smell of ozone and warm stone and hot metal. Another jagged bolt of lightning sizzled across the sky as a massive gust of wind staggered them both. The storm had arrived.

Swirls of pale mist twisted through the air around them, moving independently of the wind.

As Tyree began to turn back toward her, the wisps grew, tightened, began to coalesce. Faint outlines formed, and Amelia watched, mesmerized, as first bodies and then faces came into focus. An instant later, she realized with wonder that they were whispering to her.

Ignoring Tyree, she closed her eyes again, listening.

The wind faded. The gun, the storm—it was all distant, irrelevant. The voices were all that mattered. Young and old. Tentative and resolute. Fury and sadness and desperation, eagerness and indignation. The spirits pressed in on her—far, far more than the ones they'd found in the records.

No, this had been growing, waiting—waiting for *her*—for years. They danced over her skin, a feathery caress. A yearning.

She opened her eyes to the yawning barrel of the gun, pointed at her head. Tyree, though, must have seen something in her face, because even as his finger began to tighten on the trigger, he looked unsure.

Yes, she thought, *take me*. The world shifted as the presences around her went still, then flared into sharp relief, silvery against the dark.

Amelia flung her head back and breathed them in.

Her whole body seized with an ecstatic rush. She sobbed with the force of it, staggering. Her chest thrummed. Tiny sparks jumped from her fingertips. She could feel the women, dozens of them, moving beneath her skin.

And all of them wanted only one thing.

She looked at Tyree, and his eyes narrowed.

"What are you—" He got no further.

She thrust out her hands, and with a hollow, moaning roar, the horde flung itself from her body and roiled toward him like an avalanche. Amelia fell to her knees as they left her.

Perhaps he saw their faces. Certainly he saw something, for as they came for him, his own expression was one of terror. They hit him with devastating force, hurling him backward, his arms thrown wide. The gun cracked, the bullet sizzling into the sky. Tyree tumbled over the low parapet and fell, screaming, three stories to the stone courtyard. By the time Amelia regained her feet and stumbled to the edge, fat drops of rain were splashing into the rivulets of blood leaking across the flag-stones below.

EPILOGUE

T he little cemetery was sun-dappled and lovely. A mild breeze sent dogwood petals raining down on the small cluster of people ringing the open grave. A robed minister stood at the foot, just behind Ned Glenn. His parents—Julia's parents—stood beside him, leaning against each other and dabbing at their eyes. Half a dozen friends were gathered around them. A pair of workmen waited at a respectful distance, leaning on their shovels. They all watched as the coffin—polished oak, instead of the splintered pine that had been recovered—was lowered into the earth. It had taken several weeks of searching and an envelope full of cash to the superintendent of Hart Island, but Julia Glenn was back with her family.

Not wanting to intrude on a private grief, Amelia stood with Andrew near the front gate. Jonas, not wholly recovered from his ordeal, sat on a bench beside them.

Amelia glanced at him, still not entirely able to believe he was there. She would never have the words to describe the feeling of discovering he lived. That single instant had ripped away a boundless pall of grief and replaced it with . . . *joy* was too pale a name for it. Overwhelmed, she'd wept quite nearly as hard at learning he lived as she had when she'd believed he would die. Sidney was horrified when she recovered herself enough to explain her misunderstanding.

Jonas, when he heard the whole story, was furious.

"I cannot believe you took such a risk." He'd been too weak to shout, but he managed to inject a heavy dose of censure into the words.

"It was the only way," Amelia replied, not bothering to conceal her delight that he was there to scold her. "And it worked out in the end."

After her confrontation with Tyree, Amelia fumbled her way back down the ladder on shaking legs, fearing she would find Andrew dead in his office. Instead, he was surrounded by people, dazed from a blow to the head and cut by flying glass from the window shattered by Tyree's bullet, but otherwise unharmed. Harcourt thundered into the room, demanding explanations. Andrew's first attempt, incoherent though it was, was more than enough to set off an explosion of chatter before the superintendent grimly cleared the room, ordering them all to silence.

It didn't work. By the time an ashen-faced Harcourt left the office twenty minutes later, the whole asylum was in an uproar, with as many versions of the story spreading as there were mouths to tell it. They all had the same sensational ending: after being discovered to be a murderer, Dr. Tyree had chased Dr. Cavanaugh's new assistant onto the roof of the asylum during a storm, where a bolt of lightning had flung him to his death. Amelia told only Andrew and Jonas what really happened. And if Jonas told Sidney, Amelia found she didn't mind as much as she would have thought.

There had been an additional—if minor—drama later that day, when the completed reconciliation seemed to indicate one of the patients was missing. Andrew, despite his earlier ordeal, had insisted on helping with the recount. He searched the main office himself and managed to locate Carolina Casey's discharge form.

"It was under one of the desks," he told a relieved Winslow. "It must have slipped off the stack earlier."

Winslow thanked him profusely and processed it at once. Carolina was officially free.

In all the chaos, it took more than a day for anyone to notice Connolly was nowhere to be found. His abrupt disappearance—to say nothing of the ambulance driver's uniform found in his abandoned lodging house—confirmed his involvement in the scheme.

"That's what Blounton was trying to say," Jonas said, obviously disgusted with himself for only now realizing it. "'He finds them at the club,'" he quoted. "'He's using Connolly.' Tyree was using Connolly to find them, not Klafft."

"Wretched boy," Klafft fumed, waving off Andrew's proffered apology for suspecting him. "Think no more of it. I am only sorry to have ever employed that dreadful young man at all."

Horrified by the revelations, Harcourt initiated an investigation of all asylum staff and a thorough reevaluation of every patient. His fury at Andrew over the violation of his quarters—they elided Amelia's role in the incident—was only slightly tempered by his understanding of the quandary Andrew had faced.

The money, as it turned out, was his own, and legitimately earned. "I had planned some years ago to retire," he explained. "Then my bank failed, and I lost nearly everything I had saved. Now I keep my money in my own hands. What you discovered, through means I don't like to consider, represented several years of my salary."

Russo was similarly innocent—at least of the murders.

"He has an uncle who is a distributor of high-quality spirits. He arranged to sell some of these to me—and others here—at good prices," Harcourt said.

"He steals them," Andrew said. "He steals from his uncle and sells to you and pockets the money."

Harcourt drew himself up in offense. "I have no knowledge of any such criminal activity. And it seems to me you would do well to avoid making further unwarranted accusations."

Then, after visibly wrestling with himself, Harcourt asked Andrew to stay on at the asylum to oversee the staff and patient review.

"An entirely temporary reprieve," Andrew explained to the group outside the cemetery. "Harcourt needs an outsider to prove to the board of governors that he wasn't involved in Tyree's scheme, but he's made it quite clear that I have no future at the asylum. Once the review is complete, I expect to be in want of employment."

The review was well underway and had already borne fruit; Andrew collected enough stories of Mrs. Brennan's cruelties that Harcourt was forced to terminate her employment. One or two others had already given their notice rather than have their own records scrutinized.

Andrew hadn't found anyone else on the island who seemed to be involved in the plot. Perhaps Tyree himself was the second man who had helped haul Julia Weaver from her home, but Amelia had her doubts. Something about that conclusion rankled.

It was Sidney who found the answer.

"A friend of mine mentioned recommending his wife's nephew for a position in the clerk's office," he told them. "It seems one of the clerks recently quit without notice. I made some inquiries. He disappeared the day after Tyree died."

Jonas scowled. "That bastard. He was standing right behind me while I was making the list. He must have seen it and made up his mind to follow me when I left. That's why the 'pickpocket' had such clean hands and why he was wearing that stupid handkerchief over his face. I can't believe I let an amateur like that get the drop on me." He looked disgusted.

Although Jonas wasn't yet able to return to work, Amelia had no trouble reclaiming her position at the club.

"Sabine agreed at once," Amelia said. "It seems the customers didn't like my replacement. Too much doom and misfortune in her readings. Clients were going home early instead of staying to drink and gamble."

Jonas spoke up. "She's also fifty if she's a day, and shaped like a barrel besides. I'm sure that didn't help."

In an effort to clear their debts and sweeten Sabine's temper, Amelia dove back into work with impressive zeal. She was still trying to get a handle on her new abilities, but she was already beginning to develop something of a reputation. Even so, they would need Jonas's income while they decided what to do next. Though they hadn't yet made any long-term plans, one thing was clear.

"I don't ever want to hold you back," Amelia told Jonas. "If you want something more than the club, we'll find a way for you to have it."

Jonas squeezed her hand. "And what about you?" he asked gently. "What more might you want?"

Amelia found herself unable to answer. She and Andrew had not spoken of what passed between them in his office the evening Jonas was shot. Her cheeks colored when she thought of it, though in the wake of everything that had followed, it felt as though it had happened years before. Andrew made no further overtures, though the warmth in his eyes left her in little doubt of his regard. The possibility that their friendship might become more was undeniably appealing—more so than Amelia was ready to admit, even to Jonas. It was a question for another day.

Now, as the minister made a final gesture over the grave and the mourners began to turn away, Amelia watched with regret as the workmen stepped forward with their shovels. They'd stopped Tyree, but Julia was still dead—had been dead before they'd ever even known to start looking for her. And she wasn't alone. So far, they'd uncovered a full score of women who'd died in the asylum without any record of having ever been admitted. But with only the false names to go on, there was little they could do about it. Tyree was dead, and his minions had fled. There was no one who could tell them who those women had been and who the husbands were who had availed themselves of the doctor's ghoulish services.

Amelia had folded away the list of names. She and Jonas were resolved to act if they were ever able, but for the time being it seemed most of the men involved would face no real justice.

Including, unfortunately, Bryce Weaver. Julia's widower had recently announced his engagement to the daughter of a wealthy financier. Amelia shook her head, trying to let go of her self-reproach. They'd brought Julia home. Too late, but perhaps it was the best they could hope for from a story with so few happy endings.

As if he'd heard her thoughts, Andrew sighed next to her. "I wish we could have done more."

She reached down to squeeze his hand. "At least she's avenged. And no more women will disappear the way she did. That's all we could do."

"It might be all the two of you could do," Jonas said from her other side. "But Sidney and I decided to do a bit more."

Ned and his parents reached them in time to hear his last statement. All three stared at him blankly, too full of grief and exhaustion and resignation for curiosity. Jonas smiled his brilliant, gentle smile at them as he continued.

"A lawyer friend and I went to see Mr. Weaver last night. We found him toasting his engagement at the Union League Club. He threatened to call the police when we started talking, but we explained that if he did, every scandal sheet in the city would get a very interesting story. And since he was now engaged to the daughter of such a prominent citizen, we felt certain some of them would print it. He could sue, of course, and he might win, but the damage to his reputation would be done. His new fiancée's father would probably have something to say about it." He glanced toward the cemetery gates as if waiting for something, then turned back to them. "Once we explained what we wanted, he wasn't actually all that hard to convince."

Jonas reached into his pocket and withdrew a packet of papers. He handed it to Mrs. Glenn, who looked confused.

"What's this?" she asked.

"A notarized declaration, giving you and your husband full custody of Kitty." At their astonished expressions, he continued. "He barely hesitated. He called over a pair of friends as witnesses and signed it right there at his table. I don't think he wanted her anyway. He wants a fresh start with his new wife. A son to carry on the name, all that nonsense."

Just then a cab clattered to a stop outside the cemetery gates. The door opened, and Sidney alighted, his hair glinting in the sun. He caught Jonas's eye and raised a questioning brow. Jonas tilted his head in reply, and Sidney's answering smile made Amelia wonder how she could ever have thought him plain.

Sidney turned back to the cab and reached a hand inside. A little girl appeared, clutching a battered stuffed rabbit around the neck. Sidney swung her down as she looked around uncertainly. Then she caught sight of Mrs. Glenn.

"Nana!" The girl broke into a run, joy on her face, and flung herself at her grandmother. Sobbing, Mrs. Glenn swept her into a ferocious hug. Her husband enfolded the pair in his arms. Both of them looked a decade younger than they had only a moment before.

Unable to speak through the sudden lump in her own throat, Amelia laid a hand on Jonas's shoulder. He glanced up at her, and she saw her own understanding reflected in his eyes. With one bold stroke, he'd changed three fortunes—undoubtedly for the better. Fate might plan, but it often wrote lightly—in pencil rather than ink. Their choices mattered.

Where their own path would lead, she didn't yet know. But it didn't matter. Fate would not write their future. They would.

ACKNOWLEDGMENTS

I started writing this book on a whim. By the time I realized what I'd gotten myself into, I was far too fond of the characters and too involved in their stories to put it aside. Which is not to say I wasn't tempted. Frequently. I would not have kept going if there had not been so many people who believed in this book, and in me, and who were tireless cheerleaders along the way.

Since the first time I walked into a meeting, Michael Klein and the members of the Arlington Writers Group have been unwavering in their support and encouragement. Their criticism made me better; their praise kept me going. My thanks especially to Sarah, Dale, Richard, Lori, Paul, Evie, and Todd, who beta-read the novel--some of them more than once--and told me I had something worth putting out there.

I owe an eternal debt to everyone involved with Pitch Wars 2018. Revision is hard, querying is awful, and I'm so thankful I didn't have to ride either roller coaster alone. I'm most especially grateful for my wonderful mentor and friend, Carolyne Topdjian. Carolyne loved this story from the beginning, pushed me to make it stronger, and held my hand for four months while I broke my book and put it back together again. And her emoji game is first-rate.

ACKNOWLEDGMENTS

Thank you to my stalwart agent, Jill Marr, who told me she was determined to find Amelia a home, and to my lovely editor, Katie McGuire, who offered her one.

To Mom, Dad, and Sara, for everything, always.

And finally, my thanks and my love to my husband Alex, who once paid me what I consider the finest compliment of my life by comparing me to a wolverine, and who hasn't seemed surprised by any of this. When asked why, he just said "I knew that if you decided to do it, you would. And that it would be good."